ROLL BACK THE SUN

A NOVEL OF LOVE, MUSIC, AND THE MEANING OF LIFE

MICHAEL BALDWIN

INNER EYE BOOKS

Roll Back the Sun (A Novel of Love, Music, & the Meaning of Life)

Michael Baldwin / Inner Eye Books

Marble Falls, Texas

www.jmbaldwin.com

Cover design by 100covers.com

No artificial intelligence was used in creating this book.

Roll Back the Sun / Michael Baldwin — 1st edition.

ISBN: 979-8-9930556-0-2 paperback

Contents

Chapter One

"I Got It Bad (and That Ain't Good)"

Afghanistan, July 2002

Max was blowing Duke Ellington's "I Got It Bad (and That Ain't Good)" on his Hohner Chromonica when the IED exploded beneath them. He and his five Marine buddies had been sweating and swaying in the Doberman AMV, off and on, for a four-day eternity. The Doberman Armored Military Vehicle can withstand most ordinary combat punishment. But this uncanny IED detonated directly under them. They got it bad.

Until they were blown up, Max had been enjoying an enthusiastic camaraderie with these guys. Most of them were about half his age. They enjoyed music, jokes, and general playfulness that took their minds off their mortality for a few minutes. They were often just awkward kids until the fighting started. Then they became serious, professional death dealers.

Their unlucky AMV was in the middle of a seven-vehicle caravan. It was traveling back to Kandahar Airbase, Afghanistan, after a routine reconnaissance. They hadn't encountered the Taliban during the entire time.

Boredom had set in. The vehicle's interior was as cramped as a tuna can and equally smelly. But his companions relished Max's exuberant non-military banter and his harmonica renditions of various jazz standards. These guys were more accustomed to rap and heavy metal. Max was determined to convert them to appreciate real jazz.

While Max crooned on his Hohner Chromonica, Corporal Ramos provided an erratic but enthusiastic rhythm accompaniment on a ukulele. Private Darnell contributed an energetic drumbeat with a couple of metal rods from his body armor on various hard surfaces inside the dog, as they called the Doberman. Darnell sounded a gong off an ammo can just as the world went dark.

As an independent journalist embedded with this company of Marines, Max admired their courage and capability. America's Afghan War was now in its second year. Max had been here for four months. He had hunkered down and bonded with these Marines during several firefights and expeditions. Besides his stories about the Marines, he also produced articles about the Afghan people, whom he had quickly come to respect for their stoic dignity amid the chaos of war.

Much of the Afghan countryside reminded Max of his native North Texas, with its harsh dry prairie, sparse vegetation, boulder-strewn hills, and immense, stark sky. But the Afghan landscape also featured snow-draped mountains, jagged in the distance, which certainly weren't a Texas feature. The previous day he had spied wild camels plodding across the far, desolate plain, their images wavering with heat currents. Meanwhile, his caravan of vehicles struggled along the bare, rutted path that served as an Afghan highway.

They hadn't been expecting IEDs on this stretch of road. Supposedly, they had pacified it months before. Maybe the bomb had lain there since the Russian incursion of the 80s, waiting patiently for just the right pressure in just the right spot to trigger the charge in its old artillery shell.

Maybe some inexperienced designer had constructed the bomb since it only activated when the fourth vehicle rolled over it. Its charge must have been poorly shaped, too, because it exploded more laterally than vertically. Still, the blast sufficed to lift the heavy AMV several feet off the ground, sending it tumbling down a modest rocky incline. It came to rest topsy-turtle against some stubborn bushes near the bottom of the twenty-foot ravine.

Max, of course, wouldn't learn until much later what had happened. Strangely, however, he didn't pass out during the explosion. His eyes automatically locked shut, and his hearing turned off. He felt no pain, just a tremendous force pressing against him. He remained fully conscious, wondering coolly what had occurred, as he and his companions were shaken like dice in a cup.

He realized something extraordinary was happening but didn't know what. His questing mind perceived that he had been thrust into a vast inner space. Now he seemed to float like a feather on a nonexistent wind. He drifted toward a point of light that expanded into a luminous mist as he or it drew near. The light engulfed him, immersing him in its pure refulgence. The light embraced him like an enwombed babe as he floated within it.

Max sensed the light was a living presence. His awareness now merged with the light. The rational aspect of his mind experienced the light intellectually, while his emotional self felt an overwhelming sensation of love, beauty, and joy. Max wanted to both weep and laugh with exaltation. He understood then that the universe itself is a living conscious being, of which he is a tiny but essential aspect, and that the life force of the universe is the spiritual energy of love. In that moment, his mind expanded like a sudden supernova. Now he seemed able to encompass and comprehend the truth of everything, and, yes, it was all good.

Max wanted to remain within the light forever, ecstatic with its wonder and beauty. However, the mist now slowly dissipated. Within that luminosity he now discerned the face of his lover, Kitty. Her image was radiant, exquisite. Her long flaxen hair flowed and shimmered in the spirit wind. Her enigmatic silvery-azure eyes, glowing with urgent intensity, gazed directly into his. Kitty's lips moved silently, but he knew she was saying, "Max, Max, come back to me!" Only then did Max pass out.

***

When Max returned to consciousness unknown hours later, he found himself in a darkness so intense he wondered if he had died. But the gnawing pains in his back, shoulder, ribs, and left leg soon convinced him he was still very much alive, but a tad the worse for wear.

He realized he couldn't see because his face was planted in the dirt. With agonizing effort, he turned over. He was immediately stunned by the sight of the Milky Way, its billions of stars forming a bright lake in the darkness above him. Relaxing, Max let the stars pierce him with prickles of absolute beauty. The sight was so entrancing he could almost forget that he was in considerable pain and shivering with intense cold.

He soon noticed he could hear as well as see. The wind made a low keening through the sparse desert brush. Max imagined jinn and demons discussing his fate. There was also the faint scrabbling of anonymous night creatures. Then came the unmistakable crunch of human footsteps somewhere nearby. He was unsure whether he should announce himself to rescuers or remain silent in case it was an enemy. Just as he decided silence was the better course, a muscle twitched, and a shard of pain lanced through his leg. He gasped in pain, then forced himself to be silent. His hand slid along his leg and found an oozing wetness on his left thigh.

Jesus, that can't be good. Am I going to bleed out? Oh, well, *I'm probably about to be shot or stabbed, so I'll just close my eyes and wait for the end. Damn, I've lost Kitty. I broke my promise. I've made such a mess of my life (and* hers*) I deserve to die. At least the catfish isn't here to taunt me.*

Then he realized someone, maybe more than one, was beside him. Someone's hands investigated his body. They found his wounds. They discovered the gash in his leg, which caused him to stiffen in agony and fear. Fingers forced a tiny pebble into his mouth. It was perfectly round and tasted bitter. *A pill!? They must have poisoned me to avoid the noise of a gunshot.* Abruptly, an immense heat raced through his body. *Jesus, I'm burning!* Max gasped and passed out.

And he dreamed a dream of remembrance.

Chapter Two

"The Girl With the Flaxen Hair"

Catfish Jazz Club, Fort Worth, Texas, April 1985

Don't panic, it's no mistake. You're not imagining it. Yes, I'm the yard-long taxidermied catfish you see screwed (literally and figuratively) to the wall above the stage. And, yes, I'm talking in your head. You're not going nuts (but try the pistachios). I'm going to lay my tail (uh, tale) on you.

I'm the namesake of the Catfish Jazz Club, where a lot of this wacko story takes place. Oh, I saw you ogle at me as you entered. You laughed at my bulging eyes and this silly toy plastic saxophone protruding from my lip like a fishhook. It's okay to gawk. I'm totally used to it. As a highly sophisticated (stuffed but unstuffy) catfish, however, I've had to find ways to overcome the boredom of just hanging around like this for what seems like eons.

So, I'm noodling with your noodle. Having so much free time on my fins, I've discovered that certain rare individuals such as yourself are mentally receptive to my comments. Consider yourself privileged, not crazy.

I've magnanimously decided to introduce you to the other characters in this pathetic, all too human, romantic fiasco. Yes, indeed, there's something fishy happening here at the Club, but it's just my sly way of hooking you on this unsublime saga. You'll soon see where I'm going with this enigmatic monologue, because I'm reeling you in with it right about now. So, find a table and order a drink.

On the stage, below me, the Cowtown Jazz Trio is cruising through "'Round Midnight,*" with Larry pushing a little too hard (as usual) on alto sax; Joe is laconically thumping his stand-up acoustic bass; and Max is slipping in eager piano riffs whenever Larry deigns to take a breath—which ain't very often.*

Larry Delgado is the leader of the Cowtown Jazz Trio (Why didn't he name it the Catfish Jazz Trio after moi?) and he's the only professional musician of the three. He looks even larger than his 210 pounds in that loose, loud, floral aloha shirt and pale-yellow trousers (He simply refuses to take my fashion advice). Larry's currently in a mustache and goatee phase (very jive!). He is just back in hometown Fort Worth after several grueling years as a journeyman jazz musician in New York. But it must have been worth the gruel; it turned him into a bona fide jazz jock, and he plans to make the most of it.

This performance is a sort of belated ten-year high school reunion for these three longtime friends and their two gal-pals sitting at the band table. Larry recently decided to relocate permanently to Fort Worth, to form his own jazz combo and make some records. He persuaded his old chum, Max, to be his piano man even though their playing styles tend to diverge. But Max is becoming adept at accommodating Larry's more technical mode of play.

Max Ballard (ah, poor Max) tries to emulate the great Bill Evans' flowing pianism, always falling a bit short, of course. But then Max has made falling short in life his unconscious credo, as I often remind him. Max is not quite handsome, but his grandmother's Native American genes and his intense, gray-blue gaze can create a distinctive impression he never quite makes the most of. Tonight, Max is sporting a tad too-long mop of dark hair, black glasses, and black T-shirt imitating the Evans look. He designed the shirt himself with its infinity sign above a zero, and the message: "Everything is nothing with a twist ~ Kurt Vonnegut." That shirt could well be the harbinger of Max's fate, as you may come to understand by sticking with my story.

Max is the intellectual among these three jazz guys. He took a degree in philosophy at North Texas U. up in Denton (he's always trying to tweak my mustache with Kant about Descartes). But he belatedly realized he couldn't catch babes or moolah with just a philosophy BA (Bah, indeed!). Furthermore, the Vietnam contretemps was in full swing in the 70s. Max reluctantly opted for law school down in Austin so he would be deferred from the draft.

Now Max practices civil rights law here in Fort Worth and plays an occasional jazz gig to keep his chops polished. He would rather write poetry or fiction than con the Constitution (Heck, so would I instead of being so ignominiously nailed to this wall). But poetry won't pay his bills. He's published a couple of volumes of well-received but little-sold verses and teaches creative writing at Tarrant County College, so Max is always just sort of waiting for something to happen. And, hey, it's about to!

Joe Landers, there, on stand-up bass, (he's a stand-up kind of guy) with the crew cut, tan slacks, and green knit sports shirt, is up from

Houston for the reunion. Joe took a business degree, then completed an MBA while working as an assistant hospital administrator in Houston. Joe and wife Elaine have a five-year-old daughter, Sally (a real cutie). She's staying with Elaine's sister tonight.

That's Elaine seated at the band table with JJ Turner (don't ask what the JJ stands for). JJ is the trio's former high school sweetheart and sometime chanteuse. She also happens to be Larry's ex-wife (I'll give you the skinny on that momentarily).

The band table is just adjacent to this tiny stage where the trio is cooking (well, simmering), and where I'm hanging (don't call me a hanger-on though, that would be a drummer). From my elevated position, I can keep an eye on all the action and slip an occasional quip in Max's ear (He's the only one [besides you] who seems able to hear me, so I try to make the most of it).

JJ and Elaine are gabbing at the band table, almost oblivious to the music (they've heard it all before). JJ and Larry got hitched just before they moved to New York, must be seven years ago. But JJ divorced him when Larry got hooked on crack for a couple of years (I was hooked several times myself, so I can relate).

Larry finally realized the crack wasn't a magic charm to make him play better. He got clean and is now back in Fort Worth. And he's in JJ's good graces again. In fact, Larry wants JJ to join his new group as their singer, but she ain't having it. She's an elementary school teacher now and doesn't want to give that up to go on the road. Road trips will probably be necessary since Larry has his heart set on making a major name for himself in the jazz world. He might just do it, too. Larry's always had grit and gumption as well as talent. But watch out; Larry has a bit of a Machiavellian streak too (takes one to know one, I guess).

Let's eavesdrop on what the two girls are clacking on about.

"They're sounding better tonight than last night, don't you think?" ***says JJ, tossing down the last of her Cherry Mojito, and sucking its Maraschino cherry, the exact, artificial, ruby red of her thick, springy, tresses. She sees Elaine hasn't heard her and taps Elaine's arm.*** "Take that cotton out of your ears, girl, they aren't playing that bad or even that loud."

Elaine removes the cotton from one ear and says, "Yeah, they're sounding okay, but still too loud for me. At least the smoke isn't so bad since they put in the exhaust fans. The club could sure use some real air conditioning though. The Houston clubs are actually cold. I have to wear a sweater down there. It's like they want us to strip down in this heat." ***Elaine fans her face with a menu.***

"Air-conditioning would be appropriate for the Trio's Cool Jazz sound," ***says JJ,*** "but I reckon jazzers can't be choosers in country-western Cowtown." ***JJ's arms are flapping too, (maybe to dissipate the smoke from the crowd's Kools), but elaborate hand gestures are standard operating procedure for JJ's full-body communications style.***

"Frankly," ***says Elaine,*** "I'm glad we've moved out of Houston and Joe gave up playing so often. Sitting in shabby clubs listening to the same tunes every night just isn't my shot of tequila."

"I certainly commiserate," ***says JJ spreading her hands like a referee calling a foul.*** "But if you drink the mezcal, you got to swallow the worm. We girls are the ones who suffer for our guys' musical egos. I hope we can keep in touch and get together occasionally, honey. I'd hate to see us all lose track of each other and drift apart."

"I totally agree," ***says Elaine, putting her frozen margarita glass to her forehead.*** "And since we moved into our new house in Montgomery County, we need to invite y'all down for a party real soon. Joe's already accepted the assistant directorship at Montgomery Hospital, and he starts next month."

"Hey, that sounds great!" ***says JJ, fluffing her hair with both hands.*** "I'll look forward to it. Teaching gives me summers off. I'll be glad to come down and help decorate your new place."

"Oh, God, yes, please." ***Elaine takes too big a gulp of the margarita and pauses for momentary brain freeze.*** "Our house is on five acres out in the woods. It has a pool and plenty of room for guests, but neighbors are sparse. I prefer not to die of boredom or work myself to death. This city gal had to learn about country ways of living. We're on a well-water and septic system. Sally has a few friends there, but she would love to have her Aunt JJ visit. The house needs some serious décor work, so come on down when you can."

Now don't drowse off, folks, things are about to start shaking. As the band is winding down from its midnight rounds, a young woman slips thru the front door and looks apprehensively at the almost full house.

The audience noise diminishes noticeably as people notice her. She's not trying to make an impression, but she is so exotically beautiful that it can't be avoided. She's dressed modestly in tight jeans and a gauzy pink gypsy blouse. The overhead fans cause her long, fine, gold-blonde hair to levitate like a cloud around her head and her intense azure eyes flash with silver glints as she glances uncertainly around the room.

The band table down front is the only one with empty chairs and just the two women in possession. JJ realizes the girl's predicament, stands, and gestures extravagantly for her to join them. The girl makes her way to their table, smiles a megawatt thank-you, sits, and introduces herself.

The three musicians had observed the girl's entrance from their slightly elevated vantage point. Both Max and Larry (their hormones high on music, macho, and booze) are instantly excited by this stunning vision of the feminine mystique.

Max abruptly makes the subconscious connection between the girl's golden gorgeousness and a piece of classical music by Claude Debussy, **"The Girl With the Flaxen Hair"** *(I may have slipped that little item into his subconscious). He picks it out on the piano while his eyes follow her progress toward the band table. Larry quickly slides into the melody and turns it into a jazz improvisation. Joe adds a deep thrumming erotic background.*

When Larry takes over the melody, Max grabs the microphone and murmurs, "Ladies and gentlemen, 'The Girl With the Flaxen Hair,' in our own arrangement."

As Max emotes through the music, he glances often at the beautiful young woman. She is watching the musicians intently while occasionally turning to speak directly with JJ and Elaine. She flashes a shy but enthralling smile at the trio when she realizes the tune is a tribute to her. Max imagines she is smiling directly at him and feels a frisson of excitement surge up his spine (I'm not making this up folks. Max is already flat splat in love but doesn't know it yet).

The three women soon shift closer together and are chatting like longtime friends. JJ can see why men are gob-smacked by this semi-divine apparition. Her hair hangs to her mid-back, but it's so fine, strands are borne up by every waft of air. She must have absconded with Audrey Hepburn's swan-like neck. Her face is a soft oval with Ava Gardner's prominent cheekbones that human males find so alluring. Her unpainted lips are narrow and curved in a

naturally enigmatic smile (I wish had a smile like that instead of this bucket-mouth grin).

But it's her eyes that are truly extraordinary. They are large and wide set with a vague oriental geometry (I've got to admit, her gorgeous peepers make my glass marbles look even sillier). Her combination of intense azure eyes with their luminous silver striations makes them rare and spectacular. Those eyes give her a look of startled intensity.

Momentarily turning his gaze from the goddess, Max's eye finally catches mine. I'm regarding him with my most penetrating gaze (which is damned difficult with these bulging bobbles).

I speak to him in his father's accustomed voice of disparagement: "Max, son, she's way out of your league. Why would she be interested in a lackluster lawyer, mediocre piano pounder, and pathetic poet? Well, go ahead and find out the hard way." Max is a genuine romantic fool (with melancholic tendencies). I get a buzz out of gigging him like that occasionally, just to watch him mentally cringe.

When the musicians conclude the piece, Max and Larry nearly bolt off the stage. Max has a slight head start since Larry must secure his beloved alto safely on its stand. But Larry catches up just as Max arrives at the table, and Larry's larger bulk edges Max aside.

"Who is our lovely guest, ladies?" ***Larry queries JJ while devouring the girl with hungry hyena eyes.*** "And to what do we owe the honor of her presence?"

The girl fixes her sparklers demurely on Larry, her face flushing slightly, and she says, "I didn't really expect you to recognize me, Mr.

Delgado. It's been five years since you gave me lessons on tenor sax. I was only fifteen then. I guess I've changed some."

Larry gawks at her a moment. "Hey, that's right. I tutored several kids from Paschal High five years ago. Yeah, I remember you now! Yes, darlin', you have changed—a lot, and... I apologize abjectly, but I don't recall your name."

The girl opens her mouth to reply, but JJ touches her shoulder and says, "Let me relieve your abjectness, Larry. This is Kitty Kazinsky. She's a musician and a student at TCU. She's going to join us for the rest of the evening. Kitty, this is Joe Landers, Elaine's husband, and Max Ballard, nobody's husband, but a fine poet and a pianist of note."

"Yeah, Max's note is okay, but a pianist should really have more than one," ***says Larry, chortling at his own lame joke and elbowing Max in the ribs.***

Max manages to insinuate an arm past Larry's attempt to preempt the space and offers his hand to Kitty. "A sincere pleasure to meet you, Ms. Kazinsky. Thanks for coming to hear us play."

"I'm pleased to meet you, too, Mr. Ballard," ***says Kitty, sliding her slim, warm hand into his, which sends an electric shiver up Max's arm.*** "I hope you're going to play another set or two. I'm sorry to arrive so late. I really want to hear your stuff. I've heard good things about your trio."

"Heck, we're barely getting warmed up," ***says Larry.*** "We just need some lubrication and we'll hit it again. The later the jazz, the more it cooks. Hey, Max, it looks like the waitress is ignoring us. How about y'all get us some drinks while I renew my acquaintance with Miss Kazinsky. What would you like to drink, darlin'?"

Max and Joe take the girls' drink orders and move to the bar.

"You'd better make your move quick on that one," ***says Joe,*** "before Larry slurps her up. You know he'll try, and he's got an advantage being her ex-music mentor."

"She's a beautiful girl, all right, but she's ten years younger than we are, and we don't know anything about her. A girl that lovely probably already has a boyfriend around somewhere. Larry will just embarrass himself coming on to her like he does."

Joe guffaws, "I saw your reaction when she shook your hand, Dude; you practically turned to Jell-O. Face it man, you're smitten. I'm just saying don't let Larry's sax become sex if you get my drift. Besides, Larry doesn't embarrass himself, only his friends."

Max and Joe return to the table with the drinks. JJ catches Max's eye, arches an eyebrow, and tilts her head at him in silent severity. Larry monopolizes the conversation by elaborating on his plans for making Fort Worth a jazz Mecca with his new group and his plans for a recording studio and maybe even a jazz festival.

"When I have the studio up and running, Miss Kazinsky, you'll have to come audition for a recording with my group or your own."

"Oh, I'm not with a group," ***says Kitty,*** "and I'm not sure I'll ever be good enough to make a record. Thanks for your offer, though. I'll certainly keep it in mind."

"Well, if you have a music scholarship from TCU, you must have some pretty decent talent. I'd love to hear you play. Do you have your axe with you tonight? We'd be glad to have you sit in for a set," ***says Larry.***

"Larry, don't harass the girl," ***says JJ.*** "She's just here to listen tonight. Besides, Elaine and I are just getting to know her. We've got to warn her about you jazz wolves." ***She shoos Larry away as if flapping a towel.***

"I didn't bring my tenor anyway," ***says Kitty.*** "But I appreciate the offer. Maybe another time."

"Hey, no pressure. I'm always on the lookout for talent, and I'd sure like to give you a chance to shine."

"Come on, Larry, we need to get started again," ***says Joe.***

The trio plays two more sets, with Larry flaunting his technical chops at every opportunity. Meanwhile, the girls bond firmly with Kitty, and JJ trades phone numbers with her.

In the middle of the last set, Kitty looks at her watch and says, "I'm really enjoying the music, but I need to do some studying. Please apologize to the guys for me and tell them I'll try to catch the band again sometime soon." ***Kitty smiles and waves to the guys on stage as she makes her exit.***

Stay tuned, folks, and look for me next time you visit the Catfish Club. I'm always hanging out (or just hanging) here to observe (and comment on) this human, all too human, comedy.

Chapter Three

"Satin Doll"

Fort Worth, Texas, September 1985

Two weeks after the Catfish Club concert, JJ received a phone call from Kitty. "I hope you don't mind me calling like this, but you did give me your number, and I thought I'd ask your advice about something if you don't mind."

"Of course I don't mind, Kitty, I'm glad you called. Is this something I can answer right quick, or should we meet for coffee and have a nice long confab?"

"Well, yes, it may take some time. Can you meet me at the Purple Frog on the TCU campus, maybe this Friday?"

"Sure, my last class Friday ends at two, so I could be there by two thirty."

"That will be perfect. See you then, and thanks."

The Purple Frog was a small, recently opened coffee and sandwich shop catering to TCU students. A purple horned toad sculpture, TCU's mascot (really a lizard and certainly neither toad nor frog), menaced visitors from just above the door. JJ arrived a few minutes late due to the lack of nearby parking. As she approached the shop, she saw Kitty's face through one of the windows, looking nervous and chewing at her lower lip. Even without makeup, Kitty was strikingly beautiful, but she currently wore a frown, with a vertical crease between her arched golden brows. As JJ entered the shop, Kitty's face lit up with a huge smile, and she waved.

"Sorry I'm late," said JJ. "Thanks for saving us a table. I love the name of this place. What's good here?"

"They have coffee, soft drinks, and hot or cold tea. Their chicken salad sandwich is not bad if you're hungry. You have to order at the counter."

"I'll just have a coffee, and I'll pay if you'll order for us. I'm slightly tuckered from the walk." JJ handed her a $5 bill, slid into the chair, and flounced her hair to cool her neck.

Kitty returned shortly with two coffees and a slice of banana bread. "I thought we could share this if you like."

"Oh, I didn't notice the pastries. Good choice. I am a little peckish. So, what's the topic of discussion?"

Kitty took a sip of her coffee and looked pensive, deciding how to begin. "Well, I've had a postcard from Mr. Ballard, uh, Max, asking if I'd like to have a picnic lunch with him at the Botanic Gardens. Here's the card."

She handed JJ the postcard with a picture of the Fort Worth Botanic Gardens on one side and a little poem on the other: "Shall we picnic mid the posies?/ or better yet the roses; /but the flowers must beware,/ since they cannot compare/ with your splendor;/ they may refuse their scent to our noses."

JJ giggled and fluffed her hair again. "Oh, dear. Max is obviously ga-ga over you, girl. Look, Kitty, Max is the most creative person I know. He's actually somewhat shy, but he comes up with goofy, beautiful ideas like this all the time. It may seem like he's being forward, but he's really just being innocently playful."

"So, you think it will be okay to go out with him?"

"Sure, Kitty. He's the sweetest guy you can imagine. He's very serious, however, about civil rights and politics. He is a civil rights lawyer for the ACLU after all. But ask him about poetry or literature and you'll be on safe ground. Are you concerned he might try to hit on you?"

"Well, like you said, he seems to be infatuated with me, and I, uh, I've had problems with guys coming on too strong in the past. In fact, guys seem to hit on me no matter where I am. It really gets annoying. I haven't had a boyfriend for over a year. I'm really not interested in a relationship right now. I just want to finish school and find a job, or something meaningful to do with my life."

JJ disposed of the last bite of banana bread and washed it down. She looked Kitty directly in the eye. "Yeah, well, let me be blunt, honey. You're dangerously beautiful. College guys can be especially bothersome. At that age, most of them just want to get in your knickers and claim you as a trophy." She reached out to pat Kitty on the arm. "Maybe that's a good reason for you to go out and have some innocent fun with an older guy like Max. He won't hit on you. He's a real gentleman. But he won't bore you either."

"That sounds like what I need. I just want to get away from the grind of school occasionally and enjoy myself without getting too involved with someone. I must admit I am more attracted to older men for some reason." Kitty paused and nervously swirled a lock of hair on her finger.

Kitty let out a deep breath. "My father died in Vietnam when I was ten. Mom's been treated for depression for years, so she's not been much help. I have an older brother, but he works for Technos in California. I haven't socialized much since high school. I was late to the Catfish jam because I was afraid there might be a crowd of pushy drunks there. But I wanted to hear Larry, and I'm glad I went, since I also met you. I think I would have turned right around and left if you hadn't invited me to your table. I was a little shaky until you and Elaine rescued me."

JJ took Kitty's hand and patted it gently. "Oh, Kitty, looks like I may need to take you on as a project. I understand now why you're attracted to older men. You loved your dad, and his death must have left a big hole in your heart."

Kitty sighed. "Yes, that's probably true. I hadn't thought of it that way." She ducked her head and choked out a moan, "But it might also have to do with my being raped when I was sixteen." Kitty's eyes suddenly went wide and she gave a little gasp. "Oh! Sorry, I didn't mean to say that; it just fell out of my mouth." Kitty flushed, shuddered, and her eyes teared up. She looked around to see if anyone had noticed. Then she made several gasping sobs and glanced pleadingly at JJ.

"Oh, Jesus, Kitty, don't be sorry, dear. I'm glad you told me. No wonder you're suspicious about men. Here, take my napkin and wipe your eyes. I can see you need an older girlfriend, and God knows I've been around the block enough to qualify." JJ saw Kitty was trembling but was attempting to bring herself back under control.

"Okay, so, here's my advice," said JJ after Kitty had calmed herself. "Get some friendly socializing by going out with Max. He won't try to take advantage of you. In fact, I'll have a talk with him beforehand, if that's okay, just to let him know he had better be on his best behavior and that I have my eye on him."

"I don't know. I mean, sure, I guess; whatever you think is best. But please don't tell Max about me being raped. You're the only person I've ever told except my mom and my therapist. I don't want to be pitied or thought easy either."

"No, of course not. I won't tell him, or anyone. Let me know how it goes with Max. In fact, I think it might be good for us to talk on a regular basis."

"Oh, yes, I'd like that. By the way, there is one other thing." Kitty could smile a little now, though her eyes were red from crying. She looked at JJ sheepishly, biting her lip. "Mr. Delgado called and wants me to come over to play my sax for him next week."

JJ put her hands to her cheeks. "Oh, my God! I guess I'm going to need another coffee."

***

Max picked up Kitty at ten the next Sunday morning and drove them to the Botanic Gardens. He had told her to dress casually, so they were both in shorts and T-shirts. He wore a pale green shirt with the message: "Outside of a dog, a book is man's best friend. Inside a dog, it's too dark to read ~ Groucho Marx."

Kitty's purple TCU Music School shirt featured a design of notes and clefs. They were both a little nervous and didn't say much beyond pleasantries before they arrived. Max had not been dating in a couple of years. This was his first such foray since the Tanya incident.

Max carried a picnic basket with a quilt folded on top. "Sunday morning is the best time to visit because most people are at church," said Max. "Let's walk around the gardens while we've got it to ourselves. We can look for a good place to spread our quilt."

They walked among the flowerbeds and water features, each pointing out items of particular interest. The flowers were visually spectacular, and their fragrances wafted in the light breeze. The birds were singing and fluttering about exuberantly. By lunchtime, Max and Kitty were on easy terms with each other. They laid their quilt in some shade and ate lunch.

"Your peanut butter and honey sandwiches are yummy," said Kitty.

"Glad you like them. My mother made them for me for school. They are my go to, easy to make, comfort food. I'm not much of a cook. Try the iced tamarind juice; There's an Indian market near me. I like tamarind better than lemonade."

Kitty said, "This early Sunday excursion was a good idea. Are you not a church-going person, or do you just not like crowds?"

"Both, I suppose. I'm a devout agnostic. My mind is open regarding God. I just haven't seen any evidence that would sway me either way. The Big Guy certainly hasn't spoken to me, though I feel like He gives me a thump on the noggin sometimes."

"Maybe SHE is just waiting for the right moment to enlighten you," Kitty chuckled.

"I hope you're right. I do consider myself a spiritual person. I believe beauty is spiritual. These gardens and some wilderness areas are what I consider good places to contemplate spiritual things more so than churches. I hope that doesn't offend you."

"No, of course not. I grew up in the Methodist Church, but I've never been much of a churchgoer myself. I figure Jesus is more concerned with how I behave in the world than with my singing his praises in church. I'll bet Jesus even likes jazz."

"Well put, Kitty. I quite agree. Jesus had some good ideas even though few people can live up to them and most don't even try. He wasn't the first to say 'Do unto others as you would be done to,' either. The Buddha and Zoroaster beat him to that. In fact, I think it was best said by the Dalai Lama. Simply 'Be kind.' And the Lama could have got it from my momma, who always told me to 'Just be sweet.'"

Kitty giggled. "I like the way you can be humorous while expressing serious ideas. I liked your postcard invitation, too. It was cute and clever. I'd like to read some of your serious poetry sometime."

"Well, that can certainly be arranged. I'll bring you one of my chapbooks, uh, next time we get together. You will expand my reading audience tremendously."

"Oh, you poor, unappreciated genius!"

"You've nailed it already; you catch on fast." He pulled a peach the size of a softball from the basket. "I thought we might share it since it's so large. The Weatherford Peach Festival had a bumper crop this year. You eat half and I'll finish it."

Kitty bit into the peach. It was so juicy she got it on her cheeks and chin. Max wanted to lick it off but handed her a towel instead.

She handed him the wounded peach. "So, would you rather be a poet than a lawyer? You must be able to help many people as an ACLU attorney. I admire you standing up for civil rights and the Constitution."

"It's a living that I don't need to be ashamed of, but I can't really say I enjoy it. I suppose I would rather be a famous poet." He gnawed at the peach, letting it drip on the grass.

"Well, if you keep writing, I'll wager you'll be both."

"Says the girl who hasn't read any of my poetry yet."

"I guess I'll have to read it just to find out more about your views on life. Tell me why you became a lawyer instead of a full-time musician or college professor or something."

"Well, I do teach creative writing at the community college, but that pays only about enough to cover my commuting expenses to teach the class. When I was in college, I became caught up in the civil rights movement and the anti-Vietnam war movement, so I majored in philosophy and political science. Becoming a lawyer was just a logical continuation of that involvement. And it allowed me to stay out of the war. My dad wanted me to volunteer for Vietnam, like he did for World War Two. It really irked him that I actually opposed the war."

Kitty averted her eyes and her voice became strained. “You know, uh, my dad died in Vietnam, so it’s kind of a sore subject with me. I hope you weren’t one of those anti-war demonstrators who vilified the soldiers when they returned home.”

“Oh, gosh, no, Kitty! I’m so sorry about your father. No, I opposed the war because I thought it was totally unjustified. If my views had prevailed, we might never have invaded Vietnam. Or maybe America would have withdrawn before your dad died. And I certainly didn’t denigrate our soldiers. I think they were brave and deserving of honor. But they were also innocent pawns of the American war machine. Several of my friends, including Joe Landers, were in Nam. He came home in one piece, thank goodness.”

“Okay, then, I suppose we can still be friends,” said Kitty, her voice a little husky. “My dad was very special, and it devastated both my mom and me when he was killed. She sort of lost faith in everything. When he was drafted, he promised Mom he would come back to her. He even tore a $2 bill in half just before he left and gave half to her as a pledge he would return. She still has her half. But all we got back of his were his dog tags.”

“That’s a truly sad story. If there’s any way I can help you or your mom, as a lawyer or just as a friend, please let me know. I want to be here for you. But, let’s talk about something more pleasant on such a beautiful day.”

“These gardens hold a lot of happy memories for me,” said Kitty. “My parents often brought me here as a child, and to the zoo down the street. I liked the gardens best. The zoo was always stinky, and the animals seemed always to turn their butts toward us. I enjoyed just watching the koi here swirl in the ponds and the comical turtles with their periscope necks.”

“I had some good times here too," said Max. "Once when I was about five, I accidentally rolled down a grassy slope into the pond. The koi weren't happy with me, and neither were my parents.”

"What about your family?" asked Kitty. "Are your parents still here?"

"They are both alive, but they've been in Taiwan for the past year and will be for at least another year. My dad is an aircraft engineer. He recently retired from General Dynamics and was immediately propositioned by Taiwan to help them build an F-16 copy. I have a married sister in Denver. And, in case you're wondering, I've never been married; I'm, uh, saving myself for just the right girl; one who can tolerate my poetry and my sense of humor."

Kitty grinned. "Well, I certainly hope you don't die an old, grouchy bachelor."

Kitty and Max finished their picnic lunch, then spent a couple of hours strolling and talking among the flowers and trees. When some thunderheads began to build in the sky and the air freshened, he drove her home. They stood in her front yard, holding hands and looking deep into each other's eyes. Kitty slipped her arms around Max and gave him a tight, protracted hug.

"Thank you for a lovely outing. Maybe we can do it again soon," said Kitty.

"Yes, I'd like that very much. But JJ warned me not to be a pest, so I'll leave it to you to let me know when you would like to get together. I know you have a heavy load of classes. I'm available any time you need a break, or if I can help you with anything."

She squeezed him again before letting go. It gave him a shiver of intense desire.

"By the way, I have a piano gig at the Rondeau Club every Thursday evening," said Max. "Maybe we could have dinner together there next week before I play, if you're free. I—Yikes!" An intense flash of light and a loud bang startled them.

They fell to the ground, and Max covered Kitty with his body. He looked around, wondering if it had been a gunshot. But it had been much louder, an explosion. Then tiny pieces of metal rained down on and around them for a few seconds. Max saw a power line down across the street, whipping about, sparking, causing several small fires in the dry grass. Smoke was issuing from a transformer on a nearby telephone pole. He realized a bolt of lightning must have hit the metal transformer.

Kitty later called JJ and reported what had happened. "Max helped me up after he saw there was no more danger. He grabbed a quilt from his car and beat out the fire. Then a fire truck arrived, and they took charge. It was certainly an exciting first date."

"Wow, girl, that must have been quite a hug you gave him. Good thing y'all didn't kiss or the entire neighborhood might have caught fire."

"Yeah, I'll have to be more careful about that in the future," said Kitty, giggling.

JJ could imagine Kitty's eyes sparkling even over the phone.

***

A few days later, Kitty arrived at the Catfish Jazz Club at 10 a.m. with her tenor sax in tow. The club's owner was a friend of Larry's and had made him a partner in the club in order to have Larry as an investor and Larry's trio as the permanent house band. Larry often practiced there and used it to audition local musicians for gigs. He was alone this morning except for a couple of employees cleaning and preparing for opening that evening. Seeing Kitty enter, Larry began to play "Satin Doll." Kitty blushed at the implied musical tribute, opened her tenor case, and assembled her horn.

Larry broke off abruptly. "Now don't be nervous, Miss Kazinsky; I know you're not looking to join my band, but I sure could use some eye candy on stage to help attract a crowd, especially if you can also play."

"Mr. Delgado, I came mainly to thank you for the lessons you gave me back in high school. You were an amazing teacher. You gave me the best possible start on learning the sax. It was probably the reason I got the music scholarship to TCU. That has definitely helped my education, even though I'm majoring in math rather than music. I love playing jazz; it will be with me all my life."

Larry beamed. "Please call me Larry, Ms. Kazinsky, and may I call you Kitty? I was well paid for teaching you to play, but the instruction was a pleasure 'cause you were such an eager student. And you certainly took to jazz performance, as I recall, so let's hear what kind of chops you got."

Kitty had been moistening her reed and checking her tenor as Larry spoke. Now she put the mouthpiece to her lips and blew a strong, pure middle C, then she hit the low A-flat followed by a rapid glissando up to the high E. She came down again through some standard riffs and broke into the same version of "Satin Doll" Larry had been blowing on his alto when she entered. Larry laughed and joined her with a close harmony duet. Then he veered off with a technical improvisation. She waited for his pause, then jumped in with a similar improv featuring a creamy tone like a hot fudge sundae for the ears.

"Oh, darlin, you got to play with us sometime soon. You're way beyond what I ever taught you. You'd make Stan Getz jealous. You gotta let folks hear what you can say with that hunk of tin. By the way, does your tenor have a name? I call my alto Maria after the robot girl in the film *Metropolis.*"

Kitty blushed. "Gosh, I never realized other musicians thought of their instruments as people. My tenor is sort of my alter ego. Her name is Ellie, after my middle name: Elizabeth."

"Hey, that's a great name for your axe. You and Ellie need to come play for my combo."

"You're very kind, uh, Larry. I know I'm not up to your level yet, but I'm hoping to keep improving even though I don't plan to be a professional musician. I'd be honored to play with your group sometime. I can't make it tonight, but soon."

Larry grinned at Kitty. "Okay, now, you gotta promise me. I'm not kidding about your talent. You've got the goods, girl, and I want to be the one to show you off."

Kitty smiled shyly and her eyes sparkled like fireworks. "Thanks so much for letting me audition. I need to head back to campus for a statistics class now. I'll be in touch."

As she went out the door, Larry licked his lips like a cheetah appraising an antelope, slowly shook his head, brought Maria to his lips, and began to practice again.

Chapter Four

"Summertime"

Montgomery County, Texas, May 1986

When Max arrived at the big yellow house in the piney woods north of Houston that bright, late May afternoon, Joe and Elaine's other guests had already arrived. Larry was sitting in the shallows of the backyard swimming pool sipping a Coors and smoking a thin cigar. JJ was lounging in a lawn chair in the shade near the pool, close enough to trade quips with Larry.

JJ shook her thick scarlet curls, trying unsuccessfully to generate some cool in the humid air. She grinned mischievously at Larry after a sip of her bourbon-laced iced tea. "Why you guzzling that Colorado weak water instead of some good old Texas Lone Star?"

"Coors just recently came available in North Texas and I wanted to try it, so I brought some down. Ain't bad, but, yeah, it ain't Lone Star. Come sit in the pool if you're hot. Feels mighty fine."

"It's not the heat, it's the humidity that bothers me, and the pool is just a big puddle of humidity. Maybe I'll ask Elaine to shave my head like Sinéad O'Connor."

"I suspected you were a little crazy when we were married, now I'm certain. That red mop is your best feature."

JJ smirked. "Oh, honey-child, you haven't had any of my best feature in so long you've forgotten what it is. And speaking of which, you better not be hitting on Kitty; you're what, ten years older than her? You may have been her music mentor in high school, but I'm her mentor now, and I told her to watch out for you. So, paws off."

"I'm just her friend and maybe I'm still her musical mentor, dear. I haven't hit on her. But, hey, she's twenty-one and quite able to make her own decisions. She's sure added some glamor to our jazz combo when she played with us the last few months. She may be the shy, quiet type but, heck, she might be smarter than me; or is it 'I'?"

"It's 'I,' as you used to know until you lost all those brain cells to booze and blow."

"It was crack, not blow. And, you know I've been clean for the last three years, and I had to do it all on my own cause you bailed out on me."

JJ sat up and put away her snark. "Larry, I'm sorry. I didn't mean to diss you. You know I'm really proud of you for going cold turkey and getting off the hard stuff. But I'm not sure you would have done it if I hadn't left. You're playing in the big leagues now. Lots of money and temptation. Show me you can stay clean, and I might be willing for us to get back together." JJ grinned and flashed her eyes at Larry. "Then I could help you remember my best feature."

Larry groaned, took a last sip of beer, and slid deeper into the pool.

Meanwhile, Joe came out front to greet Max with a man hug and a back thump as Max parked and exited his five-year-old Chevy. Max eyed Larry's nearly new Corvette. It was also parked in the roundabout driveway that encircled a huge burr oak standing sentinel in the center of the front lawn.

"Max, so glad you could make it, man. Looks like fit weather for our Memorial Day weekend. It will be good to get together for a jam. Should be fun. Larry, Kitty, and JJ all drove down together. Kitty and JJ are sleeping in Sally's bedroom with her. Larry has the guest bedroom. I'm afraid you'll have to make do with a couch."

"I brought my sleeping bag, so I can sack out almost anywhere," said Max. "Heck, I may camp out in the backyard and have a campfire."

"Sure, if you don't mind a few mosquitoes, raccoons, and maybe Big Bird wandering by. There's an ostrich farm down the road, and I never know when I might find one bathing in the swimming pool some morning."

"Well, maybe I'll stay in the house then if there's that much wildlife around. Right now I could use a cold beer."

"Can do. Larry and JJ are around back guarding the drinks cooler. Kitty has been helping Elaine in the kitchen."

They walked through the house toward the rear deck. On the way, they encountered six-year-old Sally, who demanded a hug from Max and a promise to give her a piano lesson. In the kitchen, Elaine wiped her hands on her apron and hugged Max too. Kitty entered the kitchen in shorts, T-shirt, and running shoes. She smiled warmly and gave Max a long, close embrace, which involved looking deeply into his eyes. She abruptly broke away when Sally said, "Ooh la la!"

Max followed Kitty out onto the back deck, his heart hammering in double time in response to Kitty's clinch. He watched her do some stretches on the deck, then she announced, "I'm going for a jog. Anyone care to come with?"

"I'll join you," said Max. "Just let me put on my runners."

"Come with us, JJ; you too, Larry," said Kitty. "You both need some exercise; we won't go fast, and it's only a couple of miles around the big circle road."

"I eluded the Vietnam draft on account of flat feet," said Larry, "and, anyway, this water is just too damn comfortable to leave."

"I'll pass, too," said JJ. "I'm constitutionally opposed to that much sweat, especially if it's mine."

"Just you and me, then, Max. We won't have to slow down for these sissies."

"Well, I like to think I'm in fair condition," said Max, quickly fumbling into his shoes. "But I'm more of a sprinter than a distance runner like you, so let's not try to set any records."

Kitty giggled and set off at a brisk pace for the road. Sally's young yellow Lab, Rambo, decided he had better come along to protect them from any vicious armadillos they might encounter.

Max stayed side by side with Kitty for the first half mile. Rambo brought up the rear, distracted occasionally to investigate alluring odors, then racing to catch up.

"I like the message on your shirt," said Kitty, glancing at Max's blue T-shirt which proclaimed in red script "Lord, what fools these mortals be, ~ Shakespeare, *A Midsummer Night's Dream*." "Present company excepted, I hope."

"It speaks only for myself," said Max, who was breathing heavily now.

Their pace slowed on a long up-slope. Max fell behind and was admiring Kitty's sleek muscular legs when they heard barking and stopped to look around. Two large German Shepherd dogs were sprinting toward them from a side property, barking menacingly. Kitty gasped. Max stepped in front of her in the event of an imminent attack. Rambo whined and cringed behind Kitty. The two Shepherds jerked to a sudden stop at the edge of the road, continuing to bark and snarl, but coming no closer.

"Ha, Rambo, you great coward," said Max. "They have an invisible electric fence; they won't come any closer."

"Thank goodness," said Kitty, removing her hands from Max's waist. "I thought we were about to get eaten."

Rambo now understood the situation. He trotted over to the canine Gestapos, eyed them contemptuously, even as they barked hysterically. Rambo lifted a hind leg and pissed in their direction. This set the two dogs leaping, snapping, shrieking, and almost attacking each other in their frenzied desire to rip Rambo to shreds. But they wouldn't venture beyond the unseen barrier. Rambo moseyed back to his human charges and motioned for them to follow him. Kitty laughed delightedly and set off again. Max, who had welcomed the chance to take a breather after he realized they were safe, resumed his place beside her.

As they reached the top of the slope, there came a raucous laugh from the stand of dead pine trees across the road from them. A large black bird with a bright, red-feathered topknot alighted on a pine trunk near them. It began to hammer the bole with its long yellow beak, like a maniacal jazz drummer. Another bird of the same species lit on a tree close by and joined in the pounding. The two trees shivered with the beating; the sound reverberated through the forest. Suddenly, a large swath of the first tree's bark fell away, and both birds took to the air with loud squawks.

"What sort of birds are those?" said Kitty. "They must be the size of chickens."

"They are Pileated Woodpeckers, I think," said Max. "It's the largest woodpecker in the world now that the Ivory Bill is extinct. Pretty impressive, aren't they?"

Max had knelt to retie his shoe and was looking up at Kitty as he talked about the birds. She was gazing into the dead forest trying to follow the flight of the woodpeckers. Her hair was haloed by the sun, myriad loose golden filaments floating out, glowing like a sacred nimbus around her face. Her beauty suddenly overcame Max, as it had the first time he saw her last year at the Catfish Club.

"Kitty, you look like a goddess with that sun dazzle in your hair. I've got to tell you, I think—I know—I'm in love with you. I believe I have been since I first met you. And our date at the Botanic Gardens, just walking and talking with you, was the most wonderful time I've had since—well ever."

"Oh, Max..." Her voice was soft and strained. "You know I've come to care for you—as a dear friend. But I'm not ready to get serious about anyone right now. Also, it makes me nervous for you to put me on a pedestal like that. I'm just an ordinary girl. You'll be disappointed if you expect more of me than I can be." Her hands trembled a little as she brushed back her tresses. "Let's keep things light and easy for a while. I do so enjoy your company, your music, your poetry. One of the things I like—I love—about you is that you're not the pushy type."

"Of course I won't push you, Kitty. Take all the time you need. You're worth waiting for. I'll try not to idealize you, but it's difficult. To me, you're the most beautiful woman in the world. But I love you for more than your beauty. You have intelligence, humor, and a kind heart. I want to spend my life with you. You know, those two woodpeckers...They fell in love only with each other, and they mated for life."

Kitty smiled. "Well, don't go banging your head against a tree for me, please. Remember what your T-shirt says. Sometimes I think we're all fools when it comes to love. Come on, I'll race you back to the house. I'm ready for the cool of the pool."

***

Late that afternoon, the six friends sat on the back deck near the pool, under the shade of huge pines and oaks, while Joe tended a barbecue grill. Sally and two young neighbor girls were frolicking in the pool.

"Hamburgers this year instead of something more exotic, eh?" said Larry. "I really enjoyed the show last year when you put live lobsters in the pool and dared the kids to catch them. It was a hoot with the lobsters clicking their claws and scaring the kids."

"It was a hoot for everyone but the lobsters," said JJ.

"They had their last fling of freedom," said Joe. "That's more than most lobsters get before they're cooked. They were feisty enough that I had to get them out with the net."

"Do you think lobsters feel pain when they're boiled?" asked Kitty.

"Oh, I doubt it," said Elaine, bringing the buns and fixings to the picnic table. "They just sat there in the boiling water. They didn't make a fuss."

"I don't want to ruin any appetites or get into a moral argument," said Max, "but I think it's been established that most mammals and other warm-blooded creatures feel pain and even experience emotions such as love, too. Of course, lobsters aren't warm-blooded, but still...."

"Oh, come on, Max," said Larry. "You trying to turn us all into vegetarians or somethin? That just ain't gonna happen, man. Humans are supposed to eat meat."

"Just stating scientific facts," said Max. "It doesn't help to ignore them. Yes, humans are natural predators and omnivores, but I think we should strive to kill animals as painlessly as possible even if it costs extra. I've read that in the future we may be able to culture meat genetically rather than having to kill animals."

"Ah, no pain protein!" said JJ. "I like it. Then we wouldn't need so many cows taking up so much space and farting methane that causes global warming."

"And people could stop killing animals like whales, sharks, and baby seals," said Kitty.

"Is someone killing baby seals?" asked Sally, who had gotten out of the pool and was drying off.

"No, honey, it's just grown-up talk," said Elaine. "You and the girls go play inside for a few minutes. I'll call you for supper."

"Whoops, so sorry," said Kitty. "We should change the subject, anyway. Are we going blackberry picking tomorrow? I saw lots of bushes in the forest during our run."

"You bet," said Elaine. "I look forward to picking wild blackberries this time of year. Just be sure to wear long sleeves and jeans. Those bushes have plenty of thorns."

"That just adds to the adventure," said Max. "You really appreciate those berries when you've had to shed some blood for them."

"I only hope we don't run into any wild hogs or rattlers," said Joe. "Wear some boots if you have them. By the way, the hamburgers are ready."

***

After a delicious outdoor meal, they moved back into the rec room of the house and jammed some jazz. Max tickled the ivories of Elaine's upright piano. Larry blew alto sax. Joe thumped upright bass. They even persuaded

Kitty to play some tenor sax. JJ crooned several songs and got Sally to sing "Summertime" with her before Elaine put Sally to bed.

Late that night, after considerable wine and beer had been consumed, Max and Larry renewed their perennial argument about whether jazz should be technical or lyrical. As usual, neither prevailed, and everyone finally found their way to bed. Max unrolled his sleeping bag on the glassed-in back patio, where he could see some stars glittering above the trees. He made a few notes for a poem idea that had come to him earlier that evening. Finally, he sought sleep while visualizing Kitty with sun dazzle in her hair and smiling like Botticelli's Venus born from the sea.

Thoughts of Max and Larry also delayed Kitty's sleep. She somehow wanted to be with both. Larry always seemed so self-assured, like she remembered her father to be. Max was sweet and always an unpredictable adventure of mind and body. Yet she felt she shouldn't get serious with either of them until she had somehow proved herself to herself. What did she really want out of life? The world had so many problems, but no simple solutions. She wanted to do something significant and meaningful, rather than just becoming a housewife. But what and how? She felt pummeled by conflicting emotions and confusions. As Kitty drifted into sleep, she wondered how those woodpeckers fell in love.

***

The morning dawned bright and promised to be Texas torrid. Max awakened to the sounds of breakfast-making in the adjoining kitchen. The three women greeted him much too cheerily for his slight hangover as he made his way to the bathroom. A hot shower and smooth shave persuaded him to feel more invigorated. He returned to the kitchen, where Elaine thrust a cup of coffee into his hand.

"Congrats, you're the first of the guys up and around. Y'all stayed up too late last night. Did you settle anything about how jazz ought to be performed?"

Before Max could respond, Larry ambled in, rubbing his goatee, and interjected, "As usual, we couldn't agree and probably never will. I believe in constant musical innovation, whereas Max thinks jazz should merely be pleasant to the ear, like elevator music."

Max groaned theatrically, "As usual, Larry has completely misconstrued my argument. If jazz becomes mainly a vehicle for technical display, it will have ever fewer followers and will devolve into dissonant noise just as has happened to so much post-modern classical music."

"Can't jazz be many things to many people?" asked Kitty. "I mean can't it be like a tree that has many branches that are all alive and going in different directions: blues, Dixieland, swing, Cool, bop, and beyond?"

"You nailed it, sister," said JJ. "Let the listeners decide. Everyone can have their own favorite type of jazz, just so it's played with feeling."

"For that matter," said Joe, who had finally joined the group, "music itself is so various, there's a different kind for everyone. I don't care much for country, folk, or rock, but millions of people do, and that's fine."

"I agree that people are entitled to whatever music pleases them," said Max. "But it seems to me that great music itself can be one of the most powerful and significant forces for bringing people together and giving them a transforming emotional experience. The Mozart Requiem and Beethoven's Ninth always give me shivers of awe. I think jazz should do that too."

They were silent for a moment, then, "I like Alvin and the Chipmunks," piped up Sally, grinning as the adults unanimously groaned. "But I like eggs and bacon even better. Let's eat; I'm starrrving."

They devoured breakfast together around the big golden oak dining table, complimenting Elaine on the fluffiness of her biscuits.

"Well, go easy on that blackberry jam," said Elaine. "It's the last of last year's wild blackberries. That's one reason we need to go picking this morning. I want to make jam for the rest of the year."

"Yeah, and we should get going this morning before it gets too hot among the bushes," said Joe. "We don't want anyone fainting from the heat out there."

"Is Sally going to take part in Hands Across America?" asked JJ.

"What is that? I haven't heard of it," said Elaine.

"Some of us TCU students are planning to get involved," said Kitty. "It's a charity event to have people make a continuous chain of hands for three thousand miles across the U.S. It's promoting world peace. It should be fun. It will happen next weekend."

"Sounds like a good event for the kids," said Elaine. "I'll ask around."

"Maybe we should get some musicians involved," said Larry. "Entertain the chain gang in Fort Worth. Get some publicity for my group. Maybe I can turn it into a record."

"Sounds like something the ACLU should help with too, but I'm not aware of it," said Max. "I'll find out more about it and maybe join in."

An hour later, the friends were hiking the half mile to where the wild blackberry brambles grew in profusion along a stretch of public easement at the edge of the forest. They all wore long-sleeved shirts, jeans, and boots. Rambo led the way, trotting like an army drill sergeant.

"Did you name the dog after the Stallone movie or the French poet, Rimbaud?" asked Max.

"I don't read much French poetry," said Joe with a grin.

"Well, he appears to have more of a poetic spirit than a tough-guy demeanor," said Max.

"Yeah, about the only wildlife he can catch is moles and land turtles," said Joe.

"He's my sweet puppy," said Sally. "Don't talk bad about him."

"He's a good dog," said Elaine, "but he learned his lesson when he got bitten by a copperhead last year. It nailed him on the throat, which swelled up, and he would have suffocated if we hadn't got him to the vet in time. Here are the blackberries. Everyone got a bucket? Watch out for those thorns."

The group split up into singles and couples, looking for the bushes with the biggest, blackest, easiest to pick berries. Soon they were reaching deep into the tangled thorny canes for huge elusive fruits.

"Join me over here, Kitty; there are some berries in this bush as big as your thumb," said Larry.

"Yours, maybe," said JJ. "I take pride in the petiteness of my thumbs."

Sally squealed as her clothes got entangled by the thorns, and she couldn't get loose until Kitty and Elaine carefully extracted her. Then she ran to a farther bush to try her luck.

"Oh, look here," called Sally. "There's a big smooth rock in between these bushes."

Everyone gathered to see what Sally had found.

"Aha, I told you Big Bird was loose around here," said Joe. "That's an ostrich egg, Honey. We'll take it home and see if it's fresh enough to eat."

Sally, being the closest and the discoverer, reached for the egg. Just then, Rambo gave a piercing bark. Max, just behind Sally, saw the movement in the leaves and jerked Sally back. Larry grabbed Kitty, who had knelt beside Sally to see the egg. Rambo was now in full alarm mode, barking and growling.

"Snake!" said Joe. "Everyone get back. He must have been attracted by the egg, too."

They all stepped away from the nest of dirt and leaves where the egg lay. They could now discern the copperhead slithering near the egg as if guarding it.

"I'm okay, put me down," said Kitty. Larry reluctantly released her from his protective embrace. Max had placed Sally astride his shoulders. The others were keeping their distance from the snake. Joe found a long stick and pinned the reptile to the ground. Then he grabbed it just behind the head and picked it up. The three-foot long snake wrapped itself around Joe's arm and hissed impressively.

"It's hideous," said JJ, "and, woo! It stinks!"

"It's beautiful," said Max. "See the way its golden bands glow in the sunlight."

"I think it's lovely, too," said Kitty. "Look how its muscles flash and ripple."

"Joe was a biology major in college," said Elaine. "He's handled lots of snakes."

"Daddy, please let the pretty snake go free," said Sally.

"Yes, don't kill it," said Kitty. "It has a right to live too. It was just in the wrong place this time."

"You better give him a far toss; that's one disgruntled viper," said Larry. "Look at how he shows those fangs. Maybe I'll write a tune titled 'Fangs.'"

Joe walked several yards away and tossed the snake into the berry bushes beyond where they would venture. Rambo started to go after the snake, but Joe called him back.

"Well, I hope that copperhead is gruntled now," said JJ with a grin.

Meanwhile, Larry had picked up the egg. It was as big as a cantaloupe and glossy white with tan spots. “It’s heavy. How do you know if it’s fresh?”

“If it’s not dry or coagulated inside,” said Joe. “Let’s finish collecting berries and we’ll take it home to find out.”

After another hour of berry-picking, they were all sufficiently sweltered, weary, and their buckets were heavy with berries. As they walked back through the front driveway of the yellow house, Max noticed a bird perched on a thorn bush. It had a big grasshopper in its beak. As the group watched, the bird impaled the insect on one of the thorns.

“That must be a butcher bird,” said Max. “They use the thorns to store food for later.”

“It looks like a fat mockingbird,” said Kitty.

“Yeah, that’s our butcher bird,” said Joe. “That’s his regular bush. Never know what you’ll find skewered there.”

In the kitchen, Joe took a power drill and put a neat half-inch hole in the end of the thick-walled ostrich egg. He shook it thoroughly, held it over a bowl, and let the viscous yellow liquid dribble out. There was at least a quart.

“It looks fresh to me.”

“I’ll cook up a couple of pies for this evening,” said Elaine, taking charge of the bowl.

“In Africa,” said Joe, “the Bushmen use ostrich eggs as storage jars. They fill them with water and bury them in the desert to drink when they’re hunting.”

“Well, that’s fascinating,” said Larry, “but I’m gonna hunt me a cold beer and then some shade to take a nap. Berry picking in this heat is more tiring than three sets of jazz.”

After a light lunch of sandwiches, Max, Larry, and Kitty got in the pool while JJ and Elaine prepared the egg custard pies. Joe fired up the grill for hotdogs later that evening, then he, too, got in the pool. They each stood or lay in the water with a drink in a foam float.

"Did y'all hear they're gonna create a Rock and Roll Hall of Fame in Cincinnati, of all places?" said Larry. "Why don't they already have a Jazz Hall of Fame somewhere like New Orleans, New York, or Chicago? Jazz is way older than Rock."

"There's no classical music hall of fame either, as far as I know," said Max.

"There's the DownBeat Magazine Jazz Hall of Fame," said Kitty. "But it's just an annual publication. There really should be a physical Jazz Hall of Fame. Jazz was America's greatest cultural innovation, seems to me."

"Yeah," said Joe, "but you're not on the DownBeat list yet, Larry, so don't worry about a hall of fame building for jazz."

"Heck, maybe I'll 'stablish one in Fort Worth. Might help my record company succeed and put Cowtown on the Jazz map," said Larry. "I need to get on that DownBeat list and win a Grammy too."

"You'll get there in time, Larry," said Kitty. "We have faith in you. But it usually takes a lifetime to be recognized as a great musician."

"Maybe some of us can't wait for recognition in our old age," growled Larry.

"Well, bless your little old heart, Larry," said JJ. "I'll bet I could help you win that prize."

Larry seemed about to respond but shook his head and scowled.

Kitty gave them both a quizzical glance, then exited the pool and reclined in one of the poolside chairs.

Max got out and joined her. He was examining the now-empty ostrich eggshell, noticing how smooth and cool it was. "Maybe Elaine can make a hanging planter out of the shell. Be a shame to just throw it away." He put his finger in the hole and brought out a speck of the yolk. Then he noticed one of the ubiquitous little anole lizards on the arm of Kitty's chair. He reached over and put the yoke particle on her wrist near the lizard.

"Don't move. Maybe it will go for the egg," said Max.

The tiny green lizard cautiously approached, then boldly hopped onto Kitty's arm.

"Oh, he's darling," said Kitty, "and he tickles."

The anole flicked up the yoke with its tongue, then displayed the bright red fan on its throat and marched about on Kitty's arm for a few moments before moving on.

"That throat fan is the male's display to attract females. Like a peacock's tail," said Max.

"Well, he seduced me," said Kitty. "I wish I could take him home."

"I've seen a few of them up in North Texas, but they prefer this humidity," said Max. "They are sweet, friendly little critters."

Larry plopped down in a chair near them, still drying off. "So y'all are yoking around with the local jive lizards, eh?"

"Maybe the lizards have the right idea," said Kitty, grinning. "You guys should display red throat fans to attract us ladies like they do."

"What do I gotta do, baby? I saved you from that vicious reptile this morning."

Kitty's left eyebrow arched to its highest extent. "Well, you may have shown your manliness, but that poor snake wasn't about to get me."

JJ had just come out of the house. "Yeah, Larry, why didn't you grab me? I was a lot more afraid of the snake than Kitty was."

"Heck, JJ, that snake was probably terrified of you," said Larry. "Who was that female Greek myth monster that had snakes for hair and would turn you to stone if you looked at her?"

"That would be Medusa," said Max. "Surely you aren't comparing JJ to Medusa?"

"Yeah, just because you got stoned a lot in New York, don't blame it on me," quipped JJ.

"Excuse me, I think I'll take another dip," said Kitty, diving in and swimming underwater to the other end. Max and Larry watched her graceful aquatic motions.

"She could be a naiad or an undine," said Max with a wistful sigh.

"I don't know what that is," said Larry, "but she's damn pretty and she can play her tenor with me anytime."

***

That evening they dined on hotdogs, emu burgers, roasted corn-on-the-cob fresh from the garden, and egg custard pie courtesy of the ostrich. Then, Sally and her friends ran about in the darkness with sparklers, making light swirls. The adults sat up late on the patio gabbing, laughing, listening to the sounds of the forest, and watching bats flit silently through the pure white light radiating up from the pool.

"Seeing those sparklers reminds me of that Chernobyl nuclear incident in Russia last month," said Kitty. "Is it going to kill us all with radiation?"

"That was majorly bad," said Joe. "But it shouldn't affect the US much. It wasn't nearly as dangerous as a nuclear bomb explosion. But it will certainly make Chernobyl and the area for miles around it radioactive for a few hundred years. The Russians evacuated most of the population of the city, but a lot of them will get cancer in the years to come."

"Yeah, it was a real E-flat minor disaster," said Larry, forking some pie to his mouth.

"Really? Is that the way you characterize the degree of badness of a situation?" said JJ with a snort of disdain.

"It's as good as any, seems to me," replied Larry. "E-flat minor could refer to a localized disaster like Chernobyl. Now, if a nuclear missile wiped out a large city, that would be an F-sharp major catastrophe. Good things, like my stock market investments going way up, might be an A-major celebration."

"That's actually an interesting way of categorizing historic events," said Kitty. "But you would almost have to be a professional musician to make sense of it."

"Yeah, you should write up your musical scale of disastrophe as an academic paper. TWC might give you a PhD for it," said Joe. "It might even replace the Richter Scale."

"Heck, the Richter is just for earthquakes. Mine would apply to any kind of calamity or event."

"If it's musical, maybe it should be called the 'Delgado Disaster Scale,'" said JJ with a smirk.

"What about the Challenger tragedy last January?" asked Kitty. "I was in Florida with my mom and brother for a brief vacation. I heard the explosion and saw the fireball. It was horrible."

"Sure, I'd say that was definitely a B-flat minor catastrophe," opined Larry.

"You know, both 'catastrophe' and 'disaster' mean 'caused by the stars' in Latin," said Max. "So maybe your index could be related to the music of the spheres."

"Yeah, well, it sounds like ass-trology to me," said JJ, giving her scarlet ringlets a toss. "I'm ready for a non-cat-astrophic night's sleep."

***

After a group breakfast the next morning, after hugs and thanks and promises all around to get back together soon, Max left shortly after Larry, Kitty, and JJ. As he was pulling out of the driveway, he noticed a flash of red in the Butcherbird's thorn bush. The bird was absent, but one of the tiny green anoles was impaled grotesquely on a thorn, its red throat crest still visible in death.

Signs and portents? Is the universe trying to tell me something, *or is this just fodder for a poem?*

Chapter Five

"Softly As In a Morning Sunrise"

Palo Pinto Lake, Texas, July 1987

Max had invited his jazz-trio friends (now often a quartet with Kitty) for the 4th of July weekend at his parents' vacation house on Palo Pinto Lake, an hour's drive west of Fort Worth. Max wanted Kitty and Elaine to experience the lake house since neither had been there previously. The 4th was on a Friday, so they would have at least three days to party. Max arrived on Thursday evening, turned on the utilities, laid in some groceries, and listened to some Miles Davis records while he did a bit of tidying up.

It had been over two years now since Max had met Kitty at the Catfish Club. Since then, he had been on dates with her several times, alone or in the company of others. He had taken her on that first date to the Botanic Gardens and jogged with her at Joe's house in south Texas. This year, he had played jazz at the Catfish Club several times with Kitty in attendance at the wives' table or sitting-in on stage with the trio (with Carl Stokes on bass instead of Joe). Kitty played a sweet tenor sax and could skillfully improvise, though she wasn't particularly adventurous with it. She liked creamy, dreamy solos, and Max loved to help her make them shine.

Max knew Larry was interested in Kitty as well. He didn't know if they had dated, but he assumed they had. It made his heart hammer and his muscles tremble to think of her with Larry. He tried not to think ill of Larry, who had been his best friend since childhood. But Max desperately wanted Kitty to prefer, to love, to choose him.

Kitty had at least another year at TCU. Max knew she didn't want to make any plans until after she graduated. But he also knew Larry wouldn't hesitate to put a move on her if he got the chance. Larry could be quite persuasive when he wanted something. He had a certain gravitas, a force of personality that Max somehow lacked and envied. Max had never understood Larry's charm or innate authority or whatever it was.

Larry didn't have Max's creative ability with words, particularly metaphor and simile. Max couldn't remember Larry ever actually expressing an original metaphor, except maybe that musical disaster scale he had mentioned last summer at Joe and Elaine's. But Larry was a born salesman who could probably sell sand at the beach. Max knew that most people are more susceptible to emotion than to facts and logic. Maybe Larry simply knew how to appeal to selfish greed in people. Max hoped Kitty was savvy enough not to fall for Larry's enticements.

Max also had concerns about what Kitty would think of him when he got around to telling her about the Tanya episode. Surely, that debacle was completely behind him. He intended to confess to Kitty about Tanya, but when would be the right time? His relationship with Kitty seemed so fragile. She knew he was in love with her, but she had given no indication of choosing Max or anyone. She might not be ready to commit for years.

Max took a deep breath and summoned his resolve. He would tell Kitty this weekend that he wanted to marry her, however long it might take her to feel ready. And he would try to tell her about Tanya. Max had also decided how best to get Kitty away from the others in order to pop the question.

Well, the main thing right now was to make the house presentable and welcoming.

The lake house was not pretentious, but it was solidly built, with a sheet-metal roof and siding that wouldn't rot in the damp from the lake. Max's father, being an aircraft engineer at General Dynamics, had designed it himself, and the whole family had helped build it on weekends and holidays over a period of four years while Max was in high school and college. Larry and Joe, and even JJ, had occasionally lent a hand in the construction as well. Max had many pleasant memories of his time here and had written several poems about his lake-house experiences.

Walking down to the rec room, Max glanced at the picture of a mallard duck on the wall directly in front of the descending stairs to cleverly remind people to duck their heads if they were six feet tall or more. Larry had knocked his noggin any number of times before he finally learned to hunch a bit on his way down.

The house perched on a high cliff above the lake and had two levels. Its lower level gave onto outside stairs that led down to the sun deck and floating dock. The house's upper ground level featured a twelve-foot deck surrounding three sides of the building. Its deck provided a dramatic view of the lake from just above the treetops. There were three bedrooms, but the downstairs rec room also served as a bedroom. One corner could be screened off for the Murphy bed that resided upright against the wall until needed. Everyone would have a separate bedroom except Max, who would make do with his sleeping bag in the storage loft above the living room.

Early on the morning of the Fourth, Max went down to the dock to prepare his surprise for that evening. He slipped the cans beneath the boat hull, which lay bottom up on the dock. He smiled to himself, visualizing his friends' delighted reaction.

JJ and Kitty arrived mid-morning on Friday in JJ's new scarlet Mustang; Larry was half an hour behind them. Joe, Elaine, Sally, and Rambo pulled in just before noon. Seven-year-old Sally and the dog immediately ran through the house and out onto the front deck. Max hurried after them and grabbed up Sally.

"You must be careful up here, sweetheart, we're a hundred feet above the lake and I don't think you or Rambo have learned to fly." Sally giggled and looked down from their height as Max held her up so she could look over the deck railing.

Rambo had rocketed down the hill to inspect the lake. Being a Labrador, he immediately jumped in and swam around the dock before climbing out and shaking himself off. Sally giggled at his antics.

"Oh, I wish I could fly," said Sally. "I love it up here above the trees! Why didn't God give us wings like birds?"

"Well, you just slow down, young lady," said Elaine, taking Sally from Max. "Let's walk around together and see the sights. You gotta stay with the grown-ups. There are too many things around here that can hurt you. Come on, let's go down and see the sun deck. Maybe you and Dad can do some fishing if Rambo doesn't scare all the fish away."

Larry and Joe decided to play pool in the rec room, while Max showed Kitty and JJ around the property. Across the one-lane gravel road near the house were several huge gray limestone boulders mottled with multi-colored lichen. JJ opined they looked like abstract paintings.

Kitty scrambled atop the largest and grinned down at Max and JJ. "These boulders are so interesting; I wish I knew more about geology."

"I've done a lot of rock climbing on them," said Max. "They also make a great place to meditate. I wrote several poems while sitting on that very rock."

"Yeah," said JJ with a sly grin, "I remember the poem about you lying naked as a lizard on the rock and imagining the ancient past."

"Well, it does make a fine place for sunbathing, but maybe that was just poetic license. Poets do make up or exaggerate a lot of the stuff we write about."

"I know you, Max," said JJ. "You've done most of the stuff you write about. I remember your poem about cave exploring, and how you nearly drowned in one. That had to be real."

"True, but it was also accidental and foolish," said Max. "I haven't taken chances like that since I was a teenager. Let's go downstairs and I'll show you the sundeck and dock."

As they went through the house and down the outer stairs to the lower areas, Max grabbed a cooler of drinks. The outer stairs zigzagged down the steep hill through a shady grove of oaks and elms. They emerged onto the lower sundeck to find Elaine watching Sally run up and down the slanted walkway to the floating dock ten feet below. The little Sunfish sailboat hull still rested undisturbed on the dock.

"Oh, this is what I need after those mountainside stairs," said JJ, plopping into one of the deck chairs in the shade of a large umbrella.

Max opened the cooler and handed around the cold drinks, including lemonade for Sally. "You want to do some fishing, Sally? I can get you a pole, but you'll have to put the worm on the hook yourself."

"Yuck, no! I'm not going to hurt a poor wiggle worm to catch a flappy old fish. But I would like to go out in the boat." Sally batted her lashes at Max and gave him her most alluring seven-year-old going on seventeen smile.

"It's almost lunchtime now, honey," said Max. "I plan on putting the boat in the water tomorrow. I'll take you out for a sail then."

***

They gathered in the house to eat a lunch of fried chicken and potato salad the women had brought. Larry provided an ice-chest of fine wines and assorted exotic beers. Afterward, Elaine said she was ready to play some pool with the guys while Kitty and JJ read.

"Yeah, y'all do that, but I think I'll take Kitty for a walk," said Larry. "I remember that boulder up the path that looks like a castle. I want to show it to her if it's still there. Will you come, Kitty?"

"Sure, I guess so. I could use some exercise after that lunch."

"I'll come too," said Max. "You might not remember where the rock is."

Larry gave Max a frown. "I know where it is, and I'd like to show it to Kitty by myself if you don't mind."

Max spent the next anxious hour being severely beaten at pool by Joe and Elaine.

Larry and Kitty finally returned. Max rushed upstairs when he heard them come in. Kitty went to the fridge for a cold water, looking a bit flustered.

Larry gave Max a thin smile. "I remembered right where Castle Rock is. No problem. Kitty thought it was real nice. I took a picture of her leaning against it. We saw a deer on the way back. And I got an idea for a tune titled 'Castle Rock Kiss.'"

Kitty gave Larry a grimace and went out on the deck with JJ.

Larry grinned. "Hey, just kidding, Kitty."

They spent the rest of the afternoon variously napping, reading, playing in the rec room, and conversing. Larry and Max began another episode in their seemingly endless dispute about the history and aesthetics of jazz. JJ groaned and deflected the conversation.

"What do y'all think about Reagan telling Gorbachev to tear down the Berlin Wall? Do you believe the Soviets might actually do it?"

"Maybe I should offer my services to Reagan," said Larry. "I could help blow that wall down with some hard bebop and become a national celebrity."

"Fab idea, Larry," said JJ. "I'll bet the State Department is looking for you right now. Just don't let that wall fall on you."

"Gorbachev has initiated some political and economic reforms, *perestroika* and *glasnost,* that are moving the Soviets somewhat toward democracy and capitalism," said Max. "That's a pretty significant shift. If Gorbachev continues with reforms, America could actually attain a friendly relationship with Russia. Maybe we could play jazz over there to help cultivate international friendship."

"Yeah, we grew up in the world of duck and cover or the atom bomb will get you," said JJ. "It would be nice if both countries got rid of all their nukes and sponsored cultural exchanges."

"Well, there's still China with its nuclear arsenal," said Kitty, "but maybe Russia's changes will cause China to become more peaceful as well."

"I hope so. I'd sure like to be able to sing 'What A Wonderful World' in a few years, and really mean it," said JJ.

"And I'd like for Sally to grow up in a world without so much hate and fear," said Elaine.

Sally heard her name mentioned and looked up from her Nancy Drew book. "Maybe I should talk to those old Russians and tell them to be nicer. Why can't there be a world where everyone just loves everyone?"

Elaine took Sally onto her lap and kissed her. "That truly would be a wonderful world."

***

That evening at sunset, Max herded them all down to sit on the sun deck for his surprise. They saw he had placed some coffee cans at the far edge of the floating dock, which was connected to the higher deck by the sloping, hinged walkway.

They talked for a while about books, movies, and music, as they watched the sun disappear into the western hills. The air and lake seemed unnaturally calm, as if awaiting something momentous. As darkness came on stealthily, with a crescent moon low in the east, Max ambled down the walkway with a paper sack.

"Do y'all remember Halley's Comet of March a year ago?" asked Max as he prepared his surprise.

"We enjoyed it," said JJ, "all except getting up at two in the morning and having our butts frozen off by the wind on the road up there."

"Yeah, and the comet turned out to be just a bright smudge even through your telescope," said Larry. "No UFOs or shooting stars."

"I complained, but it was kind of wonderful," said JJ. "The night was so dark and the stars so bright. You don't get to see that in the city."

"Well, I've arranged for a fireworks demonstration that I hope will make up for the anticlimax of the comet," said Max as he withdrew several colored tubes from the sack. He placed them in the cans, pointing out toward the lake. "Roman candles and buzzy bees," he announced to the group. He had twisted the various fuses together into one longer fuse. Now he lit the long fuse and carefully retreated up the walkway to the deck.

As Max sat down, the Roman candles began to shoot flaming balls into the air over the lake. The buzzy bees sent bright colors whirligiging up into the night. Dazzling multicolored trails of light arced through the darkness, whistling dramatically. Fireworks were being shot over the lake by residents on the other side of the lake as well.

"Now, that's spectacular," said Joe.

"Yeah, that's what a comet should look like," said Larry. "Gotta write a tune for that."

"Oh, pretty, pretty!" Sally clapped and shouted.

Before anyone else could comment, Rambo gave a bark and stampeded down the walkway to save his people from the fire demons. The dog's weight on the lower end of the walkway caused the floating dock to tilt backward slightly, just enough that the roman candles flopped over in their cans, reversing their direction of fire: now they were aiming directly toward the watchers on the deck.

Fireballs came flying at them like tracer bullets, swooshing and sizzling. Everyone screamed and fell to the deck. Joe grabbed Sally; Larry shielded Kitty and pushed her down; Max blocked Elaine and JJ from the onslaught. After thirty seconds of fiery havoc, the fireworks had exhausted their loads. Max found the switch for the deck lights and flooded the area with light.

"Well, that was sure exciting. You said it was going to be a surprise," said JJ.

"Rambo! Where is that idiot dog?" said Joe. "He could have got us hurt. There he is in the water again. Come here, you nitwit."

"Oh, he was being brave and tried to save us," said Sally, bouncing with excitement.

Kitty said, "It reminded me of the scene in Kerouac's novel, *On the Road,* where he says he wants to burn like Roman candles firing in the dark. It was beautiful as well as exciting, and no one was hurt."

"More like *Apocalypse Now,*" said Larry. "I love the smell of cordite in the evening."

"*Mea culpa*, folks," said Max. "Maybe I should change my name to Max Culpa. I didn't mean for it to be that exciting. I should have anchored those Roman candles so they couldn't swivel. I knew the dock could tilt like that, but I didn't figure on Rambo to the rescue. Well, let's adjourn to the house."

Later that evening, after they had quaffed some vino, made some music, and were about to adjourn to their beds, Max took Kitty aside for a moment.

"Kitty, are you available for another surprise early tomorrow morning?"

"Sure, as long as it doesn't involve being shot at by fireworks or worse."

"I thought you might like to try a sunrise sailboat ride. I guarantee there won't be any fireworks involved, just the sun doing its usual lovely thing. We can't see the first moments of sunrise from the deck because of that curve of land to the east. But it should be beautiful from the sailboat."

"That sounds nice. What time should I be ready?"

"If we're in the boat by six, that should be perfect."

***

Kitty emerged from her room at 5:45 the next morning, wearing a pale-yellow Earth Justice T-shirt and green shorts. Max was in the kitchen pouring a pot of coffee into a thermos. His blue T-shirt featured Kandinsky's abstracted flying horse image with a quote from one of Max's poems: "Poetry finds beauty in everything and gives it wings."

They descended the stairs and were soon on the dock. The morning was cool, with light just beginning to pink the clouds. Max flipped over the boat, slipped it into the water, and inserted the mast into its slot. He helped Kitty onto the front swivel seat and then stepped aboard himself.

He turned the boat toward the lake and unfurled the sail. It bellied out with a snap in the light breeze. The dinghy slipped silently from the dock.

"Oh, this is delightful, Max."

As the little Sunfish skimmed toward the open lake, Kitty let her hand trail in the water. She lifted her face to the breeze and let her hair stream out behind her, enjoying the fresh air. Max was again mesmerized by Kitty's beauty and was nearly breathless. He realized he had too tight a grip on the rudder and tried to relax. His mind gradually unclenched and reached out to encompass the morning's delights.

"Have you thought about what you want to do after you finish college, Kitty?"

"I've thought about it a lot, but I haven't come to any firm decision. I still have another year to go, and I'm fully committed to mathematics, but I'm not sure what area of work I want. I'll never be a high-level research mathematician, but I'd like to make a difference for the better somehow in the world."

Max smiled. "There's still plenty of time. Don't be in a hurry. I wish I could have taken a hiatus after graduating from college. Maybe I would have gone in a completely different direction. But probably would have been drafted and perhaps died in Vietnam."

"Don't remind me about Vietnam. I'm just glad you're here with me and in one piece. I've always been interested in nature and the natural environment, even though I'm not as knowledgeable about it as you are. That's one of the things I admire about you, Max. You're interested in so many aspects of life, and you know so much about nature and science as well as philosophy and literature."

"I like to read widely in books for amateurs, but I have no real expertise. I'm a confirmed generalist. But let's go hiking together sometime, and I'll tell you all I know about nature, science, and philosophy. It won't take long."

"Oh yes, I'd like that." She hesitated, then continued in a strained voice, "By the way, Larry didn't kiss me during our hike yesterday, although he hinted he'd like to. But as to your question about my post-college plans, I think maybe I'd like to help one of the environmental non-profits like Earth Justice, Greenpeace, or the Environmental Defense Fund; maybe even the UN. They need statistical proof of the environmental degradation caused by industry, agriculture, and overpopulation. I know it's a corny euphemism, but I'd love to help save the Earth from possible ruin somehow."

"Not corny at all. I agree with you. Saving the Earth, or at least the natural environment, is going to be the great issue of the coming years in my very humble opinion. Maybe we should team up. Surely together we could save the Earth. I'll do the legal aspects; you handle the math."

Kitty grinned back at him. "Well, let's see what happens. I may have to go to grad school before I'm ready to save the Earth." She was pensive for a moment. "I've often wondered why I feel impelled to do something significant while most people are simply content to live their lives. Sometimes I think they have the right idea. No one can really save the world, and it's probably just asking for heartache to try."

"I know what you mean. ACLU work can be often frustrating as well as occasionally rewarding. But it seems to me that trying to do something meaningful in life is worth it, even if you fail, which is so often the case. I think it's our own satisfaction with what we try to do in life that matters most, not what we actually accomplish or what others think."

Max paused in uncertainty, then said, "In fact, I'm practicing to become an 'Übermensch,'" he said with a teasing grin. "That was Friedrich Nietzsche's term for a person who is more self-aware, self-determined, and tries to fulfill his potentiality in life at a higher level than our ordinary existence. It was a criticism of the uptight Christian culture of the time, which Nietzsche said caused people to be mere unthinking, obedient sheep."

"So, it's like that military slogan: 'Be all you can be'?" said Kitty, with a slight smile.

"Yes, I suppose that's part of it, but Nietzsche meant it as the long-term, ultimate goal of an individual's life. He simply wanted people to fully use their minds and to live despite society's expectations rather than just accepting what society says they should be and do. He was even suggesting that some people could attain a higher level of consciousness."

"Well, yes, I could definitely use a higher level of consciousness. But I also recognize how hard it is to buck the system," said Kitty. "I don't think I'm cut out to be a rebel or a saint."

"I don't think rebellion or sainthood is required to be an Übermensch," said Max. "It's just a matter of thinking and acting as one believes best for oneself using higher mental disciplines such as phenomenology, peak experience induction, and even ordinary meditation."

"So, you think I could become an Über wench?" said Kitty, her eyebrows arching, her eyes sparkling exuberantly.

Max laughed with delight at her pun. "Absolutely, my dear. Maybe we can help each other become more Über."

They both became quiet, watching the hills of the eastern horizon emerge from darkness.

The boat cleared the spit of land that separated their cove from the main lake just as the sun's tip edged above the far cliffs. Thin eastern clouds seemed to catch fire. The sun was like a bubble floating up from the hills, sending golden spars out across the water. A small flock of blackbirds swerved in tight formation above the lake, then swooped away in a complex swirl. Moments later, a great blue heron slowly lofted from the water's edge and glided low, mirrored by the calm water. It gave a single mournful croak as it passed near them.

"Oh, it's so beautiful and tranquil," whispered Kitty, following the heron with her eyes. "That sound it made sort of emphasized the quiet of the sunrise. It's like a single note that creates significance for a prolonged silence in music."

"Yes, exactly. The hush of the sunrise lasts only a few minutes. It's an enchanted time. Then the world gets hot and noisy again. Here, have some coffee, then we'll head back for breakfast at the house."

They watched the sun swell golden, its leading-edge rippling with heat waves, until it became too bright. Max turned the boat toward shore, tacking across the wind.

"I'll bet you've written at least one poem about the sunrise here," said Kitty, sipping her coffee. "and I'd like to hear you recite it for me."

"Oh, sure, yes, I've written about the sunrise here, but I never tried to memorize it. Let me see if I can remember it for you. The title is 'Dawn Dancer.'" Max closed his eyes for a few moments, then intoned:

"I take my coffee on the treetop deck
on a worn old wicker chair,
warm my hands around the cup,
and drink, instead, sweet morning air.
Pale vapors from the sleeping lake,
its dream-spawned incubi,
perform a sinuous ballet,
dissolve into the sky.
The still dark hills breathe up
the sun like a bubble slowly blown,
and nothing other dares to breathe
until it slips from those lips of stone.

The canyon wren jittering on the roof
now sings his arioso plea
and something of my deepest self
is, for this moment, radiant and free."

Kitty sighed. "That's a wonderful evocation of the experience. I've enjoyed the one book you gave me, but I want to read all your poems and discuss them with you."

"Gosh, I would really like that too. Maybe we could get together at my house or yours, and I'll give you a personal poetry reading. And, Kitty, uh, have you thought any more about what I said last summer during our jog at Joe's house? I—I'm falling ever more deeply in love with you and... Yikes!"

Kitty also screamed and grabbed at the sides of the boat.

Rambo's huge yellow head and paws had suddenly appeared on the rim of the dinghy.

The dog was struggling to pull himself up into the boat, but he succeeded only in tipping it toward himself. Max and Kitty tried to counterbalance but were too late. The hull tipped rapidly up and overturned, catapulting its occupants into the lake. When Max surfaced, he saw Kitty's head emerge wide-eyed from beneath the sail. She seemed unhurt and was easily treading water.

"Are you okay, Kitty? The mast could have knocked us out if it had hit us."

"I think I'm all right. I jumped clear." She chuckled, and her eyes were alight. "I'm glad Rambo didn't dump us on our way out. I would hate to have missed the sunrise and your poem." Kitty gave Max an enigmatic Mona Lisa smile.

Max realized she was probably relieved she wouldn't have to answer the question he had been about to ask when Rambo intervened. "Let's swim to the dock. I can come back for the boat later."

Sally, Elaine, and JJ had been on the sundeck talking when they noticed Rambo swimming toward the boat. They thought little about it. However, when they saw the boat flip over, they screamed in alarm. Then they realized Kitty and Max were okay. Sally laughed and bounced with excitement. JJ guffawed, her hands fluffing her ruby ringlets.

Kitty was a strong swimmer. She and Max soon reached the dock, climbed its ladder, and lay on the deck laughing a little hysterically about their adventure.

Elaine rebuked Rambo as he came ashore and shook off, spraying her.

JJ loomed sympathetically over the sodden, exhausted duo and said, "I was going to play 'Softly As In a Morning Sunrise,' for you two on the stereo, but it seems a bit inappropriate now. Maybe Larry will write a jazz tune called 'Rambo Strikes Again.'"

Sally scolded Rambo severely, then slipped him a bite of bacon from her pocket.

As Max lay dripping on the dock, shivering a little in the cool morning air, he thought about what a fiasco his plan to propose to Kitty had come to. He might not get as good a chance anytime soon. He turned his head toward Kitty and saw she was gazing at him, her eyes like sapphires.

Max felt Kitty's fingers on his and responded by clasping hers.

"Don't feel bad, Max; it was a lovely adventure. Interesting things always seem to happen when I'm with you." Kitty gave him a genuine smile this time.

Max didn't know what to say, but Nature intervened to help him avoid a possible *faux pas.* A pair of large green dragonflies with neon blue heads hovered above them for a few seconds, swirling and swooping around each other. Their glasslike wings scattered rainbow colors from the just-risen sun.

"Oh, how gorgeous!" said Kitty, clasping his hand tighter. "Are they fighting?"

"No, I think they are about to mate."

"Oh, well, uh, they're exquisite." The dragonflies whisked away on the light breeze.

Max got to his feet and offered his hand to Kitty, but she levitated effortlessly. Then she slipped her hand into his and they walked together, up to the house, through the bright new morning, into the unknowable future.

Chapter Six

"Mood Indigo"

Catfish Jazz Club, Fort Worth, Texas, October 1988

Kitty now came frequently to jam with Larry's jazz group at the Catfish Club. Max often brought her and played piano for the group. They usually had Carl Stokes on bass and sometimes Jack Perry on guitar. Max and Kitty had become much closer since Rambo had dumped them in Palo Pinto Lake that July a year ago. They had been on several dinner dates. Kitty attended one of Max's poetry readings at a local bookstore. He had given her copies of his two published poetry books, and they often discussed his poetry and her classes and ambitions. However, Max had somehow never found the courage or the right moment to tell Kitty about Tanya.

Now it was October. Larry called Kitty and left a message on her answer machine. It would be JJ's 30th birthday the next Monday and Elaine's a few days later. Larry wanted to celebrate both at the Catfish Club with a surprise private concert party. Larry asked Kitty to play with the group for the occasion, of course. Joe and Elaine were driving up to attend.

The day after Larry's message, Kitty received a phone call from Max asking if he could drive her to the party. Kitty agreed and thought the surprise party a great idea. She had often discussed with JJ the budding relationship between herself and Max. The two women had become close friends, and Kitty considered JJ her trusted mentor. Kitty felt JJ had helped her so much that she wanted to make JJ's birthday party a great success.

Max picked up Kitty and drove toward the club, which was in the near south downtown area. His route took them past Casa Mañana and the Water Gardens.

"You know, I've never been to Casa," said Kitty as they passed the massive aluminum geodesic dome of the theatre. "Let's attend a play or musical there sometime."

"Absolutely," agreed Max. "It's certainly a unique and historic venue, and they have some fine shows." Then he drove slowly by the Water Gardens, and they paused to watch the jets of its water rise and fall rhythmically.

"Let's stop a minute and get out," said Kitty. "Mom and Dad brought me here as a child, but I haven't been back since then."

Max parked, and they walked down the steps to the central fountain, where the water foamed and rushed around them to that gushing, splashing cauldron.

"Now I remember why this is so exciting!" shouted Kitty above the noise of the rushing water. She did a couple of whirls near the fountains, where the jets of water freshened the air. "But we had better get on to the club." She touched him lightly on his cheek, smiled, and they walked hand-in-hand back toward the car.

"Did you see the movie, Logan's Run? It was filmed here in the 70s," said Max. "It takes place in the far future when people are allowed to live only to age thirty. Then, they must voluntarily commit suicide. Logan and his lover escape through these Water Gardens."

"Sometimes I wish I could just run away to escape all my worries," sighed Kitty.

"I'd be glad to run away with you, anytime," said Max. "Hawaii or some tropical island might be just the thing."

"It seems quite appealing, but you know that would be the wrong thing for both of us," said Kitty, touching Max's cheek again. "But maybe we can reconsider it when I've finished my studies. I still want to become an Überwench." She grinned at him. "Instead of running away, let's talk Larry into doing a jazz concert at the Water Gardens. There's a quiet area up there away from the water noise. It would be fun, and good advertising for the combo."

They met Joe and Elaine at the Catfish Club half an hour before the start time. The tables had been set for the party, and there was a huge cake with "Happy 30th, JJ & Elaine" written on top. Soon they heard the door open, and Larry switched on the main lights. JJ gave a little shriek when she saw the others but then laughed as everyone crowded around and wished her happy birthday. They sat her and Elaine at their usual table near the stage and put party hats on their heads. Then the trio began to play.

Soon, more people arrived. Larry had invited mutual friends from high school and college, local musicians they all knew, some of JJ's fellow teachers, Odetta Randle, Max's now partner attorney, and miscellaneous other acquaintances. After about an hour, they had cut the cake, toasted with champagne, and many were chatting and dancing.

The trio was playing "Mood Indigo," which was a sad song, but a great slow dance tune. Larry was really bearing down on the melody, digging into its darkness. Max was laboring to create a sparkling sonic aura around Larry's alto solo. Then Max glanced up from the piano to see a pretty, young black woman come through the door and look around the room. She was dressed in a classy pink business suit, but her face had a somber mien rather than a party smile. She looked directly at Max for a few moments with a triumphant smirk. Tanya!

Max had a momentary falter at the piano but caught himself and continued playing. Larry cut his eyes to Max, then made the slightest of smiles around his alto mouthpiece as he continued to play. Max's heart was racing, and he hyperventilated even as he continued playing. He watched in horror as Tanya came toward the stage.

But she stopped at the birthday girls' table and pulled up a chair next to Kitty. Max saw them shake hands. Then Tanya spoke in Kitty's ear for what seemed to Max like an eternity. Kitty frowned, then gasped, putting a hand to her throat. Tanya got up, gave Max one last piercing glance, and strode from the room.

When Max looked back at Kitty, she was wide-eyed, open-mouthed, and gawking at him, her hand at her throat. Then she ran to the restroom. JJ caught Max's eye and flung up her hands in a gesture that seemed to combine question and threat. She hurried after Kitty. A few minutes later, JJ returned and whispered with Elaine while giving Max the stink eye. JJ and Elaine made their way to the lobby and didn't return.

Max's mind was blazing with anger, confusion, and self-disgust. He glanced at the catfish on the wall. It smirked at him and seemed to say in his father's voice, ***"Well, Max, you face-planted in a cow pie this time. You should have known that nigra gal would come back to haunt you. Kitty's never going to forgive you now. What a schmuck!"***

It seemed to Max that the tune was interminable. Indeed, he was sure Larry was extending it beyond its natural length. Somehow his fingers automatically found the right keys and rhythm while his mind spiraled into an infinity of anguish. As soon as the tune finished, Max rushed out to find Kitty. JJ met him at the front door.

"Where's Kitty? I need to tell her about Tanya."

"I asked Elaine to take her home. Kitty's devastated," said JJ, looking severely at Max. "Tanya told Kitty you raped her, told her she had your baby."

"Oh God, no, no, no! Should I go after her? I've got to explain, to tell her the truth."

"You should have told her weeks or months ago, Max. How stupid can you be?"

"I know. I intended to. It just never seemed to be the right time to bring it up."

"There is never a right time for something like that. You just have to swallow your pride and do it. Oh, Max, now it's going to be almost impossible to make things right with Kitty." JJ paused and gasped in sudden realization. "Oh, dear, I'll bet Kitty never mentioned to you that she was traumatized when she was raped as a teen."

"What! Raped? No, I didn't know that. Jesus, no wonder she reacted so... horrified. JJ, I've got to talk with her." Max's knees buckled. He sagged against the wall and moaned into his hands.

"Come on, let me drive you home. I don't want anyone to see you like this."

JJ pushed him out to his car, got his keys, and put him, shuddering and groaning, into the passenger seat. She was about to return to the club, intending to tell Larry and Joe what she was doing. Then she stopped, gasped again, and got into the car.

As they drove to Max's house, JJ said, "Max, pay attention. How did Tanya know about the party? You certainly didn't invite her."

Max sniffed, "Larry made all the arrangements. He must have...but why would he invite her? He doesn't even know her. All he knows is I had a brief affair with Tanya, knows it ended badly, and that we are no longer friends. Oh, shit, he did it on purpose to pry Kitty away from me, didn't he?"

"Yes, I think probably so. But Larry didn't know about Kitty being raped either. He couldn't know what a violent effect the story of Tanya's rape would have on Kitty."

"Damn it. I didn't rape Tanya. If anything, she raped me. She came on to me when we were celebrating winning an important case. I wasn't really even attracted to her, but we were alone, and she practically undressed me. It was a five-minute affair. The fact that it produced a baby was unfortunate."

"Well, I hope you did the right thing and helped her financially with the child."

Max shuddered. "I would have; I told her I would provide child support when she told me she was pregnant. But then the baby died. Tanya's husband murdered the baby when it was a few months old. He claimed it was an accident, but he was sent to prison."

"My God, Max, how tragic!"

"Then she came to me asking for money. But I refused to pay her since the child died. She said I'd be sorry. And I certainly am."

"Max, you only told me Tanya was your legal assistant, that you had a brief unhappy affair with her, and that it was over."

"Well, I certainly didn't want to disgust you or embarrass myself further about it."

"Are you certain the baby was yours?"

"She brought it to the office once. A boy. Lighter-skinned than she or her husband, Royce. I met him only once. They say he admitted smothering the baby, but he claimed it was an accident."

"Even so, there was no proof the child was yours. It could have been her husband's or someone else she had sex with. She may have already been pregnant, and you were just a convenient target. I've read that they can use DNA now to test biological relationships. Maybe you should look into it."

"Maybe, but I really don't care about anything except getting Kitty back. JJ, you've got to talk to her for me. Should I call her now or wait?"

"Let's wait until tomorrow. Then I'll call her and explain. I'll ask her whether she'll let you talk to her. Max, I'm so sorry, but you should have told her much sooner. How can a smart guy like you be such a moron sometimes?"

"Same way a musician gets to Carnegie Hall." Max smacked his head repeatedly against the headrest. "Practice, practice, practice." Then he looked across at JJ. "Oh, by the way, happy birthday."

***

The day after the birthday party, JJ called Kitty and left a message on her answer machine. "Kitty, call me and let's talk about what Tanya told you. It wasn't true. Max explained it to me, and I believe him. Let's get together. I'll be glad to come to your place if you like, or wherever. You shouldn't have to deal with this alone. Please call me."

It was several hours later that Kitty returned the call. JJ could hear her sobbing over the phone. "JJ, what that woman said was just so awful I nearly retched. I couldn't believe it, and yet I couldn't not. My stomach churns whenever I think of her words, her voice. You say she was lying? I guess come over to my apartment and tell me what Max said."

JJ went to Kitty's apartment and talked with her for several hours, consoling and commiserating with her. Then JJ called Max and said she was coming to talk with him.

"Max, I told Kitty you only had onetime, non-rape sex with Tanya and that she tried to blackmail you about the baby. I told her the baby may not even have been yours and that you never really had feelings for Tanya. I told Kitty you had intended to tell her about Tanya but just didn't know how to do it. Obviously, you didn't know Tanya would tell her first."

"What did she say? Is she willing to see me or at least talk over the phone? I really want to be with her and comfort her. Please tell me she forgives me." Max was trembling and gnawing at his fingers. He looked haggard and said he hadn't slept.

"Max, she's going to be broken up about this for at least several days, maybe weeks. She doesn't want to see you yet. I think the best way to contact her would be to write her a letter of apology and explanation. I'll keep talking with her and try to get her to see you. But don't get your hopes up."

"Yes, I'll write her a letter today. Maybe you should take it to her to make sure she reads it. If she gets it in the mail, she might just tear it up."

"You write the letter, and I'll take it to her. I recommend being abjectly contrite."

"Yes, abject contrition is becoming one of my major skills."

The next day, JJ met with Max again and read through his letter. She deemed it both eloquent and sufficiently groveling. She took it directly to Kitty. They discussed what Max had written. Kitty was still distraught and weepy.

"JJ, I want to believe Max's story. I certainly can't blame him for having had sex with Tanya before he met me. And I really don't think he could rape her or anyone. Still, I find it hard to believe she could be so mean and manipulative. And that poor baby. I know Max isn't responsible for what happened to it, but why didn't he tell me about it? It makes me wonder if I'll ever be able to trust him again."

"Kitty, I've known Max most of my life. I don't think there are any other skeletons in his closet. And he was planning to tell you about Tanya; he just didn't do it when he should have. He eventually would have told you, but Tanya got to you first. I can't believe he would ever knowingly hurt you. I think you should give him another chance."

"I really need to concentrate on finishing school and then look for a job. I've already missed several classes because of this. Maybe I should just move away. There are too many things to consider. Tell Max I'm not angry with him anymore, but I think it's best we don't see each other for the foreseeable future. I'll let you or him know if and when I'm ready."

"I'll tell him, Kitty, but it's going to desolate him. He's so much in love with you I'm not sure what he'll do. Write him a letter and give him some hope at least."

"Yes, okay, I'll do that." Kitty began to sob again as JJ left to inform Max.

***

Two days after her talks with Kitty and Max, JJ met Larry at the Paris Coffee Shop, just south of downtown, at her demand. When he slid nervously into her booth, JJ jabbed her fork at him rather than at her apple pie. "How could you have invited Tanya to that party? You must have known she would try to poison the relationship between Kitty and Max."

"I invited a lot of people. Maybe I remembered she used to work for Max and invited her, not realizing she would cause trouble."

"Don't even try to wiggle out like that. You knew Tanya had a grudge against Max."

"Well, I didn't know Kitty would take it so hard. I was just trying to make sure she knew about Max's affair with Tanya. I'll bet he hadn't told her, had he?" Larry glowered and pulled nervously at his goatee as JJ stared needles at him.

"No, Max hadn't told her. But Tanya told Kitty that Max raped her, which he didn't, and that Max got her pregnant, which may not be true. And by the way, Tanya's husband murdered the baby. The husband's now in prison."

Larry gaped at her. "Oh, Jeeze, JJ, I didn't know any of that. Max just told me he had a short, bad affair with Tanya and she had gotten preggers. I figured she either had an abortion or he paid her off. I just wanted Kitty to realize that Max ain't no saint." Larry pulled at his goatee again and kept an eye on JJ's accusatory fork.

"Well, you caused a rift between Kitty and Max that shouldn't have happened. I know you have designs on Kitty yourself, but you should play fair and let her choose which, if either of you she can really love and commit to. Your inviting Tanya was worse than Max not telling Kitty about her, in my opinion. You may think all's fair in love and war, but that's not the case. Not when it hurts those you love."

"Okay, already, I'm really sorry. I wouldn't have invited Tanya if I'd known all the facts." Larry took a shaky slurp of his coffee, spilled some on his cuff and put down the cup.

"Well, I'm going to give you a way to partially make up for it. I suspect Max wasn't the father of Tanya's baby. I've read that scientists can now analyze DNA to discover who the father of a baby is. You should pay for having that test done on Tanya's baby." JJ stabbed at her pie and took a bite while arching an eyebrow at Larry.

"But you said the baby is dead. Tanya surely wouldn't give approval for digging up the baby to be tested."

"They don't need the actual baby. All they need is some of the baby's hair or even a toy it had in its mouth or clothing it wore. So, I'm going to talk to Tanya. I'll tell her Max would like something to remember the baby by. Maybe she kept a lock of the baby's hair and would be willing to share it. If I can get some of the baby's DNA, you'll pay for the test. Right?" JJ jabbed the fork in his direction again.

Larry cringed back against the booth to avoid the fork that JJ thrust toward his eyes. The tables in these booths were much too narrow for conversations like this. "Uh, sure, I'll be glad to pay. Least I can do."

"It sure is. I'd ask you to talk to Tanya, but I think she would be more likely to do it for me than for you. I'll let you know."

Larry relaxed a little as JJ resumed her attack on the pie.

Three days later, JJ phoned Larry. "I got a few strands of the baby's hair from some that Tanya saved. She wanted a hundred dollars for it. She's a mercenary bitch. So you owe me the hundred in addition to what the test will cost. I talked to a professor of biochemistry at TWC. He gave me the name of a local lab that does DNA analysis for the police."

***

JJ hadn't visited or talked with Max after telling him he could expect a letter from Kitty. "Phone me when you get Kitty's letter and we'll talk then, Max."

But five days later, the letter hadn't come. Although he had gone in to work, Max had mostly brooded in his office. JJ had made Odetta Randle aware of the situation. She handled several of Max's clients and didn't bother him.

But as the days went by with no word from Kitty, Max grew more agitated and distraught. He couldn't work, eat, or sleep. The lack of sleep made his mind spiral into delusion and despair. He imagined Kitty had utterly rejected him, that JJ had given up on him, that Larry was laughing at him while having his way with Kitty. He felt like a worm struggling blindly under a blistering sun on a sidewalk after a storm.

Max decided that nothing in his life had gone right. Somehow, he had never lived up to his parents' expectations. His father had wanted him to become a research scientist, had encouraged him in various scientific studies and endeavors. They had built an astronomical telescope together, and Max had done science fair projects. But in college, to his parents' consternation, Max had involved himself with 'uppity Negros' in the civil rights movement. And Max had actively opposed the Vietnam war to his father's anger and dismay. Max had used his college military deferment to attend law school, even though he had little genuine interest in the law.

Now Max decided he had become a mediocre lawyer and a mere dilettante poet. His parents were still in Taiwan. They hadn't bothered to call or write for months. It seemed to Max he had lost both the woman he loved as well as his few friends. He knew Larry wanted Kitty, and that she liked Larry, perhaps loved him. His thoughts began to circle the drain of his morose imagination.

Larry is going to be a major jazz personality, *and with Kitty's beauty and talent they will make a sure-fire duo. Why would she even consider marrying a mediocre schmuck like me? I should just get out of the way of their happiness. JJ is undoubtedly exasperated with me, if not disgusted by my immature behavior. Perhaps the only noble thing I can do, like Sydney Carton in Dickens'* A Tale *of Two Cities, is to sacrifice myself for the benefit of my friends. Yes, suicide is the only answer to my failure as a son, friend, and would-be lover. I should just get out of everyone's way.*

But how should he do it? Max didn't own a gun, and a bullet was far too gruesome and messy, anyway. The same went for slicing his veins in the bath. He winced at the thought of the pain and blood. Pills might do the trick, but he had nothing on hand that could provide a fatal overdose. Drinking bleach would be both painful and uncertain. He had an electric oven rather than gas, so he couldn't emulate poet Sylvia Plath's suicide. Stepping in front of a truck might be traumatic for the driver. Max considered hanging, but that seemed grotesque. He didn't want his friends to find him hanged and be shocked. Carbon monoxide would be easy and painless, but he hadn't been able to get his car in his jam-packed garage for ages.

Max needed something that wasn't painful, wouldn't make a mess, wouldn't cause his friends anguish or disgust, and, if possible, might be seen somehow as actually noble. Finally, just before drifting into a fitful sleep that night, he hit upon the perfect method.

The next morning was a Saturday. Odetta wasn't in the office, which was the front half of his residence. He sat on his enclosed back porch, slurping coffee and gazing vacantly out the window. The sleep had done him good. He was having sober second thoughts about suicide. He had probably overreacted to his situation. Kitty's letter would surely come today, and she might even forgive him. And JJ believed him, trusted him, and was trying to save him. Yes, he would give life at least another day. Perhaps God, if there was one, hadn't given up on him yet.

Just then, something thudded against the picture window, startling him from his reverie. Looking out, he saw a little muckled brown bird lying on the ground. He rushed outside and picked up the tiny bird, hoping it was still alive. It was a Whip-poor-will, seldom seen in those parts. It had a broken neck. A few drops of blood dribbled from its beak. He recalled that Whip-poor-wills were considered precursors of death in literature and myth. *Okay, I can take a hint.*

Max returned inside, dressed, and scribbled a note. Then he drove to a nearby blood donation center and gave a pint of blood. He donated blood at least once a year and knew the procedures well. When finished there, he drove to another blood bank and gave another pint, asking them to use the other arm. Now he was feeling a little lightheaded. He had torn a page from the phone book listing all the local blood centers. He made his way to the next one, hoping they hadn't yet had time to enter him into their networked computer.

At the third blood center, he asked if they could take from his hand or wrist because his arms were sore from lifting weights. The nurse looked dubious, but they needed blood. She checked with the head nurse and then found a vein in Max's hand. When the bag was almost full, the nurse returned and saw Max was somewhat woozy.

"Go ahead and take another pint while you're at it, honey. I'll just sit here and snooze a bit," Max mumbled as he passed out. The nurse alerted her supervisor, and they tried to wake him. They noticed he was very pale and became suspicious. Checking his arms, they found the fresh needle marks.

***

Max awoke the next morning in a hospital bed with an IV in his arm. JJ was staring at him steely-eyed, her red hair flaring dramatically. "Finally, you're awake. Max, you silly fool, what were you thinking?"

"I was just donating some blood," he said, with a petulant lower lip.

"You idiot, you were trying to commit suicide. I've seen the needle marks. You lost at least three pints of blood in just a few hours. That was almost enough to kill you. Thank goodness the nurses there were monitoring donors." She was waving her arms as if conducting a presto allegro.

"Damn, I knew I should have gone to a jackleg plasma parlor. I am an idiot."

JJ slapped him hard on the cheek. "I've been worried sick about you, damn it. I chased all over town trying to find you after I saw the phonebook with the torn-out page and the note on your front porch under that dead bird. 'It's a far, far better thing I do.' What kind of melodramatic crap is that?"

"It was a Whip-poor-will. Definitely a sign. Like Keats, I became half in love with easeful death."

"Well, you're not Keats, and he didn't commit suicide as I recall."

Just then, Kitty rushed into the room. "Max, you idiot." She slapped him hard on the other cheek. Her eyes were tearful and flashed like the errant Roman candles from their infamous 4th of July. Then she hugged him fiercely. "I forgive you for not telling me about Tanya. I sent you a letter, but I forgot the stamp. It came back this morning. You must have panicked. JJ said you tried to commit suicide."

"He just donated too much blood and passed out at the blood bank," said JJ. "I don't know if it was gross incompetence or theater of the absurd." JJ hesitated, then blurted, "By the way, Max, now Kitty's here I can tell you. Tanya's baby wasn't yours. I had its DNA tested. She was probably already pregnant and saw you as a way to get paid for it."

"Well, I guess that's something of a relief to my conscience, if not my ego." Max turned to Kitty, his lips trembling. "Kitty, I promise you I could never force or hit you or any woman. I swear I didn't force Tanya. I didn't even really want sex with her. I promise I will always tell you the truth and try to honor your feelings. I love you, and I want to marry you."

Kitty stood up from the bed, still holding his hand in both of hers. "Max, I believe you, but I'm just not ready for marriage right now. And you're probably not in your right mind anyway after what you've just been through. Let's let things settle down and see what happens."

JJ heaved a sigh. "Okay, y'all kiss and make up now and let's get the hell out of here. You're taking up bed space that actual sick people need."

Kitty kissed Max obediently on his slap-inflamed cheek. Max gave them his sweetest, goofiest smile and said, "Keats also said, 'I am certain of nothing but the holiness of the heart's affections.' I love you both so much."

Chapter Seven

"Little White Lies"

Fort Worth, Texas, November 1988

JJ took Max home from the hospital after his inept attempt at suicide by blood donation. After she left, he wondered if he had been serious about suicide or if it had been some quixotic bid for attention. It had certainly worked out to bring him back into Kitty's good graces. Yet he felt a sense of shame that maybe he had manipulated her into simply taking pity on him. *Do we ever really understand why we do anything? What good did all those philosophy courses do me? I still don't know myself except as a love-sick fool.*

Max decided to accept his good luck and stopped obsessing about it. He resumed his law practice, which had languished during the past several weeks, although his law partner, Odetta Randle, had kept the office open and even accommodated several of his clients. Max had several cases pending that needed his attention. He decided the best thing he could do was show Kitty he was serious about life and was a responsible citizen rather than a romantic kook. *I hereby promise never to lie to* Kitty, either *by commission or omission, so help me... whoever.*

***

That same week, JJ called Larry to fill him in on Max's bloodletting and Kitty's forgiving Max. Larry invited JJ to dinner at *Cattleman's Steak House* in the historic Stockyards area to get the full story. As she walked along Exchange Street toward the restaurant, she encountered the twice-daily cattle roundup. A ten-gallon-hatted cowboy on horseback leisurely moved ten longhorn cattle along the street for tourists' benefit. She hadn't seen this minor spectacle in years.

Arriving at the venerable restaurant, she found the room jammed with tourists and locals. JJ made her way to Larry's table amid the clatter of silverware on plates and the locust-like chatter of diners. She eyed the life-sized murals of old Fort Worth, cattle drives, and horseback cowboys that decorated the interior walls.

Larry hopped up nervously and held her chair for her.

"I haven't been here since I was a little girl. It hasn't changed much since then. We used to come here for lunch after church on some Sundays. I always wondered why there weren't any cowgirls in those pictures. Looks like male chauvinism is still the order of the day." She glared at Larry and ordered an appetizer of calf fries, a glass of *Gewürztraminer,* and a salad.

"Calf fries, eh? You plan on busting my balls?"

"Don't tempt me. No, I just like calf fries. Couldn't find them when we lived in New York."

"Right. Well, look, seems to me Max's caper was just a crazy smart way to try winning Kitty back," said Larry, noisily masticating a bite of sirloin, then washing it down with a gulp of dark beer.

JJ fluttered her fingers dismissively. "I don't think it was deliberate on his part. Max was just so emotionally distraught he wasn't thinking rationally.

His creative subconscious may have protected him by coming up with such an ineffective suicide plan."

"So, it was deliberate, but he just didn't realize it?" said Larry, pulling at his goatee and rolling his eyes.

"I don't know, and it's not important. The main thing is he's okay, and I want you to apologize to Max and the two of you to make up." She stabbed a calf-fry with her fork, held it up, then bit into it aggressively as she eyed him.

Larry winced. "Uh, sure, I'll apologize if you think he'll forgive me. I mean, I truly didn't know inviting Tanya to that party would lead to such heavy weirdness. Heck, you'd probably be thanking me now if Tanya and Max had made nice instead of...you know."

"That's ridiculous! You must have known she would likely cause trouble for Max. Why else did you invite her? And how did she know to speak to Kitty?"

Larry swallowed hard and cleared his throat. "Well, I might have mentioned to Tanya that Max's blond girlfriend would be at the band table. But I just thought it would make Kitty jealous and Max uncomfortable."

"Right. So, you intentionally tried to cause a rift between Max and Kitty. Larry, don't let this rivalry for Kitty get dirty. Max will forgive you for this. You two have been best friends since forever. He doesn't want to throw that away. And I hope you don't want to lose his friendship either." She bit into another calf-fry and took a sip of wine to wash it down. "I explained the situation to Max, but you should do it in person. I need both of you in my life, but I refuse to be a ping-pong ball between two adversaries."

"Ha! You were always better at chunking China than playing ping-pong, uh, but I get what you mean. I'll meet with him and say sorry."

JJ put down her wine glass and grasped Larry's hand. "Listen, Larry, maybe you and I need to apologize to each other, too. Maybe I should have stayed with you when you were sick on drugs in New York. I regret leaving so abruptly like that now. But the only attention you paid me then was anger, and I was afraid you would get physical if I pushed harder." Her gaze locked with his, her eyes glistening with tears. "Larry, I...I still love you, and if there's any chance for us again...well, I'm here." She broke off, not wanting to sound desperate.

Larry averted his eyes. "Yeah, the crack really messed with my head. I thought I couldn't play without it. That was wrong and stupid. But it was your leaving that finally convinced me to get clean. Well, that and the fact I nearly burnt down my apartment trying to melt crack in a spoon. I lit one match in a book and got distracted. It caught the others on fire and burned my hand. I dropped the matches, and they caught some of my sheet music on fire. I beat out the blaze, and that caught my shirt on fire. Finally put it out. I lost some of my tunes, but it sobered me up." Larry shivered a little at the thought of having nearly burned to death.

"That's the first time I've heard that story. I'm glad it got you thinking straight."

Larry sighed. "Yeah, so I guess you did the right thing. I'll always love you too, honey. But I just don't know if we should get back together. We're kinda like gas and matches ourselves. Even though I'm clean now and playing better all the time, I feel like I need someone who can help keep me... motivated."

"You mean you want someone young and innocent like Kitty who will give you the wide-eyed admiration you crave. I could keep you motivated, but not like that."

"I know you think I'm just being selfish, and, heck, maybe I am, but if I'm going to make my mark in jazz, I've got to make it happen soon. After you left me in New York, I went to a doctor to get dried out. Besides getting me clean, he told me I had a heart murmur and should take it easy, that it could be something serious. I didn't think much of it at the time, but then I had some heart flutters again last year."

JJ gasped. "Was it something serious?"

"The palpitations weren't much, but the doctor did a full work-up on me and told me it's something inoperable. It's like a time bomb that might kill me tomorrow or maybe not for years. So, I feel like I've got to create my legacy while I can. I want to be in the jazz history books."

"Larry, why didn't you tell me?"

"I just did. I haven't wanted to think about it until recently. Please don't tell anyone else though. I don't need anyone's pity or charity. I need to know I can make it on my own talent and hard work."

"Of course, I won't say anything. Larry, you have the talent, and I'm sure you'll succeed; let me know if I can help."

Larry gave JJ a weak smile. "You going to eat all those fries?"

***

Two days after his meeting with JJ at *Cattlemen's*, Larry phoned Max, and they agreed to have a late lunch at *Hedary's Lebanese Restaurant* just down Camp Bowie from the Natural Science Museum where Max had built a telescope as a teenager. So many nights he had studied the stars and Moon with that telescope and had thought of becoming an astrophysicist. *Where would I be now if I had stayed with astronomy? So many possible pathways in life; all of them uncertain.*

It was mid-afternoon, so there were only a couple of other tables occupied in the dim interior. Middle Eastern rugs hung on the walls along with a few landscape paintings of the Levant. They took a booth in a far corner. Max noticed Larry's dour expression and smiled.

"Hey, man, don't sweat it. I know JJ told you to apologize, but it's really not necessary. I don't believe you would have invited Tanya if you had known the full story about my relationship with her. It was my own fault for not telling you, and even more so for my not telling Kitty. I was being stupid, hoping the whole predicament would just evaporate. Thank goodness Kitty forgave me."

"I 'preciate you understanding, pard, but I still want to tell you I'm sorry I did it. It was sort of juvenile of me. I did it on the spur of the moment without really thinking. You know how impulsive I am sometimes. It's kinda like I got more than one me in my head trying to drive my machinery." Larry produced a weak smile, looked about uncertainly, then said, "So, I really am sorry. Besides, JJ might break my fingers if she heard I didn't formally apologize. I sure don't want it to cost us our friendship."

"Yeah, JJ definitely has a forceful way about her." Max absently rubbed the cheek JJ had slapped in the hospital. "Look, I know you like Kitty; maybe you even love her. I was obsessed with Kitty, and when I thought she had rejected me, it was like being sucked under by quicksand. I felt so empty, so ruined, I wanted to die. I still love Kitty. I want to marry her. But it's her choice that matters. I don't want to lose your friendship even if she chooses you."

"Yeah, I agree. We've been friends since we were snot-nosed kids. And we helped each other through plenty of tough situations. How could I give up my friendship with a vampire?"

"Vampire? Oh, you mean..."

"Yeah, that time we were exploring that huge new storm sewer. Musta been seven feet high. We were thirteen or fourteen and suddenly there were those three older teens in that concrete tunnel looking to prove how tough they were."

"I remember. They had clubs. One even had a knife. But their leader was just a piss-ant, chicken-shit, wannabe bully."

"And Max, you realized they were just trying to intimidate us. You suddenly swelled up and became Count Dracula and said, 'Igor, ve haven't drunken any human blood for days. Here is a feast. You strangle this skinny one and I'll slaughter these other two. Blood! Blood! I vaunt your Blood!' Then you laughed like a maniac and ran at them. They screamed like girls and ran like track stars."

Max chortled, "Oh, man, yeah, that was beautiful. I wish JJ had been there to see us. She got a giggle out of it when we told her, but you really had to be there. Anyway, you don't ditch a friendship like that."

"When I was doing drugs in New York and JJ left me, I thought I had slipped down some sewer hole into hell. Never again, man. I think I love Kitty, but right now I'm more obsessed with my music than with her. How about if we both take it slow with Kitty 'til she finishes her master's at TCU? Then we'll let her decide whose tune she wants to play."

"Sounds good to me," said Max. "Let's continue to include her in our group activities, but neither of us will date her alone or proposition her until after she graduates. Shake on it?"

A lovely young girl with dark hair and an olive complexion, probably no more than twelve, approached the table in a flowing green robe, and asked if they were ready to order.

"Oh, gosh, I haven't even looked at the menu yet," said Max, scanning quickly through the choices. "I guess I'll have the fish with herbs."

The girl gave a little gasp, and her dark eyes went wide. "Yes sir," she whispered in a shaky voice.

"What's the matter, dear? Is there something wrong with the fish?" asked Max.

She shook her head and gave Max an apologetic look. "We have only one little fish left in the live tank, and ...well, it is my pet."

"You have a live fish in the kitchen, and it's your pet?" said Max in astonishment.

"If it's your pet fish, how come it's on the menu?" asked Larry, with a puzzled smirk.

The embarrassed girl looked down and shuffled her feet nervously. "We have not received any more fresh fish yet, and I have been hoping I could keep Ahmed alive. I know it is silly to make a pet of a fish that is intended to be eaten, but he is such a beautiful, friendly fish."

"Oh, sweetie, I wouldn't eat your pet fish," said Max.

"Well, if you don't want the fish, maybe I'll have it," Larry deadpanned.

The girl blanched again.

"Larry, quit kidding around. You can see the child is serious."

Max patted the girl gently on the arm. "Neither of us wants to eat your fish. But would you show us this amazing Ahmed?"

She brightened and motioned for them to follow her to the kitchen. Just inside the swinging door was a large aquarium containing a foot-long lonely fish. It swam to her eagerly when the girl put her face against the glass. The fish was plump, with silvery scales and bulging inquisitive eyes. It had scarlet streaks on its dorsal fin and tail. The girl looked at them and beamed a smile. "Is he not beautiful?"

"Yes, Ahmed is quite a pretty fish," said Max. "I hope you can keep him alive. Maybe you could just tell people you're out of fish until Ahmed has some edible companions."

The girl seemed pensive. Once they had resumed their seats, she sighed and said, "It would be telling a lie to say we have no fish." She gazed at Max with the eyes of a wounded angel.

Max wanted to hug her, but instead he said, his own eyes glistening tears, "You're absolutely right, dear. It's always better not to lie. Seems like bad things happen when we don't tell the truth. Why don't you tell your dad that Ahmed is your pet, and you don't want anyone to eat him? I'll bet he will understand. Now, you take good care of Ahmed and please bring us some stuffed grape leaves, the cheese plate, and some warm flatbread."

She smiled gloriously and skipped away.

Chapter Eight

"Ain't That a Kick in the Head?"

Fort Worth, Texas, 1989

Max's legal practice had thrived during the year since his failed attempt to commit suicide. His law partner, Odetta Randle, had been a real godsend. She was a savvy, hard-working lawyer and had become a good friend. He and Kitty were again on friendly terms, but per his agreement with Larry, he didn't date her alone. Max and Kitty attended many group parties, gatherings, and concerts along with Larry, JJ, Odetta, and other friends. Max and Larry had told Kitty, JJ, and Odetta of their agreement. The girls said they would enforce it as the best course of action for the two rivals.

Max threw himself into his work for the ACLU. He continued both to write and to teach creative writing. He often jammed with Larry's jazz group at the Catfish Club and other local venues, especially when he knew Kitty would be there. JJ continued to sing occasionally with Larry's combo. Still, Max felt as if he was simply marking time. Neither his work nor other activities could keep his mind off Kitty for long.

Larry was now in full pursuit of his dream to be recognized as a major jazz artist. He had received some insurance and inheritance money due to the death of his parents in an auto accident three years earlier. He used the money to open a recording studio, and he created the record label, Panther City Jazz. His plan was to record not only his group but also to invite some jazz greats to record with him. He hoped this would help him become better known among the jazz media and the public audience.

It seemed to be working. Larry often received invitations to play at major jazz festivals. He was recording with many well-known artists on major labels as well as his own. He had persuaded Kitty and Max to record with him several times.

Max was still somewhat at odds with Larry's musical ideas. They often argued at jam sessions about the direction Larry's playing should take to achieve the greatest impact. Larry inclined toward more technical, bravura alto solos like those of Charlie (Bird) Parker, Cannonball Adderley, and Ornette Coleman, a Fort Worth native. Larry had jammed with Ornette in New York and had invited Ornette to record for Panther City Jazz.

Max thought Larry would be more popular with jazz audiences if he played more lyrically, like Paul Desmond. "Desmond was not only one of the great alto players of all time," said Max. "He was also very perceptive about other musicians. Desmond said Ornette's playing was fabulous, but it was like living in a house where all the walls were red. Desmond also claimed technical complexity, such as Bird's, becomes a trap where it's more fun to play than to hear." Max demonstrated with a blizzard of deliberately ugly rhythm and chord changes in a piano imitation of Parker's tune, "Anthropology."

Larry scowled at this desecration. Max paused, then modulated into a smooth, graceful rendition of the same piece. "See what I mean? Jazz should primarily be emotionally satisfying for the ordinary listener."

"What's your take, Kitty?" asked Larry.

"I think you need to find a style you're comfortable with, Larry. It should reflect your unique personality. Otherwise, it will ring false to listeners. But that unique style should also connect with listeners. Most good jazz artists don't bother to cultivate a distinctive style even when they have complete technical control of their instruments. That's why they stay journeyman players. And there's nothing wrong with that. Not everyone wants to risk being unique or a pioneer. But you do. That's where your creativity and determination come in. If you can find a unique but interesting voice, you'll get recognized."

"You nailed it, Kittio! What would I do without you?" said Larry, smiling his tiger smile. "I've got to be me, but I need to open their ears. I'm gonna dig up a distinctive Delgado sound that will knock listeners for a loop. Hey, there's an idea! Break the tune down into small segments and loop them around and through each other. Let me try some looping runs on that Parker number."

Max rolled his eyes and glanced at the catfish. It was smirking with contempt.

***

Max's law office was also his residence, a stately two-story wood-frame building that had been something of a mansion in the 1930s. It sat on the western edge of downtown, where many legal and medical services had migrated over the years. The area had been an elegant but declining residential neighborhood until the previous decade.

The front four rooms: a large reception area, a conference room, Odetta's office, and Max's office constituted the business portion. A staircase off the reception area led to the second floor, which contained three bedrooms and two bathrooms. Max's bedroom adjoined another, which was furnished as his library/study. On the first floor, behind the law offices were the kitchen, dining room, and a music room with Max's piano. A large, enclosed back porch with picture windows gave onto a shady backyard dominated by a regal Shumard red oak.

Odetta Randle had filled the legal assistant position that Tanya Carter had held seven years previously. She was a plump, pleasant African-American matron in her forties. She had finished her law degree at SMU, fourth in her class in 1985, but couldn't obtain an attorney position. Although Max had hired her as his legal assistant, he promoted her to an attorney position after she passed the bar. Because they worked so well together, he surprised her with partnership in '87.

However, Odetta often continued to handle all the front office responsibilities since they couldn't yet afford a full-time receptionist. She brewed a great cup of coffee on Max's cantankerous espresso machine. She was also administrative assistant to Rilke, a red and black, brindled tabby that had mysteriously appeared on Max's front porch four years previously as a kitten. Rilke was lord high magistrate of the office when he wasn't snoozing on one of the storage shelves above a row of filing cabinets.

Several large Western prints by Charles Russell and Frederick Remington decorated the walls of the reception area to let clients know Max was a bona fide native Texan. In his private rooms, Max preferred images of American nature scenes by such as Frederic Church, Thomas Moran, and Albert Bierstadt. He had also hung several Texas landscapes by artist friends, and a couple of Chinese scroll paintings his parents had sent him from Taiwan last Christmas. A framed photo of the Cowtown Jazz Trio plus JJ from the late 70s, taken by a photographer friend, hung in the music room.

Max was working on his second cup of coffee of the morning and gloomily eyeing a stack of depositions he needed to review when his phone buzzed, and Odetta said Kitty needed to talk with him.

He answered eagerly, since she seldom called. "What's up, Kitty?"

"Max, it's terrible! You've got to help me."

"Sure, honey, what's the problem?"

"JJ is at St. Joseph's Hospital for...for some tests. I took her there this morning, and I was supposed to pick her up, but I'm stuck over in Arlington, and I can't get away in time. Can you pick her up, take her home, and be sure to tell her I'm so sorry?"

"Sure, don't worry. I'll handle it. What's her doctor's name? I'm on my way right now."

He arrived at the hospital twenty minutes later wondering why JJ needed a ride if she was just having some tests done. He hadn't seen her for about six weeks, which was also unusual. She had missed several jazz sessions and other events around town recently. He found JJ seated in the hospital lobby in a wheelchair. A red wool toboggan cap covered her head, but her noggin was obviously bald beneath.

"JJ, what the heck's going on? Kitty is indisposed and asked me to drive you home."

"Oh, crap! I had hoped to keep it just between Kitty and me. You might as well know. I'm being treated for breast cancer. This was my second chemo treatment, and I'm not supposed to drive."

"Cancer! My God, JJ, why didn't you tell me? You're going to need more help than just a ride home. Let's get you in my car." He waved off the attendant and pushed her wheelchair to the car. She was a little weak and wobbly when he helped her in.

As they drove to JJ's house in the Meadowbrook neighborhood of East Fort Worth, she said, "Max, I'm sorry to get you involved, but I need to ask for your help. The school district has put me on sick leave, and when that runs out, if I can't work, they won't renew my contract. I'll lose my health insurance. So, I may have to sell my house and car. Can you help me sell if it comes to that?"

"Of course, JJ, don't fret about it. Let's hope that selling won't be necessary. Right now, you need to rest and not worry about anything." He helped her into the house. JJ immediately made for the bathroom, where Max heard her retching.

"Damn it, JJ, this won't do. Pack a bag. You're coming to live at my house while you're under treatment. That way I can take you to your appointments and keep an eye on you. Where's that hound, Barkly?"

"He died of cancer four months ago. That's why I finally went to the doctor myself."

JJ argued but finally gave in. Max soon moved her into his music room at the back of the house. He converted it into a comfortable bedroom with its connecting bathroom. JJ wouldn't need to climb the stairs, and she could watch the wildlife in the backyard from the picture windows. Max examined her finances and found out what the treatments might cost. It didn't look good.

***

A few days after she moved in, Max and JJ were having breakfast on the back porch. He gave her the news that she might indeed have to sell her car and house. Max was fuming.

"Medical care is one of the major things wrong with America, and it's so stupid. In Canada or any European country, all this medical treatment would cost you little or nothing because they have universal health care through general taxation. But in America, you are free to get sick and go bankrupt or die. How does that help the economy or anyone but the insurance companies? Back in the forties, President Truman proposed national health care, but it was rejected by the doctors and Republicans as socialism, and it's been off limits ever since. Cancer treatment is just another profit center for rapacious capitalism." He waved a piece of toast in a sweeping arc that came perilously close to his coffee cup.

"Max, settle down. Since you are so generously letting me stay here free, I can sell my house and car, and maybe that will pay my bills until I recover. I wish you would let me pay you rent or at least let me help out around here."

"You know that's not going to happen, not until you get your strength back. Besides, I think I've figured out how to beat this rotten system." He looked at the photo of the jazz group on the wall, took a gulp of coffee, then blurted, "I want you to marry me. Then they can't deny you health insurance."

"Marry you!? Max, only you would come up with such a loony idea." She put her hand gently on Max's cheek as he glowered into his coffee. "You know I love you as a dear friend, but I consider marriage a bit more sacred than a business deal to save money. Besides, I also know you love Kitty, and she loves you. I refuse to be an impediment to your eventually marrying her."

Max groaned. "I wish I could be as sure as you that Kitty will choose me. Well, my offer still stands if worse comes to worst."

JJ sighed. "I do appreciate the offer, and I agree the health insurance situation in America is totally screwed up. But this was really my own fault. I failed to get an annual mammogram for the last several years. The doctor said if the cancer had been detected even two years ago, it would have been caught before it became serious, and some minor surgery would have gotten rid of it."

Max grimaced and moaned, "How many times have we wished we could go back in time and make a simple change like that? Well, if you won't consider marriage, I'll just consider your being here part of my devious plan to spend more time with Kitty. She's joining us for lunch today to see how you're doing. I had better get some work done before then."

***

Later that morning, Max's intercom buzzed. There was a note of strain in Odetta's voice. "Mr. Ballard, there's a Mr. Royce Carter here to see you. He doesn't have an appointment, but, uh, he says you know him, and he demands to talk with you."

Max put on his best fake smile as he entered the reception area. Royce, at six-foot-three and well over two hundred pounds, seemed even larger than Max remembered from the one time they had met six years previously.

"Hello, Mr. Carter. Let's step into my office to talk."

"We can talk just fine right here. Won't take long. I want that five thousand dollars you promised Tanya and me for support of your baby." Royce shifted nervously yet menacingly as he spoke, clenching and unclenching his fists.

"Mr. Carter, if the baby had lived, I would have been glad to provide child support, but the baby—died, and I've since discovered that, uh, he wasn't in fact my baby."

Royce's eyes flared. He abruptly punched Max in the face. Max collapsed to the floor, his nose bleeding extravagantly. Odetta screamed and grabbed the phone. "I'm calling the police!"

"Get up here, you coward, so I can hit you again." Royce loomed over Max menacingly. "Tanya said it was your baby, and she ain't lying. You better pay me that money."

Max remained sprawled on the floor, but managed to say, "Royce, a DNA test proved the baby wasn't mine. I did have sex with Tanya just one time, but she was the one who came on to me. You should leave before the police get here. You're on parole. They'll send you back to prison. Leave now, and we won't name you to them."

"If I got to go back to prison for hitting you, I might as well mess you up good." Royce drew back his leg to kick Max in the head. Odetta screamed again. Royce's kick grazed Max's ear as he rolled slightly away. Then Royce screamed as twelve pounds of brindled fury landed on his head, slashing at his face. Rilke leaped back onto his shelf before Royce could grab him. Raging, Royce produced a switchblade knife and bent toward Max as if to stab.

"Drop that knife and leave right now or I'll shoot you deader than a door-mouse!" JJ stood in the hallway to the living area, fifteen feet away. She held a gun in both hands, its barrel pointing at Royce's chest. "Go, or I shoot you at the count of three. One, two...."

Royce didn't drop the knife, but he did make a hasty exit, banging the front door behind him. They watched him lope across the lawn to a waiting car. It peeled out with a screech of tires and a plume of blue exhaust.

Max was still on the floor with blood oozing from his nose and ear. He looked at JJ with his mouth agape. "Damn, JJ, I always knew you were one tough babe, but I didn't know you carried a gun. Would you really have shot him?"

"Not with this," said JJ, holding up the extra-large Sharpie marker with its gray barrel. "People see what they think they ought to, especially when you give them a little encouragement."

Odetta cackled with glee as she reached down to help Max up. "Now that's some quick thinking, JJ. I'll get you some ice for that nose, Max."

Max grinned up at JJ, who was dressed in bunny décor pajamas, fuzzy slippers, and her red turban. "I think what really scared him was you threatening to shoot him 'dead as a door-mouse'."

"Well, that's all I could come up with on the spur of the moment." JJ wasn't smiling. She knelt next to Max to examine his wound.

"What's the matter, JJ? It turned out fine. You saved my life—again. Are you okay?"

"Yes, but I'm in some—moral anguish. I lied to you about that DNA test. It indicated you were the baby's father. I didn't want to tell you then because you were so broken up about Kitty. Since the baby had died, it seemed sort of a moot issue anyway. I didn't realize Royce might come around and stir things up again."

Max groaned, and his eyes slid from side to side a few times. "Oh, JJ, don't beat yourself up. You did nothing wrong. Royce and I are the ones who will always have to live with the shame of it. Let's just hope he doesn't come back."

Max had now gotten to his knees and was checking to see if there was blood on his tie. JJ put her hand on his cheek. Odetta returned with ice in a towel for Max's face.

Suddenly the front door flew open. Odetta gave another squeal and let the ice cubes slip from the dishtowel, clunking onto Max's head.

"Good lord, what's going on?" said Kitty, astonished by their Three Stooges tableaux. "Max, you're covered in blood, and JJ, shouldn't you be in bed?" Rilke slipped into Kitty's arms with a plaintive meow, needing to be cuddled after his exertions. Odetta chuckled, “Lord, why did I ever think this job might be boring?”

Chapter Nine

"Perfidia"

Catfish Jazz Club, Fort Worth, Texas, November 1990

The lights in, on, and around the Catfish Jazz Club glowed eerily into the night as chilly November rain pounded Fort Worth and all North Texas. However, the parking lot was well-populated with vehicles because Larry was hosting a private party. It was mainly a celebration of Max winning a poetry book prize. They were also quietly celebrating JJ's remission from breast cancer. She had been living with Max for almost two years. She had sold her house to help pay for the cancer treatments, but also because Max needed her full-time help with the office. Max, Kitty, and Odetta had all helped shepherd JJ through her cancer treatments while Max labored to maintain his law practice. Larry, too, had often visited JJ and assisted with her recovery, sometimes taking her for treatment.

Tonight, Joe and Elaine were up from South Texas for the party, leaving ten-year-old Sally with an aunt. JJ, Kitty, Max, Elaine, and Odetta sat together at the traditional band table near the stage. Various friends, colleagues, and musicians occupied several other tables and even a few of Max's poetry students. Larry, Joe, and a technician were arranging the stage and making sure the recording equipment was operating properly.

"JJ, I see your hair has almost completely grown back," said Elaine. "But now it's more strawberry than scarlet."

"Yeah, I haven't applied the crimson hair color I used before. I think I'll stay natural for a while. It's a bit frizzier too, but I'm just glad to have my hair back. I got tired of trying to find hats for my cue ball," quipped JJ.

"I thought you looked cute bald," said Max. "Maybe I just got used to it."

"Well, I think your new hair is gorgeous," said Kitty. "I've never seen quite that shade of red on anyone else."

"Yeah, orange and fuzzy like our squirrel's tail," said JJ. Then, seeing Kitty and Elaine's puzzlement, she said, "Max and I saw a squirrel one morning a couple of months ago. It had its tail caught in that wire sculpture in Max's backyard. The poor little thing was exhausted from trying to get loose. It was just lying there with its tail all twisted in the wire. We got a bath towel and wrapped the squirrel in it so she wouldn't struggle. She was so sweet and calm. Her eyes were pleading with us. Well, you tell them what you did, Max."

"There was no way to undo the tail from the wire," said Max, "so I got a pair of limb loppers and cut the squirrel's tail off at the base while JJ held her. We were afraid she might bleed out, but there was no blood at all. The tail must be all tendon. She sat there for a few moments after the surgery just looking at us, then she wandered off, tailless."

"Oh, I feel for the dear thing," said Kitty. "I hope she'll be all right. I wonder if she can keep her balance in the trees without a tail."

"We didn't see her for several days," said JJ, "but a couple of weeks later she showed up again foraging for bird seed along with some others in the backyard. So, I guess she'll be okay. Max removed the wire sculpture to prevent another such incident. Now I sort of identify with that squirrel.

We both lost our crowning glory, but we both lived to tell the tale of the tail."

Larry waved to Max that they were ready to play and record the first set. "Come play with us, Kitty," said Max.

"You go ahead. I'll just listen for a while and chat with the girls. I may play later."

Max joined Larry and Joe on stage. Jack Perry, their sometime guitarist, was also there. They had decided to begin with some older, slow, smooth tunes that would be easily danceable. As Max, Jack, and Joe provided an intro, Larry whispered into the microphone, "Folks, thanks so much for joining us on this miserable night. But it's dry here inside, and we have some warm, cozy music for you, beginning appropriately with that great old standard, 'Stormy Weather.'"

As they migrated through "Naima," "Autumn Leaves," "In a Sentimental Mood," and "These Foolish Things" (on which Joe played a lovely extended solo), several couples danced, and wine flowed. JJ circulated around the room to thank her friends for coming. Even her cancer doctor was in attendance. When she returned to their table, she found the girls in avid conversation about Mikhail Gorbachev having been awarded the Nobel Peace Prize the previous month.

"Seems to me not only the Berlin Wall, but Communism in general is falling," said Kitty. "Russia just can't hold it together. The Eastern European countries are breaking away. What do you think, Odetta? You majored in Poli-Sci didn't you?"

"I did, but Communism wasn't my specialty. Still, it does look like Russia's hold on Eastern Europe has collapsed, and Russia itself may change drastically. That could be a good thing, but on the other hand, they still have all those nuclear missiles. I'd hate for some crazy military faction to get control of those nukes."

"Gosh, you've got a point there," said Elaine. "I hope there's not a Dr. Strangelove in Russia. Oh, by the way, Kitty, congratulations on your upcoming graduation with your master's degree. Sorry, Joe and I won't be able to be here for the ceremony."

"It's no big deal," said Kitty a little hesitantly. "There will be so many people at the ceremony; it will be pretty chaotic. I may decide to skip it myself."

"You should attend, Kitty," said JJ. "It's a once in a lifetime thing, and you really earned it. Larry, Max, and I will be there if you are."

"I guess Max and Larry will soon start pestering you for dates again," said Elaine.

Kitty's eyes widened briefly. She blushed and said, "Uh, I'm going to get a refill on my drink. Can I get something for y'all while I'm up?"

The quartet had just finished playing "Winelight." Larry took the microphone and announced, "We'll do another set in a few minutes, but I want to remind everyone that one reason for our party tonight is to congratulate my piano man, Max Ballard, for an outstanding accomplishment. Besides being a fine pianist, Max is a talented poet. He recently won the Wallace Stevens Prize for his new book, *13 Ways of Looking*." The crowd applauded politely. "I'll bet Max could be persuaded to inflict—I mean, honor us with a reading from the book." More applause.

Max took over the mic and held up the book. "Thanks, Larry, and thanks everyone for coming out on such an awful night to help us celebrate. We're so happy and thankful JJ has recovered. She has been my anchor in an often-stormy sea, and I know many others feel the same." Max slipped on his reading glasses.

"I won't impose more than a couple of poems on you, just to give you a flavor of my writing. The book title is a tribute to Wallace Stevens' famous poem, '13 Ways of Looking At a Blackbird.' I wanted the book to emphasize that there are many ways of looking at life, love, and reality in general. One of the poems is written from a ghost's perspective. Another is what a person's shadow might say. And one is about abandoned angels. The title of this first poem is 'Waiting,' which is self-explanatory." Max opened the book and read:

"I wrote this poem as usual,
at the last minute,
waiting for inspiration,
waiting, unamused, to be mused,
to be infused with winged fire.
But, of course, I had to hobble instead of fly.
Such is the pattern of my existence:
always waiting for a sign that I should
do some wondrous, some worthy thing,
waiting for a more appropriate time,
a more propitious occasion,
yet, somehow, never recognizing it,
until far too late.
Never sure what *diem* to *carpe*.
Always waiting for the *deus ex machina*
to appear and rescue me
from life's wretched ambiguity.
So it seems my moments
have merely dripped away
rather than riding me high
on a tide of momentousness.
And my story comes down to
an extended series of ellipsis,
a neat, bleak row of ink dots leading

nowhere, and only there to indicate
the absence of what might have happened
if only I hadn't waited for...."

Max rapped the piano top to indicate the futility of waiting for opportunity to knock. He read two more short poems but saw that many of the audience would much rather be listening to music. He said, "This will be the last one for tonight; it's dedicated to a very dear friend." Max smiled at Kitty and read:

"When I Think Of You
When I see long-stemmed lilies
adorned with morning dew
I think of you
When fragrance of fresh roses finds
my olfaction what can I do
but think of you
When the moon almosts the glisten
of your eyes gazing on us two
I think of you
When that solitary lark sang
so yearningly before she flew
I thought of you
When leaves unlimb and languish
quilt the earth with variegated hue
I think of you
When stars sang last night's nocturne
blazing brighter as my tears imbue
I thought of you
When geese in gaunt geometries
groan longing on the high bleak blue

I think of you
and when the sky is empty too"

After polite applause for Max, Larry took over the mic again. "Thank you, Max, for those, uh, artful words. Maybe I'll write a tune based on that poem of yours, 'Flying On Love.' There's a table near the door with copies of the book, folks. I'm sure Max will be glad to sell you a book and sign it for you during intermission. We'll be back with music in just a few minutes."

Max started for the book table, then turned back to Larry and said, "We need to have a party here to celebrate Kitty's graduation next month, don't you think?"

Larry hesitated. "Uh, yeah, sure, great idea. We'll do that, Max."

Max went to the book table and signed books for several people. Then Kitty was beside him, her eyes shining, her smile radiant but restrained. He handed her a book. "I've already signed it for you, Kitty. Read the inscription."

"'To Kitty, my heart will always be your haven.' Oh, that's so sweet, Max, thank you. I'll cherish it always."

"Kitty, now that you're about to graduate, my agreement with Larry not to date you will be finished. That last poem I read was about you, of course. I think about you constantly. I know I'll never be rich or famous, but I will be a loving and attentive husband if you'll have me."

"Max, you know I love you, and—"

Suddenly, Larry was there. He grasped Kitty's arm and said, "Kitty, we need to do our sax duet. The natives are getting restless." Larry pulled her toward the stage while Max gazed after them open-mouthed. She looked back at him as if a little frightened.

Max followed them onto the stage and sat at the piano. Kitty took out her tenor sax and joined the group in the tune, 'You Don't Know What

Love Is.' She and Larry provided a daring saxophone duet in which she wandered lasciviously through the tenor's low register with an occasional extended low D that had become a Sonny Rollins' trademark.

When they finished, to much applause, Larry hugged Kitty, then continued holding her hand. "Friends, another reason I threw this party is to announce that Kitty and I are engaged to be married. As you just heard, we already have a great sax life."

Kitty blanched, looked at Max wide-eyed, her hand to her throat. She jerked her hand away from Larry's and hurried to the band table. Max saw JJ and Elaine were surprised but were hugging her and talking excitedly.

Larry was grinning like the Cheshire Cat. He turned to the musicians and said, "What shall we play next, guys?"

Max hissed, "'Perfidia'!"

Larry glared at Max for a long moment, then covered the mic with his hand and spoke low but emphatically, "Hey, man, I didn't betray our deal. The day after Kitty received her graduation notice, I called her to come record with me, and I proposed to her. She accepted. Simple as that."

"But we agreed we would wait until after her graduation to date her. She hasn't even had her graduation ceremony yet."

"Yeah, well, I guess maybe we each interpreted our deal somewhat differently, but I didn't cheat on it."

Max stood up from the piano and would have confronted him, but Larry had turned to the musicians and said, "Okay gentlemen, 'Perfidia' it is." The group jumped into the tune.

Max joined in, his jaw clenching. A maelstrom of confusion, agony, anger, and frustration battered him. His mind raced in several directions toward oblivion. He played the familiar tune automatically, unable to pay full attention to the ensemble. He stared at the keys without really seeing them. Then his glance was arrested by the catfish on the wall above the stage. Surely it was leering at him. Max blinked as he seemed to see the fish take the toy saxophone from its mouth. It winked at him and said, ***"Ah, perfidia, self-pittia. Did you really think Kitty would marry a lame- ass lawyer, mediocre pianist, and piss-ant poet, when she can marry the next great jazz wizard?"*** The fish smirked and resumed its accustomed immobility.

When the piece ended, Max beckoned to Roger Thorne, another pianist who often played with the combo. Roger took over the piano, and Max made his way unsteadily to the band table, still in a daze. Kitty immediately stood and hugged him. She was pale and agitated.

"Max, I'm so sorry. I didn't know Larry was going to make that announcement tonight. I wanted to tell you myself when we could be alone. Yes, we are engaged. I was going to explain just as he pulled me away. Larry told me he has a heart condition and probably has only a few more years to live. He said he wants me to help him become a major jazz artist and win a Grammy before he dies. Max, I'm so confused. I love you too, but I just feel he needs me more right now. Please don't hate me." Her voice was strained, and she was fighting back tears.

Max held her at arm's length and sought her eyes. "Kitty, darling, I could never hate you. I'll always love you. I'm just stunned and in shock. I feel like he tricked both of us. I've never heard anything about a heart condition. Larry seems able to create a logical justification for whatever he wants. Well, I had better go sell some books. Can we talk tomorrow?"

Kitty nodded and hugged him again, long and tight, felt him tremble against her, then she released him. She gazed into his eyes for several seconds and collapsed into her chair with a moan of anguish. Max staggered over to the book table, still in a fog of bewilderment. The girls watched him for a few moments, then resumed their interrogation of Kitty. Minutes later, JJ looked toward the book table, then around the room.

"I don't see Max," said JJ. She went to the book table. Max's car keys were holding down a note that read: "Free books. Please take them."

JJ rushed back to the band table and showed them the keys. "Max must have walked out into the damn storm. Odetta, let's you and I drive around and find him before he catches pneumonia. No, Kitty, you stay here. We'll find him. And you can tell Larry I'm going to slap him up, down, and sideways first chance I get."

Odetta and JJ grabbed umbrellas and then found Max's car. They drove slowly around the neighborhood, peering about intently. The rain was still falling in sheets, making anything in the darkness even less visible. Occasional lightning crackled through the monstrous clouds, illuminating for an instant the empty streets. Finally, they came to a vacant lot a few streets from the club. The lot was the exercise yard for a horse stable. Lightning flashed, and there was Max, leaning against the fence, his face pressed to that of a skinny horse that must have been left outside. Both were drenched and miserable.

Odetta said, "I'll get him, JJ. You drive. You certainly don't need to get a soaking and catch pneumonia, yourself."

"Max is probably thinking about his favorite philosopher, Nietzsche," said JJ in exasperation. "Nietzsche hugged a beaten carriage horse after being rejected by Lou Salome. I'm sure all this will soon become poetry."

"I hope I can get him in here before one of us is struck by lightning," said Odetta as another bright flash ripped through the rain. "That man is one love-crazy human—or maybe just crazy."

Chapter Ten

"Something Else"

Palo Pinto Lake, Texas, May 1991

JJ asked Max for the keys to his parents' lake house so she, Kitty, and Elaine could have a girls-only outing prior to Kitty's wedding to Larry, which was now only a month away. Max was happy to comply but told her to be careful out there in the wild, and to call his cell phone if they needed anything. He knew JJ was now completely recovered from cancer, but he would relish coming to their rescue. Max had recovered from his devastation at the news of Kitty's pending marriage to Larry, but he was still desperately in love with Kitty and hoped they could eventually be together. Perhaps Kitty would change her mind before the wedding or divorce Larry after. Or maybe Larry would actually die of the heart problem he had used to persuade Kitty to marry him.

JJ wanted to get Kitty away from both Larry and Max to a locale where the three girls could relax and open up with each other as trusted friends. JJ had been surprised Kitty had agreed so quickly to marry Larry. She recalled how Larry and Max had agreed to let Kitty finish her master's before they began dating her again. Their engagement seemed to JJ, and to everyone else, to have come like a bolt from the blue. JJ had been surprised Kitty had said yes to Larry without giving Max an equal chance to court her.

So, JJ wanted to make sure Larry hadn't coerced or unfairly influenced Kitty in some way. Having once been married to Larry for four years, JJ knew Larry all too well. She knew how persuasive he could be when he wanted something. JJ also knew Kitty and how vulnerable she was. But if Kitty was determined to marry Larry, JJ wanted to prepare her for his foibles. Perhaps Kitty would have more success with him than JJ had. JJ still loved Larry, but she wanted him to be happy, even if it had to be with someone else.

The three girls rode together in JJ's red Mustang (which Max had insisted she keep during her illness). They gabbed like teens and sang along with Ella Fitzgerald on the tape deck. Arriving at the lake house, they stored away their groceries and began their hen party with wine, cheese, and fruit out on the treetop deck.

"Oh, this is so pleasant, girls," said Kitty. "Thanks so much for arranging it. My mother and Larry's aunt Lucy are doing most of the planning for the wedding, but it's been quite stressful for me, anyway."

"Yeah, weddings are the worst," said Elaine. "I'd rather go to a funeral. Everyone says nice things about the deceased or stays quiet. At weddings, everyone gets drunk and catty, and the guys try to hump the bridesmaids. At least that's what happened at mine."

JJ guffawed. "I remember yours vividly, hon. Dan Renfrew followed me around until Larry told him to bugger off. He got so drunk he barfed on Janet Creston."

"Well, I'm trying to keep it simple," said Kitty. "I'm not having any bridesmaids. Just Sally to hold my train. I had to talk Larry out of an elaborate ceremony. He wanted to turn it into a jazz commercial."

"I'm glad he listened to what you wanted. He'll try to bully you if you let him," said JJ. "By the way, now that it's just us girls, tell us how he persuaded you to say yes so quickly."

Kitty made a little grimace, and her face reddened. "Larry called and asked me to come to the Catfish Club three days after I received my notice of graduation in the mail. He must have called TCU and asked them when the notices went out. The graduation ceremony was over a month later."

JJ rolled her eyes and twisted a lock of hair. "So, Larry broke his agreement with Max not to put a move on you until after you graduated. He'll say it's a technicality since you had gotten the official graduation notice. Larry's notorious for his self-serving logic that often defies common sense. He once admitted to me that he took blowjobs from groupies when he was on the road with Rocking Raven. But he justified it, saying Raven expected his crew to live up to the mystique of rock musicians and anyway, it wasn't really sex."

Elaine snorted so hard wine came out of her nose. "Maybe some musicians think they blow their best when they've been blown!"

Kitty was biting her lip. "At first, I thought he asked me to come to the club just to help him plan the little jazz festival he's been talking about. But he seemed very quiet and serious. I was afraid he had some bad news, that he was in trouble, or that someone had died. Then he said he was sure he could become a major jazz personality, but he needed me to be his partner and his muse. He said he gets his best ideas for music when I'm with him."

"Classic Larry setup," said JJ. "Then he told you about his heart condition, am I right?"

"Yes, he said he was afraid he didn't have much time to make his mark in music because he has an inoperable heart condition that could kill him any time. He swore he loved me. I probably should have reminded him of his agreement with Max, but I was just stunned by the whole thing."

"Sounds like he had it all planned out," Elaine chortled, still dabbing her nose.

"Yeah, he told me about that heart condition over a year ago," said JJ. "But he made me promise not to tell anyone. I think he's probably telling the truth about his heart, but he's bad about making shit up if it serves his purpose. Larry once tried sucking up to Miles Davis by claiming he had run with a black gang as a kid. Far as I know there was only one black kid in his neighborhood, and I never saw Larry with him."

Kitty took a long, shaky drink of wine and held up her left hand with its engagement ring. "He presented me with this huge sapphire engagement ring, went down on his knee, and asked me to marry him. I was actually afraid if I said no, he might have a heart attack right there. He seemed so sincere. I guess I said yes without really thinking it through."

"Well, he obviously had thought it through," said JJ. "He must have planned it well in advance. Max said he was called out of town about that time to meet a client for some emergency that didn't materialize. Max realized later Larry had probably arranged it just to make sure Max couldn't be there to preempt Larry's preemption."

"Good gravy, girl, you were definitely set up," said Elaine. "He didn't wait until you actually graduated like y'all had agreed. You can still get out of this wedding. Do you want to call it off?"

"I'm not sure. I don't think so. I mean, I have true feelings for Larry. I feel secure with him even though I realize he's very self-centered. He knows what he wants, and I guess I'm it. And maybe I really can help him succeed. I guess I can wait a few years to help Max save the world if I can help Larry become a jazz great before he dies."

"But it's what you want that's important, Kitty. And what about Max?" asked JJ. "You know he would marry you in a New York minute if you would have him. He told me he's been in love with you since he first saw you and that he's told you his feelings several times. I remember his exact words, in fact. He said he would marry you in a minuet (or in a minute if you preferred a waltz)."

Kitty giggled at the pun, then wrung her hands and began to tear up. "I know! I feel so bad about Max. I love him very much. If I'm totally honest with myself, I probably love him more than Larry. I just feel Larry needs me more. I guess I've always been a sucker for needing to be needed. Why do I feel so awful when I'm engaged to be married and have two great guys in love with me?"

JJ patted Kitty's knee. "Yeah, lots of girls think that would be a great problem to have, but it's agonizing, isn't it?"

"I think we're going to need more wine," said Elaine, going inside to find another bottle. "Hey, what's this noise in here? It sounds like an animal is inside the cast-iron stove."

JJ and Kitty joined Elaine in the living room. There were scrabbling, scratching noises coming from the closed-up Franklin stove that hadn't been used since the previous winter. They got up close and listened.

"I'll bet it's a bird," said JJ. "Max said he found a dead one in there one spring when he went to clean it out. Wrote a poem about it, of course. I'm going to open the grate. Stand back. It might be a rat or something."

"I've got a poker to hit it with just in case," said Elaine.

"Well, don't get excited and whack me," said JJ.

JJ eased open the stove grate, looked in, then reached in. She brought out a chimney swift enclosed carefully in her hands. It was trembling and looking around in desperation.

"Aw, poor thing," said Kitty. "She must have wanted to nest in the chimney. She fell down the stovepipe and then couldn't climb or fly back out."

They took the little bird outside, and JJ placed it on the deck railing. It sat there for a few seconds, panting, then launched into the air and was gone.

"Yea! We did good," said Elaine. "Now let's have that wine."

***

That evening, they watched a wonderful rose and gold sunset against some low western clouds that later moved in to provide a gentle pattering rain after dark. They ate a candlelight supper, drank more wine, listened to some of Max's romantic records, and made more girl talk.

JJ said, "I don't mean to embarrass you, Kitty, but have you and Larry, uh, done it yet?"

Kitty's cheeks reddened in the candlelight. "No. And frankly, I haven't had much experience with sex. After I was raped at sixteen, I was afraid and disgusted by the idea of sex for years."

"Raped! Kitty, you never told us you had been raped," said Elaine.

JJ said, "She told me, but I promised I wouldn't tell anyone else. I told Max that night Tanya created the scene at the Club, so he would understand Kitty's extreme reaction. Then I felt I needed to tell Larry so he would realize he had screwed up royally by inviting Tanya."

Kitty was biting her lip and nodding. "That's okay, I understand. I certainly don't blame you. You did right under the circumstances. Thank God Max's suicide attempt failed. That might have really driven me over the edge."

"Gosh, Kitty, you must have been terribly damaged emotionally as a teen," said Elaine.

"Yeah, I was. I was very wary of men for years, and the idea of sex nauseated me. I deliberately had a brief fling with a fellow student at TCU the year before I met y'all. It was just to prove to myself I wasn't frigid. I certainly wasn't in love with him, and he didn't really do anything for me. So, I decided to wait until after I married, if that should ever happen."

"Gosh, Joe and I went at it like rabid weasels before we were married," said Elaine with a smile of remembrance. "I guess that's because I knew he was the one. But I've always been kind of highly sexed. I was with several guys and, uh, girls before I met Joe."

JJ ogled Elaine. "I never knew that about you, girl. Didn't you go to Catholic school?"

"Yeah, an all-girls school. We had to defy those uptight, knuckle-rapping nuns somehow. It was no big deal, just a fun, rebellious teen thing."

Kitty's eyes were large and luminous in the candlelight. "Do you think there's only one true love for each person? If so, I'm not sure Larry is mine. I mean, I think I love him, but it's not like an earthquake in my heart when I'm around him, like romance novels portray it. And I also have very warm feelings for Max."

"But you and Max haven't made love either?" asked JJ.

Kitty looked wistful. "No, I kind of wish we had. Then, I might have chosen Max. Now I guess I'll never know."

"Max and I made out some when we were in high school together," said JJ. "But we never went all the way, which is strange now I think back on it. I was kind of wild and, uh, experimental back then. I was just a year at North Texas State, two years behind Max, before transferring to TWC to be with Larry." She paused to take a sip. "I think Larry may have been jealous of Max, not only about me, but because Max was in one of the lab bands. Larry said NTSU was the best jazz school in the nation. But Larry had to stay in Fort Worth for family reasons, so he went to TWC on a music scholarship." JJ gave a smile of rueful remembrance.

"Larry's jealousy may have been justified," JJ continued. "I had feelings for Max, too. But Max got involved in the Civil Rights movement and had affairs with a black girl I knew, Louella Lacy, and a Hispanic girl later, I think. But those were just flings. He was never serious about anyone until you, Kitty."

"What about you and Larry?" asked Elaine.

"Larry and I had sex several times before we were married. You might want to do the same, Kitty, just to see if Larry is really right for you, at least in that respect."

"He said he wouldn't ask me to since he's trying to be a good Catholic now."

"Ha! That didn't seem to bother him before we were married," said JJ, fluffing her hair. "I wanted to make sure we were compatible and really in love. I guess I sort of seduced him. Not that he required much persuasion. But Catholicism sure never entered into it."

"Well, maybe you should give Kitty a heads up about Larry," said Elaine with a grin.

"Yeah, well, don't expect lollipops and rainbows," said JJ. "Larry's like a jazz tune in 6/8 time. He goes at it hot and heavy for a couple of minutes, then he finds the coda and falls asleep pretty quick. You're probably going to have to handle your own orgasms."

"Well, that's standard operating procedure with just about any man, ain't it?" said Elaine grinning again. "They just don't have the staying power women need. I keep my little friend vibrator by the bed even though Joe is still pretty attentive."

"Since we're having this discussion, I wish one of us had done it with Max," said JJ. "If he can make love like he writes poetry about it, he might just be the exception to the rule. Maybe I'll try to seduce Max after you're married, Kitty. But I think he's so much in love with you he may not go for it."

"Gosh, now you've got me all hot," said Kitty, fanning herself. "I think I'm going to take a shower and hop in bed. But first, I want to say thanks for this wonderful time together. I feel kind of like that bird we set free earlier."

"Bed for me, too," said Elaine. "But I'll cook breakfast in the morning. You can both sleep in."

"Sounds good to me. I'm going to stay up a while longer and read," said JJ.

Fifteen minutes later, Kitty was in the midst of her shower when JJ stepped into the stall with her.

Kitty gasped in surprise. "JJ, what are you doing?"

"I remembered the hot water here doesn't last very long, so I thought I would ask you to share."

"Oh, well, sure, I just...." JJ slipped her arms around Kitty and kissed her gently, then passionately. Kitty hesitated, then moaned and responded with equal passion. When they came up for breath some minutes later, Kitty trembled in JJ's embrace and said, "Wow, girl, that was something else!"

"When you said you've had only one small sexual episode, I thought you should experience the real thing before you consign this exquisite body to Larry's clumsy clutches."

"Oh, JJ, I never suspected you liked girls too. I've never really been attracted to women, but, gosh, this is so nice."

"I'm mostly attracted to men myself, Kitty, but face it, you're a major love magnet. You were asking earlier about whether there's just one real love for each person. I think that may be true sometimes, but for most people, and I'm one, love can be multiple and can have degrees of intensity. I don't think love cares much about gender. I hope you will experience a ton of love and happiness in your life, Kitty. You deserve it." JJ slipped her hand between Kitty's thighs. "Now, just relax. I'm going to help you have a real orgasm."

"Oh, I don't know if I can. I've never actually had one. I...oh, oh. Oh, my God, Yes!"

***

The next morning, Elaine was up early and busied herself in the kitchen for half an hour making chorizo eggs, biscuits, juice, and coffee. She tapped on Kitty's door, then opened it and peeked in. Kitty and JJ smiled sleepily up at her from their naked entanglement.

"Damn, I might have known all that wine and sex talk last night would lead to this. I just wish I had gotten in on it. Uh, is three a crowd?"

Chapter Eleven

"Our Love Is Here To Stay"

Fort Worth, Texas, June 1991

Although the sun was fierce in a cloudless sky, the June morning was mild. It had rained gently the night before, freshening the air and caressing all outdoors with a light, sweet breeze. It was a perfect day for the wedding. Max, JJ, and Elaine entered All Saints Catholic Church together. They saw Odetta Randle and her husband were already seated, so they slid into the pew with them on the groom's side.

"Maybe we should be on the bride's side since it has fewer people and, uh, we really know Kitty so much better now, after our weekend last month," said Elaine, giggling a little.

"I agree," said JJ. "But it would probably offend Larry, since I'm his ex."

"What enigmatic female stuff are y'all alluding to?" whispered Max. "That's why men see women as so mysterious. You demand total honesty from us males, but you retain the right to remain secretive among yourselves."

"Very insightful, Max. You might actually deserve that philosophy degree someday," said JJ. "It's not exactly secret; it's just girl-talk that the feeble male mind wouldn't comprehend."

They gazed around the large, dim, airy space. There were only about twenty other people in the church, but there was still some time before the ceremony was scheduled to begin.

The stained-glass windows glowed with multi-hued radiance. A gold-edged white cloth covered the altar, which was empty except for one large candle. It was already lit and flickered golden in the gloom. The spicy aroma of incense pervaded the chamber. An organ groaned softly in the background, working through some basic chord progressions. More people gradually entered and filled the pews on both sides.

Elaine said, "This is a lovely church for the wedding. It's much more serene than our church in Conroe."

"This is my first time in a Catholic church," whispered JJ. "Larry and I had a civil ceremony. I hope I don't make a faux pas. Will you show me what to do if I hesitate?"

"Sure, just watch me. It won't be anything difficult, just a lot of kneeling and standing as well as sitting," said Elaine. "You don't really have to say anything."

"Max, why aren't you acting as Larry's best man?" asked JJ. "I thought you and he had resolved your issues and were on good terms again."

"We made up—again," said Max a little grumpily. "I forgave him for announcing their engagement at my party, and he forgave me for saying he betrayed me. In fact, he asked me to be his best man, but I just didn't feel I could do it. Besides, Joe is Catholic, so he's the better choice for a Catholic wedding."

"At our gals' weekend," said Elaine, "Kitty said Larry is not only having a Catholic wedding but wants to be serious about their being Catholic. He wants Kitty to convert."

"Gosh, I hope Kitty resists that," said Max. "Surely Larry's not serious about them doing the church thing. She doesn't need the fear of sin they peddle, all the while the clergy itself acts like an immoral mafia." JJ elbowed Max in the ribs.

"Ough! Sorry, Elaine, I didn't mean to offend."

Just then, Larry, in a light blue summer suit and tie, approached the altar from the right alcove. Joe followed him a few seconds later.

Odetta reached over to tap Max on the knee. She pointed up toward the far, dim ceiling. "Do you see something white moving way up there? They don't release doves inside the church, do they?"

The other three peered into the gloom above them. Indeed, something small and white was wafting about erratically up there, shimmering in and out of the high shadows.

"I don't think it's a bird," said Max. "The movement seems different. Also, they wouldn't want bird crap on the furniture or people's heads."

"A bird might have gotten in accidentally," said JJ.

"I think it's a butterfly or moth," said Max as the creature spiraled down closer above the candle-lit altar. "Wow, it looks like a Luna moth. It must be attracted to the candle flame. Luna moths are rare, at least around here—and not Catholic, as far as I know."

JJ elbowed Max sharply in the ribs again.

The white-robed priest and two altar boys entered from the left alcove. The priest stood behind the altar and took the golden chalice and then a ciborium bowl, containing the host, from the boys. He placed them on the altar.

The four friends glanced back up and saw the moth fluttering ever closer to the altar. It was now some twelve feet above it and slowly, uncertainly, descending toward the candle flame.

Max whispered, "It's definitely a Luna moth, but they are usually light green. This one must be an albino; it's pure white and the largest one I've ever seen. Its wings must be over six inches across."

"It's so beautiful," said Odetta in awe. "I hope it doesn't land on the altar or disturb the wedding."

The organ broke off its random ruminations and struck up Mendelssohn's wedding march from *A Midsummer Night's Dream*. All the attendees stood and looked toward the rear entrance. Kitty, exquisite in a white satin dress and veil, walked slowly toward the altar. Her brother Jeff was her escort. Ten-year-old Sally Landers walked behind her, holding up the train of her long gown.

All eyes were on Kitty as she advanced. She turned her head toward her four friends as she passed their pew, but her veil hid her face. She made a slight motion to them with her hand. Their gaze followed her toward the altar. They could see the moth was now directly above the candle flame and spiraling toward it. The girls gave a collective gasp as the moth seemed to dive deliberately into the flame just as Kitty arrived next to Larry.

The moth caught fire, rose a foot or two into the air again, desperately fluttering, its wings spectacularly aflame. Then it crashed onto the altar cloth. One of the altar boys must have been watching it; he reached over and smacked the flaming moth with the flat of his hand and rubbed it into the cloth. That put out the fire but left a black blotch on the white fabric. The priest ignored the incident and began the service.

Elaine said, "Oh, that poor thing. Wrong place, wrong time."

"*Au contraire*," whispered Max, "I think it must be God's opinion of this marriage." Max gave an audible cough as both JJ and Elaine simultaneously jabbed him in the ribs.

The wedding proceeded to its conclusion half an hour later with the married couple showered with rice as they emerged from the church.

"You're going to take me to the reception, aren't you?" said JJ as they walked to his car.

"I suppose so, if you're determined to go," sighed Max. "You can imagine what kind of mood I'm in."

"Max, you're their best friend. Both Larry and Kitty will expect you to be there. So, put on a brave face and show them you have no hard feelings. Besides, I need the ride."

"You just want the free wine now that you're fully recovered."

"Yeah, but not only that—I plan to catch the bouquet."

***

Max and JJ drove to the National Hall, which was only a couple of miles away down Jacksboro Highway. As they drove, JJ said, "Wasn't she exquisite in that white wedding dress? She looked like spun sugar. I could have eaten her up myself."

Max glanced at JJ quizzically. "She always looks beautiful. But I think there was one too many troths plighted today."

"Is that an arcane part of the Catholic wedding service?"

"No, it's not necessarily Catholic, but neither are they."

JJ punched him on the arm and he swerved a couple of times, pretending to lose control of the car.

"Okay, let's agree on no more snide comments from either of us for the duration of your ordeal," said JJ.

"Gosh, I haven't been here in ages," said Max as they parked and walked across to the large rectangular, yellow brick recreation building. "Remember when our high school jazz combo played here for dances on Saturdays?"

"Sure. I loved dancing to swing and singing those old 40s and 50s tunes the adults demanded. That's still the most romantic music there is, in this gal's opinion."

"I loved the swing tunes too; honed my piano chops on them. Oh, but do you remember the time the Mexican Mariachi group showed up and claimed that they were booked for that night? Larry wouldn't back down, so we settled it with our fists in the parking lot. Losers had to play the others' music for the gig."

"You and Larry looked pretty foolish playing Mariachi with black eyes."

Max grinned. "Heck, Larry said it added a whole new musical genre to his repertoire. It's a good thing he could play with one eye closed. It's a wonder he didn't start another fight when he did his Yakety Sax version of Mariachi."

"I wonder if Larry would have said the same if it were Czech polka music he had to play. It was the Czechs who built National Hall after all. They were a pretty tight-knit community, but generous with use of the building."

"I guess they couldn't make much money renting it only for polka music," said Max.

The capacious interior of the National Hall was already prepared, with tables for about fifty guests. The elevated stage was empty, but classic smooth jazz played through speakers located around the room. Many of the guests were already there. Max had dawdled, taking the scenic route. Still, the bride and groom had not yet arrived. Max procured glasses of wine for JJ and himself while she secured a table. They circulated separately around the room, greeting various friends. A few couples danced on the polished wood dance floor.

Fifteen minutes later the newlyweds arrived, having changed into clothes more appropriate for the party. Larry wore a white sports coat over a pale-yellow shirt with no tie. He had shaved his face clean for the wedding. Kitty was radiant in a knee-length lavender strapless that complemented her eyes. Her finger sported a gold band and the huge sapphire ring, which caught the light as she waved to everyone. Larry seated her at the head table and began the speeches as the food was being served.

Joe Landers gave a fine, funny speech, which included the story of their blackberry picking and finding an ostrich egg and the copperhead snake near the Montgomery house. When Larry rose to speak, Max gritted his teeth, praying Larry would refrain from making that stupid pun about their "sax life." Larry thanked several people and made a few standard innocuous remarks. Then, "Wasn't that a gorgeous ceremony? Probably the only Catholic wedding ever accompanied by fireworks. That butterfly must have been so dazzled by Kitty's beauty it accidentally stumbled into the candle flame. It gave me a great musical idea. I'm going to name my next album *Burning Butterfly*. I bet it will be a chart-topper. Kitty will play the butterfly part, and I'll provide the fireworks."

During the speeches, Sally Landers, now nearly eleven and pretty in a pink ruffled party dress, wandered over to visit with Max and JJ.

"Uncle Max, you haven't visited us in so long," she pouted. "I need another piano lesson. I don't much like the woman who gives me lessons now. I miss you and JJ, too. I'm so sorry you've been sick, JJ."

"Thank you, sweetie. I'm feeling much better now," said JJ. "You did a great job as Kitty's maid of honor."

"We both miss you, too," said Max. "I've just been awfully busy at work and helping JJ get well. We'll plan to come visit you soon. I'll give you a lesson then, okay?"

Sally hugged them both and was about to move on but turned back as if with a new thought.

"Kitty looks so beautiful. I hope I look like her when I grow up. Maybe you and I can get married then, Uncle Max, since you didn't marry Kitty. That way I'll get all my piano lessons free."

Max swallowed hard and choked up. Before he could reply, JJ said, "What a brilliant idea, Sally. I'll bet Max will wait for you. And you'll be even prettier than Kitty."

Sally grinned widely and skipped back to her table. Max looked morose. He and JJ picked at their lunch, saying little. Roger Thorn and his wife came over to share their table, and the four made desultory conversation until the dishes had been cleared away. Then Larry and Kitty took the dance floor, dancing to 'Can't Take My Eyes Off Of You,' sung by Frank Sinatra.

"I didn't realize Larry was such a good dancer," said JJ. "He was never much interested in dancing when we were married. He must have been practicing lately. Kitty's no slouch either."

Now other couples joined them on the dance floor, and several men took their turns dancing with Kitty.

"You should go get in line and dance with her."

"I don't know. I don't want to embarrass myself or her."

"You'll be fine. It's just for a few minutes. I'm sure she wants to dance with you. Come on, let's you and I dance, then you can change to Kitty when we get close."

Max reluctantly walked JJ to the dance floor. They shuffled about to "Let's Face the Music and Dance."

"You're doing fine. Let's maneuver closer to Kitty," said JJ.

Soon, they were near Kitty, who was dancing with their guitarist friend, Jack Perry. The tune finished, then Billie Holiday began to croon, "Our Love Is Here To Stay."

"Time to make your move, Max. I'll see you back at the table," whispered JJ, shoving him in Kitty's direction.

Max tapped Jack on the shoulder and took Kitty in his arms. She smiled gloriously and hugged him close. "Max, thanks so much for coming. Both Larry and I appreciate it. I know this has been awfully hard for you. I wish I could lessen your pain somehow."

"Kitty, I can't deny I'm sad and disappointed, but I understand your decision, and I certainly wish you every happiness. Don't worry about me. I'll be fine. This song says it all better than I could. My love for you is here to stay. If ever you need me, for any reason, I'll always come to you."

Kitty laid her head against Max's chest as they danced. Then she looked into his eyes, hers glistening silver with tears. "Why is the world so complicated? I wish I could somehow be married to both of you. I feel like the person in that poem by Robert Frost who wanted to go down both paths in the woods but had to choose just the one. You know that poem, of course."

"Yes, it's one I teach in my poetry class. But it's sort of a trick poem. The traveler says he will look back on the choice he made ages hence and say that it made all the difference. Yet the two paths were almost exactly the same, and in the future, he couldn't know what would have happened if he had taken the other path. But for you, Kitty, those paths are very different. I wish you every happiness, but I truly believe you are on the wrong path."

Kitty frowned and was about to reply when Larry laid a heavy hand on Max's shoulder.

"We need to cut the cake now, Kitty, and throw the bouquet. Great to see you, Max. Glad you could make it. Come visit us after we get back from our honeymoon in Vegas."

"I'll certainly come visit. But Larry, I'm disappointed you didn't ask me to give you a toast during the speechmaking."

"Oh, uh, gosh, Max, sorry about that. I really should have asked. I guess I didn't notice you way over there and just forgot in all the excitement."

Larry signaled to a server with a tray of drinks, grabbed a glass of wine, and handed it to Max. "Would you like to toast us now?"

"Sure," said Max, raising the glass to them. "May bad luck and trouble follow you all the days of your life." He took a sip of wine. "But may they never catch up to you."

Larry frowned and Kitty gasped when she heard the first of the toast, then sighed with relief at the ending after Max's long pause. Max smiled wanly, avoided Larry's eye, and walked silently away.

Max returned to JJ's table. "Come on, let's leave, JJ. All this partying is making me a little nauseous."

"Well, it looked like you and Kitty had a pleasant talk. She was certainly happy to see you. Let's stay for the bouquet toss at least."

The newlyweds did the ritual cutting of the cake, then left its serving to Kitty's mother and aunt. Kitty soon returned to the dance floor with a ribbon-bound bouquet of red roses. Max looked on as the unmarried girls formed a semicircle around Kitty. Max was thankful Larry hadn't insisted on the tradition of removing and throwing the bride's garter to the unmarried men.

Kitty turned her back to the girls and tossed the bouquet high over her shoulder. JJ was in perfect position. Max realized she had probably made a deal with Kitty beforehand. The bouquet sailed directly toward her. JJ stretched forward like a baseball fan snagging a foul ball. She caught the roses, only to notice she had reached directly over Sally's head. JJ held up the bouquet for all to see, then handed it to Sally, who squealed in delight.

"You keep it as good luck for your wedding, sweetie," said JJ.

"Yeah, I'm going to save it for when I marry Max," she shouted to the laughing crowd.

Chapter Twelve

"How High the Moon?"

Fort Worth, Texas, December 1992

JJ had insisted that she and Max arrive at the Delgado house an hour before the party was to start so she could help Kitty with preparations. JJ had whipped up some special jalapeno and cream-cheese poppers for the occasion.

Although it was early December, it was to be an outdoor party for viewing the only lunar eclipse of the year. Fortunately, the weather was cooperating by providing a crisp, mild, cloudless evening. Only sweaters or light jackets would be required for comfort.

JJ sported a multi-colored ski sweater while Max wore a light blue sweatshirt patterned with luminescent phases of the moon. The party was also celebrating the recent release of Larry's new album, *Burning Butterfly*, which had gotten rave reviews from *Downbeat* and *Jazz Times.*

"Larry and Kitty's new house should be a great location for a moon-watching party since it's on that high bluff above the Trinity," said JJ excitedly as they turned onto Northside Drive.

"Yeah, it should be a perfect, clear sky tonight for the eclipse. It's still a couple of hours before the eclipse begins. Larry will be in high spirits about his album. I hope Tiger Blakely will be there, as Larry claimed. I've admired his records, but he was in Europe for many years and did little recording during that time."

"He's the pianist Larry put on the album instead of you?"

"Yeah, but that was a smart move on Larry's part; I didn't mind at all. Blakely is better-known and a better pianist than I am. He was big during the 70s, moved to Europe, then disappeared from the jazz scene for years. There's a rumor Blakely worked for the CIA in Europe and that he was briefly held in a Chinese prison until the *Tiananmen Square* incident in '89. This is his first recording since returning to the States. Everyone who knows jazz will want it. He not only plays piano, his tenor sax work is also legendary. I heard he's teaching musicology at TCU next year. I think he has a doctorate from the *Sorbonne*."

"Wow, he sounds like a real musical mystery genius, but that's not why you're so nervous."

"Well, I haven't seen Kitty in a couple of months, and she seemed kind of sad then. I think this marriage is not doing her any good. I feel like Larry is using her rather than making her happy."

"Max, that's their business. I know you can't help loving Kitty, but you have to let her make her own decisions. Don't pick a fight with Larry. And don't go mooning over Kitty. Hey, that's a pretty good pun for a moon-watching party, *n'est pas*?"

"Okay, I'll be good. But I worry about her. And I've just found out something that will keep me from seeing her and you for a while."

"Don't worry, I'll come visit you in prison," JJ giggled.

"It's not quite that bad. I'm being appointed to a minor position in President Clinton's Justice Department. Since I worked for his campaign, they decided they could use an experienced, if not very successful, civil rights lawyer. But it means I'll be back and forth to Washington a lot for the next couple of years, and maybe longer if Clinton is reelected."

"That's good news, Max! I'm proud of you. But what will happen to your law practice?"

"I wanted to ask you about that. Odetta has been a real anchor to me as my partner. She has agreed to stay on and run the practice while I'm away. She'll need an office manager, and since you're already living there and don't have a current teaching position, I hope you'll consider it."

"Well, I have gotten used to living at your place. I guess dealing with bail jumpers can't be any worse than herding crumb crunchers. Sure, I'll help Odetta hold the fort."

"You're quite the dominatrix with a Sharpie marker, too, as I recall."

***

The Delgado house was a two story, modern, modular structure that included Larry's recording studio and their residence. The circular driveway currently held only a couple of other cars.

Before they exited the car, JJ put her hand on Max's arm and looked him in the eye. "I really am proud of you, Max. I know it's hard for you to take your mind off Kitty, but you've been so good to me these last few years, I've kind of fallen in love with you. Our cuddling on the couch really helped me recover and kept me going. If there's ever anything I can do to ease your pain—well, anyway...." She leaned over and kissed Max lightly on the lips.

"JJ, you've saved my life twice and kept me mostly sane the last five years. I guess we're both pretty good for each other. You want to have another think about that marriage thing?"

"You and I both know Kitty will always be the only one in your heart. But I appreciate the offer." They kissed again, smiled at each other, and climbed out of the car.

"This is my first time here," said JJ as they walked to the front entrance. "Looks kind of Frank Lloyd Wrightish. And it's very Larry. I'm glad he's becoming a success. He's been working to be a jazz biggie so relentlessly."

Kitty met them at the door, in jeans and a jade-green turtleneck sweater. She gave JJ a hug and said, "Oh, thanks for bringing goodies, JJ; please put them in the kitchen, through there."

As JJ sought the kitchen, Kitty quickly wrapped Max in a long, close hug and whispered, "Max, I'm so glad you came. Try not to let Larry get on your nerves. He's just excited about his new album."

Max didn't want to let her go. *I could just carry her to the car and drive away.*

"I promised JJ I would be on my best behavior. But while we have a moment alone, I have something I need to tell you."

"Max!" boomed Larry, striding into the room in a flamboyant western shirt and cowboy boots, his arms gesticulating manically. "Great to see you, Chum. I feel like I'm on the moon myself tonight!"

"Larry, congrats on the success of your new album. Well-deserved."

"Thanks, Max. I want you to meet Tiger Blakely. He's my special guest tonight." A tall, gray-haired, black man appeared from behind Larry. He wore a vibrantly patterned, long sleeve *dashiki* that dramatized his angular face and penetrating eyes. "Tiger, this is my old pal, Max Ballard."

"My great pleasure, Mr. Ballard." Blakely smiled a large, sincere smile, his very white teeth contrasting with his ebony skin. He gazed deep into Max's eyes as they shook hands. Max had the impression Blakely was scrutinizing his soul.

"I understand from Mrs. Delgado that you are a fine poet as well as a pianist. I hope you will honor us with a poem or two this evening. My mother nicknamed me 'Tiger' after William Blake's famous poem. I've been trying to live up to it my whole life. I love poetry almost as much as music."

"Well, you certainly burn bright on the recordings I've heard," said Max. "I'd be happy to read a poem later, but I definitely want to hear you play."

"And you gotta meet our group's chanteuse, my ex-wife, JJ." Larry grabbed JJ by the arm, almost lifting her off the floor, and drew her to Blakely.

"Wonderful to meet you, Mr. Blakely," said JJ, as Blakely gently clasped her hand. "Max told me you're one of his favorite pianists, right up there with Bill Evans."

"That is a compliment both undeserved and of the highest order," murmured Blakely. "Please call me Tiger. And I would be so pleased to accompany you if you care to sing for us tonight."

"Oh, gosh, thanks, I'd love to, Mr., uh, Tiger."

Kitty rejoined them, beaming her thousand-watt smile, and said, "Sounds like we have more than the moon to look forward to. Let's adjourn to the patio, and we'll have some wine and snacks until the other guests arrive."

She led them through the house to a stone patio and multi-level deck. It had an expansive view to the southwest of the night sky above the Clear Fork of the Trinity River. JJ brought glasses of champagne for Max and Tiger, who quickly fell to discussing music, poetry, and Hindu philosophy when Max learned Blakely had spent time in India. Blakely barely sipped at his wine; Max drained one glass and took another from a nearby tray.

"Slow down, Max," said JJ, who was monitoring him while chatting with Kitty. "You don't want to be snockered when you recite."

"You've never seen me drunk, have you? Besides, all great poets have been imbibers."

"Max, you're a good poet but not yet a great poet," said JJ. "Don't drown yourself before you get there. Remember, that's why Larry and I split."

Blakely put his hand on Max's shoulder, pulled him close, and said, "I nearly ruined myself with drugs and drink, many years ago, Max. Don't allow your disappointments to control your life. Oh, excuse me, I think Larry wants me to meet someone."

Max frowned at JJ and said, "How does he know about my disappointments in life?"

JJ rolled her eyes. "Max, it doesn't take a Dr. Ruth to see you're ga-ga in love with Kitty. Try to scrape your eyeballs off her occasionally."

"That's one reason I've taken the job with the Justice Dept. I've got to put some distance between Kitty and me or.... Oh, look, nightjars!"

Max was pointing at the bright, newly risen full moon. Several birds could be seen flitting in dark spirals across the moon's bright visage.

"The birds must have found a swarm of insects attracted to the moonlight," said Max.

Larry had fired up the stereo with a playlist of tunes featuring the moon, starting with 'Moon Glow.' Now Aretha Franklin was belting out 'Blue Moon.'

"I've never seen a blue moon," said JJ. "Is there such a thing?"

"It doesn't refer to the moon's color," said Max. "The term applies to the rare second full moon in one month. It happens only once or twice a year. This is the first full moon of December. There won't be a second."

"Sort of like true love. Happens rarely, and you miss it if you're not looking at the right time or place."

"Shouldn't that be my line?" said Max.

"Friends, while we're waiting for the eclipse, Tiger Blakely has kindly agreed to play a few pieces with me and Kitty," Larry announced. "So come on into the music room."

A nine-foot Yamaha electric grand piano dominated the room. It could be played either manually or automatically with pre-programmed tunes. Blakely opened the keyboard and sat down on its bench. About fifteen guests were now assembled to listen.

"While I'm waiting for Larry and Kitty to get their instruments, I'll play a classical moon tune for you that's rarely heard as a jazz arrangement. This is my rendition of 'Clair de Lune' by Claude Debussy."

Blakely suddenly created a delicious sonic mist on the piano, his fingers a blur as the piano became an orchestra. The complex classical melody was still recognizable, but now it gyrated to a subtle jazz beat that also evoked the emotional exoticism Debussy intended. When it came to its quiet conclusion and Blakely relaxed, Max led the group in applause and hoots of pleasure.

"Thank you all so much," said Blakely. "I see our hosts are ready to join me now. Shall we do a couple more tunes inspired by moonlight?"

The trio played "Moonlight Becomes You" and "How High the Moon." Then Blakely called JJ up to sing "Fly Me To the Moon." JJ crooned and capered as if she were flying, herself. At its conclusion, she and Blakely hugged while the crowd applauded exuberantly.

Kitty announced the eclipse was about to start, so they adjourned to the deck again. The Earth's penumbra had already advanced beyond the moon's edge, slightly dimming it. During the next hour, as the group nibbled, sipped, and conversed, the moon darkened and reddened, was obscured, reappeared as a sliver, then swelled to full brightness again.

Larry and Tiger were comparing alto sax technique. Larry explained his new method of breaking the tune into fragments and stirring them sonically. Tiger was interested but skeptical that it would capture audience approval. "Sounds a bit like atonality in modern classical music."

"No, it's mostly tonal, but I like to break the machine down to nuts and bolts before I build it back again," said Larry.

"I never conceived of a jazz tune as a mechanism," said Tiger, frowning. "But I suppose that's one way of thinking about it. You'll be going beyond Train or Ornette in that direction."

"It may be an extreme, but it's a logical extreme," said Larry.

Max, overhearing them, winced, and said to Kitty, who had joined him and JJ, "I hope you can convince him to return to something like lyricism, or he's liable to implode."

"He's beyond my influence now that he's tasted success," said Kitty. "He often talks about himself as if he's a machine of some sort."

JJ chimed in, "Sometimes, in New York, when he was high, he acted as mechanical as a robot."

Kitty saw the eclipse was finished. "Okay, friends, now that we've seen it, let's hear Max's poem about an eclipse that happened some years ago." She handed Max her copy of his book containing the poem "Moondrunk Lunar Eclipse."

"This is a somewhat unconventional poem," said Max. "It has no punctuation or capitalization. It is supposed to reflect the thoughts of a person viewing a lunar eclipse who is inebriated both by wine and by the beauty of the moon itself." Max opened the book and intoned the poem:

"nothing more naked than moonlight
she dances Salome's solemn bacchanal
upon the wine-dark night while
we and the stars drown moondrunk
nothing more drunk than moondrowned
while we prattle on of stock picks   politics   jazz licks

until brightness fails as she unveils
and blushes with shadowed innocence
nothing more innocent than moonblush
yet as she unmirrors the sun
and echos earth's lesser lumination
ah if love could thus reflect if only in eclipse
nothing more reflective than moonlove
so we see her shed her last
bright sliver shivering mindless
perhaps not only with the cold
nothing more shiverous than moonmind
then slowly she hurtles
homeless as a god-thrown stone
lost on her always falling circle
nothing more homeless than moonlost
and we stagger blindly back inside
only to find her stranded in the television
wonder-wounded   time-trammeled
nothing more"

Kitty led the applause when Max finished the poem. As he handed the book back to her, he noticed she had written at the bottom of the poem, "Yes, I feel that way too."

"While I have your attention," said Max, "I want to announce that I've been appointed Assistant U.S. Attorney for Civil Rights in President Clinton's Justice Department. It's no big deal, but it means I'll be in Washington much of the time for the next few years. I'll miss you all very much, but I'll try to get back here whenever I can." Max glanced anxiously at Kitty, who was watching him, wide-eyed, with her hand to her throat.

Larry boomed, “Hey, that’s great, Max. We’ll miss you, Buddy. Say, maybe you can arrange for me to play at the White House. Clinton is a pretty fair sax man himself, you know. He and I could play a duet with you as our pianist.”

Chapter Thirteen

"Search for Peace"

Fort Worth, Texas, 1994

Max had now been working at the Clinton Justice Department for two years. He mostly wrote or reviewed proposed legislation. Sometimes he helped prepare civil rights cases for trial. It was boring but necessary work. He even assisted with a couple of Supreme Court cases. The work kept him from obsessing about Kitty, at least sometimes. When not working, he wrote or visited museums and historic sites in the D.C. area. He also played a few piano gigs in the D.C. area.

Because Max was a native Texan, he was sent to observe the aftermath of the Branch Davidian siege debacle in Waco in April 1993. The FBI killed David Koresh and 75 of his cult members, including many children, when Koresh's compound caught fire. Three FBI agents were also killed during the operation. Before Max returned to Washington, he, JJ, and Odetta were guests for an outdoor barbecue at Larry and Kitty's house. Max was in a somber, pensive mood and had to be cajoled to describe the horrors of the Davidian massacre. "It was a shameful episode. And I'm afraid it will probably trigger future acts of domestic terrorism. There are a lot of crazies with guns out there with a grudge against the federal government."

"Hey, I played a concert with Koresh," said Larry. "It was there in Waco back in the early eighties when I was touring with Rocking Raven. I even visited his compound. He had a shitload of audio equipment and often invited local musicians out there to jam. Koresh wanted to be a rock star. He played fair rock guitar, but he was beyond weird. Always quoting scripture and spouting 'pocalyptic garbage. But the women and kids thought he was right up there with Jesus."

"Those poor innocent children that died," said Kitty.

"Heck, it was probably for the best," said Larry. "The cult physically abused and brainwashed those kids. They would'a been totally warped if they'd lived."

"That's cold, Larry. We shouldn't ever give up on children," said JJ.

Odetta said, "Koresh sounds a lot like Charles Manson and Jim Jones. I wonder how men like that have such persuasive power that others follow them into obvious craziness?"

"Maybe a few men exude charisma like some women exude sexuality without even realizing it," said JJ, glancing at Kitty momentarily.

"Until they do realize it and take advantage of it," said Max. *I wonder if Larry could have become like Koresh and Manson if he had been less successful as a musician? He has at least some of that charisma.*

"Koresh didn't seem charismatic to me," said Larry. "He was just a nutjob. Oh, dang! Now you made me burn the shrimp."

***

In February 1994, Max received a summons from his boss, who sent him over to the White House to meet with several of Clinton's advisors.

In March 1994, Max called Odetta from Washington and told her he would be out of the country for several months. He asked Odetta to let all his friends know he might be out of touch during that time, that he was being sent on an assignment overseas.

"They're sending you to Bosnia, aren't they, Max?" said Odetta with a worried whisper. "That's where all the trouble is. I hope you haven't made enemies there in Washington."

"I'm not allowed to talk about it, but I don't think it's that dangerous. I'm just to be an observer. Tell Kitty and JJ not to worry. I'll try to phone you when I can."

Max called Odetta a few times between March and July 1994, to check in, but he could do little more than let her know he was still alive. In late July, he called from Washington to say he was back in the U.S. He had to report to his superiors and answer their questions, but he would be home in a few days. He arrived at his house in Fort Worth at ten a.m. to be greeted joyously by Odetta, JJ, Kitty, and Larry.

Kitty slid into his arms and gave Max one of her patented whole-body hugs. He wanted to just hold her the rest of the day, but Larry grabbed his shoulder and said, "Max, we've got a great party planned for this evening. It will be here in your music room with just a few of us close friends. We want to hear all about Bosnia, or wherever you've been, wink, wink. It better be Bosnia, 'cause I've written a tune called 'Bosnia Bop.' Here, let me pick it out for you on the piano."

"Back off, Larry," said JJ. "Max is probably dead on his feet."

"Yes, let's let him get some sleep," said Kitty. "I'm sure you're exhausted, Max."

"Yes, I need some rest, but it's so good to see all of you. Come by this evening. We'll party down, and I'll tell what I can."

Max went to his bedroom and fell into a deep sleep without even removing his clothes. JJ came up a couple of hours later to look in on him. She covered him with a quilt, slid a lock of hair off his face with gentle fingers, and kissed him tenderly on the temple.

***

That evening, Max's closest friends showed up for the party. Joe, Elaine, and fourteen-year-old Sally were driving up from Conroe. JJ and Odetta had spent the afternoon decorating the music room with flowers and strands of party lights. It looked like a high school sock hop. They made a variety of finger sandwiches and had wine and beer at the ready.

Max came down about five, freshened up and smiling. JJ embraced him, and they kissed enthusiastically. Then he slipped his arms around Odetta and gave her a great smacking kiss as well. "Is it unethical to kiss your law partner?" Max asked.

"Ethics be damned!" Odetta cackled, hugging him to her ample breast. "We love you, Max, and we're so glad you're back safe."

Max was idling at the piano with a beer when Kitty and Larry arrived. Larry had insisted on bringing a huge tub of Bar-B-Q ribs from Riskie's. While Larry stowed the ribs in the kitchen and instructed Odetta on how he wanted them served, Kitty and Max reveled in a fervent hug and kiss.

The Landers arrived soon after. Sally whooped and launched herself onto Max, wrapping both her arms and legs around him, smooching him several times. "When are you going to marry me, Uncle Max? Dad's thinking of moving up here, so I can live right here with you!"

"You've got way too much energy for me, chickadee. But I'm glad you may move up here. Then we can definitely have more frequent piano lessons."

"I wish I could get away with that," Kitty whispered to Max when Sally untangled herself from him and ran into the backyard with Rambo.

"Maybe JJ can distract Larry, and we'll give it a try. Oh, hi, Larry. Thanks for bringing Riskie's. I haven't had their ribs for ages."

"Yeah, I thought you might 'preciate some actual guy food instead of just these little sissy sandwich bites. Well, everybody's here. Let's party down. Tell us about your exploits."

JJ brought Max a glass of Shiraz and a tray of eats. The others settled in and looked expectantly at Max. He gnawed a rib while gathering his thoughts.

"Well, I can't tell you everything because some of it is classified. But you were right, Larry; I went to Bosnia. I don't know why they picked me. Maybe I was just the most gullible or expendable guy they had. However, I think it partly had to do with my being a poet. I'll explain why in a minute. Anyway, Clinton got the Bosnians and Croats to sign what's called the Washington Agreement last February. That was supposed to bring some peace to the Bosnia-Herzegovina region. Clinton wanted some nonpartisan observers on the ground there to report on how the agreement was working. That was me. They wanted me to be incognito, however. So, they seconded me to the UN peacekeeping team already in place there."

"I read the UN troops sometimes came under fire from all sides," said Odetta. "I hope they weren't shooting at you."

"I was mostly behind the lines. I arrived in March and just traveled around the new republic of Bosnia-Herzegovina for a couple of months, observing and learning about the area. The republic is about the size of South Carolina. Its capital city is Sarajevo, which has a population of about half a million. But Sarajevo has been under siege by the Serbs since 1992. It doesn't have electricity or other utilities and has been continually bombarded by artillery."

Joe asked, "What the hell started the war in the first place? We thought the world would be more peaceful when the Soviets got out of Europe."

"I guess that was just wishful thinking," said Max. "Bosnia is part of the former Yugoslavia, which, before that, was several ethnic territories controlled by the Ottoman Empire. Then it was part of the Austrian Empire until the First World War."

"Ironically," said Odetta, "the First World War started because a Bosnian Serb assassinated the Austrian Archduke, Ferdinand, in Sarajevo in 1914."

"Right you are," said Max. "After the war, the region became the Kingdom of Yugoslavia. During World War II, Nazi Croats, who were opposed by the Communist Serbs, took it over. Josip Tito fought against the Nazis and became the strongman of Yugoslavia until he died in 1980. Tito was a Communist, so the Soviet Union continued to control Yugoslavia until the USSR broke apart in 1990. That's when the Serbs, Croats, and Bosnian Muslims all decided they couldn't live together in peace any longer. That region has been a powder keg for the last hundred years, and the ethnic animosities actually go back several hundred years."

JJ said, "Did the Washington Agreement bring about peace?"

"It helped, but it only applied to the Bosnian Muslims and Croats in Bosnia-Herzegovina, which is just one of the six former Yugoslav republics. The Serbs wanted control of the entire region, so they continued to make war in Bosnia-Herzegovina while I was there."

"So, what were you supposed to do?" asked Odetta. "Sounds like a futile assignment just to observe the chaos there."

"Yeah, I observed plenty of scary and sickening violence. The Serbs perpetrated many atrocities. But I eventually found out I wasn't there just to observe. The Serbs had created several concentration camps and engaged in ethnic cleansing, in which they massacred Muslims. One of those being held in a prison camp was a prominent Croat writer and former diplomat. I'll call him Radicek, although that's not his real name. The UN wanted to rescue him for political reasons."

"So that's why they chose a poet-lawyer?" asked Kitty.

"Maybe that figured into it. I think Clinton and the UN thought the chances of getting Radicek out were actually rather slim, and they didn't want to send anyone well-known who might get killed or captured or who would cause Clinton embarrassment when they failed. That might cause an international incident. There wouldn't be any fuss or bad publicity if I disappeared over there."

"My God!" said JJ. "How callous can they get?"

"They told me about the risks and that I wouldn't get much help if I got in trouble," said Max. "But I figured it would certainly be less boring than writing legal briefs, and, uh, it might take my mind off other things."

Kitty tried to hide a little gasp, then got up to get more wine.

"Thanks, Kitty, I could use a refill," said Max, gazing into her eyes as she poured his wine with a trembling hand.

"Did you rescue the writer man?" asked Sally.

"I did indeed, but I had a lot of very special help. One friend I made shortly after arriving there was a young man named Dylan Moonbear. He was raised as an American Indian, although he is Caucasian with natural red hair. He was a UN observer like me, but he was also an ace helicopter pilot. Dylan's a natural adventurer and has a genius IQ. We became good friends and began coptering around together. We saw a lot of conflict, some from a distance, some a little too close up."

"You promised you would stay out of harm's way," said Kitty, with a catch in her voice.

"Well, it was sometimes unavoidable. Other times it became almost addictive. I found that when I was close to the fighting, or in danger myself, life seemed to become more focused, more real. All my senses were on high alert. I was charged with energy and had a sense that everything was more meaningful somehow."

"I've heard that's the way soldiers often feel when they're in battle," said Joe. "It's an intensity that becomes addictive for some of them. That's why so many go back into combat. They feel most alive when they're close to death."

"Well, I definitely lost all my boredom," said Max, "but I don't think I would become hooked on the danger. The atrocities I witnessed sickened me. The Serbs were making the same moral mistakes as the Nazis and Communists and even us Americans when we massacred Native Americans and persecuted blacks throughout our history. All 'civilized' cultures seem to be lured too easily into violence, revenge, and even genocide." Max was silent for a while.

"This Moonbear guy sounds like a real cowboy," said Larry. "I'll bet he enjoys playing fast and loose with danger. When I was on tour with Rocking Raven, there was a drunken brawl about once a week. Sometimes you just can't avoid violence. I used to keep a tire iron on my sax rack and had to use it a few times to protect myself and Maria."

"Well, Moonbear didn't rush into peril. He's an adventurer but not reckless. He abhors violence too. When I told him about my rescue mission, he immediately volunteered to help, and he developed a plan to rescue Radicek that wouldn't require violence."

"How did you meet Moonbear?" asked Elaine. "Did he just come up to you and say he heard you are looking to rescue Radicek?"

"No, I met him in a bar in Tuzla, which was the only city in Bosnia not controlled or under attack by the Serbs. It was just a couple of weeks after

I arrived; I was still getting my bearings. He recognized me as a fellow UN observer and struck up a conversation. He and I became friends almost immediately because we have similar interests. Turns out he loves poetry too. He was named after the poet Dylan Thomas. He dropped out of college, but he has probably read more philosophy and literature than I have. Dylan also writes some fine poetry. So, we had plenty to gab about while we observed the atrocities and chaos as we traveled around together, mostly in his helicopter."

"I wish I could ride in a helicopter like that," said Sally, hugging Rambo.

"It was quite exciting seeing the countryside from the air. We could admire the natural beauty of the mountains and valleys. Then we would observe the explosions and streamers of artillery fire in battles. And crowds of people trying to escape the carnage."

JJ said, "It must have been frustrating not being able to help the refugees."

"Yes, Moonbear and I both were repulsed by the violence and horror, but it was also fascinating. We tried to decide why the danger was so compelling. I think it was because it gave us a god-like perspective on the chaos. The risk and uncertainty were so radically different from the routine boredom of ordinary life that it was exhilarating. It seemed to make life much more intense. We observed the violence, the misery, the horror from relative safety above it all. We were empathetic toward the refugees, but somehow we were both stimulated and horrified by the spectacle. It was like watching a war movie, but more real." Max paused to bite a sandwich and quaff some wine. Then he continued.

"Moonbear believes humans are just naturally aggressive, and that paradoxically, war has been the primary driver of technology and of civilization in general. All civilizations have made war so as to acquire more territory and resources. But it also has to do with the way our brains work. Moonbear said that most people have several different mental selves competing for control of the conscious mind, often pulling in different directions. When we have to concentrate on something intensely, such as in sport or playing music, we unite our multiple selves into one stronger mental self that can experience life more deeply and meaningfully. That's what happens in war, too. When life is in danger, sometimes those selves scatter and we freeze, or we merge all our various mental selves and live more completely and deeply in that moment."

Max paused thoughtfully and took another sip. "I think that's what the existential philosopher, Heidegger, must have meant when he said people have to learn to live more authentically, to rise above the routine mental habits in which most of us live our lives. But he didn't explain how that could be done. There must be better ways than war."

"Isn't that authenticity also the state of higher consciousness you mentioned several years ago at the lake?" said Kitty. "Moonbear must be what you call an Übermensch. I remember reading that Nietzsche claimed the Übermensch needed danger and strife to realize himself. You have to live in the moment and be able to embrace the danger and hardship of a situation. Maybe that's why you and Moonbear enjoyed the danger of the war. It forced you to rise above your ordinary selves." Max decided not to mention that the Serbs had fired a shoulder-rocket at their helicopter. Only Moonbear's skill as a copter-jockey had saved them from going down.

Odetta frowned and said, "It's all well and good to talk about living 'in the moment' when you're not really immersed in the horror like those refugees who were fleeing violence. They were simply running scared. I doubt they had time to be philosophical about it."

"You're right about the refugees, of course," said Max. "I think soldiers can consider their situation and accept it because they have training and some control over their fate. Refugees have no real choices. I think both

Nietzsche and Moonbear would say you have to deliberately choose to live with danger and hardship in order to rise to the level of the Übermensch."

"Wow! That's heavy, man," said Larry. "But I think Moonbear's on to somethin. I often feel like my mental gears don't mesh; my wires are pulling in different directions. But when I'm blowing my alto, it all comes together and I just become the music itself. Then everything seems so easy and perfect. That's living in the moment. Hey! Maybe I'm one of them Übermen-cheeses too."

"I agree with you about music," said Max. "Playing and listening to music can help people attain an expanded sense of self, of living more fully. And music does it more positively than seeking danger. Probably, intense engagement in any sort of artistic activity could have the effect of attaining a higher consciousness. If we could learn to view our ordinary life with sufficient intensity and freshness, maybe we could live more often in that higher consciousness."

Joe said, "Sports can give you that feeling too. When I played on the tennis team in college, I often felt a sense of oneness or calm, mental intensity during a match."

"Why do you think people are so mean to each other?" asked Sally.

"I'm not sure, honey. Moonbear thought our tendency to fear strangers too often outweighs our impulse toward love and kindness. Ironically, civilization has made us more strangers to each other and thus more fearful of each other. In prehistoric times, people lived in small groups of fewer than two hundred. Everyone knew and depended on everyone else. Now, many people don't even know their next-door neighbors."

"Dylan Moonbear sounds like a real hunk," said Sally. "And I'll bet he's super cute, too. I hope I get to meet him sometime. I might decide to marry him instead of you, Uncle Max."

"Wait until I tell you about the others we worked with," said Max. "Dylan brought in two of his friends who are also extraordinary people. One claims to be half-Neanderthal. His name is Brant Lasker, and he is both very intelligent and probably the most dangerous hand-to-hand combat fighter in the world. Lasker was attached to the British Indian Gurkha regiment of the UN, along with his friend, Gurung, another tough Gurkha soldier."

"A half-Neanderthal?" said Larry. "That just ain't possible. Somebody musta been pulling your leg, Max. Did Bigfoot show up too?"

"Neanderthals are supposed to have died out thousands of years ago," said Odetta. "How could he be half-Neanderthal?"

"Lasker claimed he grew up in a hidden Neanderthal village in the Altai Mountains of Siberia. An American woman anthropologist, who was also a medical doctor, found the village in 1972. She married one of the Neanderthal and produced Lasker. Russian soldiers wiped the village out in 1983. Lasker and his Neanderthal uncle were the only survivors. They wandered for several years, with Lasker being trained in Neanderthal hunting and fighting skills. Lasker ended up in northern India, where he was Western-educated and later joined the British Gurkhas. He trained them in hand-to-hand combat. Lasker's a strange fellow, but very personable. He speaks multiple languages and can pick up any language in just a few days. That's why we needed him. He was both our interpreter and protector."

"Did your Neanderthal super-soldier have an opinion about the causes of human violence?" asked Elaine.

"Yes, he had a somewhat different view from Moonbear. Lasker said that in ancient human and Neanderthal history, tens of thousands of years ago, both were hunter-gatherers. They all were pantheists who worshiped nature as God, and they got along with each other pretty well. They understood nature and its dangers. Those people lived much more intensely than we do now because they had to be constantly alert for threats from predators and a hostile environment."

"I've read that prehistoric humans were actually more intelligent than we are because they had to know so much more about their natural environment and its dangers," said Joe.

"Right, and Lasker claimed Neanderthals died out because modern humans traded the hunter-gatherer lifestyle for agriculture," said Max, taking another gulp of Shiraz. "That caused us to become more acquisitive and more aggressive. We humans had to have more children to work the land to raise more food and then needed more land to feed more people. We went to war to steal other people's land. So, war became standard operating procedure, and it's still too much with us."

"Sounds like Lasker has it about right," said Odetta. "Does he think we should all become hunter-gatherers again?"

"He knows that's impossible. But he thinks it would help humanity become more peaceful if we adopted pantheism and worshiped and protected nature. He thinks all the monotheistic religions promote violence and war because each says its god is the only real one and the other religions should be eliminated. He thinks religious violence has been one of the primary drivers of war. Christians and Muslims are indoctrinated to care more about the afterlife than caring for the natural world and its peoples. So, we still have the evils of crime, war, slavery, and destruction of nature."

"Tolstoy said evil is simply the absence of love," said Kitty.

"Sure," said JJ, "but there must be some actual cause of the absence of love. I think love is always there if you just look for it." She and Kitty grinned at each other as if sharing a secret.

Odetta said, "It's ironic that all the major religions are based on the idea of love but they have also been the source of so much hate and violence throughout history."

"So, this Lasker is a warrior-pacifist?" quipped Larry.

"That's not far from the truth," said Max. "Lasker never looks for a fight, but he's always ready for one. Moonbear and I were in that Tuzla bar one day when Lasker and Gurung came in and Dylan introduced us. We four were having a great conversation when a burly British soldier came over and began to hassle Lasker. The Limey was there with several rough-looking buddies. Evidently, the Limey was big in the martial arts and had been goading Lasker for some time to fight him. Lasker wouldn't rise to the bait. The Limey called Lasker a coward and even said Lasker's mother must have mated with a monkey. Lasker just laughed and tried to ignore him."

"That Limey sounds like a nasty bully!" said Sally.

"Finally, the Limey threw a drink in Lasker's face. Lasker sighed and got up. The Limey tried to get in the first punch, but Lasker was ready and easily avoided it. Then suddenly Lasker was like a blur of buzz-saw motion. In about thirty seconds, he had smashed not only the Limey, but three of his friends into a tumble of broken bones and blood. He didn't kill any of them, but they were going to need some serious medical attention. Lasker wasn't even breathing hard. He said, 'Shall we adjourn to another tavern, gentlemen, where we can converse in peace?'"

"I'll bet Lasker is a hunk, too. I think I'll marry him instead of Moonbear," said Sally.

"Over the next few days, Dylan, Lasker, Gurung, and I became good friends. I told them about my rescue mission, and they all wanted in," said Max.

"So, how did you rescue Radicek?" asked JJ eagerly, taking a chomp of sandwich.

"Well, the concentration camp where Radicek was being held was about ten miles away. The guards regularly came into Tuzla on leave. We grabbed one, interrogated him about the camp, and had him draw a diagram of it.

Then we gave him some money, told him to say nothing, and put Gurung in his uniform. Gurung escorted Lasker and me to the camp the next day. Lasker was my interpreter. He explained to the camp commandant that I was there as a UN representative to remove Radicek from the camp. If they didn't let him go, the UN would be unhappy. We didn't plead or threaten."

"Oh, I'm sure they just handed him right over to you since you asked so nicely," sneered Larry.

"No. The camp commandant had a good laugh and said I'd have to get permission from the Serb regional commander, who was up in the mountains slaughtering Croats. We had expected, of course, that they wouldn't give Radicek to us just because we asked." Max paused to sip his wine, then continued.

"The camp was built around a former high school that had an auditorium with a piano. I offered to play a recital for the commandant and the camp guards before I left. They didn't get much entertainment in the camp, so he jumped at the chance. The commandant pulled in many of the guards for my performance. I played a quodlibet of some high-energy boogie-woogie for them for half an hour. They really enjoyed it, and we actually got quite friendly."

"A quodlibet, really?" said Larry, rolling his eyes. "Well, of course, that made them change their minds and give you Radicek."

"No, but before I played, I told them their rifles made me nervous, so could they stow them by the door. They had us outnumbered ten to one, and we were unarmed, so they must have figured it was no big deal. The commandant carried the only pistol. While my playing distracted them, Lasker eased back there and deployed a couple of long bike lock cables he had brought. He locked all the rifles together through their trigger guards. So, their guns were useless. Meanwhile, Gurung, dressed as the guard, found Radicek outside among the detainees. He took Radicek to an out-of-the-way open area, marked it, and radioed Dylan to bring in the helicopter."

Joe frowned. "Weren't there still some guards with rifles who would shoot at a helicopter showing up out of nowhere?"

"Moonbear had thought of that, too," said Max. "He had been in Bosnia with the UN forces several months before I arrived. He knew the UN had confiscated a lot of counterfeit American money the Serbs had been making. The UN was planning to burn it. Moonbear convinced them to mark it and let us use it for the rescue."

"So you bribed the guards with fake dollars?" asked JJ.

"No, that would have taken too much time and been too uncertain. Moonbear simply dumped it out of the helicopter as he flew over the camp fast and high a couple of times. So, there were thousands of dollars fluttering around in the camp. The guards couldn't resist. They went for it, along with many of the prisoners. It was pandemonium. Then Dylan landed the copter where Gurung had brought Radicek."

"Wow! That must have been quite a sight," said JJ, with a guffaw. "I wish I could have seen it. You should have filmed the entire operation."

"Yeah, I wish we had thought to do that," said Max. "When we heard the chopper buzzing the camp, the guards in the auditorium thought they might be under attack. They went for their rifles. Lasker had to break a few heads, but they couldn't use their rifles anyway since they were all locked together. We disarmed the camp commandant and took him hostage. He was scared witless and ordered his men to stand down."

Odetta cackled. "Max, it sounds like that Moonbear boy has the same kind of crazy imagination as you!"

"Well, it was still a little scary. We marched the commandant out to the chopper and took him with us. His men would have to take a chance of shooting him to stop us. They didn't have much incentive to shoot at us.

Most didn't have rifles and were happy to go for the cash. We just whisked Radicek and the commandant out of the camp in the chopper. We set the commandant free when we got back to Tuzla."

"So, you rescued Radicek with no one getting hurt," said Kitty. "That was both genius and heroic, Max."

"I can't really take credit for it. It was mostly Moonbear's ideas and Lasker's muscle. They are both remarkable individuals. I'm glad they were there to help. I probably couldn't have done it without them. I hope I can meet them again someday and that you all can get to know them too."

"Did they give you a medal, Uncle Max?" asked Sally.

"No, honey, but I got a pay raise and a week's leave to come home to see you guys. Thanks so much for this party. Now, let's forget about politics and play some music."

Publisher's Note: The character, Brant Lasker, the half-Neanderthal, is the main character of Michael Baldwin's novel of exotic high adventure, *Neanderthal Gita*.

CHAPTER FOURTEEN

"DESAFINADO (A LITTLE OFF-KEY)"

FORT WORTH, TEXAS, 1995

Max sneaked onto the front porch of his law office and threw open the door. He sprang into the reception area, loudly announcing, "Look busy, the boss is back!"

JJ was behind the reception desk with her back to the door. She gave a startled shriek and whirled around, accidentally squirting Max with the sprayer she was using to water the plants.

"Damn, Max, don't do that! I nearly peed my pants."

The commotion must have frightened Rilke, too; the cat leaped into JJ's arms to be consoled.

"Sorry, JJ, my bad," said Max, shaking water from his shirt. "I wanted to surprise you, but I didn't mean to scare you like that. Come here, Rilke, my lad, I haven't seen you in ages."

JJ handed the cat to Max, but when Rilke encountered Max's wet shirt, he hissed disdainfully and retreated to his shelf.

JJ handed Max some paper towels. "Well, I'm glad to see you're back. I can't believe it's already been four months since you last returned home."

"Now don't make me feel bad. You and Odetta are probably doing better without me moping around, anyway."

"Yeah, we've been getting along just fine, but we have missed you. They won't send you to another war zone, I hope."

"No, I'm just doing boring stuff like writing proposed civil rights legislation. I've prosecuted a few cases. That's no more interesting than my work was here, but, well, you know."

"Yeah, I hope distance dulls the pain a little. But, as a matter of fact, I have news for you, Mr. Lovelorn. Kitty is pregnant, and she said to bring you over when you're in town."

"Pregnant! She and Larry finally did it?"

JJ grinned. "Oh, I think they've been doing it for years. It just took a while to make a baby happen. I'll give her a call. I can close the office. Odetta is in Dallas for a case, and there aren't any client appointments today."

"Sounds like business is booming. I hope Odetta is holding her own. Be sure to let me know if you or she needs money. My expenses are rather modest, even in D.C. I mostly just write or haunt libraries and museums in my spare time."

***

Max and JJ arrived at the Delgado house at about eleven that morning. Kitty smiled dazzlingly as she opened the door and gave them both enthusiastic hugs that made them aware of her as yet slight baby bump.

"Oh, Max, JJ, it's so good to see you. Larry doesn't want me getting out much during my pregnancy, so I get bored just piddling around here reading, cooking, and gardening. By the way, he's out for the day in Denton, meeting with some student musicians."

"In that case, allow us to rescue you from this mire of sloth and take you to lunch," said Max. "Is that Italian place on Beach Street still open?"

Later in a booth at Luigi's, Kitty and JJ gossiped and giggled outrageously as they swirled spaghetti on their forks. JJ and Max sipped the house red; Kitty had iced tea. Max beamed, remaining mostly silent, content to savor the nuances of Kitty's radiant face and melodic voice.

"So, Tiger Blakely—remember you met him at our eclipse party?" said Kitty. "We've had him to the house several times for dinner and music. Tiger brought along his dog, Bix, recently. He's named after Bix Beiderbecke, the '20s jazz cornetist. Bix is both the ugliest and the smartest dog I've ever seen. He seems to understand everything we say." Kitty twirled a forkful of spaghetti into her mouth, then continued.

"So, one evening Tiger played that Bossa Nova tune, '*Desafinado*,' on the piano. The title means 'a little off-key.'"

"Yeah, there are several notes that the tune deliberately flats," said Max.

"That's right," continued Kitty, with a grin. "Well, Bix ignored the intentional flats. But when Tiger would occasionally throw in another wrong note, Bix would give a little warning bark. He knows more about music than most people."

"A real canine critic," quipped JJ.

Kitty sighed. "I asked Larry if I could have a dog to keep me company since he's out of town so often now. He said maybe. What kind do you think I should get?"

"Don't get a Lab like Rambo," said Max. "I might want to take you sailing next time we go to the lake house."

JJ snorted. "You both looked like drowned rats swimming to shore after Rambo overturned that dinghy."

Kitty grinned. "Yeah, I was flung out of the boat before I realized what had happened. You're right; I don't want a big, dumb pooch like Rambo."

"Big dogs are better with kids though, I've heard," said JJ. "Maybe get a sheepdog that will keep an eye on the little tyke and make sure he doesn't get into trouble."

"Good idea," said Max. "But you should either get a dog now or wait until after the baby is crawling around. Maybe you can find one like Bix. A smart one that will know how to protect a baby and be a good companion. I'll be glad to visit Dr. Blakely and ask him where we might get another like Bix."

Kitty smiled, reached out, and covered Max's hand lightly with hers. An electric thrill raced up Max's arm and quivered in his heart.

"That's really sweet of you, Max," she said with a sigh, "but I doubt Larry will actually let me have a dog before the baby is a toddler, if then. I guess I was just sort of daydreaming."

"Please stand up for yourself and don't let Larry steamroller you," said Max. "He will give you his expert opinion about anything, even when he knows almost nothing about it. And he will try to control your life if you let him. He's always been Mr. Do-it-my-way."

"Is Larry playing somewhere tonight?" asked JJ, quick to change the subject.

"Yes, he's going to be downtown at the Black Dog Tavern with the Johnny Case Trio. I hate that place. The jazz is usually great, but that basement is so shabby and always full of smoke."

"Well, maybe we can hang around at your place to keep you company this evening, have an extended chat, and drink some of Larry's expensive wine," said JJ.

Kitty giggled and said, "That sounds like fun. Let's us mice party while the jazz cat's away!" Then Kitty gave a little frown. "Max, one of your letters said you went to Oklahoma City to investigate the bombing of that federal building in April. I remember you telling us there would be increased domestic terrorism because of the Branch Davidian massacre two years ago. Do you think the bombing had to do with that?"

"Absolutely," said Max. "The McVeigh fellow they arrested has admitted the Waco and the Ruby Ridge killings inspired him to take revenge on the federal government. There are just too many guns and too much hatred being fomented by our divisive politics. It will only get worse, I'm afraid."

Kitty suddenly gripped Max's hand tight. He thought she must be disturbed by what he had just said. Kitty gasped, then stared at Max with wide, frightened eyes, as if looking into a vast distance. She grimaced, dropped her fork, and doubled over with a groan of pain. She straightened up, looking at her hand, her eyes wide with fear. Her trembling fingers were wet with red. "Oh my God, I think it's the baby. I'm bleeding!"

Max jumped up and shouted at the staff to call an ambulance. JJ scooted over and hugged Kitty to her, pulled her down into a fetal position in the booth. A server rushed over with towels. Kitty cried and keened hysterically as JJ held Kitty's head in her lap.

***

JJ wanted to ride in the ambulance with Kitty, but the medics wouldn't allow it. Max and JJ followed the ambulance to the emergency room. Once at the hospital, the staff wouldn't give JJ or Max any information since they weren't Kitty's family.

"Kitty said he was in Denton or downtown at the Black Dog," said Max. "But it's so loud there he might not hear his cell phone even if it's turned on. I'll try to call the Black Dog itself."

"I'll call Kitty's mother," said JJ.

An hour later, Kitty's mother arrived and talked with the doctor. Kitty was in surgery. There were complications beyond the miscarriage. Mrs. Kazinsky thanked JJ and Max profusely for helping Kitty. She sat fretting, trying to knit. JJ sat with her, hoping to calm her anxiety. Max and JJ took turns calling Larry. When he didn't answer, they left messages telling him to come to the hospital. After another hour, Larry arrived. He was wild-eyed and manic.

"What happened? Is Kitty okay? Where is she?"

"Take it easy, Larry," said JJ. "She had a miscarriage. Evidently, there were complications. She had some bleeding, but they said she'll be okay. She's in Room 405 down the hall. Her mom is with her. We looked in on her briefly, but she was asleep."

His face ablaze, Larry glared at JJ, then Max. He clenched his fists as if about to explode. The irises of his eyes were large, his pupils, pinpoints of intensity. He gave an angry growl and stalked down the hall to Kitty's room.

JJ watched Larry for several seconds. She grasped Max's arm. "Jeeze! I hope Larry's okay. I thought he was going to punch you there for a moment."

"He's probably just upset about not being with her when she miscarried. I guess there's nothing more we can do for now," said Max. "Let's go home. Maybe we can see her tomorrow."

***

Max and JJ arrived at the hospital again about ten the next morning with a bouquet of red and yellow hollyhocks from Max's garden. They asked at the nurses' station if they could visit Kitty and were told Larry had spent the night in her room. The door to 405 was partially open. They saw Larry sprawled on an armchair, asleep. Kitty looked to be asleep, too, her face pale, her amber hair like a glowing nimbus around her head. When they approached the bed, Kitty opened her eyes and offered them a weak smile.

"Hi, guys," Kitty whispered. "Try not to wake Larry; I think he didn't get much sleep."

"You sure gave us a fright, Honey," JJ whispered back. "How are you feeling?"

"They have me doped up, so I'm not in much pain." Then her face crumpled. "Oh, JJ, I lost the baby!" Kitty wept quietly, her body shuddering. Max could hardly restrain himself from embracing her despite the IV-line snaking into her arm.

JJ patted her shoulder. "I know, honey, but you can try again. We're just so thankful you're okay. You rest now and get well. We brought some flowers to cheer you up. Max, see if you can find something to put those in."

"Never mind the flowers; just take them with you and go," growled Larry, now standing behind them. "What the heck were you thinking by taking her out to a restaurant? I told her to stay home and rest. She could have died because of you."

"But, Larry, she was only four months along," said JJ. "She said there had been no problems with her pregnancy. It should have been good for her to go out dining with us. It's not like we had her running the Cowtown Marathon or something. Did her doctor advise her not to go out?"

"No, but I wanted her to be extra careful. And frankly, Max, I didn't want her to be around you. Somehow, you always cause her to become emotionally agitated." He hesitated and then scowled at Max. "In fact, it makes me wonder if the baby could have been yours. I mean, Kitty was four months along, and it's been four months since you were last in town."

"What! Jesus, Larry," said JJ, "how can you say that after Kitty nearly died?"

"That's exactly why I said it. It's not like Max hasn't been in that situation before. His affair with Tanya. She said it was Max's baby. For that matter, JJ, I always wondered if you and Max maybe did it behind my back."

JJ gasped and stepped toward Larry to slap him, but Max held her back. "Larry, you're totally out of line, man," said Max, trembling and reddening. "You know I love Kitty, but I swear to you that she and I have never been intimate."

From her bed, Kitty whispered, "Larry, Max is telling the truth. You were the father. You're just upset and looking for someone to be angry on. The doctor told me the miscarriage wasn't because of anything I did wrong. It would have happened at the house if I had stayed there. I'm just so thankful JJ and Max were with me. It came on so quick and hard, I might have died if they hadn't been there to help me."

Larry stiffened, and his eyes bulged as if two opposing forces were struggling within him. Then he relaxed slightly, still breathing heavily. "Okay. Okay, I...I'm sorry, Max. You too, JJ." Larry grimaced. "It's just that sometimes my mind gets to churning and goes down a drain hole or something. It's like I'm playing in the wrong key and don't realize it. The gears in my brain just locked up, and I got a little paranoid. This scared me so bad. Sorry."

Max and Larry shook hands. Then Larry hugged JJ and said, "Sorry, JJ. Thank you both for being there to save her." Larry turned to the bed and touched Kitty's cheek tenderly.

"Thank you, Larry," said Kitty. "Now I'll tell you what you can do. Go give some blood. The nurse told me I had lost a lot of blood. Then I heard her tell the doctor that their blood supply was running low."

"Gosh, I'll go right down and donate," said JJ. "And you will too, Larry. I know you have no fear of needles."

"Yeah, only because you've been needling me all these years," Larry growled.

"I'll offer to donate," said Max, "but I think they have me black-listed since I tried to, uh, give too much blood that time."

"Well, you can give me those flowers," said Kitty. "I love hollyhocks."

Max placed the flowers in Kitty's arms and kissed her tenderly on the forehead.

Chapter Fifteen

"I'll Be Seeing You"

Fort Worth, Texas, July 1996

The little Methodist church was hushed despite the fifty or so people seated in its pews. Max, on the aisle of the second row from the front, glanced around at the silent congregation. Many he didn't recognize. Joe, Elaine, and sixteen-year-old Sally were at the other end of his pew. Odetta sat next to Max. He and Odetta were holding hands. She patted his hand to make him realize he was squeezing hers too tightly. He relaxed a little, released her hand, and faced front again. The polished wooden casket lying on a rolling table in front of the center aisle drew his unwilling gaze. Max shuddered and raised his gaze to the stained-glass image of Jesus, which seemed to glower at him.

The pastor finally finished his seemingly interminable standard remarks about the certainty of the resurrection for believers. Max forced himself to look again at the casket. The top half was open. Max was glad he couldn't see the body within it. He trembled, and tears sprang again to his already red-rimmed eyes.

As the pastor stepped away from the lectern, Larry made his way to it. His eyes were dry but had an unfocused stare. He gripped the lectern with both hands, hesitated, took a deep breath, and spoke in a hoarse whisper.

"She was my wife and my rock during the storms of my life. I let her down so many times, but she was always there for me. It was only when she left me, I realized what a mistake I had made; that I had driven her away. But JJ's absence caused me to kick my drug addiction and get myself back on track again. Even though we didn't remarry, we remained good friends, and she always gave me good advice and support. I never stopped loving her. I will miss her beautiful voice and her sassy conversation. She has left an empty place in my soul."

Larry seemed to have more to say but could not continue. He shuffled back to his seat beside Kitty, who was convulsed with tears, a handkerchief to her face. Max had to restrain himself from going to her. But he was up next.

The pastor motioned for Max to come to the lectern. Max felt as if he were in a bad dream, struggling through some thick, impeding substance. At the lectern, he too paused, trying to gain control of himself. He could now see JJ's pale, dead, impassive face in the coffin. He shuddered and forced himself to look out over the audience. Max began haltingly, unsure where he was heading; he had meant to give the speech more thought beforehand.

"I met JJ in high school. She was two years behind me. JJ, Larry, Joe, and I were in the orchestra and marching band together. We became close friends. We all enjoyed jazz, so we formed a jazz combo. JJ was a wonderful singer. She had such a warm, effervescent personality. She was the soul of our group. JJ was the glue that kept us together. It was her encouragement that kept us improving." Max felt his throat tighten but continued.

"JJ became a teacher. She inspired hundreds of children during her tenure. She came down with cancer but didn't let the illness slow her down. JJ continued to teach and to sing with our combo. During her chemo treatments and subsequent lengthy recovery, she couldn't keep teaching. But she wanted to continue to be active, so she came to work for my law firm. She quickly became indispensable there." Max paused to clear his throat.

"JJ was so brave. She was always upbeat during her convalescence. She once faced down a knife-wielding hoodlum in our office by pretending she had a gun. JJ left us far too soon. The recurrence of her cancer took her and all of us completely by surprise. It was too aggressive even for her indomitable spirit." Max wiped his eyes, sighed heavily, and then went on.

"JJ was the best of us. We will think of her and miss her every day for the rest of our lives. I wrote a poem in which I tried to express JJ's wonderful, special personality. It is of course inadequate, but perhaps it will resonate with those of you who knew and loved her."

Max took a paper from his shirt pocket and unfolded it with trembling fingers and hoarsely intoned:

"For JJ
I knew a lovely, sweetsome girl,
but the world was too much with her.
She was a brightsome, prairie flower,
flaunting the sun too brief an hour.
She was a frolicsome colt, kicking the wind,
racing her fleeting time, everyone's friend.
She was a lovely sweetsome girl
but the world was too much with her.
She was a trillsome lark, her song soft as a feather.
Now that she's flown, there's only gloomy weather.

She was a blissome butterfly, embellishing the air.
To know her was to love her and her blessing share.
She was a lovely, sweetsome lass,
but the world was too much with her.
Now we've just her memory, and it must last,
for the world is no longer with her."

Max spoke slowly, trying to keep from breaking down as he read the poem, but he was sobbing as he finished it, and he heard Kitty, Elaine, Sally, and Odetta weeping as well. The service ended with Max, Larry, Joe, and three other friends carrying the now-closed coffin to the waiting hearse. They drove to Greenwood Cemetery for interment.

***

It was a day too beautiful for a funeral. The sky should be weeping. Instead, the sun was glorious and somehow mild instead of the usual brutal July heat. A gentle breeze lifted the leaves of the trees as if waving goodbye. Crape myrtles were in full bloom in red and purple. Birds regaled the world with song despite the somber human occasion. Cicadas thrummed the air with a subtle choir of grief, or maybe something more hopeful. The cemetery seemed pleasant with its resident mossy standing stones and statuary among lush green grass. It could have been a lovely place for a joyous picnic.

The crowd encircled the open grave. There were fewer here than in the church, but still quite a few. JJ's parents had passed, but her only sister was up from Houston. Several of her teacher colleagues and former students were there. And several musician friends were in attendance. Odetta stood on one side of Max, holding his hand. Kitty and Larry were on his other side. Kitty touched Max's hand; they interlaced their fingers for a few moments.

The coffin had been placed just above the grave, supported by straps that would allow it to be lowered. Several sprays of flowers adorned the coffin lid. The pastor spoke a few more comforting words and the Lord's Prayer. The attendants then began lowering the casket into its cavity.

With a sudden flash of red, a scarlet tanager landed on the coffin lid and snapped up a berry from among the flowers. It looked around at the mourners for a moment, shivered its feathers, gave a raucous squawk, and sprang into the air again to disappear.

Those gathered nearest the coffin gasped in surprise. Sixteen-year-old Sally gave a delighted squeal. "I think JJ's spirit is still very much with us!" The mournful mood was broken. Kitty smiled at Max and squeezed his hand, then quickly turned her attention to Larry.

***

Larry had arranged for a memorial wake at the Catfish Club that evening. He had invited everyone who had attended the funeral services. So, the club was well-packed. Larry had hired a caterer to provide refreshments. Larry, Kitty, Joe, and Max took the stage to play some of JJ's favorite tunes.

Sally had found a redbird soft toy and hung it from a string above the stage, where it wheeled and twirled in the breeze from a couple of fans. There was an enlarged photo of JJ on an easel to one side of the stage.

Toward the end of the evening, Larry announced the combo would play "I'll Be Seeing You," which was one of JJ's favorite songs, and which she had recorded in Larry's studio. Larry had removed the instrumental tracks from the recording, leaving only JJ's vocal. The combo would play the tune live to accompany JJ's recorded voice.

Larry turned to the combo and counted for the start. They played the tune at a slow tempo, with complex instrumental interaction, in a melancholy minor key. After several minutes of somber instrumentals with solos by each of the players, JJ's smoky soprano slipped in to capture the melody and made the whole tune bloom with exotic beauty like a scarlet orchid illumined by a sunbeam in the jungle.

The exquisite yearning expressed by the lyrics seared Max to the heart and gathered to a choking sensation in his throat, even as he caressed the piano keys with delicate passion. During the entire performance of "I'll Be Seeing You," Max's gaze had been locked on Kitty. With her eyes mostly closed, Kitty and her tenor, Ellie, were in deep communion with the music. Toward the end of the tune, as JJ's singing became breathlessly tender with longing, Kitty opened her tear-glistening eyes and looked directly at Max. She gave him a slow, sad smile. Surely she was saying, "Yes, I will be seeing you."

Max looked up at his old nemesis, the catfish. It seemed genuinely sad itself. ***"Well, bozo, first you lost Kitty, now you've lost JJ. Maybe you should quit while you're behind. Find a bigger wallow for your self-pity."***

When the tune ended, Max closed the keyboard cover, leaned his head against it, and wept silently. Sally came to sit beside him. She put her arms around him and whispered in his ear, "Uncle Max, JJ wouldn't want you to be so sad. JJ always tried to find some gladness in everything. She and I had so many happy times together, and I know you and she did too. Don't do anything she would frown about. I'll bet she's got her eye on us right now and is saying, 'I'll be seeing you.'"

Max lifted his head and hugged Sally. "You're so right, sweetheart. I think a lot of JJ must have rubbed off on you. I think I'll be fine now."

When Larry went off to pay the caterer, Kitty came over to the piano and touched Max's cheek. "Whatever Sally told you goes double for me. I love you, Max. I know it's been hard, and now it will be even harder—for both of us. JJ was my best friend, and I loved her more than you know. I don't think I could live with myself if I lost you too. Surely love will find a way for us, eventually."

"Yes, darling, I guess you and I have to be here for each other somehow since we can't take our problems to JJ now. I'll never give up on us."

Most of the people had left. Sally untied the redbird toy from its string. She turned toward Max and Kitty with a sly grin and said, "Catch!" She tossed it high between them. They both reached up and caught it at the same time. They looked at each other, both holding the bird.

"I think JJ is still here for you two," said Sally.

"I certainly hope so," said Kitty. She looked around and, seeing no one else watching, kissed Max quickly on the lips, then stepped away with the bird in her hand.

CHAPTER SIXTEEN

"SEPTEMBER SONG"

FORT WORTH, TEXAS, SEPTEMBER 1998

The Landers had finally moved back to Fort Worth! Now the Cowtown Cool Jazz Combo could play together more often. All except JJ, of course. The three Landers had recently moved into a new house in Benbrook on the southwestern edge of the city. Joe had been appointed assistant administrator of Harris Hospital. They were throwing a homecoming party for their Fort Worth friends.

It was one of those rare, lovely days in late September in North Texas when both the heat and wind moderated to almost pleasant. There had been rain two days ago, so the fields and roadsides were verdant, and troops of wildflowers continued their parade. A flock of huge puffy cumulous clouds wandered about playing tag, or perhaps something more romantic, in the blue immensity of the sky.

Kitty arrived at the Landers' early with a seafood salad to assist Elaine with preparations. Elaine met her at the door with a grin and a hug. "Thanks for coming early, dear. Don't you look stunning in that sundress? Violet is a great color on you, but of course, you would make a potato sack look fabulous. Maybe Sally will take a cue from you about attire. She wants to show off those teenage legs of hers in short shorts. Have you cut your hair? Love the wave. Will Larry be along later?"

"Larry sends his regrets. They called him at the last minute from TWC to lead their jazz band concert tonight. The regular conductor took sick, and Larry is their go-to guy since he's a famous alum. He, uh, gave me permission to come without him."

"Well, how generous of him. We'll miss him, but I'm so glad you're here. We can sure use that seafood salad too. The party will be on the back patio since the weather is cooperating. Go on through, and Sally will show you where to put your dish. Let's try to have some girl-gab before the others show up."

Kitty made her way through the house to the back patio. She waved to Joe, who was preparing to barbecue some skewered chicken and shrimp. Sally intercepted Kitty as she placed her dish on the serving table.

"Oh, Kitty, I'm so glad to be back in civilization!" said Sally with dramatic hauteur. "It was *trés amusant* growing up in rural Texas, but now that I'm a mature woman of eighteen, I require a more sophisticated environment for my multifarious interests."

Kitty grinned and hugged Sally. "You mean you need a larger pool of boys to slaver over you. Your mother told me to warn you off those short shorts, but you've sure got the legs for them. Are you going to college sometime soon?"

"I can't decide whether to take some time off to work or maybe travel or start at TCU next year."

"Well, I enjoyed my time at TCU, but don't be in too much of a hurry. I wanted to get my math degree so I could work for an NGO and help save the environment. Look what happened to me! Marriage, and not even a baby to show for it. Now I'm drudging for an insurance company."

"You sound annoyed, Kitty, but I admire your accomplishments. You've made some great jazz records too. Hasn't she, Dad?"

Joe was now squinting into the glowing mound of charcoal like a tribal shaman. "Kitty is one of the most intelligent and accomplished women I know. She's an excellent role model for you. So, you should follow her advice and change out of those shorts."

Sally giggled and then, a moment later, squealed as she saw Max amble onto the patio. She rushed over to give him an enthusiastic hug. "Uncle Max, how do *you* think these shorts look on me?"

"Now, that's a loaded question if ever I heard one! Anything would look great on you, pumpkin. And those shorts would definitely distract my gaze if you weren't standing next to the most beautiful woman on the planet."

"Well!" said Sally in mock anger as she marched into the house. "I'll go change, but I expect a piano lesson while you're here."

Max and Kitty smiled at each other, then Kitty gave him one of her long, close, full-body hugs that made him almost faint with love and desire.

"Where's Larry? I expect to have my head taken off at any moment," said Max into the intoxicating fragrance of Kitty's hair.

"Jazz concert emergency at TWC. And frankly, I'm glad. Now, maybe you and I can have a proper conversation. It's been far too long since we could talk alone."

They walked around the large backyard, admiring the flowers and shrubs, and stopped in one of the more secluded areas, holding hands.

"Well, Kitty, my self-imposed exile to D.C. hasn't really done what I had hoped. I still think of you almost constantly. I've decided to leave the Clinton administration and return to my work here. I—I hope we can see more of each other even if it's frustrating for me."

"For both of us. With JJ gone, I feel like you're the only person I can talk to about anything serious, so I'm awfully glad you're coming back. I've missed you terribly."

"You sound unhappy. Larry isn't—abusing you, is he?"

"No, he tries to control me too much, but he isn't physically abusive. He just cares more about his career than about me. It's my own fault. I knew when I married Larry he wanted me to help him become a major jazz personality. It seemed important at the time. But it turned out that he mainly wanted an attractive wife to flaunt and a child to carry on his legacy. After my miscarriage, Larry was upset that I couldn't have children. We talked about adopting a child, but he's not interested in adoption. I guess he thinks his talent is only hereditary."

"None of that makes any sense to me. Have you tried therapy?"

"We went a few times to couples therapy, but Larry thought it was worthless. So now I have a dog I don't like and a meaningless job as an insurance actuary. Nothing helps. I feel like my life has been a waste. I've gotten tired of attending jazz festivals and concerts. Even though it's often exciting to play in them and meet famous musicians. The dazzle of it all has worn thin."

"Kitty, divorce him and marry me. You know I've loved you since forever, and I'll never stop. You deserve love. Obviously, Larry can't or won't give you what you really need. You and I can still save the world together like we discussed at the lake all those years ago."

"Oh, Max, I love you, too. I realize now I should have chosen you. But I worry a divorce would kill Larry. He does have a fragile heart, and he angers too easily."

"I almost wish he would have that heart attack he's been prophesying all these years. Frankly, I think he's a fake. That's just his way of controlling you. But I won't pressure you, darling. Whatever you decide, I'll always be here for you. I have no ambition but to give you all the love you need."

"Max, Kitty, here you are." Sally, now in a slightly longer skirt and blouse, approached carrying a tray with glasses of white wine and some nibbles. "Odetta and her family are here, and several others, but it will be a while before we eat. I brought you some wine, and *I'm* having some too." Sally grinned mischievously at them as if she were still ten years old. "Have you been discussing philosophy or poetry or maybe music?"

Max cleared his throat and said, "Since I'm here with two such beautiful women, I've been thinking about beauty. Where do you think beauty comes from?"

"Gosh, I haven't ever thought about it," said Sally. "Something is either beautiful, or it isn't, and we just kind of know beauty when we see it, don't we?"

"Ah, the Justice Potter Stewart argument. He was a Supreme Court justice who famously said he couldn't define obscenity, but he knew it when he saw it."

"Let's not have a legal lecture, Mr. Attorney," said Kitty. "Where do *you* think beauty comes from?"

"I believe it comes from right here," said Max pointing to Kitty's and Sally's heads. "We actually create beauty with our minds. People say, 'Beauty is in the eye of the beholder.' It's a cliché, but it's true in a way people don't realize. It's not just a matter of taste, but of creative imagination. Most people don't use their imagination very much. Ordinary people as well as great artists can create beauty. Our imaginations are engines of beauty if we just use them. Most people consider Van Gogh's *Starry Night* beautiful, and Michaelangelo's *David*, and Beethoven's *Ode To Joy*, but there are many things we might consider beautiful that other people find bland or even repulsive."

"That's going to take some proving," said Sally, squinting. "Kitty and I are skeptical."

"As a matter of fact, I think I have the perfect example right here in your backyard," said Max. "Let's walk over to those bushes. When we strolled by them earlier, I noticed something and meant to show you, Kitty, but we were discussing, uh, something else. There, look closely and tell me what you see on those plant stems."

The girls leaned close to the greenery, then quickly backed away. "Yuck!" exclaimed Sally. "That's bird poop!"

Kitty looked puzzled. "Yes. Why is there bird poo on this particular bush?"

"If you look more closely, you'll see it's not bird poo, but caterpillars," said Max. "Those little guys will get fat, then weave cocoons, and hatch as exquisite swallowtail butterflies. They have evolved to look like bird poo to fool birds into ignoring them."

"Oh, gosh, you're right. They're eating the leaves. They just look like poo at first," said Sally. "But they aren't beautiful themselves; they will only become beautiful when they change into butterflies."

"Keep looking," said Max. "Notice the white pearl on their backs. See the intricate pattern of black and white markings, how ornate they are. They are very un-poo-like when you look closely and appreciate them as fellow creatures. See them as beautiful with your creative intentionality. Now tell me if you still think they're ugly."

"I see what you mean," said Kitty with a smile. "I remember reading about seeing the world with creative attention. These caterpillars are still ugly, even comical, but they are sort of beautiful in their ugliness once you know what they are and will become. Once you get over your initial disgust and get to know them a little, they are fascinating."

"Keep a close eye on them for the next couple of weeks, Sally," said Max. "Take some pictures of them as they develop, form chrysalises, and become butterflies. I bet you'll be in love with them by then. And your loving attention will make them beautiful to you."

"Okay, Uncle Max. You convinced me. But you just said I'll love them, and that's what will make them beautiful. So, beauty must be a kind of love."

"Yes, my dear, clever girl, beauty is created by love, by who and what and how we love."

"Well then, what is love?"

"Love is probably the greatest mystery of all," said Max with a sigh, glancing at Kitty. "I think it's why we exist: to love and to be loved. Love is the most important thing we can do, but we don't really know why. It must be more than just the urge to reproduce. Have you ever wondered why almost every popular song is a love song? Most movies and TV shows involve love somehow. Most novels contain romance. Love is a primary concern of society. It always has been since the earliest times, yet we don't really understand why. We just take love for granted."

"Gosh, that's true. I hadn't ever thought about it," said Sally. "It's almost like a fish not knowing about water."

Kitty said, "Maybe the arts emphasize love so much because we all long for it, but love is actually so rare in real life."

Max said, "Yes, I think you're right. I wrote a poem that ends: 'When will we learn that love is ***not*** the ***most*** important thing? Love is the ***only*** important thing.' I don't know why I wrote that line, but it seemed absolutely true to me. It came from my subconscious mind. Our subconscious is as vast as the universe itself. And I'll bet the answer to the mystery of love is in there somewhere. Perhaps you, Sally, will be the one to explain the importance of love to humanity and how we can have more of it."

"Wow! Yes, that seems like a worthy goal. The world certainly needs more love. Maybe I'll study philosophy at TCU. I thought it was supposed to be hard, but you make it seem easy, Uncle Max."

"Well, there's a lot more to it than my little demonstration, but I certainly won't discourage you from studying philosophy. You just have to learn to question everything."

"Question everything? Why?"

"Good! Oh, look, Kitty, here's our old nemesis, Rambo. You've mellowed in your old age, boy," said Max, patting Rambo on the shoulder. "You must have come to tell us supper's ready. Let's head for the patio."

Sally gave the old dog a back scratch that made his hind leg jitter. "Rambo, don't you bother those caterpillars. I've seen you eat poop before, so don't mistake them for snacks."

Sally and Rambo ran on ahead while Max and Kitty strolled hand in hand to the patio, gazing often into each other's eyes.

"Max, you are so good with Sally. And your comments about love...."

"Well, I've had a lot of time to think about love, darling— in much more than just a philosophical sense."

***

After a delicious patio supper and convivial conversation, darkness descended gently on the Landers' backyard. Max and Kitty found a secluded alcove where they could hold hands, whisper endearments, and occasionally kiss while the others hashed over sports, politics, and the weather. Kitty saw Odetta cock her head at them in warning and gently pushed Max away.

Kitty said to the group, "Why don't we go in and have some music?"

Sally agreed with a whoop, so the party moved indoors. The twelve of them fit nicely into the Landers' capacious living room. There was a new baby grand in one corner, with posters from various band concerts decorating the wall above it.

"Do some tunes for us on the piano, Uncle Max," said Sally. "I'll bet Dad will play too."

Joe got out his bass, and he and Max played a few standards for the group. Then Kitty said, "Play 'September Song' and I'll try to sing it if Sally will help me. It was one of JJ's favorites. It was so wonderfully sad the way she sang it. Come on, Sally, sing with me."

Max and Joe played the slow, somber intro, establishing the song's melancholy mood. Kitty and Sally stood together holding hands by the piano. Rambo lay down at Sally's feet and closed his eyes. Sally entered the melody with her light, sweet soprano. Kitty harmonized with a husky, almost whispered contralto.

Max and Joe evoked the swirl of autumn leaves and the chill of winter's wind as the melody progressed and repeated several times. The thump of Joe's bass was like a heartbeat on the edge of eternity. The girls explored the ache of love's loss a little more intensely with each repetition. As they lingered on the last few words, and the melody faded, Rambo raised his head and emitted a high, tender howl that somehow seemed both hilarious and utterly appropriate. Kitty and Max once again found themselves gazing into each other's tear-glistening eyes.

Chapter Seventeen

"Cast Your Fate to the Wind"

Fort Worth, Texas, November 1999 - January 2001

It was a dreary, raw, late November day in Fort Worth, but few people were worried about the weather for a change. Everyone was excited about the coming transition to the new millennium. Experts sagely asserted that 2000 would not be the beginning of the new millennium; that would properly occur in 2001. But most people reckoned it began with 2000 and all those zeros, like the odometer of a car rolling over. What might this rare historic moment portend? Would the Y2K computer bug cause the Internet and maybe the world economy to crash? Religious zealots prophesied Jesus' Second Coming or the end of the world? Both anxiety and elation abounded.

Max's law practice was flourishing now that he was permanently back from D.C. Both he and Odetta had full caseloads, including several wealthy clients that were quite lucrative. Profits from these high-end clients allowed Max and Odetta to take on worthy pro-bono cases in the area of civil rights. They were even thinking of adding another attorney to the practice.

Max saw Larry and Kitty every couple of weeks. He visited with the Landers often as well, to chat or dine with Joe and Elaine, and to give Sally piano lessons. Max also had his friends over to his house for meals and parties frequently.

Max still sat in on jam sessions at the Catfish Club or the Caravan of Dreams, the premier music venue of Fort Worth, which often invited Larry's combo to perform. Max usually attended when he knew Kitty would be there. Sometimes Max and Kitty met in the Caravan's rooftop garden to walk and talk while another pianist subbed with Larry and the group.

Kitty had agreed to email with Max sporadically from her work email at the insurance office. It was mainly friendly chit-chat, usually light and non-amorous. They both missed being able to talk with JJ.

Thus, Max kept up with the Delgados' doings and plans without arousing Larry's potential disapproval. Max knew if he pestered Kitty to break up with Larry, she would likely become annoyed. Max knew she loved him, but she was conflicted and ambivalent. He felt frustrated that Larry could dominate Kitty so effectively. Max, even using his lawyerly skills, had so far been unable to persuade her to leave Larry, despite her admitted unhappiness. Sometimes he wondered if she preferred having both Larry's security and the excitement of Max's attentive devotion.

Today Max was at Chicotsky's Grocery on West 7th, shopping for Thanksgiving. He had hoped to be with Larry and Kitty for Thanksgiving, either at his place or theirs. But Kitty had emailed him that her brother was in town from California. She and Larry would have Thanksgiving with him and their mother at her mother's house. Odetta came to the rescue by inviting Max to spend Thanksgiving with her family.

Chicotsky's was the only gourmet grocery in Fort Worth. Max wanted something special to contribute to their feast. He selected a strawberry-rhubarb pie, a crisp Alsatian wine, and some oriental fruits to make an exotic fruit salad. As he approached the checkout counter, he looked across to the opposite lane, and there she was, like a divine apparition.

"Kitty," Max stage-whispered over the general noise of the store.

"Oh, hi, Max!" She turned to him in surprise, then smiled gloriously. "I didn't see you. I'm a bit zoned out. Let's meet outside."

Max waited at the door for Kitty, then walked her to her car and helped unload her basket. "Do you have time to talk, Kitty?"

"Sure, for a few minutes. Larry usually comes shopping with me, but he's at the studio working with a new guitarist today."

They sat in her Mercedes and gazed at each other with hungry eyes. Max put his arm around her and scooted closer, hoping to kiss her.

"Not here, Max. Someone might see us." Kitty glanced around nervously. She was trembling a little and biting her lip. "When I'm near you, I have to restrain myself from wanting you completely, and, well, I mustn't do that."

"I feel the same way, darling. I'm always ready to give myself to you totally. Why do you hesitate? Just tell Larry you're leaving him and come live with me. It's that simple. I'll take care of arranging the divorce, or we can just live together if you prefer. I'm desperate to be with you. We've both wasted years that we should have been together. I swear I'll devote myself to your happiness if you'll just come with me."

"I want to be with you, Max, but I don't want to hurt Larry. He's not a monster. Larry has been good to me in many ways. He's just more self-focused and driven toward worldly success than you. I'm afraid it will make him sick, maybe even kill him if I leave him."

"Kitty, I know you take your wedding vows seriously—to cherish and obey and all that stuff. But has Larry kept his end of that bargain? As you say, he's completely obsessed with attaining his success in music, and you've just been a means to that end. JJ left him when she realized he was becoming a drug addict for his music. That was actually an act of love. You should do the same. You're his ego crutch, not his lifesaver."

"Oh, Max, I wish I could believe that. Maybe I think I'm more important to him than I really am. Maybe I'm indulging my own ego. It's all just so confusing. Let me think about it. I'll try to make a decision. I'm sorry, but I'd better go now."

Max reluctantly opened the door. Kitty squeezed his arm. "I love you, Max. Just give me a little more time." He saw she was trying not to tear up. He watched her drive away as he walked to his Chevy. Once inside, he laid his head against the steering wheel until another car honked, wanting his parking space.

***

The 2000 Millennium came and went with no major disasters or miracles. Y2K was a fizzle, and the Second Coming didn't come for the 2000th time. Life went on much as before for the world, for America, and unfortunately, for Max. Four months after their meeting at Chicotsky's Grocery, Kitty still hadn't made a decision about leaving Larry. Max often visited with the two of them and his other local friends. They had celebrated the turning of the millennium in grand style at the Catfish Club and had gotten together for meals several times. Max hadn't yet had another chance for an extended talk with Kitty alone, however. Larry was always cordial with Max when they were together, but he never gave Max and Kitty an opportunity to be alone together if he could subtly thwart it.

Now it was late March 2000. Max was home alone this evening reading the *Inferno* from Dante's *Divine Comedy,* sipping a smoky Scotch whisky, and listening to Franz Liszt's *Dante Symphony* through headphones. He was in his ground-floor music room with its window-wall view to the back garden. A thunderstorm was raging in the night. Lightning crackled, and wind lashed the trees furiously. The storm made him remember that night eleven years before when Larry announced his and Kitty's engagement and Max stupidly wandered into the storm. *Thank goodness JJ was there to keep me from attempting suicide again. Oh, JJ!* God, *how I miss you!*

But warm and cozy inside, Max was actually enjoying the storm. With headphones on, he could concentrate on the music and on Dante's magnificent *terza rima* stanzas, letting his eye and tongue luxuriate around their delicious syllables, while occasionally glancing up at the extravagance of the storm. It and the music were the perfect accompaniment to Dante's monsters, demons, and damned souls.

As nearby lightning caught Max's attention, Rilke suddenly bounded onto his lap.

"What's wrong, old son? Did the lightning scare you?"

Rilke stood on his hind legs, put his front paws on Max's chest, and stared intently into Max's eyes. Something was wrong. Max took off the headphones, and now he heard it: a roar like a jet engine. He looked into the garden, where a swirling wall of debris was quickly bearing down on them.

"Jesus, it's a tornado!" Max grabbed Rilke and raced to the hall. He heaved up the door in the floor beneath the stairs that led down into the bare concrete basement. The tornado smashed into the house just seconds after the cellar door slammed into place above their heads. Then the single basement light went out, leaving them in utter darkness. Max felt his way to a corner and huddled there, hugging Rilke to his chest.

Max heard and felt the house explode above them. The floor that was now their ceiling shook and clattered as part of the structure collapsed onto it. But the floor held, and the twister passed, leaving only the sound of rain pattering dully just above their heads.

"Rilke, you sure saved our hides tonight. I'm going to promote you to chief of security and start feeding you fancy tuna. I guess we'd better stay down here until the storm is over. Damn, I don't even have my cell phone. I wish I could call Kitty and make sure she's okay." Rilke meowed in sympathy, or maybe it was a more critical comment. Max opened his cardigan sweater, then closed it around Rilke so they both were a little warmer. Rilke was soon asleep against Max's chest, purring heavily.

***

Max awakened hours later to the sound of footfalls and wreckage being shifted above them. He was stiff and cold, but unhurt. The basement had a couple of small, high windows that let in a faint light. It must be morning. He carried Rilke up the steps and pounded on the cellar door. A minute later it was opened by a grinning firefighter.

People were wandering around the ruined neighborhood, some obviously official, some volunteers, some dazed survivors. He saw wreckage strewn about at random like a hallucinatory landscape from a Hieronymus Bosch painting. Max gave his name to a worker who was making notes on a clipboard. Then he walked away from the devastated area, still carrying Rilke inside his sweater. Along the way, he saw the mangled remains of his piano and many of his books, now ruined. His elderly Chevy had disappeared. That was no great loss; he had planned to replace it soon, anyway. He made his way to an office building that had been spared, borrowed a phone, and called the Delgados.

Larry answered and hollered for Kitty to get on the line too. Max could tell she had been crying. Now he could hear her smile.

"Oh, Max, we were so worried! We saw your neighborhood on TV as the tornado arrived. Did it hit your house?"

"It destroyed my house. But Rilke warned me a few moments before it hit, and we got into the basement just as the house blew apart. I didn't have time to get my cellphone, or I would have called you. It was cold, dark, and scary, but Rilke and I are unscathed."

"Max, we'll come get you," said Larry on the other phone. "You can crash with us for a while. Tell us where to pick you up. We're on our way, bro."

They found Max an hour later. Kitty giggled to see Rilke carried like a baby inside Max's sweater. Rilke was delighted to see Kitty and quickly slid into her arms for cuddling.

"Goodness, Rilke, you've had a scary adventure. Thanks so much for saving Max." Rilke gazed lovingly at Kitty with emerald eyes and purred contentedly. Kitty stared anxiously into Max's haggard eyes and silently mouthed, "I love you."

"Man, you are a total mess," said Larry as Max collapsed onto the back seat. "Let's get out of here. It may take a while. That twister devastated the entire southwest downtown area. You're probably still in shock. Hey, I'll have to write a tune to commemorate this event. It's definitely a G-minor catastrophe. Yeah, I'll call it 'Cowtown Tornado.' Bet I can get some good publicity from it. Maybe do a whole album."

"I'm just so glad the tornado didn't come your way. Thank God you're safe," mumbled Max. "Have you checked with Odetta and the Landers to see if they're okay? Let's call them when we get to your house." Max lapsed into dazed silence and simply observed the damage as they picked their way through Fort Worth's littered streets.

Kitty let her hand dangle into the space between the seat and door and wiggled her fingers to attract Max's attention. Max slipped his trembling hand into hers and held it contentedly all the way to their house.

***

Max stayed with the Delgados for only four nights. Sleeping overnight in the same house with Kitty quickly became too nerve-wracking for him. He was afraid Larry might become suspicious of his obsessive attention to Kitty. Max was mesmerized seeing her in a dressing gown as she moved about the kitchen fixing breakfast. The ubiquitous scent of her perfume intoxicated him. He was enthralled as she brushed her hair while discussing a book she was reading. Max wondered if Larry was taunting him somehow with Kitty's proximity, daring Max to say or do something for which Larry could take offense.

One evening the three of them were discussing the Beat Generation and how it had influenced both jazz and popular music.

"Did you know that the Beetles' name comes from the Beats rather than the insects?" said Max. "The Beat poets had a huge influence on mass culture even though there were only a few of them. Jack Kerouac, Alan Ginsberg, and William Burroughs—he's the one who wrote *Naked Lunch*—were the main influencers. But there were other poets, writers, and musicians, who helped make it happen." Max suddenly realized he was staring at Kitty's naked feet and had an erection about the size of Oklahoma, as he noted in an email to her the next day.

"Seems to me the Beats were more influenced by jazz greats like Dizzy, Bird, Train, and Miles," said Larry. "Those cats were burning with Bebop in the 50s."

"It was the times," said Kitty, nearly making Max faint by wiggling her tantalizing toes at him from the coffee table and taking Rilke into her lap to be caressed. "The end of the war must have brought a tremendous sense of freedom and possibility. Bebop somehow caught the mood just right. The poets, writers, and movies all got on board. The Beats were so far beyond ordinary they couldn't help but get noticed and emulated. It must have been a wild time to be alive. Our culture is getting awfully tame again. Maybe the two of you can start a whole new counterculture with poetry and jazz."

"I can see your mechanistic riffs, Larry, as reflecting the spirit of our technological age," said Max, "but I think what's really needed is a new romanticism directed toward revering nature and, uh, loving kindness instead of the cynical materialism that is all too rampant."

"Argh, Bro, give me a break. I just want to make a buck playing the music I'm good at and love," said Larry. "Let's have another brandy."

Although Larry offered to accommodate him longer, Max decided to move into a hotel until he could rebuild on his property. Still, Max spent more time with the Delgados, the Landers, and the Randles, taking meals with them alternately several nights a week for the next several months.

One night after dinner at the Delgados, Kitty presented Max with a Hohner Chromonica, a beautiful silver professional harmonica.

"It will give you something to play until you have another piano," said Kitty.

"Yeah, you don't hear harmonica much in jazz, so maybe you can do some real innovatin' with it," said Larry.

"Wow, thanks, guys, for such an unusual and interesting gift. I don't know if I can learn to play it at a proficient level, but I'll sure give it a try. Odetta may think I've gone over the edge if she hears me practice at the office."

Max had car, residence, and business insurance to replace what he had lost, though it took a while to receive payment. He and Odetta immediately rented office space and reopened their law office. He replaced his lost Chevy sedan with a new Chevy van. Max threw himself into his legal work and the rebuilding of his house. He and Kitty now emailed each other on an almost daily basis. She used her office email exclusively for this, although their messages remained primarily friendly rather than romantic. Max scrupulously avoided cajoling Kitty to leave Larry.

By the end of the year, Max had moved back into his rebuilt house, which was very similar to his previous house plan. He made sure it kept the basement that had saved his life. Again, it accommodated his law offices, but they redesigned the house with an enlarged front area for three attorneys. The music room and glassed-in back porch were replicated, but the backyard had changed dramatically. The tornado had uprooted the big Shumard red oak, leaving a large empty spot. Max put in a koi pond where the tree had been.

Rilke decided to give up his law-office duties to remain with Kitty, who spoiled him brazenly and didn't subject him to tornadoes. That was fine with Max. He still visited Larry and Kitty often and took supper with them almost weekly. Max and Larry no longer argued about jazz performance. Larry was becoming quite successful with what he called techno-bop, which involved breaking a tune into tiny fragments and repeating them in polyrhythms with tonal and accent variations. To Max it was almost unlistenable, but Larry had gained a considerable audience for it.

Max had been Larry's lawyer for several years since Larry had become a jazz business entrepreneur as well as performer. Their business gave Max further excuse to visit the Delgados and to see Kitty, even if he couldn't be alone with her for an extended time. It had been a frustrating year for Max in many ways. Although George W. Bush narrowly lost the total popular vote, he narrowly won on electoral votes. The U.S. Supreme Court halted the vote count in Florida with Bush slightly ahead. The completed Florida votes might have swung the election to Al Gore. Both Max and Kitty had been pulling for Gore because of his promises to protect the environment and reverse global warming. Despite these disappointments, the real millennium would arrive on a brighter note.

***

Max invited the Delgados, the Landers, the Randles, and a few other friends to a 2001 New Year's Eve party in his recently completed house and law offices. Although the house was still only sparsely furnished, Max had immediately replaced his demolished piano in the music/recreation room. Their new attorney, a young Vietnamese-American woman named Nancy Nguyen, provided *Ha Cao* Dumplings, spring rolls, spicy fried noodles, pot stickers, and cream cheese wontons. The group washed these goodies down with spiked eggnog, beer, and Vietnamese bubble tea.

Larry hovered at the snacks table, noshing avidly on the Asian *hors d'oeuvres*. When Nancy brought out some additional spring rolls, he struck up a conversation with the pretty, petite woman.

"So, you were born here but also speak Vietnamese?"

"Yes, I've tried to keep up with some of my Vietnamese heritage. I still have relatives in Vietnam and have been there twice to visit them."

"Are they still Communist? Seems like I heard they took up capitalism."

"They still claim to be Communist, but they've learned the economy does better when it's not totally government controlled. The Chinese are much the same. America should have stayed out of Vietnam and saved a lot of grief on both sides."

"Well, I reckon hindsight is always 20-20. We thought we were doin' the right thing, trying to save Vietnam from Communism."

"But we didn't, and it was a tragedy for both. Maybe it will have been worth something if it makes America think twice next time an unnecessary war beckons."

"Yeah, I guess the end don't justify an unjust war," mumbled Larry.

"That the end doesn't justify the means is a mistaken cliché," said Nancy. "Actually, only the end can justify the means. But it has to be a noble end and appropriate means. Somehow that seldom seems to be the case."

Larry pulled at his mustache. "Hummm. Maybe that's the reason God had Jesus crucified. Sacrificing Jesus to a cruel death justified the end of saving all the world's sinners."

Odetta, who had been listening to their conversation, said, "Larry, maybe you should have gone into the priesthood. That would have solved so many problems. You could have been the jazz priest."

Larry sucked on a beer and opined, "You might have something there, Odetta. Maybe I should have married the church instead of JJ. In fact, it seems to me the world's main problem is all the different religions just don't get along. If the world were totally Catholic, we wouldn't have so much conflict. Aren't most Vietnamese Catholic, Nancy?"

"Many Vietnamese are Catholic. The French colonized Vietnam in the 1800s and inflicted Catholicism on them. But there are still many Buddhists, and there is a native Vietnamese religion to which I belong. It is called *Cao Đài*. It was established only in 1926."

"Wow, I've never heard of it. Uh, so how *did* your cow die? Heh, heh."

"Gosh, that's the first time I've heard that one—this week."

"Hey, don't mean to offend, but why does the world need a new religion? As I said, seems like there's way too many now, and Catholicism is the oldest and best."

Nancy hesitated, then snapped, "Well, Zoroastrianism, Hinduism, and Buddhism are much older than Christianity. Furthermore, the old religions like Catholicism have too much nasty baggage, like war mongering, witch-burning, book burning, heretic torture, suppression of scientific truth, buy-your-way-to-heaven scams, massive priestly corruption, rampant priestly pedophilia, suppression of women. Just trivial things like that!"

"Okay, don't get your temperature up, darlin'. I didn't mean to start a religious war."

"Don't worry, *Cao Đài* teaches complete non-violence," said Nancy. "No holy crusades for me except legally speaking."

Max had overheard their conversation and now made his way over to them. "Larry, are you hitting on my new attorney? I should have warned you she's one tough lady. Best remove your foot from your mouth and stuff a spring roll in it. Everybody take a seat. Sally and I have some entertainment planned."

It was about half an hour before midnight. Sally, twenty now and studying philosophy at TCU, called for everyone's attention and, grinning Cheshire kittenishly, said, "Uncle Max and I are going to play a demure little ditty for you that we've been practicing together. I think you'll agree it represents some of what has happened this past year." She took the piano, and Max pulled the Chromonica from his coat pocket. No one except Odetta and Sally had yet heard him play it. Kitty had thought he might have gotten frustrated and put it away. She had been reluctant to ask him about it. Now she was delighted to see him hold it up with a mischievous grin.

Sally provided a few introductory chords, then Max entered with the melody of "Cast Your Fate To the Wind" on the Chromonica. They played it straight and simple the first time through. Then, Sally gradually embellished the melody and increased the tempo, expressing the gathering force of a storm. They gradually built the tempo, volume, and complexity of the tune. By the ultimate repeat, Sally was hammering the piano in a furious tornado of notes in the lower registers, and Max's Chromonica had become a howling tempest. They brought the song to a wild, chaotic conclusion with several explosive chords from the piano and some hair-raising shrieks from the Chromonica. Everyone hooted and applauded excitedly.

Sally stood to give an elaborate bow, then hugged Max, who smiled and flashed the Chromonica to the group.

Larry said, "Damn, Max, I've got to record that piece for my Cowtown Tornado platter. Kitty and I can add some wind to it as well with our saxes. Great playing, Sally. Max has sure turned you into a fine jazz pianist. I told you, Max, that harmonica might really make jazz sizzle! You just proved it."

A few minutes later, it was midnight. Max and Sally played "Auld Lang Syne," and everyone toasted the New Year with champagne. While Larry was explaining to Nancy why she shouldn't have taken offence, Kitty gave Max a heavy-duty hug and an extended, passionate kiss under the mistletoe. That made his millennium.

Chapter Eighteen

"Stolen Moments"

Fort Worth, Texas, Spring 2001

Max and Kitty's love affair began inadvertently, even though both had been aching for each other for months and years. They had established a routine during the past year of Max coming for supper with Larry and Kitty on most Fridays. On a Wednesday in early May, however, Max told them he needed to be out of town on business that Friday. Larry decided to go out jamming with some musician friends who had a gig in Dallas. He told Kitty not to wait up.

Max's client cancelled late that Friday afternoon, so Max called the Delgado house to say he was free for supper after all. He was elated when Kitty told him Larry was out for the evening and to come on over. This was his first chance in months to visit Kitty alone. He took her to the Raja restaurant for supper, where he plied her with Indian delicacies and held forth on the philosophy of the *Bhagavad Gita* and the story of the *Mahabharata*, which featured a princess with five husbands at the same time.

"Five husbands would sure keep a girl busy," said Kitty, dipping some naan bread in spiced yogurt.

"I think I could keep you contentedly busy just by myself," said Max, "but I'd reluctantly be willing to share you with Larry if he agreed."

"We both know that's not likely."

"Well, polyamory has worked for lots of famous people, particularly artists, writers, and musicians. The poets Percy Shelley and Lord Byron, and the novelist, George Eliot, who was a woman, Mary Ann Evans, advocated and practiced free love and women's liberation."

"Okay by me. You run it by Larry and see if the top of his head stays in place."

They returned to her house for a nightcap. Kitty poured glasses of Rainwater Madeira for them. Max turned on the electric player piano and selected several romantic classical pieces. They cuddled together on the leather couch, sipping the wine and making shy small talk, neither quite sure what to do next. Rilke sprawled on Kitty's lap knowing exactly what he wanted. Kitty picked up one of Max's poetry books and asked him about a poem whose title puzzled her: "Music as the Ontological Dynamic of the Universe."

"Well, the title is maybe a little pretentious," said Max. "'Ontology' is the philosophy of being. So the poem is saying the universe is alive as music in a sense, and we are an integral part of its music. Would you like me to read the entire poem?"

"Yes, please. I always enjoy it more hearing you read your poetry."

"Okay, then, close your eyes and savor the words:

Before humanity was born,
before the pulse of life entire,
before the very world was torn
from foaming, sun-spun fire,
before shining nebulae arrayed
and waltzed upon the void,

was the sound of a lover's serenade;
so, singing, were bel canto stars deployed.
We are the music and the players.
Some are notes and some whole phrases.
And we are the instruments--the resonators.
Some are rests--the necessary silent places.
Then, as cadenzas in polyphonies,
our syncopated lives we improvise,
souls with infinite possibilities,
the music of the universe to realize.
Were I not I yet I would be
some other I who still is me,
a recurring rhythmic entity
of the melody of eternity.
Yes, the Cosmos melodic
moves and loves in music."

"Oh, Max, it's both lovely and profound. But that last stanza: 'Were I not I, yet I would be, some other I who still is me.' What does that mean?"

"Ah, you've got me there. It just came to me and insisted on being included in the poem. Sometimes that happens. Words and ideas appear from some hidden corner of the mind. I guess I'd say that just as certain phrases recur in music, we as individuals may recur in the universal music of being, even if we don't realize it."

Kitty looked puzzled. "Are you talking about reincarnation?"

"Well, there is scientific evidence for reincarnation, but no, I was thinking of the possibility of other universes. Quantum physics speculates there may be an infinite number of almost duplicate universes with us in them, maybe living a slight variation of our lives in this particular here and now.

So, there's probably another Kitty and Max out there somewhere who have been happily married for years."

Kitty smiled up at Max. "That seems a little spooky, but also quite appealing."

Max looked deep into Kitty's eyes, suddenly magnetized by her nearness. Her pupils had expanded enormously, leaving only a tiny rim of azure. He saw in those depths something he could never describe or explain, something sacred, something her, but more than, and he felt it pulling his soul toward hers. For a moment he couldn't breathe, and an electric tsunami surged through his entire body.

Kitty must have perceived something similar as she gazed into the depths of his eyes too. She was trembling in his arms, her heart seized by some intense force. Then, she said in a husky whisper, "I want you—Now!"

They stared, amazed, into each other's eyes for a few more seconds, then began fumbling at their clothes. Max made to pick her up, but she said, "Not the bedroom—under the piano."

Kitty grabbed a quilt from atop the couch and handed it to him. Max flung it flat under the Yamaha grand, which was now playing Debussy's "The Girl With the Flaxen Hair," the same tune Max had played the first time he saw her, at the Catfish Club, fifteen years before. Kitty joined him there, beneath the piano's music—to make their own music—to help create the music of the universe.

They made love for over an hour. Afterward, they lay in an exhausted, blissful tangle.

Max was overwhelmed with an ecstasy beyond anything he had ever expected, even in his fantasies.

Kitty sighed and whispered to herself, "Gosh, JJ was sure right about you, Mr. Poet."

"What's that, darling? I didn't hear you."

"Just something JJ and I discussed shortly before my wedding."

Before Max could ask her to explain, Rilke put his paws on Max's backside and gave him a little claw.

"Ouch, Rilke, what the heck!"

"I think he's telling us we had better call it a night," said Kitty, reaching out to caress Rilke with her own claws, which were also much in evidence on Max's back. Then she caressed Max's cheek with trembling fingers. She looked into his eyes. "Go before I won't be able to let you go."

"Yes, I'd better vamoose. Rilke, you're like the angel with the flaming sword, driving us from Eden. Shall I help you clean up, darling?"

"No, I can manage. You go on before Larry somehow shows up early." Kitty now seemed nervous. Her fingers trembled as she dressed. "I'll try to call or email you tomorrow," she said, her gaze now unfocused, her breathing ragged.

"You could just come away with me now. Leave a note for Larry that you want to be with me. Kitty, I want to be with you openly and always."

"Oh, Max. That wouldn't be honorable or fair to Larry." Kitty's eyes pleaded with his. "I know that may seem strange since I just broke my marriage vows to him. But I don't hate him. I don't want to humiliate him. Surely you don't either. I owe it to him not to simply abscond. I'll talk with him...soon. I promise."

Max gave her a long kiss and hug goodbye. She finally pushed him gently away, with a worried frown.

***

When Max left the Delgado house, it was almost midnight. An unaccustomed light mist freshened the air. Rather than being tired, he felt extraordinarily energized. Max felt younger, and for the first time in years, he felt optimistic. He paused on the dark driveway to gaze up at the stars, still in a blissful reverie. He recalled Dante's joyous viewing of the stars as he emerged from the caverns of Hades. The night was magnificent with star-spill. Then Max looked to the other side of the sky and saw the full moon encircled by a rare double night rainbow. He stared at it awe-struck. Surely that meant the universe approved of his and Kitty's love affair. Surely now she would choose him, and all would be well.

***

By the next afternoon, however, Max had not yet heard from Kitty. He sent her a short poem by email:

Ever I'll recall that fateful, tender night,
your eyes held some vastness of sacred light,
and we made love beneath the piano on your dare.
Your oceanic eyes near drowned me there,
while on the piano, Rubenstein played Debussy:
"The Girl With the Flaxen Hair."

When Max hadn't heard from Kitty by Sunday evening, he was frantic with worry and fear that Larry might have found her out and harmed her somehow. Max was about to call when his phone rang. Kitty just whispered, "Come to my office tomorrow at noon." Then there was only the dial tone's ominous hiss.

***

Max spent a fitful, sleepless night. When he pulled up to her office building the next day, she was waiting outside. She looked around, then hurried to his van and quickly slipped inside.

"Let's drive somewhere more private and talk." She was biting her lower lip, and a vertical crease showed between the arches of her golden brows.

Max drove to a nearby secluded street and parked. Kitty moved to the bench seat behind the driver's chair. Max joined her there. She reached for him and hugged him close.

"Is something wrong, darling? Did Larry find out or suspect?"

"No. It's not that. I'm sorry I couldn't contact you until Sunday evening. Larry got home about 2:00 a.m. Friday night. We both slept late Saturday. When we got up, he wanted to take me out for breakfast. That's when he announced he's been nominated for an International Music Association Award. He said he'll need my help during the next few months for him to stand a chance of winning. We drove to Austin on Saturday to meet a record promoter. We stayed overnight down there and didn't return home until late Sunday afternoon. I was exhausted." Kitty trembled in his arms, then continued.

"Larry said he needs to schmooze with music industry bigwigs and make some major venue appearances to stay in the running for the IMAA. He had hoped to be nominated for a Grammy, but it didn't happen this year. Max, if I remain with him, perhaps I can help him get this award. He's been working toward recognition all these years. If I leave him now, he will probably lose the IMAA. He would be devastated, and his heart problem might become critical."

Kitty looked at Max with pleading, tearful eyes and a worried frown, then hugged him hard again. "Please be patient until September, when they have the awards. Then, win or lose, I'll tell him I want to be with you."

Max clasped her tightly. "Kitty, I've waited fifteen years; I guess I can wait another few months. I wouldn't want to be the cause of Larry's losing an award—or having an attack. But I need to see you and...be with you in the meantime. Do you think that will be possible?"

"I hate to continue deceiving Larry, but if he goes out of town without me, perhaps we can be together. We'll find a way somehow."

"The rear seat of my van folds into a bed. You could take the rest of the day off, and we could drive somewhere remote."

"Darling, I'm sorry. I'm just too upset today, and I have some work to catch up on in the office. But that's a good idea. Maybe we can find a free day to get together later this week."

***

Kitty was as good as her word. That Thursday she called Max from her office and asked him to meet her at noon. Max picked her up and drove to a shady, isolated street still mostly in ruin after last year's tornado. He had already folded out the bed and pulled the curtains across the windows. A sunscreen across the windshield finished converting the van into a love mobile. The van may have quivered some, but no one saw. The van's stereo system played a series of jazz tunes low in the background as they made love.

"Is that Bill Evans playing 'Stolen Moments'?" whispered Kitty. "I guess these are our stolen moments. I just hope we don't regret them later."

"I'll never regret this time with you, my darling. I only hope we won't need stolen moments much longer."

They made love in the van or some other secluded place about once a week during the next three months. Max worked extra hours on the other days and rearranged his schedule to keep up with work. Odetta may have suspected something, but she didn't question Max as long as he held up his portion of their workload. They had separate clients now anyway, and Nancy was helping them both. They had also hired an administrative assistant to handle the reception desk and record-keeping.

Larry traveled out-of-town several times that summer, playing jazz festivals or meeting with music agents. He usually took Kitty with him. One day in July, however, Kitty told Max that Larry would be out of town for several days. She had pleaded that she had work to catch up. Larry agreed he didn't need her with him on this occasion. So, she had several days free. Max suggested they take a day trip to Clark Gardens, west of Weatherford. "It has fifty acres of beautiful botanic gardens and very few visitors or staff during the summer."

There were only a couple of other cars in the parking area when they arrived at Clark Gardens. Kitty was delighted by the beauty of the landscape. She, too, was blooming with a sense of freedom after the recent claustrophobic quality of her life. She had brought a picnic basket and a quilt. They strolled about the near-deserted grounds for half an hour, holding hands, admiring the flowers and shrubs, the birds and butterflies. The fragrance of mountain laurel, Mexican plum, and lilac mixed pungently in the heavy air, causing bumblebees to stumble about as if inebriated, among the cornucopia of blossoms.

Then Max directed them to an isolated nook he had discovered on a previous visit. It was a small grassy alcove completely hidden behind some thick abelia bushes, now blushing with hundreds of tiny pink flowers. The hideaway bordered a portion of the stream that wandered through the gardens. Several low-hanging willows provided shade.

Max had also thought of how to make this little paradise even more private. He had brought a sign that read "Danger, Snakes!" which he now hung on the bushes secluding the nook.

"You're incorrigible! What if the staff sees that?"

"They won't, darling. The grounds-crew is minimal in the summer, and they're working in other areas. Don't worry. Be adventurous. Even if someone happened to see you naked, they would be stunned by your beauty and think a goddess had miraculously appeared."

She gave him a playful shoulder punch and pushed through the bushes to the verdant area by the stream. They laid the quilt on the grass and reclined on it together.

Max asked, "Lunch first, or shall we work up an appetite?"

"Let's make love first since we're being adventurous."

"Okay, but let's watch out for those snakes."

They divested their clothes. Max saw that Kitty's eyes were the same soft azure as the sky and her skin glowed radiantly in the splash of sun-dazzle through the leaves. They made slow, tender love for not nearly long enough.

As they lay caressing each other afterward, Kitty asked, "Max, did you ever make love with JJ? She told me shortly before Larry and I were married that she hadn't but wished she had."

"Funny you should ask. JJ was my dearest girlfriend during high school. I had the hots for her then, and I think it was mutual. She and I often made out, but we never went all the way. Then she fell in love with Larry. After she divorced him and returned to Fort Worth sans Larry, I thought I might have another chance. But then I met you and, well, here we are. Now I can't imagine desiring anyone other than you. But..."

"But?"

"When JJ came to live with me during her cancer treatments, we often got cozy with each other. We did a lot of kissing and cuddling but didn't make love. After she fully recovered—a couple of months after you married Larry—we had a nice dinner together at Bill Martin's Seafood. When we got home, we had a couple of drinks, and she just came on to me. I was still awfully broken up about your marrying Larry. She said she still loved Larry, and she knew I loved you, but she said we should console each other. So, we made love. And it was good—very good. I remember after that first time, we were cuddling together, and she quipped, 'I may suck at fellatio, but, as a poet, you are certainly a cunning linguist.'"

"Well, I can attest to that," said Kitty with a giggle.

"We made love on a couple more occasions," said Max. "That night after the eclipse party at your house for one. But I finally admitted to her that I was thinking about you each time. She didn't get upset, but we just didn't do it again after that. Then her cancer came back, and, well, that was that. God, I miss her so much."

Both of them were getting misty-eyed. Then Kitty smiled and touched his cheek. "Well, I've got a confession to make too. Remember when JJ, Elaine, and I had that weekend at your lake house just before my wedding? JJ told me then she regretted that you and she had never made love. She said she might try to seduce you after I was married to Larry."

"So, she had it all planned beforehand."

"Yes, but that's not the real confession. She, uh, told me while she and I were making love."

"What!? Why, you randy little minx! I never suspected you swung both ways."

"I didn't either. And I really don't. She seduced me just as she did you. And it was really good. She helped me have my first orgasm. You've given me all my subsequent ones."

Max was about to make an enormously witty reply when they were startled by some strange, almost musical, sounds, like a baritone saxophone, coming from the stream. Two black swans were gliding together only a few feet from them. The swans crooned shyly as they rubbed and twined their long necks around each other, kissing with rosy beaks.

Kitty gasped, then laughed in delight. "Aren't they the most beautiful things you've ever seen?"

"Yes. They must have come to welcome and worship their goddess, as have I."

Kitty frowned. "Max, you've got to stop idealizing me like you do. I know I'm physically attractive, but I also have qualities that are—less than ideal. I'm just an ordinary woman who's madly in love with you."

"Darling, you'll never be ordinary. Besides, as I said in my love-beneath-the-piano poem, I saw something extraordinary, something sacred in your eyes that night. I'm in love with the beauty that radiates from your soul even more than I am with your physical qualities. Sex with JJ was wonderful fun, but my lovemaking with her didn't have the sacred quality you and I always seem to have together."

"Oh, Max," Kitty sighed. "We had better get dressed and eat our lunch before God sends the snakes to find us."

***

Kitty was mostly quiet on their drive back to Fort Worth.

"Are you all right, darling?"

"Yes, I'm fine. It was such a lovely day. You—we were wonderful. I'll cherish it forever. I'm just a little tired."

Max saw they were nearing one of his favorite places to stop during this stretch of highway. They pulled into a roadside rest-stop with a scenic overlook onto a long valley. No one else was about. They watched as a thunderstorm came gliding toward them a mile down the valley, spitting lightning. Beams from the lowering sun punctuated the storm's green-black clouds and scrim of rain.

"I know how to cheer you up, Darling, said Max." He backed the car near the edge of the overlook. They opened the doors, which contained stereo speakers. Max turned on a CD of Antonio Vivaldi's glorious *Gloria* and played it at full volume into the valley. It sounded like a thousand love-crazed angels rending the universe asunder with song. Kitty laughed in delight, and the two merged like magnets; their bodies seemed charged with the same energy as the music and the storm. They hugged and kissed and watched the storm until the end of the *Gloria's* fantastic first movement.

"This is what I intend to make our life feel like after we're married, my goddess. I know you don't like that term, but to me you are a goddess, and I want to worship you as one."

"Oh, Max, my dear, sweet Max. I guess I had better try to be more worthy of your worship. Let's just see if we can get there first."

"Yes, let's go off together right now. There's nothing to stop us but your fear that Larry will have a heart attack. He's been making that claim for years, and he's still as healthy as a hippo. Your leaving might actually be good for him. He became a better man after JJ left him."

"Oh, Max, you know I can't. Please don't press me about it. In fact, the reason I was so quiet in the car was because I need to tell you that today has to be our last time until after the IMAA awards. Our affair is making me nervous around Larry. I'm afraid he'll notice and start interrogating me. As it is, he's so focused on the award that he hardly notices me. But he's no fool. Let's not push our luck. What we've been doing is probably wrong, but I simply couldn't help myself."

"Kitty, darling, I believe true love can do no wrong. Saint Augustine himself said, 'Only love and do what you will.' But love is also patient. Our love will surely bring us together soon. Visualize the beautiful life we'll have. Remember what we heard and saw and felt today. I will try to make it real for you. And we're not too old to adopt a child if you want. I believe God means for us to be together and to have a wonderful life."

"So now you've gotten religion?"

"Not religion, but a belief in the spirit of love. Remember my poem that ends: 'Love is the only important thing.' We are, we will be, that love."

Chapter Nineteen

"Sack O' Woe"

Los Angeles, California, September 2001

The night of the International Music Association Awards finally arrived. Larry, Kitty, and Max were in Los Angeles at the Staples Center along with several thousand other music industry folk and hangers-on. The three had seats near the front reserved for the nominees and their guests. They were surprised and delighted to find seated in the row just in front of them, Dr. Tiger Blakely, Tiger's recently acquired wife, the former Lili Rendon, Missy McKean, the young violin prodigy who was Tiger's and Lili's protégé, and Missy's fiancé, Dylan Moonbear.

Max was astounded to see Moonbear there. The two immediately grabbed each other like long-lost brothers. Max introduced Moonbear to Kitty and Larry. Dylan introduced Missy to them, and Tiger introduced Lili, who was also Missy's violin mentor. Dylan was now a federal Secret Service agent. He and Max sat together for a while, reminisced about Bosnia, and caught up on their doings since then. Dylan told Max about how he had met Tiger and Missy on a jazz tour, while they were trying to avoid a mysterious someone eager to murder Tiger. Dylan had gone undercover and was tracking the same killer for other reasons. Dylan gave

Tiger's dog, Bix, all the credit for convincing the villain to jump to his death from the roof of Bass Concert Hall in Fort Worth during Missy's concert debut.

Missy, overhearing Dylan's story, grinned and said, "Yeah, Dylan just relaxed there on the roof while Bix did all the work, and I worried about being blown up or shot during my performance. Talk about playing under pressure! Dylan's still in my doghouse."

It was an exciting night for all of them. The program revealed Tiger was to receive a Living Legend Award, having been a major performer and jazz influence for nearly 50 years. While waiting for the show to begin, Larry said almost nothing. He was visibly nervous; his feet were constantly tapping in triple time, his fingernails in danger of bleeding as his teeth ripped at them intermittently. Kitty tried to distract and calm him, but to little avail. Larry had several cocktails as the servers worked the aisles.

"Larry, slow down on the alcohol," said Kitty. "You don't want to be drunk when you accept the award."

"I'm not drunk, I just haven't gotten much sleep lately," Larry snarled.

Max, a little concerned about Kitty, exchanged seats with her. Now beside Larry, Max could also converse more easily with Tiger. They discussed historic jazz performers Tiger had known, and Tiger's travels in Europe and Asia as a musical ambassador for the State Department. They tried to bring Larry into the conversation, but he hardly made a comment.

Kitty and Missy were soon laughing and chatting like long-time friends. Dylan Moonbear was content to smile and listen to the conversation while covertly assessing their surroundings as if he were protecting the president.

Kitty touched Blakely on the shoulder and said, "Tiger, I'm miffed that you haven't brought Lili, Missy, and Dylan to visit us. You're all invited to our next party, which I plan to have very soon."

"We would be delighted, my dear. But check with Lili for a date when I'm not required by the Cliburn Contest planning committee and Missy doesn't have a concert scheduled. We've all been far too busy this past year. I'll be happy to slow down and visit with friends for a change."

Then the ceremonies began, and for the next two hours they listened to the nominated music and acceptance speeches by the winners. When at last they announced the winner of the Best Jazz Album of the Year, it wasn't Larry. They all groaned but applauded the winner. Larry was utterly deflated. Kitty tried to hold his hand, but he wouldn't respond.

Tiger turned his head to address Larry. "Don't let it get you down, man. You're young. There will be another chance next year. Maybe even a Grammy. You've got the good stuff. Just keep it coming, and you'll be recognized. I've had to wait fifty years. That makes it all the sweeter."

"I don't have fifty years to wait," spat Larry. "Maybe I won't even have next year."

Kitty stared at Larry anxiously. "Don't say that, dear. Tiger's right. You just have to persevere. Most nominees probably don't win the first time."

Max said, "Larry, a Zen proverb says, 'Fall seven times and stand up eight.' You—"

"Shut up, Max. I don't need your stupid platitudes. I know what's up with you and Kitty. She talks in her sleep. You should know that since you've been sleeping with her! That's prob'ly why I lost; she was sneaking around with you when I needed her."

Kitty gasped and flushed. Her eyes became huge and fearful. There was a momentary silence that felt like falling off a cliff. Then Kitty blurted, "Tiger, Missy, I think we had better take Larry back to the hotel. He's not feeling well. I'm so sorry we can't stay to see your award."

Tiger frowned and cleared his throat but suppressed a comment. Missy looked distressed but didn't speak. Lili was silent, though her dark eyes probed Kitty's sympathetically. Dylan was taciturn, a raised eyebrow his only reaction.

Larry followed Kitty sullenly as she tugged at his sleeve. Max trailed them both, worried as always for Kitty's welfare.

***

The three took a cab to their hotel, with Max sitting up front next to the driver. None spoke until they arrived at the Delgados' room. "You come in too, Max, I want to settle this," Larry snarled, breathing heavily, barely controlling his anger.

Larry immediately went to the room's bar cabinet, opened a pint bottle of bourbon, and swallowed half of it in a few gulps.

Kitty said, "Larry, what's this all about? Please don't get drunk and don't be angry. Let's talk like reasonable adults."

"Why shouldn't I be angry? You and Max have been—having an affair behind my back while I've been working my butt off to win that damn award. Which was all for nothing! As I said, you talk in your sleep. Usually I'm asleep before you, but I've been so nervous the last few weeks, I've had insomnia. I've heard you whisper: 'Max, Max, Max.'" Larry downed the rest of the pint and went back to the cabinet for more.

"I've always known you were in love with him, but I thought you were both loyal enough to me and moral enough not to act on it. I guess I've been a fool thinking mere church vows would keep you true to me."

"Look here, Larry, you've brought this on yourself," said Max. "Yes, Kitty and I have been in love for years, but we refrained from acting on it until just a few months ago. From my point of view, you married her under false pretenses. You told her fifteen years ago you needed her because you didn't have long to live."

"Well, it was true, damn it," said Larry. "The doctor said my heart might go any time." He drank off a vodka mini like a shot.

Max continued, "So, all this time Kitty and I have assumed we could be together after you died. I hate to put it that bluntly, but it needs to be said. She married you mostly because she thought she could help you become a major jazz performer before you died young. Then, she and I could be together. You've accomplished a lot with her support. She even tried to give you a child, but that tragically didn't happen. Now Kitty's miserable, and she can't really do much more for you. Let her go. Let her be with me. I can make her happy. You and I can still be friends. She can still work with you, still help you get an award. But let her have a chance for happiness with me."

Larry downed a second vodka mini. His words had now become slurred. "I achally thought if I won this award I'd be set and could be mang--mag-nanmonus, maybe let Kitty decide what she wants to do. More fool me. Now I'm back at square one. My wife and best friend have betrayed me. I'll prob'ly be the laughingstock of the jazz world. They'll never consider me for an award again. This is all a huge conspiracy against me. I should be playing 'Sack O' Woe.' That's what I feel like right now."

Larry's eyes were glassy, red-rimmed, and unfocused. He staggered to the balcony's sliding door and looked out into the night. "Heck, I might as well just end it right here. This is the pin—pintacle of my so-called career." He slid open the door and stepped onto the balcony. He leaned against the balcony rail, five floors above the ground, gazing out over the city. Then he turned and bent backwards over the railing. "Tell them it was an accident, that I was drunk from celebrating my almost-win. This is the only way for me to make the news," he sneered.

Kitty screamed. Max lunged to the balcony and grabbed the front of Larry's jacket. Larry made as if he were trying to topple over. Max jerked the bigger man away from the rail, pushed him back into the room, and shut the door. Larry collapsed onto the sofa, put his head in his hands, and wept. Kitty sat beside Larry and pulled his head into her lap. She looked at Max with pleading eyes.

"Larry, you're not thinking straight tonight," said Max. "Let's talk in the morning. Things will look better then." Max and Kitty stared at each other, not sure what to do.

Kitty said, "Let's put you to bed, Larry. Max is right. Things will look different in the morning."

Max helped her maneuver Larry to the bed, removed his outer clothes, and got him under the covers. She closed the door and hugged Max, weeping against his chest.

"Shall I spend the night here on your couch, just in case?" asked Max.

"No, I think he'll sleep through the night. I'll sleep on the other bed."

"You could come sleep in my room, just to be safe. I'm worried he might wake and try to harm you."

"I don't think he would hurt me. He's too far out of it now, anyway. He'll sleep through the night. I don't want him to wake up in the morning and find me missing. Let's hope he'll be more reasonable when he's sober. I'll see you then." Max hugged her desperately, not wanting to release her, tasting her tears as he kissed her cheek. His own tears met hers. He would have held her for much longer, but she released herself.

"Go on," said Kitty, her voice strained. "I'll be okay. Let's talk in the morning."

***

The next morning, after much thought and a little fitful sleep, Max woke early. He had coffee and a light breakfast in his room. He called Kitty's room about nine. They needed to leave for the airport in an hour. The three were booked on the same flight back to DFW.

Kitty answered the phone, her voice a little shaky. "Max, I think you had better go on to the airport separately from us. We'll meet you there. Everything is okay, but Larry and I are—discussing our situation."

Max was hesitant, then said, "Okay, I'll see you there. Better get a move on to be there in time. Kitty, I love you. Please don't let him intimidate you into doing something you don't want."

"I—I'll see you at the airport."

***

Max took a cab to LAX and checked through to the departure area with only a small carry-on bag. He paced about nervously near the departure gate. Half an hour later he saw Kitty and Larry walking toward him. They carried only their instrument cases, having checked their other luggage. Max met them at the edge of the gate area, some distance from the other passengers. Kitty's eyes were red-rimmed, and she avoided looking Max in the eye. Larry, his right cheek twitching, his upper lip curling, regarded Max with obvious but suppressed antagonism.

Larry growled, "Let's don't have a scene, Max. Kitty is going to stay with me. I've forgiven her infidelity. I can't say the same about you. You are no longer my attorney or my friend. I don't want you coming to our house or seeing Kitty. Don't phone or email either. We're finished. I wish you would take a separate flight home, but that's up to you. Just don't try to talk with Kitty."

"Now, wait a minute, Larry. You may be her husband, but you don't own Kitty. She can make her own decisions about whether to talk to me. Try not to make a total ass of yourself like you did last night."

"I had too much to drink. I had an emotional crisis because of your betrayal. Kitty and I have discussed it, and she is committed to our marriage and to helping me win an award next year."

"Larry, think about Kitty's happiness for a change, not just your damn award! Maybe I should have let you flop over that balcony last night. If you were serious about suicide—which I very much doubt—then I saved your life. Now you tell me not to contact either of you—ever again? You're sick, man. You need more help than Kitty can provide. You should see a therapist."

"As a matter of fact, I plan for Kitty and me to attend couples therapy, to keep her out of your clutches, if nothing else."

Max looked at Kitty, who was trembling, her eyes on the floor. "Listen, Larry, have some compassion in your heart for Kitty and for me. We didn't want to hurt you. But we couldn't help ourselves. We're in love. But I'm not jealous or possessive. Why can't she be with both of us? She could stay married to you, could help you with your music, but she could also be with me when she wants to. No more subterfuge or anxiety. It should be her choice. Many people have had arrangements like that. Even famous people. Edna St. Vincent Millay had several lovers while she was married, with her husband's knowledge and consent."

"Well, Kitty ain't no Saint Edna, and I'm not about to share her with you like some two-dollar bottle of booze. Besides, it would violate our Catholic faith."

"What?! Larry, you've never let Catholicism stand in the way of anything you wanted to do. I doubt you've been to church since you were married. Don't pull out your phony religious crap now to justify your ass-holiness."

Larry's eyes blazed. He balled his fists and moved toward Max. "You're just a damn serial seducer, maybe an actual rapist. That's what Tanya said. I'll bet you had JJ too. And that little slant-eyed slut lawyer of yours has probably been in your bed."

Now Max was trembling with adrenaline. "Spew your lies and paranoia, Larry, if that's all you've got. But if I ever hear you've hurt Kitty, I'll come after you every way I can."

The other people in the waiting area had been eagerly eavesdropping on the quarrel as it grew louder and more protracted. Larry was about to snarl a rejoinder, and his hands were clenching at his sides as if wanting to strangle Max.

Kitty stepped between them, wringing her hands. "Larry, Max, please don't say such nasty things. I know you really don't mean them. Can't we just wait until we get home and talk this out together? I care about you both so much. Larry, there's got to be a better way than shunning Max. You're both too angry to think straight right now."

Max pleaded, "Kitty, surely you haven't really agreed never to see me again. Please don't let him bully you."

"I have promised to stay in our marriage for another year," said Kitty. "But let's wait until our emotions cool down and we can discuss it without getting so upset. Please, Larry, don't be so harsh. Let's—"

Loud gasps, screams, and shouts from the lobby interrupted her. Curious, they moved to where a crowd had gathered around a large wall-mounted television monitor. Two airplanes had hit the World Trade Center towers in New York. The replay showed the towers belching smoke and collapsing into rubble one after the other. Then there was a picture of the Pentagon having been hit by yet another airplane.

Everyone was stunned. Some were cursing, a few were praying, many were weeping.

Kitty said, "Oh, my God. There must have been thousands of people in those buildings."

Max said, "This is madness. It's either an act of war or terrorism. They might attack here too. We should try to get you somewhere safer, Kitty."

Larry said, "Damn, I'll bet our flight is gonna be delayed. Hey, what's that music?"

Over what was now a general pandemonium in the passenger area, they heard the nearby sound of a piano and violin playing "This Land Is Your Land." Looking down the corridor, they saw the grand piano that was available for public use. Playing it was Tiger Blakely. Standing atop a large ceramic planter of tropical greenery next to the piano was Missy McKean, sawing away at her violin like a demon. Lili Rendon stood protectively beside Missy. Dylan Moonbear leaned against a nearby wall, talking into his cellphone while keeping a protective eye on the other three. A crowd was gathering around the musicians, singing, and clapping along with the music.

"Let's get down there," said Larry. "This is gonna be historic!"

The three moved through the crowd to the piano. Tiger saw them and said, "Join us. Let's help people cope with this tragedy."

Larry and Kitty unpacked their instruments. Max quickly retrieved the Chromonica from his bag and joined Missy, who acknowledged him with a wild intensity in her eyes. She was now improvising feverishly, all over the tune, her shoulder-length honey hair billowing around her head as she gyrated precariously atop the planter. Max joined her, supplementing her lead with his Chromonica. The two soon meshed and created a trio with Tiger. Then Larry's alto and Kitty's tenor joined them. Now the tune really bloomed, and the crowd was singing it, chanting it, shouting it, intoxicated with the fury and emotional release of it.

When they brought the song to its close, after several choruses, someone in the crowd shouted, "God Bless America." Missy immediately jumped into the tune, and the others followed along. The impromptu concert lasted over an hour, and included "America the Beautiful," "My Country Tis of Thee," "America," "Take Me Home," and concluded with "The Star-Spangled Banner."

When they finished, Dylan came over, lifted Missy down, and then gathered the musicians around him. "I've been talking with my Secret Service team in D.C. They think this is some sort of terrorist incident rather than the first blow of war. But they sent the president to a secure bunker. All the airports have been ordered locked down for today and maybe for several days. They want me to return to Washington ASAP. I've requisitioned a small federal passenger jet. I can fly you all back to Fort Worth. Then I'll go on to Washington. The plane will be on the tarmac soon. Decide now if you want to come with me."

"I hate to leave all these other people stranded, but we can't really help them by staying, so I'm in favor of going with you," said Tiger. Lili and Missy nodded their heads.

"Heck, yes," said Larry. "Me and Kitty will ride with you. I sure hope the media got pictures of the concert."

Max looked at Kitty, who had been playing with passion during the performance, but now she seemed deflated and unfocused. Max grimaced. "You all go on. I'll return by car or bus. It was wonderful jamming with you, Tiger, and you, Missy. I think we helped folks here cope a little with this horror. Be safe. I'll see you back in Fort Worth in a few days. Kitty, Larry, please think about my proposal. I don't want to lose your friendship. Don't let this be a day of personal as well as national tragedy." Max made as if to hug Kitty, but Larry pulled her away, turning their backs on him.

The others walked away, leaving Max, head bowed, leaning against the piano. A young woman who had been in the listening crowd was lingering in the area. She tapped Max on the shoulder. "Hey, you're one of the musicians. Thanks so much for the music. It was rad. Are you anyone famous?"

"I'm a total nobody," said Max, "unknown even to myself. 'Look for me under your bootsoles.'" §

The young woman frowned and gazed quizzically after Max as he trudged, like one of the New York bombing survivors, down the corridor toward the exit.

§ Walt Whitman, 'Song of Myself: "I bequeath myself to the dirt to grow from the grass I love, / If you want me again look for me under your bootsoles."

Publisher's Note: Tiger Blakely, Dylan Moonbear, Missy McKean, and Lili Rendon are also four of the main characters in Michael Baldwin's mystery novel, *Murder Music.*

Chapter Twenty

"My Man Is Gone Now"

Chicago & Fort Worth, Texas, 2001-2002

It took Max five days to return to Fort Worth from Los Angeles. He was in no hurry. He wanted to give Larry and Kitty time to talk between themselves. Hopefully, Larry would cool down and change his mind. He and Max had reconciled before. Hopefully, too, Kitty would find the courage to defy Larry or persuade him to relent. Max also needed some time to think, away from his mundane professional concerns, time to regain some emotional equilibrium.

When Max got to the car rental area of LAX the afternoon of September 11, all the rentals had been taken. He hopped on a shuttle van into LA, then caught an interstate bus toward Chicago. That took three days. A train from Chicago took him home to Fort Worth. During those long hours and days, Max read Virgil's *Aeneid.* It seemed doubly appropriate since Aeneas was fleeing the fall of Troy while Max was fleeing the fall of the twin towers as well as the probable fall of his love affair with Kitty. He was also reading Ovid's *Metamorphosis* (*Am I being transformed by fate into some awful otherness?*). Max felt as though he was living in a Greek myth, like Sisyphus or Tantalus, ever striving for Kitty but never quite able to attain her. He tried to take his mind off Kitty by discussing the 9/11 events with people he encountered along the way. He worked on several poems about the tragedy.

Max was sitting on one of the massive wooden benches in Chicago's Union Station, waiting for his train to Texas. The station's classical Greek architecture and arching glass roof duly impressed him. Soon he turned his attention to writing a poem about 9/11 tentatively titled "This Is How the Millennium Begins."

A tiny, elderly black lady eased down onto the other end of his bench with a sigh. She was immaculately dressed in a gray pantsuit. A string of small pearls accented her neck. He glanced at her, and they exchanged smiles and nods. Atop her white hair was a black pillbox hat with a jaunty little redbird perched on top. She watched as Max concentrated on the poem, his pen scratching out, substituting, scribbling. She scooted closer, as if to better see what he was writing.

"Oh, I see you're a poet. I love poetry. I knew Gwendolyn Brooks here in Chicago. She was the first black woman to be U.S. Poet Laureate, you know. She died just last year. Are you anyone famous?"

"No, ma'am. I've published a couple of books, but they haven't gotten much notice. Poetry isn't as popular as it once was. Brooks was a wonderful poet. I wish I could have met her."

"May I read what you've written?"

Max handed the notebook to her; she read the poem slowly, the wrinkles of her face crinkling as she whispered the words to herself.

"This is a good poem. I especially like these lines:

'the crush of crumbled towers' humbled pride,
in streets begrimed with grief for strangers,
in the grotesque smoke of thousands
of innocent souls, ascending.'

Could I buy this poem from you?"

"Well, it's not finished yet. If you give me your address, I'll be glad to mail you a copy free when it's finished."

"Oh, I insist on paying. Would $2 be enough? I have a new $2 bill my nephew, Darrell, sent me from New York. He died in the collapse of the North Tower that day. I'd like to read this poem at his memorial service next week. I think he would like the idea of his money buying this poem. And it might help folks deal with their sadness."

Max gave a little groan. "I'm so sorry about Darrell. Yes, $2 would be perfect. I'll finish the poem today or tomorrow. I should be home in Fort Worth by Sunday. I'll put it in the mail to you the next day. And I'll dedicate it to Darrell." She wrote her name and address in his notebook and handed it back to him.

"So kind of you, Mr...?"

"Oh, sorry, I'm Max Ballard, itinerant poet, honest lawyer, and utter fool."

She looked at him with flinty eyes that knew how to deal with sorrow. "Well, we're all fools one way or another, Mr. Ballard. Most people can't admit it. As you said, poetry doesn't get much notice these days, but when something enormous like this New York tragedy happens, people look to poets for the words to cope with it. I'm glad to have found you. God must have brought us together. What do you think about that?"

"To tell you the truth, I've never been much for organized religion. But I do believe there are mysteries of spirit beyond our understanding that sometimes affect or use us."

"That's good enough for me, son. You be sure and send me that poem now."

***

The train arrived in Fort Worth late Sunday evening. Max had phoned Odetta from Los Angeles and again from Chicago to let her and Nancy know what he was doing. He took a cab home from the train station. His own bed welcomed him like a heavenly cloud after his restless sleep on buses and trains. Late Monday morning he came down to the office to confer with Odetta and Nancy. They were both busy with clients. Max decided to bite the bullet and call the Delgados. Kitty answered.

"Max, Odetta told us you were taking several days to make your way home. I'm so glad you're back safe. I—"

Larry interrupted. "I'll take that, Kitty. Max, nothing has changed from what I told you in LA. Kitty and I have been to a couples' therapist, and he recommended we cut off all contact with you. So don't try to communicate with Kitty or me ever again. Go find some other woman to hit on. If you try to contact Kitty, I'll get a restraining order against you. Goodbye."

Max was stunned and devastated. Odetta found him slumped over his desk after getting no response from her knock on his office door. He was trembling and staring into an infinite distance. Odetta shook him, trying to get him to respond. Then she pulled him up by his collar and slapped him hard on the cheek.

"It's Kitty, isn't it? Everyone knows you love her. You and she must have been getting together behind Larry's back. Now he's found out and cut you off. Right?"

He couldn't meet the terrible pity in her eyes. He simply moaned and tried to pull away from her. Her long red nails dug into his shoulder.

"Max, I know this must seem like the end of the world to you, but it will pass. When JJ knew she was dying, she asked me to keep an eye on you and make sure you don't try to commit suicide again or do some other fool thing. She figured Kitty wouldn't be able to stand up to Larry despite loving you. She knew both him and Kitty better than any of us. And she knew you."

"Yeah, well, if JJ hadn't divorced him, Kitty and I might have been married long ago."

"Don't you be disrespecting JJ. I think she loved you as much as she loved Larry. She told me Kitty probably sees Larry as a father figure, since her father died in Vietnam. Also, Kitty told JJ that she had been raped as a young teen. It traumatized her severely. She will always be fragile because of that."

"Yeah, JJ told me about Kitty being raped after Tanya told Kitty I raped Tanya. It wasn't true, by the way. I hope you know I could never do something like that."

"I know. JJ told me all about your Tanya episode. But that's why Kitty reacted so extremely then, and it's probably why she still clings to Larry as her authority figure."

"I can't blame her," said Max. "I can see why she's reluctant to break away from Larry. He gives her stability and security, but what she needs is love, my love." He dropped his head onto the desktop.

Odetta jerked him up again. "Max, you've got to get over this anguish. You've got so much good to give to the world. You hired me and even made me a partner when a middle-aged, black woman lawyer didn't stand a chance anywhere else. Now it's my turn to help you, even if I have to smack you around some."

Now she had Max's attention. But he still looked stricken. He picked up the knife-like letter opener from his desk and eyed it quizzically.

Odetta shook him again and grabbed the letter opener. "You mustn't let Larry defeat you. If you commit suicide or become some kind of addict, it will hurt Kitty even more and doom her to unhappiness. She would probably blame herself. She truly loves you, Max, but she's emotionally frail. You've got to find something productive to do until either Larry dies or Kitty finds the strength to leave him. Come on, get up. Let's walk outside. It's a beautiful day."

Odetta finally got Max to talk about what had happened in Los Angeles. They spent the rest of the day walking in the neighborhood, talking about Max's dilemma and life in general.

He told her that during his trip home, he had become increasingly depressed about 9/11, his desire for Kitty, the decaying political and social climate in America, and the worsening of the world's natural environment. He wasn't suicidal, but he saw little worth living for. Everything seemed to be collapsing around him like the Twin Towers.

The Twin Towers; the poem! Max stopped and smacked his forehead. "Damn, I haven't posted my poem to Mrs. Longacre in Chicago. She needs it for Darrell's memorial service." He told Odetta about the lady who had purchased his poem.

"You met Ida Longacre? Max, I grew up in Chicago. I knew Ida Longacre when I was a teenager. She's been a leader of the Chicago civil rights movement forever. Was she wearing her trademark pillbox hat with a redbird on top? Yes, she's a wonderful lady. You see, your poetry is doing more good in the world than you realize. Let's go back to the office and express mail your poem to her."

***

During the remaining weeks and months of 2001, Max tried emailing Kitty at work but got no reply. He wrote Larry a letter arguing that it was unfair and cruel for him to cut Max off from seeing Kitty. He pledged not to subvert their marriage. Max emphasized that their long-time friendship was too precious to destroy. Still, there was no response from Larry or Kitty.

Max became more desperate and depressed as he realized Larry intended to exclude him permanently from his and Kitty's lives. Furthermore, he was concerned about the recent US invasion of Afghanistan seeking Osama Bin Laden. That could only lead to long-term violence and more terrorism. In April 2002, frustrated and desolate, Max offered his services as an independent war correspondent to the Associated Press. They agreed to send him to Afghanistan.

Max decided he must try to see Kitty one last time before his departure. He emailed her at work, telling her he was leaving the country for an extended time and would like to see her for just a few minutes before he departed. He got no reply.

Max arrived outside Kitty's workplace just before noon on the day he was due to depart. Twenty minutes later, Kitty appeared at the door and looked at him pleadingly. Then she bit her lip and came to him.

"Can we go get a cup of coffee and talk for just a few minutes?" asked Max.

"I...yes, I suppose so. I'm already breaking my promise just by seeing you."

They walked to a nearby coffee shop and took a table in the back. Kitty was trembling, her fingers twisting at her wedding ring, and her eyes reluctant to meet his.

"Kitty, I'm going to Afghanistan as a war correspondent for a while, maybe a year."

She gasped. "Oh, Max, no! This is all my fault. I shouldn't have let Larry talk me into staying with him another year when we were in LA. But he was so pathetic, and then so persuasive. I would even have been willing to be with both of you, as you proposed, but he couldn't tolerate that idea."

Kitty groaned and forced herself to meet his eyes. "Now we're causing you to go into danger in Afghanistan. It was so unfair of Larry and that arrogant Catholic therapist to demand complete estrangement, but they didn't give me any other choice." She was weeping silently now.

"Don't blame yourself, darling. I'll be fine." He gently touched her arm, wanting to pull her into his embrace, but didn't want to risk a rebuff. "It's just that I feel the need to do some thinking in a completely different environment. And maybe I can actually do some good over there. At least I won't be constantly tempted to try to wrest you away from Larry. But I will be thinking of you and wanting you my whole time there. Please don't give up on us."

"Max, I'm so sorry that I can't seem to stand up to Larry. My mother is on his side. He's always on his best behavior around her, and she no longer has fits of depression like she used to. I'll try to help him win an award this year, but he really doesn't need my help for that. He tells me he needs my moral support, but he seldom asks for it or takes my advice. I believe he just can't stand the thought of losing to you."

"Yeah, we were always both rivals and friends in high school and after. We have different ideas about music and most other things in life. Larry and I were like a pair of scissors that sharpened itself as the blades scraped together. We pushed each other to do better."

"I guess I broke your scissors."

"It would have happened, eventually. He and I are just too different. We grew even farther apart when he was in New York. I think his drug addiction may have permanently affected his mind, even though he finally kicked it. He was different when he returned from New York. I wish he had stayed there. But you and I might never have met in that case. Oh, Kitty, if you truly still love me and want to be with me, come with me now. I can get out of this assignment. We can go to a different city. I can be a lawyer anywhere."

The vertical worry crease between her eyebrows deepened. "Max, you know how I feel about violating my vows and promises. I just can't do it, much as I want to be with you. My mother would be furious. And if Larry had a heart attack because of it...."

"I understand, and I respect you for it, darling. But I can't help feeling we have both wasted our best years in empty, meaningless activity apart from each other. Happiness has always been possible, just by making a simple choice that we've never made. Kitty, life is too real, too important to take the easier path. We're like birthday candles, burning for a few moments, then snuffed out. We should be dancing to the music of life instead of being devoured by it. We need to take that other path the Frost poem described. It's right here in front of us."

Kitty was weeping now and couldn't face him. "Max, please don't punish me. I know I'm too pathetic to do what you want. Even if I believed it's truly moral, as you say. Please don't get yourself killed because of my weakness. I couldn't live with that."

"Darling, never blame yourself for my choices. I fully intend to come back to you. I'll never stop waiting and hoping for you. May I give you something to remember me by while I'm over there?"

Kitty sniffled, wiping her eyes and nose. "If it's not something Larry might see and get angry about."

"Would he hurt you if he found out you've seen me? Has he ever hurt you before?"

"Larry's never hit me. He grabbed my wrist tight once and bruised it. He apologized. He's more verbal than physical. He's sometimes critical of how I dress and keep house."

"If he physically or mentally abuses you while I'm gone or if you just decide you've had enough, call Odetta and she will help you. I'll write to her while I'm there, and she can keep you informed about me."

"Okay, yes, I'll keep in touch with Odetta to find out about you. What is it you want to give me?"

"Do you remember telling me about how your father tore a $2 bill in half and gave half to your mom as a pledge to come back to her?" Max took out the new $2 bill he had received from Ida Longacre and showed it to Kitty.

"Oh, Max, of course I remember. But Dad didn't come back. I don't want the same thing to happen to us. It might be like tempting fate." Her tears sprang again, and she wrung her hands.

"I'm not going into battle. I'll be on the sidelines. And I'll be careful. I just want to give you something to help you remember me." He took out a pocketknife. "Here, I'll cut it in half. When I come back, maybe things will have changed for the three of us. I hope we can tape this together again and then be together ourselves for the rest of our lives." He kissed her half and put it in her hand.

"Yes, I hope so too, my darling. I'll keep my half hidden away. Please, please be careful and come back to me. I'll be thinking of you every day."

***

Four hours later, Max flew out of DFW, bound for Germany, then on to Bagram Air Force Base, Afghanistan. While waiting for his flight at DFW, he wrote a little poem and emailed it to Kitty:

I am lonely as half of a two-dollar bill,
which, taken as a token
of our love, more than spoken,
was torn on our leaving,
can't undo our grieving.
In God we trust, true love's surrender,
surely to reunite our legal tender.
Yes, I'm lonely as half of a two-dollar bill.
Now I find all but your absence absurd.
Can our poem form lacking your word?
What shall I feel without your touch?
How will I live sans your nonesuch?
How can I sleep if our dream is nil?
I am lonely as my half of our two-dollar bill.

***

For the next three months, Max acclimated himself to Afghanistan and the American military operations there. He made friends with other journalists and with many of the troops. He often played the piano at the base restaurant. Eventually, he was invited to accompany troop patrols and saw several firefights. The Associated Press accepted and distributed his stories. Then came the day Private Darnell saw Max just as Darnell's caravan of vehicles was leaving for a week of routine patrol, just to be showing the flag.

"Hey, Max, we've got room for you. Should be a smooth few days. Come play some tunes for us."

Max climbed aboard, high-fived his Marine buddies, and played his Cromonica for them as the caravan lumbered into the desert.

Chapter Twenty-One

"Moanin'"

Afghanistan, July 2002

Max vaguely recalled being in the AMV with his Marine pals an eternity or two ago. Something had happened that caused him to black out. Someone or something must have attacked their Doberman. He remembered waking to find himself alone in the frigid night desert of Afghanistan. Everything was jumbled and hazy in his mind. Except, yes! He vividly remembered his vision of cosmic love, and of Kitty soundlessly begging him to come back to her. That memory was etched deeply in his mind in sharp detail.

Now, something was happening, but he wasn't sure what. Max had an indefinite feeling of the passing of time and distance as he wavered in and out of consciousness. There was jostling movement, the torrid weight of the sun, the pungent odor of animals, water sometimes dripping deliciously into his mouth, someone muttering in Pashto, the penetrating cold of the Afghan desert night again.

When he regained full consciousness, he found himself in a building of some sort, but it obviously did not belong to the American military. He lay on a pile of soft, thick pillows. The interior was dim, but he could discern that it was a rectangular room, about twenty feet by fifteen. The walls were plaster or mud with two high, narrow, glass windows. Elaborately ornamented woven rugs of many colors covered the floor. Several rugs also hung on the walls.

A copper samovar sat on a small iron stove, which in turn resided on a shallow wooden platform in the middle of the room. Turning his head in the other direction, he was startled to see a handsome mocha-faced boy of about ten staring at him with dark, flashing eyes. Max noticed a moaning sound that must have attracted the child's attention as well. Then Max realized the sound was coming from his own throat. He paused, cleared his throat, and smiled at the lad. "*As-salamu alaykum*," Max croaked. The ubiquitous Islamic greeting was about all he knew of Arabic.

"*Wa-Alaikum-Salaam*," the boy whispered automatically in reply. Then he bolted out the doorway jabbering in excitement.

A few minutes later, a man entered and gazed intently at Max. His dark eyes probed Max's face like lasers. The boy's face peeked in through the partially opened door. The man had a short salt and pepper beard and a colorful woven skullcap on his otherwise bald head. He might have been anywhere in age from forty to sixty years, his face and hands roughened by frequent outdoor work.

The man stood about five foot six and wore a long, rough-weave white shirt over baggy cotton pants of light beige. Around his waist was a wide multicolored sash, but it contained no weapon that Max could see. Thin leather sandals completed his garb, which Max recognized as typical clothing of rural Afghan villagers.

However, the man's demeanor seemed anything but ordinary. His eyes sparkled with keen intelligence, and he carried himself with casual dignity. Max felt no sense of threat, so he summoned up his courage and gave the Arabic greeting again.

"Points for trying," the man said with a grin, "but it is obvious you don't speak Arabic or Pashto. Let us then employ English." He spoke with a slow, distinct voice, slightly accented, but easily understandable.

"That would indeed be welcome," responded Max. "Although I consider myself a poet and thus an aficionado of language, I'm really lousy at learning foreign languages."

"What! You are a poet?" The old man's face suddenly bloomed. "You must know then that poetry is the great art and treasure of Afghanistan. Do you perhaps know anything by Master *Jalāl al-Dīn Rumi*?"

Max held up a finger seeking a moment to recall a favorite strophe by the great Sufi Afghan poet, then recited: "That which God said to the Rose, and caused it to laugh in full-blown beauty, He said to my heart, and made it a hundred times more beautiful."

The Afghan beamed, clapped his hands, and recited first in Pashto, then in English:

"On the seeker's path, wise men and fools are one. In His love, brothers and strangers are one. Go on! Drink the wine of the Beloved! In that faith, Muslims and pagans are one."

"I hope that means you don't intend to sell me to the Taliban," said Max solemnly.

The old man took Max's hand in both of his, looked deep into his eyes, and said, "My friend, I am Dawud al-Balhki, and I certainly could not betray one who can quote Rumi to this tired old Sufi. The Taliban are no friends of mine. You shall have true Pashtun hospitality in my house and this village. Rest now. Refresh yourself. Have no worries. We shall talk again when you are stronger."

Max took some water offered by the boy and drifted back into a more restful sleep. During the following days, Max learned that Dawud and his son, Salim, had been searching for stray goats when they heard explosions and gunfire. Watching from a distance, they had seen the Marine caravan in a firefight with the Taliban for over an hour until a pair of American fighter planes came to the rescue. Three helicopters then arrived to evacuate the remaining Marines and their casualties.

Why did the rescuers not find me? Max wondered. He remembered then that he had encountered his Marine friends as they were just leaving the base. Private Darnell had said the convoy was off on a routine outback excursion for a few days and had invited Max to join them. Evidently, Max's inclusion had been unplanned, unofficial, and unrecorded. He hoped his friends had survived, but if they did, they might not have thought to mention Max.

Dawud and Salim had approached the abandoned wreckage that night. Their dog sniffed out Max, who had been thrown into a shallow, brushy depression away from the AMV. They realized he was only unconscious, tended his wounds, and put him on a *travois* pulled by the dog. After two days of slow progress, they had brought Max back to their rural village, where Dawud was an honored elder.

Salim brought in a tray with a thin soup he called *chorba*, and some lumpy flatbread of irregular shape he said was *naan*. Both were delicious, but since Max was famished, he would have enjoyed anything edible. The boy watched him with dancing eyes as Max ate, then took the dishes away. Later Dawud returned, and they shared a pot of strong, sweet tea.

"I am so grateful to you for saving my life and bringing me to your home," said Max. "I'll leave as soon as I am able. I know I must be putting you in considerable danger by being here."

"You may know that the Pashtun are famous for their hospitality," said Dawud. "You are our honored guest. Please do not worry about us. You and we are quite safe. The Taliban do not know you were left behind. They will not be looking for you. Also, you have several wounds that must heal before you can return to your people. So, I must insist that you rely on our meager resources for a while."

"It is I who am honored by your generosity," said Max. "I must be incredibly lucky that you were close by and found me."

"Obviously it was God's will," said Dawud. "You were sent to us for a reason. It will all be made clear in *time, inshallah* (God willing)."

"Maybe it was simply to bring together two lovers of poetry. I will be delighted to hear more Rumi from you."

"Ha! You shall be thoroughly sick of Rumi when I am done with you," laughed Dawud. "You must acquaint me with your American poetry, of which I am mostly ignorant."

***

At first, Max was still somewhat suspicious that Dawud al-Balhki might be a member of the Taliban or was holding him for them. Maybe Dawud was trying to gain Max's confidence to obtain information about American forces, or to hold him for ransom. In the subsequent days and weeks, however, Max found Dawud to be much more than Max had assumed on first meeting. Dawud became a genuine, trusted friend.

Dawud explained he had been raised in a well-to-do family in Kunduz in northern Afghanistan. He showed much promise as a student, learned English, and was sent to England to attend secondary school and then Oxford University. There, he took a degree in history and literature and returned to Afghanistan in the late 1970s to teach.

When the Russians invaded Afghanistan in 1980, the war disrupted Dawud's family. His parents and several of his brothers died in the war. Dawud traveled abroad to seek support for Afghanistan. While in America, he met, fell in love with, and married Suraya, an Egyptian woman working for the United Nations.

Dawud and Suraya returned to Afghanistan toward the end of the war with Russia, and Salim was born in 1992. Shortly afterward, however, the Taliban fundamentalists began their violent takeover. The Taliban murdered Suraya because she had advocated for women's rights. Her death devastated Dawud. When a relative invited him to join their clan and village, Dawud decided it might be safer to do so. Thus, he returned to the hard, simple life of his ancestors and raised Salim as a pastoral herder. Because of his prestige as an educated man, however, Dawud soon became one of the esteemed elders of the village. Now, Dawud had found a kindred spirit in Max.

Chapter Twenty-Two

"Don't Get Around Much Any More"

Afghanistan, July 2002

In the first few days after Dawud installed Max in his house, Max mostly slept. They determined he had one or more cracked ribs, but no broken bones. His left knee had a strained ligament, his lower back had been badly bruised, and his left arm had been dislocated at the shoulder. But the major wound in Max's left thigh, which had been bleeding copiously when Dawud found him, was now only a scar. That was strange since it had seemed quite serious. Dawud said he had simply compression-wrapped it. Max remembered fearing for his life just before he passed out from loss of blood that night. He also recalled swallowing a pill of some sort. He remembered thinking it might be poison since its heat had knocked him out. Max decided not to ask about that.

In fact, all of Max's wounds seemed to heal more rapidly than he thought possible. Dawud and a villager, who had been a medic during the Russian war, wrapped Max's ribs and put his shoulder back in place. They treated his back and knee with a stinky salve Max suspected was used mainly on their animals. Perhaps there was something therapeutic about the air or water here. Or maybe it was that noxious salve.

Soon Max could sit up with his back against a wall. There were no chairs in the house. It would still be some weeks before he could stand and walk without difficulty. He had to get over his initial embarrassment to use a chamber pot for bodily functions during those first weeks. Max longed to walk outside in the open air. His confinement became somewhat more bearable when Dawud introduced Max to his small collection of English books. Dawud gave Max a pencil and invited him to write on any of the books' blank pages.

Dawud and Max soon became genuine friends. They found they both shared a passion for poetry, literature, music, and the life of the mind. Max had known no one at home who was as intellectually compatible as this Afghan goatherder. Dawud evidently felt the same way. They often talked for hours about literature and philosophy. What sealed their friendship, however, and took it to a higher level was their shared experience of mystical spirituality.

One morning the three were enjoying a breakfast of tea, naan bread, and an egg and potato omelet. Salim asked Max what it had felt like to be blown up. Max described his sensation of floating while blind and deaf, yet still conscious. Then Max turned to Dawud and, with some trepidation, mentioned his experience of merging with the divine light, his recognition that the universe is an entity of pure love, and the image of Kitty pleading with him to return to her.

Dawud stopped eating and looked at Max with mouth agape. "This was a very true and important experience, my friend. Do not disregard it. This was not simply a product of your physical trauma. Allah was speaking to you thus."

That was all he said at the time. Dawud had chores to attend to; but Max could tell from Dawud's pursed lips and knitted brow he meant to pursue this subject farther.

Now, for the first time in his life, Max had encountered in Dawud someone of high intelligence and in whom he felt he could confide his innermost thoughts. Furthermore, he and Dawud had the leisure to explore their mutual intellectual proclivities. Max still had weeks of recuperation before he could become fully physically active again. He had plenty of time to consider the vagaries of life that had propelled him into this strange situation. His love for Kitty was his touchstone, but how could he become more worthy of her? How could he change his catfish subconscious to become more worthy of himself? Would this predicament lead to his destruction or his salvation? Such thoughts assailed him often during his recovery.

Max remembered discussing religious matters with Kitty during their picnic at Fort Worth's Botanic Gardens and on other occasions. He had told her he was agnostic, but he hadn't felt comfortable mentioning his long spiritual quest for some truth beyond mundane reality. That search, more than anything else, had turned him toward poetry. He found poetic contemplation, with its imaginative exploration of ideas, both consciously and subconsciously, more useful than philosophical rationality for delving into the realm of spirit. The French poet Mallarme claimed the essence of poetry is mystery. Max felt that applied to philosophy and spirituality as well. Max's mind now probed the mysteries of his innate being and his love for Kitty. Was God guiding or goading him toward some mysterious purpose, as Dawud seemed to think?

***

Dawud's village duties seldom required much of his time. The pace of life here was leisurely; Dawud devoted large parts of his day to reading, socializing, and now to developing his friendship with Max. Salim, too, grew very close to Max.

While Max was incapacitated, Salim usually brought him food and drink and tended to his basic needs. The boy spoke some English but had no formal schooling in it, unlike his father. His mangled syntax often amused Max. But Salim was eager to learn more English. The boy listened intently during extended conversations between the two adults. Max sometimes used a slate and chalk to teach Salim to write English. The boy was a quick study. In return, Salim taught Max some words and phrases in Pashto and Arabic. Salim also provided Max with information about the village and its activities. Salim was a natural gossip.

After they attended to the basic daily chores of the camp and dealt as needed with other residents of the village, Dawud and Salim would usually repair to their dwelling to drink tea and talk with Max. Sometimes Dawud would invite a male friend or two from the village to join them. The villagers could thus get to know Max and come more readily to accept him as an honored guest rather than holding suspicions of him. Islam prohibited women from socializing with males outside their families, so it was always a strictly male gathering. Although Dawud didn't smoke, one or more of the guests often did. They usually used a *shisha* water pipe. Max found their *Latakia* tobacco quite spicy and intense. It made for a slightly oppressive, noir ambiance in Dawud's abode. But Max found these gatherings exotically interesting and stimulating. Salim was elated at being included.

Often at these confabs, Dawud and his friends would recite Afghan poetry and folktales. Dawud, or sometimes Salim, would translate for Max, who would sometimes contribute one of his favorite poems or stories.

Dawud conveyed Max's stories to his guests, revising them as necessary to make sure they didn't violate any cultural norms.

One story Max told was of a man stranded on the roof of his house during a flood. "This man prayed to God for a miracle to save him. Soon afterward, a motorboat came by that had room for one more person. The man waved them away, saying he would wait for God to send help. Later, a decrepit rowboat arrived. The man told it to go away too. He said God would surely save him with a miracle. Hours later, the man was getting desperate from thirst. Suddenly, an eagle swooped down and landed on the roof. It spoke to the man. 'Why did you not take one of the boats to safety?' The man said, 'I was waiting for a miracle from God.' The eagle said, 'I sent two boats to rescue you. Was that not miracle enough?' The man said, 'I thought God would send an angel or a Biblical miracle.' The eagle said, 'Such miracles are reserved for those who have faith but no other choice.' With that, the eagle flew away, and the man remained on his roof for another day before being rescued by a rusty scow."

Dawud translated this tale a little differently for the villagers, who knew nothing of floods. "A man was traveling through the desert. A snake bit his horse, which died. The man trudged on, carrying his possessions on his back. He was very thirsty. He prayed to Allah for a miracle to save him. A rider on a camel found him, gave him water, and offered a ride, but how could a dirty camel have been sent from God? He walked on and later encountered a man on horseback who offered him a ride. He feared the man was a bandit who would steal his goods. Surely Allah would send a miracle rather than a bandit. The rider departed. The man soon grew desperate with exhaustion." Dawud paused for a sip of tea. The guests looked at him expectantly until he continued.

"An eagle flew down and landed near the man. 'Ah, here is my miracle,' thought the man. The eagle asked why the man had not accepted the help

Allah had sent. 'I awaited a true miracle, and here you are.' The eagle replied, 'Miracles are usually reserved for the humble faithful who have no other hope. But you shall indeed be given a miracle.' The eagle flew away. Soon, a dust devil came swirling across the desert. It swept the man up and delivered him to hell."

The villagers grinned and nodded their heads appreciatively at Dawud's version. Salim giggled. After they had smoked and drunk some more tea together, the villagers left, patting Max on the shoulder. Max asked Dawud whether he had changed the story.

"I had to change a few details so they could relate to it. They liked the story. But I gave it a less ambiguous ending." Salim cackled with glee.

***

Max also sometimes played his Chromonica for villagers and his two hosts. Salim had noticed the harmonica shining silver in the moonlight near Max when they rescued him. Salim had shyly presented it to Max soon after they became acquainted. Max was amazed the harmonica had survived the explosion intact with only a few scratches. He blew some jazz and classical tunes for Salim, who became fascinated with this little polished metal box that produced such strange, wonderful sounds.

Salim was a natural musician himself. He was accomplished on the *rubab*, a stringed instrument about the size of a guitar, but with a thick, boxy body and many strings. The boy often played the *rubab* for Max while Dawud sang and thumped a *tabla* drum. Max would join them with the Chromonica, though it was a very different sort of music. When Max offered to teach Salim to play the Chromonica, the boy was ecstatic.

Chapter Twenty-Three

"Girl Of My Dreams"

Afghanistan, September 2002

Max was eager to recover as quickly as possible from his wounds. He knew Odetta and Kitty would be frantic when they didn't hear from him for several weeks. Dawud's one-room house was both uncomfortable and claustrophobic. Afghans were accustomed to simply squatting on the floor or reclining against pillows. He had never been much of a squatter and couldn't squat because of his injuries.

Max's injured knee was the primary obstacle to his mobility and comfort. But the knee was now almost fully healed. The Afghan medic continued to treat his knee with ointments and recommended exercises. Within three weeks after arriving at the village, Max could hobble about on an improvised crutch.

Finally, Max could limp outside with a cane and enjoy the fresh air with increased mobility. He often leaned against the outer wall of Dawud's stone house and gazed into the immense distances of the Afghan prairie. After his several-week confinement, it was exhilarating to be outside and view the vastness of the countryside. He wrote a few short poems about life in the Afghan village:

No electric   no inside plumbing
Only sweat to cool in desert heat
No motor vehicles   going   coming
Fruits fresh from a tree   so sweet
No fancy clothes   no rush to succeed
Faces smile thru wrinkles and scars
A cup of honeyed tea is all I need
for reverie and at night   ah such stars

The landscape was monochromatic brown in one direction. Only a few bushes interrupted its rock-strewn plain. But in another direction, swaths of green showed where a tiny spring bubbled up. It meandered a short distance before disappearing again into the rocky soil. Trees and bushes clustered near the spring, and a large community garden had been located there with vegetables and fruit trees. Beyond the endless stretches of barren plain, far mountains jutted into the blue haze toward heaven, and clouds like gigantic fantasy creatures plied the skies. Max realized he was contented here despite his longing for Kitty.

The houses of the village ascended the slight incline of a hill. All were constructed of stone, the most plentiful local material. A few structures were whitewashed. Two of the larger buildings had shallow domed roofs. Max learned these were the school and mosque. A few scraggly pine trees subsisted at the edge of the village.

Men and women went about their daily chores in the winding alleyways among the houses. Old men sat gossiping in the shade. Children chased about, kicking a soccer ball, or hitting a smaller ball with sticks, like field hockey. Other youngsters squatted in a circle playing marbles. Sometimes Max also saw groups of children flying kites, vying to force rivals from the air. Kite flying, Max learned, was the primary children's sport of Afghanistan.

Dawud had procured for Max some Afghan clothes that almost fit him. These included a jaunty brown cloth cap, baggy gray trousers, and a long white shirt that hung low over the pants. The wreck of the AMV had destroyed his glasses, but they had been non-prescription reading glasses, so he could manage without. He had also lost his backpack with his notebooks, camera, passport, wallet, and credit cards. He could replace all those if he survived and returned home.

By some miracle, his Texas boots had stayed on his feet. Max was thankful for the boots because he had inserted his half of the torn two-dollar bill in the inner lining of the right boot. The bill was still there. He took that as a sign that he would survive and return to Kitty to reunite the bill halves and themselves.

All Afghan men wore beards of some sort. Max let his beard grow to better fit in with their culture. Each day, Max ventured farther into the village from Dawud's house. Many of the villagers came to recognize him and greeted him in a friendly fashion.

One sunny morning, Salim and his great shaggy dog, Kaj, found Max walking near Dawud's house. Salim said, "Come, Father want you see goats."

Max followed the boy and dog around the edge of the village to a stonewalled enclosure. Dawud was sitting atop the three-foot high wall. He beckoned to Max as they approached. Max and Salim mounted the wall and gazed into the enclosure. The interior had been excavated into the earth another few feet. It formed a circular corral about thirty feet in diameter. The corral contained some fifty shaggy goats, milling about or nibbling at piles of hay. A few other men sat on the wall or moved about in the enclosure examining the goats.

"So, these are your goats?" asked Max.

"They belong to the entire village," said Dawud. "We hold many things in common and provide for everyone. You Westerners might revile it as communism, but it has worked well for us for hundreds of years."

"I like to think I'm a pragmatist in politics and economics," said Max. "If it works for you, that's really all that matters. Do the goats always remain in this corral?"

"No," spoke up Salim. "Other boys and I take goats for graze. We keep away from vegetable gardens near our water."

"But everywhere else seems so barren," said Max. "Is there enough for them to eat out on the prairie?"

"They eat any vegetation," said Dawud. "The children know where there is low-growing grass and brambles that the goats can eat. They bring them into the corral in the evening to keep them safe and so they don't wander. We have hay stored here to supplement their foraging."

"And do you shear the goats for their hair? I read that cashmere from goats is one of Afghanistan's exports."

"A few of these goats are cashmere," said Dawud, "but most are just ordinary goats. The women make rugs and jackets from the hair. Some goats we eat. Some we milk. We try to be self-sufficient. Today we are culling the goats we don't need."

Salim jumped down into the enclosure and picked up a tiny black goat that had huddled in the shadows. He brought the kid to Dawud, cradled in his arms. "Father, this one need milk, but mother not nurse."

"Well, it must be put down then. More goat meat for the stew pot."

"Father, let me try help baby nurse. Will you hold baby, Max, while I find mother? I think is the black and white one."

Max eased himself down into the corral. He took the tiny goat awkwardly in his arms. It looked up at him and bleated. Salim grabbed the mother goat by its horns and dragged her over. Max then held the mother still while

Salim positioned the kid to suckle. It glommed onto the teat and sucked greedily.

"Perhaps the mother will accept the baby now," said Max.

"Goats are stubborn, but maybe after several feedings," said Dawud. "By the way, Max, that goat saved your life. It is the one we were searching for when we found you. We had just recaptured it when we heard your explosion. Pregnant goats sometimes wander. She also alternated with the dog in pulling your travois."

Max bent down and looked the mother goat in the eye. They were large, bulbous, yellow eyes with elongated horizontal pupils that seemed to look in several directions at once. "Thanks, Nanny, for helping save me." The goat bleated irritably in reply.

"You will have to keep an eye on these two, Salim," said Dawud. "Let her sniff the baby when it is finished feeding. You may need to bed down with them in the corral tonight to help them bond. Now, Max, come walk with me toward the gardens and let us talk."

The two men walked down a well-worn path toward the garden acreage near the trickling spring. Max now used a cane that a neighbor had given him. He was gaining strength and stability every day. When they reached the verdant level area, Max saw well-tilled gardens of various vegetables and melons. Some low-growing trees displayed large pink fruits he recognized as pomegranates. "These are our pride," said Dawud, caressing one of the softball-sized fruits. "We will sell and trade these in a few weeks when the *Kuchis* trade caravan comes. We've had a good year. You have perhaps brought us luck."

"It would be nice to think I brought someone good luck," said Max. "But it would probably be the first time. You had best thank Allah instead."

"Yes, of course, but I'm sure you are part of God's plan. You should not denigrate yourself. Allah has his eye on you. In fact, that is why I brought you here. You must tell me again about your vision when you were blown up. I have been considering what it might mean."

"Surely it means only that I desired to be with my lover, Kitty."

Dawud pulled his lower lip and gave a little shake of his head. "We Sufis have learned that such visions are important messages from the More-Real-World-Than-This. Rumi had several such visions. He warned us: 'We live in a ruin, this body, where treasure is buried. You are that treasure. Try to wake from this dream we live....' So, your vision, Max, may be more true than this delusion we think is reality."

"Well, I have been recalling it as you suggested, considering it in detail," said Max. "The vision was so real and intense that I can remember it much more clearly than anything else that happened. I recalled something I hadn't mentioned previously. I hadn't really noticed it myself at the time since I was concentrating on Kitty's face. She wore a thin gold chain around her neck. It held a glossy blue oval that matched the color of her eyes. I had never seen it before. Its shape and the lines on it made it look like a beetle of some sort."

Dawud looked so intensely at Max that he was afraid he had said something offensive.

"Can you draw the oval for me?"

Max took Dawud's book of poetry by William Blake from his pocket. He found a page that had some empty space. With a pencil nub, he drew a rough oval. He added two horizontal lines parallel across the top, one vertical line down the middle to a third horizontal line at the bottom. Then he added a curved vertical line on each side. Max considered it for a few moments and said, "I've never been much of an artist. There were a few more minor details, but I think that's basically how it looked."

Dawud examined the drawing and growled as if clearing his throat. Then he reached into the neck of his shirt and pulled out a gold chain holding a plump blue oval, its markings identical to those Max had drawn. "Is this the same one you saw?"

Max's eyes went wide. His mouth gaped. "My God, yes, that's exactly the one Kitty was wearing. But how? I've never seen yours before now."

"This is indeed a great mystery, my friend. And I believe it must be freighted with some great significance. Let me tell you the story of this amulet." Dawud removed the necklace and let Max hold the strange object. It was heavier than Max expected, with a well-rounded dome on top. The amulet was some two inches long. It was formed from a single precious stone. The black lines incising it made it look indeed like a beetle.

"This is an Egyptian heart scarab amulet and quite ancient. The Egyptians worshiped the scarab beetle as a god who was responsible for rolling the sun across the sky each day. Dung beetles roll dung balls along in the dirt, so the Egyptians thought that must be how the sun progressed across the sky."

"Yes, I remember reading about that and thinking it peculiar but somehow also rather *àpropos*," said Max.

Dawud said, "Such scarab totems were very common among the ancient Egyptians. The heart scarab symbolized hope for life after death. Most of them were made of clay or common stone. This one was carved from *lapis lazuli* about three thousand years ago. It was gifted to my Egyptian wife, Suraya, by her brother, Gyasi, who is an Egyptologist. He told her that the amulet came from the tomb of a priest of *Khepera,* the scarab beetle god." Dawud paused, seeking Max's reaction.

Max fingered the amulet, feeling the smooth crystalline surface warm to his touch. Some characters decorated the flat gold reverse side. "Do you know what the hieroglyphs on the underside signify?"

Dawud nodded. "It reads, 'Within is life beyond death.' Gyasi told Suraya that the amulet contained seeds or pills that the Egyptians believed could heal the dying, bring the dead back to life, or assure them of the afterlife. You can feel them move inside if you shake it. Gyasi said there were indeed legends of Egyptian royals returning to life after eating a scarab seed. Gyasi never opened it and told Suraya to open the amulet only if someone dear to her was fatally ill or injured. To have them swallow just one pill."

"You said the Taliban murdered Suraya. Did she not have a chance to take one of the pills herself?"

Dawud groaned and hung his head. "I was not close by when it happened. She did not have time to open the amulet, or if she took one, it had no time to take effect. Her body was badly mutilated. The amulet was still around her neck and locked when I found her in the rubble of her school. If only I had been there to help her, perhaps it could have saved her as it saved you." Dawud sighed and moaned again.

Max frowned. "What do you mean, it saved me? The scarab? Did you give me one of its pills?"

"Yes, your leg was bleeding badly. You would have died. Seconds after I put the pill in your mouth, the bleeding stopped."

"My God! I remember something being forced into my mouth and feeling a wave of heat throughout my body. Then I passed out. The scarab really works."

Max clasped Dawud's shoulder. "Thank you so much for giving it to a foreign stranger. I'm so sorry you couldn't save Suraya, but you probably would have died yourself if you had been there. Who would have taken care of Salim then? Surely it was Allah's will that you serve some greater purpose." Max paused in thought. "But what could be the meaning of my seeing the amulet worn by Kitty in my vision?"

Dawud smiled through his obvious sadness. "Yes, we must investigate this mystery. In a few weeks, some other Sufi friends of mine will visit us. They are holy mystics who may be able to explain it for us."

Dawud put the amulet around his neck again and tucked it inside his shirt. As the two friends walked back toward his house, Dawud picked one of the ripe pomegranates and split it between them. It was juicy and delicious.

"Rumi said, 'When the fruit ripens sweet, it lets go of the branch. Holding tight to this world is a sign of immaturity.' You must ripen, my friend, into the mystery of true love's being. It is our only real reality."

Chapter Twenty-Four

"Caravan"

Afghanistan, October 2002

Two weeks after the revelations about the scarab amulet, Max sat reading in the shade of Dawud's house waiting for Dawud to return for lunch. He heard a shout and saw two distant figures racing toward the village from across the rocky plain. As they drew closer, Max saw it was Salim and his big lanky dog, Kaj. The boy arrived beside Max breathless and panting. He seemed excited rather than frightened. Max gave Salim and the dog some water from the goatskin flask he carried. Before Max could question the boy, Dawud came ambling home from the village.

"Father, *Kuchis* caravan arrive tomorrow! We were with goats in far pasture and saw dust of caravan coming down from hills. I left others to come tell."

"Ah, the caravan is early this year. We must gather the crops immediately so we will be ready for the *Kuchis.* I don't want them to stay here longer than necessary. Salim, run and tell your friends to spread the word. Everyone must come to the gardens to harvest."

Salim was off like a rocket, Kaj racing close beside him. As soon as they were alone, Dawud put his hand on Max's arm and looked him in the eye, frowning.

"Max, these *Kuchis* have been nomadic traders for hundreds of years. They travel the whole of Afghanistan. Each caravan usually takes the same route every year. They trade not only in commodities. They often provide information to us, but also to the Taliban, to the enemies of the Taliban, perhaps even to the Americans if they are savvy enough to know how to deal with the *Kuchis*."

"So, they might know if the Taliban are looking for me?"

"Yes, but obviously, I cannot ask them directly or they will know you are here. They might tell us if the Taliban are active in this vicinity. They might also know if the Americans are searching in this area. We must be extremely careful not to let them even suspect you exist. They would not hesitate to sell you to the Taliban."

"I suppose I should stay in the house while they are here."

"That would be best. However, I am also concerned one of our villagers might let the snake out from the bag."

"We say let the cat out of the bag, but I understand what you mean. How can you prevent that?"

"We must keep both the cat and the snake in the bag. It will not be easy. I will remind everyone to say nothing about you. It could go hard on the entire village if the Taliban come here for you. They are truly the unbagged snakes."

"Could I help with the harvest today before the caravan arrives?" asked Max.

"Humm. We do need every hand we can get. Yes, I think it will be acceptable for you to work with us today. In fact, the villagers will then better understand you are one of us. Let us go to the gardens and get to work."

By the time Max and Dawud arrived at the gardens, a small crowd was already busy there. They were filling cloth bags and woven baskets with vegetables, melons, and pomegranates. Max pitched in, plucking pomegranates and easing them into a sack so as not to bruise them. After everyone arrived, Dawud went around speaking to the men, who then told their wives and children not to mention Max to the *Kuchis*.

The villagers were still working as sundown approached. One villager gave a shout. Three riders were approaching on horseback. Dawud looked annoyed and warned Max just to keep working and try not to be noticed. Dawud and two of the other village elders went to talk with the riders. The *Kuchis* had come to make sure the village knew the caravan would arrive the next day. Max avoided looking toward them. He edged away from the *Kuchis* trio, who were now talking with Dawud and the other village elders. They stood about a hundred feet away. Then, from the corner of his eye, Max saw one of the *Kuchis* point directly toward him.

Damn! Has someone given me away already? I'm wearing my Afghan clothes. I'm suitably bearded and tanned. Have I moved in some subtle way different from how they would move?

Then Max realized he was wearing his American boots, which were obviously different from the usual Afghan sandals. His too-short pants on his lanky, six-foot frame didn't quite cover them. They weren't fancy boots, but they were hand-tooled Texas Western walking boots, which his Marine buddies had admired and inquired about on several occasions.

Salim came up to Max and whispered, "That *Kuchis* want see your boots. Father says pretend you mute and feeblemind." Then Salim led Max by the hand to the *Kuchis*.

Max hunched over slightly and limped, though he had ceased using the cane weeks ago. He turned his head away from the Kuchis who was interested in the boots. Max stuck out his lower lip and let drool run into his beard. The *Kuchis* asked him something, then squatted to touch one boot. Max made some grunting noises and pulled his foot away. Dawud spoke Pashto in a soothing manner to Max and patted him on the arm. Then he spoke more emphatically to the *Kuchis*. He motioned for Salim to take Max back to the pomegranate grove.

When they reached the trees again, Max could see that the *Kuchis* were no longer watching him. Salim said, "Father tell them you his brother. He buy boots for you when we visit Kabul two years ago. You do very good. They think you moron." Salim giggled a little and rushed off. Max felt a shiver of relief run down his spine. Then he returned to his fruit picking and moved deeper into the grove.

***

Max slept fitfully that night. On waking before dawn the next morning, he remembered dreams of being lost in a forest and being pummeled with exploding pomegranates by men wearing his boots. Just as the sun's rim wobbled up red from the hills, the *Kuchis* caravan arrived at the village. They encamped near the gardens, pitching large low tents. They loosed their animals into the now empty gardens, where their manure would help enrich the soil for the next season. It was a day of festivities for everyone.

Village children romped with *Kuchis* children, who let them pet and even mount the resting camels. The men of the village traded their garden produce for the *Kuchis'* tea, spices, tobacco, small tools, medicines, leather goods, and many other items not locally available. The village women intermingled with the *Kuchis* women and traded cloth, rugs, and small crafted items.

Dawud had instructed Max to stay with the goats in the corral and to act simple-minded if any of the *Kuchis* should accidentally see him. Dawud said he would try to keep the *Kuchis* away from the village and the goat corral. Thus, Max was surprised when, early that afternoon, Salim came vaulting over the corral wall. Salim jabbered excitedly that Dawud was bringing a *Kuchis* who wanted to trade for some goats.

Max immediately went into his feeble-minded act. Salim grabbed the black baby goat he had been nurturing and thrust it into Max's arms. Max retreated to the far edge of the corral and huddled in the shadows, petting the baby goat.

A few minutes later, Dawud and one of the *Kuchis* came through the corral gate. Max watched them out of the corner of his eye. This *Kuchis* was not the one who had been interested in his boots. Still, Max tried to keep his boots out of sight by kneeling with his feet behind him. The kid, much stronger now, bleated and struggled to escape. Max kept a tight grip on the little goat and tried to calm it.

The *Kuchis* pointed to a shaggy brown goat among the herd, and Salim fetched it for him to examine. The man slipped a cord around the animal's neck. He inspected several more goats and selected two of them. He examined but rejected the mother of the black baby goat. She then came over to Max as if in response to her baby's cries of distress. Max pushed the mother goat away and, in doing so, lost control of the baby.

The kid scampered toward Salim, with whom it had bonded. Max arose and took a couple of steps to make a grab for the kid. The *Kuchis,* who had been discussing his selections with Dawud, looked toward the commotion. As Max stood bent at the waist, the mother goat butted him in the rear and knocked him sprawling. Max stayed on the ground. The mama goat stood over him, staring at him with her crazy yellow eyes. The *Kuchis*, Dawud, and Salim had a good laugh. Then Dawud and the *Kuchis* led the chosen goats back toward the encampment.

Salim remained behind, petting the baby goat. He walked over to Max. "You get up now; *Kuchis* gone."

Max stood and dusted himself off. He patted the mother goat, who was now licking its baby in Salim's arms. "I believe you've saved me again, Nanny. But let's hope this doesn't become a regular thing."

Salim grinned at Max, his dark eyes sparkling. "I think you safe from *Kuchis*. Now they sure you are moron!"

Chapter Twenty-Five

"Everybody's Jumping"

Afghanistan, October 2002

Max was now getting around well without a cane. He considered himself fully recovered. Most of the villagers now knew and trusted him. He usually took a morning walk for exercise either alone or with Salim or Dawud when they were not otherwise occupied. Max had made friends, too, with Salim's dog, Kaj. The dog sometimes accompanied Max if Salim had duties where the dog wasn't welcome.

This morning, with Dawud and Salim elsewhere, Kaj came along with Max. The dog was part Afghan Hound and other parts unknown. He was tall, skinny, mottled gray, and had a long, tangled coat. Max sometimes saved a morsel from his goat soup for the dog. Kaj was devoted to Salim, although the boy seemed to take little care of the animal. Dogs were not considered pets in the same way they were treated in America.

The village houses sat in rows that ascended the slight incline of the low hill like stair steps. Crooked little streets and alleys broke the rows in places, allowing pedestrians to move higher or lower along the hill. Some of these streets were mere rough steps or rocky pathways, but the villagers knew them intimately and negotiated them without difficulty.

Max and Kaj were laboring up one of these stony paths. Max saw Dawud and Salim near the top and stopped to wave. Kaj suddenly jumped around Max and rushed to join Salim just as a village woman carrying a basket of apples was coming toward Max about fifteen feet away. The dog must have caused the woman to misstep on the rough path. She gave a yelp and juggled the basket for a moment, spilling some apples. Max jumped forward and grasped her arm to steady her.

The woman gasped and jumped back. As she did, her *hijab* veil came away from her face. Most of the village women didn't bother to wear the veiled *hijab*, just the headscarf. The veil was a custom observed in cities where the Taliban could enforce the practice. Max saw she was not a woman, but a young teenage girl. She stared at him with wide-eyed terror for a moment, then quickly pulled the veil back over her face and knelt to pick up her apples.

Max realized he must have made some sort of social error. Then he saw Dawud hastening toward him, waving his arms and whispering urgently, "Max, step away and don't look at her!"

Max complied, quickly ascending the pathway to meet Dawud, who grabbed him and said, "Go on up, then return to my house by another path. Say nothing to anyone." Dawud looked around to make sure no one was watching, then hurriedly followed Max.

The girl was still picking up the apples. Salim came bounding down the path to help her. Kaj stood panting, wanting to be of service as well.

Max was in the house when Dawud arrived panting from his unaccustomed hurry. He grimaced at Max, then went to pour some tea for them from the samovar.

"Did I do something wrong? I was just trying to keep her from falling and hurting herself and spilling all her apples."

"You did nothing wrong. I know you were just trying to help," said Dawud. "But adult men are not supposed to look upon an unveiled, unmarried young woman, much less touch her. It is a stupid custom, but an old one that some of these people still adhere to. To make matters worse, she is the daughter of the *mirab*, the water master, who is very conservative about these customs. If he finds out you saw her, he may beat her and will resent you. She will say nothing, but if someone else saw, they may tell the *mirab*."

"Beat her! That's insane. Maybe I should go apologize to him and let him know it was an accident, not an insult."

"Great God, no! That would make matters even worse. He would consider it an affront to his honor. He might actually kill her."

Salim entered the house. He put his hands on his hips and said, "Do not worry about Ferhana. I think no one saw. But I tell Ferhana if anyone tell her father she must say it was Salim and his dog, not Max."

"That is good thinking, Salim," said Dawud. Then he said to Max, "It is okay for Salim to see her face since he is but a child. Let us hope that makes an end of it." He reached for a ceramic bottle in the back of a high cabinet. "Perhaps we should have something a little stronger in our tea for a change if we are violating old Islamic traditions."

Chapter Twenty-Six

"Unsquare Dance"

Afghanistan, November 2002

It had become noticeably cooler in the village, especially at night. Early-morning frost often speckled the stone houses until the sun asserted itself. This morning, Max awoke to find Dawud and Salim leaving with their prayer rugs under their arms. Nothing unusual there. They were both observant Muslims, although Dawud had told Max the Sufis were not as strict as many other sects, and certainly not extreme like the Taliban's *Wahhabism*. Ordinarily, however, Dawud and Salim performed their morning prayers at home.

"Ah, Max, we hoped not to wake you. We will do our morning prayers at the mosque today because tonight we shall see the crescent moon and Ramadan will begin. I must consult with the *malik* and the *mullah*. I will tell you more about it when we return. Make yourself some breakfast."

Max recalled that the malik was the elected headman of the village, whereas the *mullah* was the religious leader and teacher. These, along with the *mirab*, the water master, were the primary authorities of the village. Because this village had easy access to water from the little spring, the *mirab* had little to do, and resented his lack of power according to Dawud.

The *mirab* was also the man whose daughter Max had seen unveiled when she spilled her apples a few weeks ago. Nothing had come of that episode. Evidently, no one had seen it happen except Dawud and Salim. Max certainly hoped the *mirab* hadn't found out about the incident. He hated the thought that the *mirab* might harm the girl for being seen unveiled.

By the time Max finished preparing porridge, dates, and tea for the three of them, Dawud and Salim had returned home. As they sat at breakfast around the samovar, Dawud explained what was about to happen. "Ramadan is the high holy time of Islam. It lasts for a full month. From the first sighting of the crescent moon at the start of the ninth month to the next crescent moon. During the month, we fast from dawn till dark. So, we will eat a predawn meal and nothing else until after sundown. You are not obliged to comply with the fast, of course."

"Well, I'll try to join in the fasting," said Max, "although I've never missed a meal all day before, much less every day for a month. I wouldn't want to eat in front of people who are fasting."

"That is both kind and wise of you," said Dawud. "The villagers know you are not Muslim, but they will appreciate you sharing their fast."

"Somehow I had the idea Ramadan occurred in the spring," said Max. "Why is it happening now?"

"Can you explain it to him, Salim?" said Dawud.

Salim hesitated a few moments, then said, "Muslim calendar is based on phases of moon. There are twelve and one-half moon months in year. So, ninth month of Ramadan is move two weeks backward each year. Ramadan move through every season of year."

"And what does Ramadan actually celebrate, Salim?" asked Dawud.

"Ah, first revelation of Quran to Mohammad."

"Very good, Salim," said Dawud. "Now, Max, let me tell you why this Ramadan is particularly significant."

"Let me tell!" blurted Salim.

"Yes, alright," said Dawud, caressing the boy's hair.

"Dervishes will be here!" said Salim. "This my first chance to see them. They come only seldom."

"Dervishes? Whirling dervishes? I've heard of them. The ones that spin around in circles? Are they entertainers of some sort?"

Dawud threw up his hands with a snort. "No, they are not entertainers. Dervish dancing is a form of meditation and worship. It enables dervishes to enter a trance state and commune with Allah. It takes many years to learn to dance properly and enter the ecstatic trance. Rumi invented the dance himself, and it has been a Sufi tradition since your Thirteenth Century."

"And they come here this year to dance during Ramadan!" shouted Salim.

"It sounds exciting," said Max. "Will it be possible for me to see them perform?"

"You will do more than just see them. Usually, non-Muslims may not watch. But because you and Salim are musicians, you will actually be invited to take part. You will help provide the music. The dervishes usually bring their own musicians, but this time they cannot bring all their people."

Salim let out a yelp of excitement. "I will play *rubab* for dervishes!"

"Yes, now go see to your goat while I talk with Max. Oh, and Salim, you must tell no one that the dervishes are coming. That is very important. Tell no one."

"Yes, father. My lips are stitched."

Dawud sipped his tea and turned to Max. "I had word from the dervishes that they would come because they heard from me that you are here. These are the friends I mentioned some weeks ago. I am a member of the Dervish order, although I am not one of its dancers. They must be extra careful these days. The Taliban hate us dervishes because, as Sufis, we believe in love of humanity and tolerance of all religions. Sufis are anathema to Wahhabism. The Taliban would exterminate all Sufis if they could. These dervishes live in a hidden monastery, and they perform publicly only on special occasions. I invited them because I think they may be able to help solve the mystery of your vision. They may also be able to help you return to the Americans."

"But how did you contact the dervishes? By magic? Neither you nor Salim has been away recently."

Dawud chuckled. "A little bit of magic, perhaps."

Dawud lifted the edge of the rug covering the low wooden platform on which the stove resided. He inserted his finger into a hole in the side, which opened a small compartment. He withdrew a chunky black satellite phone and showed it to Max. Then he returned it to its hiding place.

"Your CIA approached me when I was in the United States trying to gather support for Afghanistan during the Russian incursion. I refused them at that time, not wanting to become entangled in foreign intrigue. Suraya and I returned to Afghanistan when the Russians left. We wanted to help rebuild the country. Then the Taliban took over the government and murdered Suraya. The CIA contacted me again before I came here. They asked me to provide general information about Afghanistan and about the Taliban when I see or hear of them. The CIA gave me the phone for that purpose. The dervishes also have such a phone. Now, America is at war with the Taliban. If America can rid us of these devils and establish a democracy here, I am proud to help. In fact, I was there on purpose to observe the Taliban when they attacked your convoy, and you were blown up."

Max stared at Dawud. "Good Lord! I was rescued by a spy."

They both broke out laughing.

***

It would be several more weeks, near the end of Ramadan, when the dervishes were expected. Dawud had told no one except the *mullah* and the *malik* about the dervishes. They swore to tell no one else. They both knew the entire village would be in danger if the Taliban found the dervishes here. The dervishes would dance in the mosque, which was the largest building in the village.

During the weeks of waiting, during the daily fasting, Dawud taught Max and Salim some of the special music the dervishes required. Salim took to the dervish music immediately with his *rubab.* Dervish music had similar cadences, harmonies, and rhythms to other Afghan music with which Salim was already familiar.

Dawud would establish the rhythm for them on his tabla drum. It took Max some time to learn how to blend in appropriately. This music sure wasn't jazz. It had little melody; its sonorities wove a droning matrix of sound in a minor key. However, Max soon found his Chromonica worked well to help produce this strange, hypnotic music.

***

Finally, the dervishes arrived on the penultimate day of Ramadan. Dawud, Salim, and Max had been up before dawn so they could eat the pre-fast meal. Dawud sent Salim up on the roof to watch for the dervishes. He soon called out that he saw riders. Five horsemen rode into the village soon after dawn. Dawud, Max, and Salim walked down to meet them.

The dervish leader, Hassam, was an old friend to Dawud. They hugged each other exuberantly and kissed cheeks. Then Dawud introduced Max and Salim. Hassam spoke to Max in good English, then introduced the other four dervishes to him.

"Hassam speaks fluent English, Max, as you see," said Dawud. "But he will prefer to speak in Pashto and have me translate for you when we are among the villagers."

Salim saw to stabling the horses while Dawud and Max walked the dervishes to the mosque. They encountered several villagers along the way, and Dawud explained about their guests, telling them to spread the word that the dervishes would dance that night.

The *mullah* met them at the mosque with a bow and arm clasp. He ushered them into its interior. Max remained outside since the dervishes would be refreshing themselves and performing their morning prayers.

As he walked back toward Dawud's house, Max sighted the *malik* and the *mirab,* making their way toward the mosque. Max ducked into the shadows of an alley to avoid being seen by them. Max noticed the *mirab,* the water master, was scowling and vociferating at the *malik.*

***

The dervishes were to perform that night after the daily fast was completed. The *mullah* invited Dawud, Max, and Salim to join them for the evening meal. Soon afterward, the entire village population showed up to watch the dervishes perform. The rugs had been removed from the floor of the mosque's main prayer room for the ceremony. The floor was of smooth, polished concrete. The men gathered on one side of the room; the women and children occupied the opposite side. Dawud, Max, Salim, and two village musicians who knew the music, sat on the platform from which the *mullah* usually preached.

The music began slow and solemn, barely a murmur, but the silent crowd could easily hear it. After a few minutes, the five dervishes entered through a side door. They were dressed in floor-length black capes and tall, cylindrical brown hats made of camel hair. Each crossed his arms in an X on his chest. After circling the dancing space three times, each bowed to the *mullah.* They removed their cloaks and handed them to the mullah. Dawud had explained to Max that the black cloak symbolized the human ego and, with its removal, the rejection of ego, so the soul can quest for spiritual truth.

When the cloaks were removed, everyone saw that the five dervishes were appareled in long-sleeved, white linen jackets over a white gown with a skirt down to the floor. They wore loose white linen pants underneath the skirts. Their feet were shod in black slippers. A wide black waistband completed their costume. The five formed a large circle on the polished floor. They stood very straight and tall, extending their arms out and up above shoulder height. Their right hands pointed up toward heaven, their lefts toward earth.

In unison, they slowly turned from right to left by stepping with the right foot completely over the left and rotating on the ball of the left foot. Dawud had told Max before the ceremony that the whirling represented revolving around the heart, which symbolized embracing all humanity with love. "As Rumi told us, 'Humanity has been created with love, to love. All loves are a bridge to Divine Love.'"

The music now increased in pace and intensity, and the five dancers whirled more rapidly, their skirts flaring out wide around them. Their dance looked effortless and exquisitely graceful. Max, although totally immersed in the flow of the music, was also fascinated by the dance. The experience was magical. He wished Kitty could be here with him to see it.

Now Hassam, the lead dancer, glided to the center of the circle, still whirling. The other four revolved around him, equidistant, rotating slowly counterclockwise in perfect synchrony. It soon became obvious to Max that Hassam had entered an ecstatic trance. He was whirling twice as fast as the others, his face was toward the ceiling, his skirt fully extended. His face radiated rapture. Max wouldn't have been surprised to see Hassam levitate into the air. Dawud kept up the rapid tempo with his tabla for several minutes, then gradually slowed the pace. The dancers slowed their rotation accordingly.

The music volume slowly decreased, became a sustained tone, and then silence. The dancers spiraled to a stop, stood immobile for a few moments, then walked from the dance floor with their arms again in the X position. There were murmurs of approval from the crowd, but no applause since this was a serious religious ceremony rather than entertainment.

The *mullah* came forward and said a prayer. The villagers dispersed quietly until they were outside. Most had candles or lamps to light their way home. Max, Dawud, and Salim watched as the multitude of small lights scattered into the surrounding darkness like a swarm of lightning bugs.

Returning to the mosque, the three found the dervishes dressed in their traveling clothes. Salim translated for Max as Dawud spoke with Hassam. "I thought you would stay the night, brother. Why are you dressed to travel?"

"Two things were revealed to me during the dance," said Hassam. "Max's vision was strong and true. I will speak with him later about it. But

I was also made to know that someone among the watchers has betrayed us to our enemies. We must leave tonight before the Taliban arrive."

Max touched Dawud's arm. "This morning, I saw the *malik* and the *mirab* coming toward the mosque. The *mirab* seemed angry. Perhaps it is he who informed the Taliban."

Dawud growled. "Yes, he is the most likely one. He resents his lack of influence in the village. He may even know of your affront to his daughter. And he has a horse. He may have sent one of his sons to the Taliban during the dancing."

The *malik* had remained with them at the mosque. He confirmed the mirab had been angry about not being told the dervishes were coming. Dawud turned back to Max. "We must ride with the dervishes tonight. The village will no longer be safe for you or us. Let us pack a few things and be off. The *malik* will provide horses for us."

Salim ran to get the horses. Dawud and Max returned home and packed clothes, food, water, a few favorite books, and the satellite phone. Salim brought the horses. His *rubab* was slung over his shoulder. Kaj stayed close to Salim, knowing something was afoot.

They mounted and joined the dervishes on the road leading away into the desert. Dawud had a powerful flashlight to help show them the way since there was no moon tonight. However, Hassam told him to turn off the light. Soon their eyes had acclimated to the darkness, and they found they could see well enough by the light of the Milky Way, radiant as a lake of light above them.

"We seem to be dangerously exposed," said Max. "Won't the Taliban come in vehicles?"

"Probably," replied Dawud, "but they may be quite a distance away. And they will assume the dervishes would stay the night. They are likely to come at dawn. If we make it to the hills without being observed, we should be safe, *inshallah*."

Hassam dropped back beside them and spoke to them in Pashto, which Dawud translated for Max. "Rumi said, 'The deepest love is one with many difficulties. Who avoids those is not a real lover. It takes great courage to do the dance of lovers.' Embrace these difficulties. You are protected by universal love."

Chapter Twenty-Seven

"Night and Day"

Afghanistan, November 2002

The eight riders proceeded slowly along the hard road for several miles. It was merely a bare dirt path, almost indistinguishable from the surrounding desert in the swallowing darkness. The leading dervish must have excellent night vision to keep them on this faint track. Max couldn't discern it even after his eyes fully adjusted to the moonless dark.

The frigid night bit into their exposed faces and hands. Max was thankful there was no wind to make it worse. Like the others, a long wraparound Afghan *pagray* turban covered his head and neck. He kept it over his face as well, except when he exchanged a few words with Dawud. The group traveled in silence, concentrating on the trail. Max soon allowed his mind to wander. He gazed often at the immense radiance of the Milky Way. He imagined it as a friendly spirit, guiding them to safety.

Max must have dozed for a while, relaxed by fatigue and by the gentle rocking motion of the horse. He sank into a dream that he was in a small boat. Kitty was there at the other end. But when he tried to go to her, the boat rocked as if to turn over. Max jerked awake when he felt himself losing his balance. He felt Dawud's hand on his shoulder pushing him back upright.

"We will soon leave this path and cut across the plain, so you must be alert."

A few minutes later, the leader turned them toward the jagged line of hills that were just a darker silhouette against the night sky. One dervish lagged behind to erase or confuse their tracks where they turned off. Soon, the going became even slower, requiring them to navigate around boulders and ravines. After several hours of carefully picking their way, Max noticed that the sky was becoming a little lighter. The hills were now looming large.

They arrived at the strange rock hills just as dawn sent their shadows streaking out across the barren plain. These hills were really a tangled labyrinth of enormous boulders, natural megaliths. They progressed in size from shoulder-high stones to granite immensities soaring hundreds of feet vertically. The bleak beauty of these gargantuan standing stones amazed Max. Their geometries had no consistent form but were like a jumble of half-constructed toy blocks some giant child had abandoned. The pathways through this city of stone were often narrow and branching, very much like a maze. However, their dervish guide obviously knew where he was going.

"I see what you meant when you said we would be safe in these hills," said Max. "They are like none I've ever seen. Armies could hide in here."

"These rock formations extend for miles in all directions," said Dawud. "Not only is the dervish monastery well-hidden, but the people who have lived here for many generations also protect it. We call them bandits, but they are just descendants of runaway slaves, outcasts, and renegades from society. They seldom venture beyond this safe haven. We dervishes are non-violent, but these other residents could decimate any army that attempted to invade. The Russians learned that lesson here early on and gave up on it."

"But the Taliban?" asked Max.

"These bandits defend us dervishes against the Taliban as well. They refuse to live under Taliban *Wahhabism* or any other imposed governance. They have been watching us since we entered."

Max glanced around but saw no evidence of being observed.

It took another hour of slow riding before they entered a narrow, grassy valley where water trickled from a small spring-fed pond to irrigate some gardens. A few horses, goats, and camels grazed on the far side of the water, watched over by children. Several men and women were working in the gardens. The travelers unsaddled their mounts and turned them loose to join the other animals. Salim turned Kaj loose in the valley where he could range about by day and crawl into a haystack to keep warm at night.

Max was stiff and sore from the unaccustomed riding. He looked around for the monastery. There were no buildings in the valley. Then he saw a large wicker basket attached to several ropes ratcheting down from an opening in the rock face fifty feet above them. Two by two, the dervishes and their guests ascended in this Afghan elevator.

The basket brought them to a wooden platform against the opening in the rock. The cave-like interior was refreshingly cool after the heat that had radiated from the high boulders during the last part of their journey. Dawud, Salim, and Max were shown to a room with a window to the outside. The wall between the window and the room was about six feet thick. The sparsely furnished room was much like Dawud's house, with rugs on the floor and pillows on which to sit or recline.

A young acolyte, a little older than Salim, brought them a basin of water with which to freshen themselves. The boy stared at Max, then spoke to Salim. The two boys were soon in an animated conversation, laughing with each other. After the travelers had washed their faces and hands, the child escorted them to a refectory where they took tea, fresh bread, and fruit with Hassam.

They ate and made small talk about the journey for a while. Max thanked Hassam for rescuing them from the probability of capture by the Taliban. He also apologized to Dawud for disrupting his life and putting him and Salim in danger. “I hope the Taliban won’t punish your village for harboring me. Do you think you will be able to return and resume your life there?”

“We Afghans have become accustomed to disruption,” said Dawud with a grim smile. “And we Sufis accept that life is an ordeal with anguish and suffering that are essential to a soul’s growing into deeper love, which turns disappointment into joy.”

Hassam chuckled and added, “Sufis say that just the right disaster comes at just the right moment to break us open to what the heart requires.”

“I am in sympathy with your philosophy,” said Max. “It surely requires more courage than I can muster. However, I feel my entire view of life has transformed during my months here with Dawud and now you dervishes. I learned to slow down and enjoy life’s simple pleasures. Now I see more beauty in the world and in all people. I was running away from life when I arrived in Afghanistan. Now I am learning to walk toward life. And Rumi is winning me over to the love of, well, everything.”

“I hope you still feel that way when I tell you more about your vision and its meaning,” said Hassam. “But that must wait just a little longer. For now, let me show you around our monastery. You must endure our hospitality for at least a few more days. There is no need to hurry now. You are safe among friends.”

Hassam led them down a long hallway with rooms off to each side. The rough gray granite walls of the hall and those of the other rooms sparkled with grains of quartz that caught the light. Every twenty feet or so, a square, white ceramic tile had been set into the walls at adult eye-level. The tiles featured Arabic calligraphy in dark blue.

"What do these tiles say?" asked Max.

"Ah, each is a poem or saying by Rumi or one of our other Sufi saints," said Hassam. "This one by Rumi says, 'Submit to love without thinking, as the sun rose this morning recklessly extinguishing our star-candle minds.' These sayings remind and inspire us continuously."

Most of the rooms to their right featured large open windows to the outside, like that in their room and the refectory. The windows could be closed with wooden shutters that would keep out the elements but allow breezes to enter. Some rooms were lit by oil lamps or candles. Several rooms were spacious. One looked to be a prayer room. In another, dancers and musicians practiced, several of them unveiled women. A third was a crafts room with weavers and potters, including more women. The rooms on the other side of the hallway must have been smaller, private bedrooms or apartments. Their wooden doors were spaced closer together and were closed.

"How long has this monastery existed?" asked Max.

"Since your 14th century, about one hundred years after Rumi founded our *Mevlevi* Order of Sufis," said Hassam. "We were persecuted during that time as now. This cave had been here for centuries before we came. It was a redoubt of the bandits. They offered it to our founder and his small group of refugees, who had wandered here looking for a safe place to build a monastery. It was of lesser size then. Over the centuries, our people enlarged it. We have a mutually beneficial relationship with the bandits. We provide religious and educational services for them. Some of them have become dervishes."

"I noticed women among your dancers and crafters. So, you are not just a male monastery?"

"Women may be Sufis too. We have many families here. The boy who brought you water is my son, Kabir." Hearing his name, the boy came forward, and Hassam tousled his hair affectionately and kissed his forehead.

At the end of the hall, a stairway led down to a lower level of storage rooms. One featured a large cistern fed by the same trickling spring that created the pond in the valley. Hassam conducted them to another room on that level, the door to which was closed. When they entered, Max understood why. The air was warm and moist. There was a depression in the floor about twelve feet square and three feet deep containing warm water. The interior walls of the pool were of the same smooth, white ceramic tile as those that decorated the walls of the corridors. Pipes from a cast-iron box stove extended into one end of the pool. Steam rose from the pool's surface. The four dervishes who had journeyed with them were relaxing in the water, grinning up at them.

"This is our *hammam*, our hot water for bathing. If you care to join us there, I think you will find it refreshing after your travels."

Dawud and Max looked at each other, shrugged, and began removing their clothes. Kabir took Salim off to show him more of the extensive interior and then outside to romp with some other children in the grassy valley. The seven men were soon soaking the soreness from their muscles. They also scrubbed themselves with rough homemade soap. A few minutes later, an attendant came in, took away their soiled clothes, and provided fresh ones.

"How do you heat the water?" asked Max. "It feels wonderful!"

"With some difficulty," said Hassam. "The animals in the valley provide ample dung for our gardens. We dry the excess and bring it up here to fuel the kitchen stoves and ovens, and the furnace that heats this water. But there are also coal deposits nearby for which we trade with the bandits. We heat the water only once a week. Another reason I wanted to return today. The Taliban provided us with an excellent excuse." Dawud and Max chuckled and sighed with the contentment of unaccustomed luxury.

***

After soaking in the *hammam* for an hour making small talk, Hassam guided Max and Dawud back upstairs to their original room. They reclined on the pillows and were served tea and sweets. Hassam said, "I will now tell you what was revealed to me about your vision as I danced in the mosque yesterday."

Max scrutinized Hassam's face. He saw Hassam was hesitant, as if not sure how to proceed. "Was it a bad omen?" Max blurted. "Is Kitty in danger?"

"No, quite the contrary," said Hassam. "But it will require some explanation since it is a complex and sensitive subject." Hassam sipped his tea, then continued. "That you saw your lover wearing Dawud's scarab amulet is puzzling. It means that she is calling to you from a future time when she possesses the amulet rather than Dawud. I cannot tell you how that comes about."

"From the future!" exclaimed Max with a nervous chuckle. "How can that be? The vision itself is extraordinary without the idea that it comes from the future."

Dawud interjected before Hassam could reply. "It is extraordinary, but quite possible. Many Sufi mystics and seers from other spiritual traditions have had visions of the future—prophecies, premonitions. Even modern science supports the concept of the future affecting our lives. I had a college class in quantum physics for non-physics majors. One thing I recall from it is that time is really a unity rather than progressive. We usually experience time in a serial manner, from present to future, because we are immersed in it. But the future already exists somehow and can influence the present."

"Yes, I've read about Einstein's theory of the unity of time," said Max. "I've always thought of time as being like a phonograph record. The needle of time moves along the groove of life. We experience only the momentary sound, but the entire symphony is already there. Does that imply we have no free will? That everything is already determined?"

"No, I think not," said Dawud. "The future depends on our freely decided actions. But there is a constant interaction between the present and the future. So, our individual experience of time is more like us playing the music for the dervishes. We improvise within a general context. We experience only the present moment, but we can change the music as we go. That changes the ending, which influences the way you improvise."

Hassam smiled. "Rumi voiced that same idea hundreds of years ago: 'The beginning of eternity and the end of eternity arch into Union.'"

Dawud continued, "Occasionally, a hugely significant effect will reflect strongly back to us from our future. We experience it as both now and then. That is what happened with your vision of Kitty. It was—or will be—so intense that it resonated back to you through time."

"Intense? Does that mean that she somehow knew, or will know, that I was blown up and nearly died?"

"Perhaps that, or perhaps it will involve some extraordinary future event," said Dawud. "I've read that many people had premonitions of the 911 tragedy. You and Kitty are intimately connected mentally and spiritually. Some powerful, emotional, future event will cause—did cause—your vision of her."

Max slowly shook his head, awed by their words. "What sort of event could be of such importance?"

"We cannot know what the event is. Our knowing would surely alter it," said Hassam. "Perhaps the vision is significant because you and your lover are of great importance to the world."

"I love Kitty more than anything," said Max, "but I can't imagine that our love is of any historical significance. I just want to have a normal married life with her."

"All love is important," said Hassam. "Love is really the most important thing there is. We, Sufi, and most notably Rumi, teach that human love and divine love are one. Love is a spiritual energy both dispensed and required by God. The evils of this world are caused by insufficient love energy. When people express love in any manner, they generate love energy for God. But particularly when couples make love, they generate love energy most strongly. Our love energy nourishes God, of whom we are an intimate aspect. That is the purpose for which humans evolved. Love energy helps heal this broken world through God's mercy."

Max gasped. "That's amazing. I've never heard of that belief. Is it unique to Sufis? If it is true, and if it were widely known and practiced...."

Dawud interjected, "The Jewish and Christian Kabbalists also believe in the need to heal the world through love. They call it *Tikkun*. We Sufis believe there are certain couples that are particularly powerful generators of love energy. God intends their union for that purpose. When they make love, good things happen in the world. Evil will be diminished significantly."

Hassam continued, "Dawud and his wife, Suraya, were such a couple. We believe their love helped end the Russian occupation of our country."

"You never mentioned this," said Max, staring in amazement at Dawud.

"It is not something to advertise," said Dawud with a frown, "and Suraya's death is a continuing sadness for me."

"So, you believe Kitty and I are one of these special couples that can help heal the world?"

"Yes, that is what was revealed to me," said Hassam. "Tell me, when you and Kitty first became lovers, did anything unusual occur?"

"Well, I have been in love with Kitty for years, but she married my friend, Larry. He convinced her he might not have long to live and needed her help. She is very tenderhearted and easily persuaded by someone as self-assured as Larry. So, Kitty and I remained only good friends for many years. Then one night Kitty and I were alone together by chance when Larry was out of town. I remember looking into her eyes and seeing some strange, wonderful thing that I can't describe. She must have seen it too, because she said she wanted me, needed me. We immediately made love."

"Yes, you saw God looking at you from her eyes, compelling you to make love," said Dawud. "Something similar occurred between Suraya and me. You and Kitty were making love not only to each other but to God as well. You were generating love energy to the God Cosmos."

"And did the world seem more peaceful during your love affair?" asked Hassam.

"That was an ecstatic few months for me, so I didn't really pay much attention to the world situation. However, a few weeks after our affair ended, the September 11 terror attacks occurred."

"Love energy from only one or a few couples can suppress but not eliminate the evils of this world," said Hassam. "The world needs thousands of couples like you and Kitty."

"Perhaps it is your mission from God not only to generate love energy yourselves," said Dawud, gazing intently at Max, "but to persuade other couples that their love can help heal the world."

"My inability to persuade people of anything has always been my dominant quality," said Max with a snort.

"Do not be so self-deprecating, Max," said Dawud. "You can inspire people through your poetry, which is powerful. I can quote Rumi, but you could be, should be, a modern Rumi."

Max gulped. "I wish, but surely not."

"Only about five percent of people are dominant personalities," said Hassam. "They usually seek to dominate others. Your friend Larry is probably one of those. But perhaps five percent of those dominant personalities are what I would call independent seekers, what the psychologist Maslow called self-actualized. They do not pursue dominance over others but truth in things and ideas. They often become major artists and thinkers."

"And, perhaps five percent or even less of those few combine art and ideas with the genuine ability to express selfless love," said Dawud. "That is who you are, Max. You must embrace your true nature and employ it for the good of humanity."

"Yes," said Dawud, "you can attain that transcendent consciousness that Nietzsche believed humanity is developing toward. Rumi was such. So must you be."

Max flushed, his eyes blinking with incredulity, his body trembling.

"We must return you to the Americans as soon as possible," said Hassam. "You and Kitty must be reunited. The better destiny of the world may depend on you and her being reunited and persuading other couples to generate love energy."

Max yelped as he spilled hot tea onto his lap.

Chapter Twenty-Eight

"The Golden Striker"

Afghanistan, December 2002

Three days after Hassam's revelation about Max's vision of Kitty, preparations were complete to return Max to the American military base at Kandahar. Dawud had radio-phoned his contact in the CIA, who said they would arrange for a military helicopter to meet them. But they would first have to travel to the confluence of the Kushk-I-Nakhud River, flowing from the mountains where the Sufi's redoubt was hidden, and the larger, longer Arghandab River. The meeting place was about fifty kilometers northeast of Kandahar Air Base. This would involve a horseback trip of perhaps thirty kilometers over rugged country. Hassam estimated it would take eight to ten hours.

Max would be accompanied by Dawud, Salim, and two of the Dervish guides with whom they had traveled to the monastery. They would travel light to make the best time. The guides would return with the horses after the Americans picked up Max, Dawud, and Salim.

"How can we be sure there are no Taliban in that area?" asked Max.

"We can't be sure, of course," said Dawud, "but the Americans said they did a high flyover yesterday. They took pictures of the area without drawing attention to it. They will let us know if there was any unusual activity."

"Don't be in too much of a hurry," said Hassam. "You will want to stay here until the day after tomorrow. We are hosting a *Buzkashi* tomorrow."

"*Buzkashi*?" asked Max. "Is that more dervish dancing?"

Dawud threw up his hands and groaned. "No, this time it really is entertainment."

"It is the national sport of Afghanistan," said Hassam. "Ten men on horseback fight over the carcass of a goat and try to throw it in a goal circle."

"It's like American football on horseback but with much more violence," said Dawud. Then he turned to Hassam. "But surely your dervishes don't engage in *Buzkashi*!"

"No, it is our neighbors, the bandits, who play. Our valley has a perfect natural arena for the game, so we host their play two or three times a year. It helps us maintain good relations with them. We get a few players from outside the bandit maze as well."

"Sounds exciting," said Max. "Let's stay another couple of days and watch the game."

***

The next day, the sun rose golden into a thin scrim of high clouds. Hassam opined it would be a perfect day for *Buzkashi,* cold but bright with little wind. Horsemen appeared from several directions and mingled in groups on the far side of the valley, which featured a flat field about three times as long and wide as a football field. They soon scribed a ten-foot chalk circle at each end of the arena. There were no other markings.

A crowd of men, women, and children assembled along the sides. They sat on and stood atop boulders that had long ago been cleared from the field to create boundaries and rough stadia for viewing the game area. Max, Hassam, Dawud, Salim, and Kabir occupied one such boulder. Kaj was glad to be with Salim again and stayed by his side as they watched the action.

Soon, five horsemen gathered at each end of the field, one group costumed in yellow, the other in red. The men wrapped themselves heavily in cloth and each wore a leather or metal helmet. Each held a short whip. The horses snorted and cantered about with nervous energy. A man plodded onto the field, dragging the goat's headless, gutted carcass and deposited it midway between the two teams. As he hurried to the sidelines, a bugle blew; the riders galloped toward the goat at breakneck speed.

The two teams crashed into each other, slashing with their quirts at their opponents as well as at the horses, which bucked, whirled, and reared in frenzy. Several minutes into this chaos, one man leaned down and grabbed the goat. But the other team quickly set upon him, causing him to drop the prize before he could go far. The teams repeated this occurrence several times during the next half hour as they pushed each other about the field, slashing, slamming, and bashing their opponents.

During the constant brawl, several men and horses were injured. One man fell from his mount, and the frenzied herd trampled him. Unable to remount, he limped to the sidelines, leaking blood as a fresh member of his team rushed into the melee.

The action moved back and forth toward one end of the field, then the other, until, with a shout of "*Allahu Akbar*!" one of the yellow-clad horsemen broke away, galloped with the goat, and tossed it into the chalk circle. The crowd erupted with cries, whistles, and ululations. Kabir and Salim leaped about screaming wildly with the other spectators. Kaj wanted to go for the goat himself and had to be ordered back and reprimanded by Salim. The teams regrouped, brought in fresh combatants, and, after an intermission, resumed the game.

Max was amazed. "My God! I've never seen anything so vicious. Aren't there a lot of serious injuries or deaths?"

"Oh, yes," said Hassam. "Our medical people always get plenty of practice with *Buzkashi*. There have been a few deaths over the years."

"This is actually a mild version of the sport," said Dawud. "In the past, *Buzkashi* was often played with the bodies of vanquished enemies."

The game went on until dark, with the yellow team winning by two goats. Before that, Max, Dawud, and Hassam had retreated to the monastery for lunch and final preparations for their journey. Kabir, Salim, and Kaj stayed to watch the game in fascination to its conclusion.

***

That night, chaotic dreams troubled Max's sleep. Stampeding horses menaced Kitty and him. He awoke sweating in the pre-dawn dark and lay awake meditating until Dawud arose yawning and stretching from his bedding. They ate a last breakfast with Hassam, who informed them that some of the *Buzkashi* riders had volunteered to accompany and protect them on their journey.

"How did they know we were leaving this morning, or why?" asked Dawud.

"I'm not sure," said Hassam. "Perhaps one of the dervishes mentioned it during the games yesterday."

"Will it be safe traveling with these strangers?" asked Max. "I hope they know we won't be carrying anything valuable."

"I will speak with them and with your dervish guides before you leave," said Hassam.

An hour later, the travelers assembled in the valley below the monastery. Besides Max, Dawud, Salim, and the two dervish guides, five of the *Buzkashi* men arrived to travel with them. Hassam conversed with his dervishes and then with the *Buzkashis*.

"These five say they came from near Kandahar to take part in the *Buzkashi.* They must return the way you are going, so they agreed to accompany and protect you on your journey. They don't know you are meeting the Americans along the way. One of them overheard Salim and Kabir mention the trip during the game yesterday."

Dawud asked Salim if this was true. "Yes, Father, I am sorry. I not realize it put us in danger. Kabir say he was glad I am staying for the game and not leave for Kandahar until today. We were petting *Buzkashi* horses that were not yet ride in game. One attendant must have heard us."

"It seems innocent enough to me," said Dawud. "Let us be on our way."

Soon the ten riders were weaving their way through the stone maze toward Kandahar. Kaj ambled along beside Salim. Soon after they exited the jumble of granite megaliths, Salim looked back. Something had caught his eye above the towers' heights.

"Look! A kite!" said Salim, pointing to a large red box kite trembling in the breeze hundreds of feet in the air above one of the inner spires. "Maybe Kabir is saying farewell."

"Let's hope it is as innocent as that," growled Dawud.

The riders now advanced onto the open plain. They arranged themselves with the five *Buzkashi* men in the lead, the two dervish guides next, and Max, Dawud, and Salim bringing up the rear.

Max scrutinized the *Buzkashis,* who seemed relaxed and amiable, often conversing animatedly among themselves. One was an older man, or so it seemed by his gray beard and heavily lined face. He carried a long, narrow leather bag strapped to his back. The other four were younger, with shorter, dark beards. They each cradled a rifle or AK47 on their laps or hung from their saddles.

Travelers in these little-known regions never knew whether bandits or rogue militias might set upon them. So, everyone traveled armed if they could. One of the *Buzkashis* still wore a yellow helmet from the previous day's game. The others covered their heads with standard *pagray* turbans, as did Dawud, Max, and Salim. Neither of the dervishes was armed. They were avowed pacifists. Max carried only his Chromonica, food, and water. Salim had his *rubab* case slung on his saddle. Dawud likewise was unarmed but had the satellite phone and binoculars in his pack.

After several hours of riding, Max had relaxed and was conferring with Dawud about what he had learned from their conversation with Hassam. "Why are such visions as I had so rare, do you think?"

"I can only conjecture, of course, but I think it happens only to those few people who are mentally open to God even if they don't know it. You have a questing mind and a kind heart. God had His eye on you. Then, when you were blown up, there was the opportunity to expand your mind into the spiritual realm. Some philosophers call it cosmic consciousness."

"Yes, I've read about peak experiences and cosmic consciousness," said Max. "Poets such as Blake and Whitman had such spiritual episodes. If more people could learn how to experience cosmic consciousness, maybe humans could finally live together in peace."

"True, but I think humans are still evolving," said Dawud. "Most of us are like primitive lungfish that can come out of the water but are yet too weak to live full time on land. We are stuck between our animal consciousness and our potential spiritual consciousness. Only on rare occasions do the strongest of us experience spiritual, cosmic consciousness, as you did. So, we mostly stumble about yearning for the unattainable spiritual possibilities we intuitively sense exist. You may never have such an experience again, but that one has changed your life, has elevated your ordinary consciousness."

Max chuckled. "Well, I do often feel much like a fish out of water."

"What are those dust trails over there?" asked Salim.

There were indeed seven spumes of dust in the air several miles ahead, coming toward them in parallel. Dawud examined them through his binoculars, groaned, then turned to the others.

"There are seven vehicles coming this way. I believe they are probably the Taliban. They will reach us in maybe fifteen minutes," Dawud gritted his teeth and looked around. "Let us make for yonder promontory. The Taliban prefer to capture rather than kill us, so maybe we can delay them until I can call the Americans." He shouted to the *Buzkashis,* and they all galloped toward the nearby rocky mesa.

As they neared the mesa, the man in the yellow helmet pulled alongside Max, reached out, and grabbed his reins. Max tried to push him away, but his horse had come to a stop. The man pointed his rifle at Max and shouted in Pashto. He tried to pull Max toward the oncoming vehicles.

Salim, from behind Max, saw and called an order to Kaj. The dog latched onto Yellow Helmet's trouser leg, growling. Yellow Helmet released Max's reins to hit at the dog with his rifle butt, dislodging him with difficulty. Kaj circled the man's horse trying to attack the man's leg again. Finally getting his horse under control, Yellow Helmet shot Kaj before he could latch on again. Max and Salim were now alert and moving quickly away toward the up-thrusting mesa.

Yellow Helmet glared toward Max and Salim and again barked something in Pashto. Then, he spurred his horse toward the Taliban vehicles. Salim looked back and hesitated, wanting to check on Kaj.

"Leave him, son. He's dead. Kaj saved us. He's a hero. We must escape."

Max and Salim galloped to the steeply rising granite mass. They were the last to arrive. Salim was still raging about the killing of his beloved Kaj as they dismounted and scrambled up the steep-walled mesa.

The dervishes and *Buzkashis* were already near the top. Dawud was waiting halfway up for Salim and Max. He pointed out the easiest path for them to climb. They all finally made it over the top of the promontory just before the Taliban convoy halted several hundred yards away and expelled its passengers. Max lost count at twenty-five. All were armed with rifles and automatic weapons. Yellow Helmet met the convoy and pointed to the mesa as he talked with the leader.

Dawud lost no time in contacting the Americans with his satellite phone. "It is the Taliban. They will come at us from all sides soon. Please hurry. We are on top of this plateau, but we are far outnumbered and outgunned," said Dawud. "Yes, I will leave the phone on so you can home in on its location."

The top of their mesa was almost circular, fairly level, and about fifty yards in diameter. It rose from the surrounding plain, about sixty feet high. The sides were nearly vertical in most places, but there were a few steep yet climbable areas. Several boulders lay scattered about on the mesa's surface along with some sparse dry bushes.

Dawud had his arm around Salim, who was still raging about Kaj being killed. They and Max crouched together behind one of the central boulders. The dervishes were talking to each other near another of the rocks.

The old bearded man had moved near the edge closest to the enemy vehicles. He appeared very calm and deliberate. He removed the rifle from its long leather case. The other three *Buzkashis* had their guns out, but they were just observing the Taliban. They knew the enemy was too far away to bother shooting at them yet. They scouted about for good defensive positions near the perimeter.

Max looked around anxiously, desperate to do something useful, something decisive. He felt utterly helpless. Max watched the old Buzkashi with intense curiosity. He seemed too much at ease for such a dangerous situation. Max recalled his days helicoptering with Moonbear in Bosnia. This somehow felt much more perilous. Max feared for himself and his friends.

The old *Buzkashi* laid his rifle carefully atop his boulder, from which he could view the enemy vehicles. Max saw the rifle was an old-fashioned, long-barreled, heavy thing that only fired one shot before reloading. He doubted that such an antique could be of much help. The gun had a strange iron sight behind the firing mechanism. The sight could be lifted several inches high, where it would be close to the shooter's eye.

The old man adjusted this sight and squinted down the barrel. He tested the wind with a wet finger, tweaked the sight, exhaled, and then squeezed the trigger. Two seconds later, the betrayer's yellow helmet exploded, spraying the nearby Taliban leader with blood. The Taliban soldiers scattered like drenched cats. Most fell to the ground, seeking their attacker. Gray Beard chambered another long, fat cartridge.

One of the Taliban grabbed a four-foot-long metal tube from one vehicle. He aimed it at the mesa and fired. The rocket round whistled toward them but hit the side of the mesa several yards down from the top. The detonation threw up a cloud of dust. As the dust cleared, the old man fired again. Bazooka man's chest gushed blood as he flew backward while pulling its trigger. The second bazooka round went high and exploded in the desert well beyond their mesa. The Taliban crowd was now like a stepped-on ant bed. They ran about crazily, many trying to hide behind the vehicles. Others sought boulders or depressions for cover.

Dawud crawled over to talk with the old man. After a few minutes' discussion, Gray Beard removed a large revolver from his belt and handed it to Dawud. Then he took aim and downed another of the Taliban, who had been creeping forward in foolish bravado.

Dawud came back to the rock behind which Max and Salim were hiding. "The elder there came in 4th for rifle shooting in the '80 Olympics. He returned home to become a sniper. He killed many Russians with that rifle. He called it a Sharps Buffalo Gun."

"I've heard of those," said Max. "The U.S. Army killed Indians and buffalo at long range with them in America's Old West. That gun must be over a hundred years old."

"Seems to work well for him," said Dawud with a grimace. "Maybe he can hold them off until help arrives. He gave me this in case they get close." He showed Max the huge pistol.

"Let's hope you don't need to use it," said Max.

"They are move!" shouted Salim, who was standing atop their boulder.

The two end vehicles, a Land Rover and a pickup, went in opposite directions to circle around the mesa. Gray Beard put a bullet through the engine grille of the Land Rover. It came to an abrupt halt in a geyser of steam and disgorged its passengers. They came scampering toward the mesa in crouching zigzags. The pickup went around to the far side of the hill. One of the other *Buzkashi* relocated there with his AK-47.

The Taliban leader must have realized the sniper could not do rapid fire. He sent his men charging toward the mesa. The old man picked off two of them before they reached the base of the mesa. Now he would have to expose himself in order to get off a good shot.

Dawud told Salim to stay put and joined the sniper at the edge of the mesa. The old man would quickly peek over the edge to see where they were, duck back as they fired, then reappear to shoot one he had targeted.

He was obviously a seasoned campaigner. Dawud used the sniper's strategy to track the progress of one coming steadily up the steep slope. As he neared the top, Dawud moved to a closer position and shot the man in the chest before he could clear the crest of the mesa.

As Dawud walked back from the rim, a hand-grenade came arcing from below and landed near him. He quickly kicked it back over the edge, so it exploded somewhere below.

Max stayed with Salim and gathered a pile of fist-sized rocks just to be doing something. He watched as the *Buzkashis* dispatched several more of the enemy as they emerged at the rim of the mesa. Then the nearest *Buzkashi* shrieked, jerked back and collapsed. Max ran to him and saw that his chest was gushing blood. Max grabbed the man's AK. He had never used one. He assumed it was ready to fire.

As Max was examining the weapon, a black-bearded face appeared above the edge of the mesa. Max brought the gun up and pulled the trigger. Nothing happened. *Oh, I must need to cock the gun by pulling back this little handle on the side*. The attacker, thinking Max's gun empty, grinned and levered himself up over the rim. He brought his rifle to bear on Max. They fired simultaneously, and the other lurched back over the edge with a scream. Max grimaced in triumph. *Now maybe I can do something useful*. But he felt strange. He shivered. Time slowed. His mind found itself in a hallucinatory fog. Everything now appeared unnaturally bright, and the others were now moving in slow motion. *This must be how* soldiers *feel in battle.*

Max heard chanting. In the middle of the plateau, he saw that the two dervishes were dancing. They did a slow synchronized rotation, their arms extended, right foot stepping over left, slowly turning, their voices intoning a prayer. Max gazed at them in amazement. Then he realized: *Oh, my side is wet and sticky. Damn! I've been shot. Why didn't I feel it? This can't happen.*

I've got to get home to you, Kitty. I promised you I'd return. And Hassam said it's vital you and I are together. I love you, Kitty. I'm coming back to you *somehow, my darling.*

Max was groaning and gazing about aimlessly when Salim screamed. Max turned to see the boy throw a rock at an attacker. *Where did he come from?* Max raised his gun to shoot the man, but Salim stepped forward and swung his *rubab* at the attacker. The Taliban had a bayonet on his rifle. Max froze. *No, Salim! I can't get off a shot without hitting you!*

In slow motion and excruciating detail, Max watched the *rubab* smash harmlessly against the man's shoulder. The bayonet blade, undeterred, slid into Salim's stomach as if into warm butter. As he withdrew the blade, the man's head blew apart in a gusher of blood. Dawud had raced over and shot him with the big revolver. As Max ran toward them, another grenade dropped nearby. Max kicked it back over the cliff and reached his friends.

Dawud cradled Salim in his arms and howled in anguish. Salim's stomach wound was welling blood. The boy was unconscious. Max felt like he was in a nightmare. He was acutely aware of the movements of everyone around him, as if he were viewing everything from above. But it felt like his body was struggling through quicksand. Noticing motion from the corner of his eye, he saw another marauder come charging toward them. Max tried to fire, but his rifle clicked empty.

The attacker raised his AK and howled, "*Allahu Akbar*!" But the last syllable was cut short as he jerked, spun, and collapsed. Gray Beard waved from the other side of the plateau. The dead man's blue turban fell from his head and tumbled to within a few feet of Max. ***Blue!***

The image of Kitty wearing the blue scarab flashed in his mind.

"The scarab, Dawud, the scarab!"

Dawud, his eyes blazing, abruptly understood. He tore open his shirt and ripped the scarab from his neck. He opened it with shaking fingers.

Max took up the pistol Dawud had dropped. He watched Dawud while glancing around for enemies. Max saw that the scarab contained some ten shining golden pills. They looked like the BBs Max had shot from his air rifle as a child. Dawud put one in Salim's mouth, but the unconscious boy couldn't swallow it.

"Put one directly in the wound," shouted Max.

Dawud did so, and rocked the lifeless boy in his arms, weeping. "He's gone! My sweet boy. These devils have murdered my son and my wife!" He held Salim tightly for a few moments, then laid the slack body tenderly next to the rock and covered it with his jacket. Dawud got to his feet, shaking with anger.

"Here, take the scarab," Dawud barked. "God must want you to have it. It has only been a curse for me." He snapped the scarab closed and handed it to Max, who took it in a daze and slipped it into his pocket. Max noticed again the blood on his shirt, but he still felt nothing. He turned back to his friend.

"Dawud, don't do anything foolish. If we can hold them off a little longer, surely the Americans will come."

"It does not matter now. I have tasted too much of this bitterness. I must go to be with Suraya and Salim." Dawud stood, took a few staggering steps, and quoted Rumi one last time. "I place one foot on this plain of death, and some grand immensity sounds on this emptiness."

Another attacker clambered over the rim of the mesa and was creeping toward Dawud. Max held the pistol in both hands and fired. The Taliban doubled over and sprawled on the ground, still writhing, but rapidly bleeding out. Max decided not to waste another bullet on him.

Dawud took no notice. He walked toward the center of the butte where the two dervishes were dancing, chanting, slowly rotating in their holy circles, oblivious to the sounds of gunfire, explosions, and the screams of the dying.

Then Max perceived another sound, a low rumble like distant thunder. He looked for its source and saw an airplane flying low, perhaps only a hundred feet above the ground, coming directly toward them. As it drew close, he recognized it as an A-10 Thunderbolt, what his Marine buddies had affectionately called a Warthog.

"Dawud, the Americans are here; come back."

Another grenade bounced, skittered, then came to a stop between Dawud and the dervishes. Dawud gazed at the small iron globe for a long moment, then fell upon it as if in prayer. The blast lifted his body like a rag doll. Max screamed and ran to him, but it was obvious his friend was gone.

Now everyone except the still-dancing dervishes watched as the plane drew near. The Warthog circled the mesa just thirty yards away, looming enormous, a nightmare monster. Some of the Taliban fired at it with their rifles to no effect.

Max could easily discern the shark's teeth and angry demon eyes painted on the A-10's nose. Then the shark's gaping maw spewed gouts of golden flame, raking the sides of the mesa. The Taliban became shredded bodies raining from the granite walls. The few survivors ran or crawled for their vehicles.

The plane turned toward the line of vehicles and pounded them with depleted uranium bullets in a staccato stream of yellow lightning from its Gatling-canon. The line of vehicles exploded like a string of firecrackers.

The Warthog gave a lazy wave of its wings to them and wandered off toward the southeast. A few minutes later, Max heard the distinctive whapping of helicopter blades. He was now trembling uncontrollably from the effects of the adrenaline that had been sustaining him against his loss of blood. With his tension released, he now noticed the stench and taste of cordite, blood, and hot metal in the air. Max stared amazed into the sky. Bright billowing clouds massed like an audience of gods above them, showing magnificent indifference to the scene of human violence. *Perhaps they view our madness like a Buzkashi game.*

The American troop copter circled the scene and landed atop the mesa in a plume of dust. A squad of Marines came boiling from the chopper as it touched down. They spread out over the area, ravenously seeking hostiles, and checking bodies for survivors.

Max put down the pistol, raised his hands, removed his burnoose, and shouted that he was American. His side was burning fiercely now but had stopped bleeding. His side didn't hurt nearly as much as his pain at the loss of Dawud and Salim.

The dervishes had quit dancing and stood with folded arms. The two remaining *Buzkashi* laid down their weapons and raised their arms. Max found the captain in charge and explained that the dervishes and *Buzkashi* were friends who had fought against the Taliban.

Fortunately, there were a couple of Pashto speakers among the Marines, so they could interrogate the dervishes and *Buzkashi.* They permitted *t*he old sniper to keep his Sharps, but they confiscated his horse pistol and the other men's weapons.

Max said, "Captain, will you take the bodies of my two friends back to base to be buried?"

"Yes, of course. In fact, Mr. *Al Balkhi* was a valued asset and colleague. We will provide for his funeral. Did you think we went to all this trouble just for you?"

Max forced a thin smile. "And his son?"

Just then a Marine said, "Hey! The boy is alive."

Max spun around to see Salim being carried by the Marine. Salim was awake and wide-eyed. "Max, we won. We are rescue."

"Let's get you all in the chopper and get airborne," said the captain. "I don't want any Taliban stragglers tossing a grenade at us. You and the boy need medical attention."

Salim shrieked in horror when he saw his father's body mangled on the ground. Max distracted Salim while they put Dawud into a body bag. Then they got everyone into the helicopter. Max hugged and comforted Salim. The boy's wound was now just an angry red scar on his stomach. Max was incredulous but said nothing.

A Marine medic attended to Max's wound. "The bullet must have glanced off a rib and made a shallow exit. No major damage, Mr. Ballard, but it will require some stitches and compression. You've lost considerable blood."

"Oh, I'm quite used to that," said Max.

The helicopter delivered the dervishes to the edge of their stone forest in only twenty minutes. Then it turned toward the air base with the *Buzkashis,* Max, and Salim.

Max remembered the scarab and took it from his pocket. He examined it in silent wonder. He tied the chain's ends together and slipped the amulet around his neck. It lay like an anvil against his chest. He took out his Chromonica, and, to make sure it was undamaged, played a solemn, grateful rendition of the 'Marines' Hymn.'

Chapter Twenty-Nine

"I'll Be Home for Christmas"

Afghanistan, Germany, America, December 2002

On arriving at Kandahar Air Base, Max and Salim were rushed to the hospital. Max had advised Salim not to mention that he had been stabbed. If they asked about the scar, he should just say it was an old wound and plead ignorance of how he got it.

Max had a cracked rib and a shallow rip where the bullet had lanced through his side. His old leg wound from the explosion had been re-injured. He had numerous minor cuts and scratches that required treatment. However, the doctor opined that Max was miraculously unscathed for having been in a major firefight with the Taliban.

They allowed Salim to stay with Max in the base housing. Intelligence officers interrogated them both, hoping to glean information about the Taliban and Al Qaida. They provided Max and Salim with new clothes, simply basic chinos and sweatshirts. Max was desperate to call home, but the military wouldn't allow it. The base tightly controlled communications. Max got the impression that the intelligence officers didn't quite trust him. He would have to wait until he was back in the States to make a call.

They held Dawud's funeral the day after their arrival since it is Islamic custom to bury a body as quickly as possible. A local Sufi mullah officiated at the funeral. Salim tried to remain impassive but cried and buried his head in Max's chest as his father's body sank into the ground. Max, too, shed many tears for the remarkable man who had become such a dear friend in such a brief time. It was grotesquely ironic to Max that Dawud had committed suicide thinking Salim was dead, that the scarab pills hadn't worked. *If he had just waited a little longer....*

The military scheduled Max to fly to Ramstein Air Base in Germany in a few days. They provided him with a temporary passport. He wanted to take Salim with him, and Salim wanted very much to go with Max. But they told Max the boy would have to remain at the base.

Max wanted to adopt Salim formally and take him home to the U.S. He knew that would be difficult since Max was not married nor related to the boy. Salim had no passport, birth certificate, or any other documents. Max spoke to the captain who rescued them. He promised to keep Salim on base and well looked-after until Max could either send for him or provide otherwise for the boy.

Salim soon acclimated to his strange new circumstances. The air base with its planes, helicopters, and variety of new experiences fascinated him. He quickly reverted to his naturally friendly, talkative self. Many of the airmen and Marines befriended him as he regaled them with his adventures in his rapidly improving English. He was also becoming more skilled at playing the Cromonica. He chatted and charmed everyone with whom he came into contact. Several of the military women were ready to adopt him themselves.

The day came when Max had to leave. He promised Salim that he would send for him as soon as possible. As he was about to board the plane, Max gave Salim a last hug, handed him the Cromonica, and told him they would play jazz together in America sometime soon.

***

The layover at Ramstein was supposed to take five days. It was getting close to Christmas. Max was eager to be home with his friends for the Christmas holidays. Military intelligence agents interrogated Max once again. They still wouldn't allow him to call home. The doctors reexamined his wounds, which seemed to be healing well. The doctors planned to keep him in the hospital for several days to test him for any contagious diseases he might have contracted. Still, they assured him he would be home well before Christmas.

Late the second night, as Max lay dozing in his hospital room, a hand touched his shoulder from behind. Thinking it was a nurse, he started to complain about being awakened.

A man whispered, "Quiet! Don't look at me. I'm a fellow journalist. I have a favor to ask. It may involve some danger. I hope not much, but I don't want you to be able to identify me."

The back of Max's neck tingled. "What is it you want?"

The man showed Max an ordinary, sealed, blank business envelope. "When you get to the U.S., just open this envelope and mail the inner envelope. It's already addressed and stamped. All you need to do is drop it in a mailbox."

"Why can't you do that?"

"They would know it was mailed from here and figure out who sent it."

"What if I'm searched? Will they find something illegal?"

"No. Just information that will embarrass the government about Iraq. The U.S. is planning to invade there soon. That's why you won't be suspected. You've only been in Afghanistan. They should have no reason to consider you. The inner envelope contains a micro-card. Only touch the outer envelope and dispose of it separately. That way, there won't be any fingerprints or DNA on the inner envelope."

"Those are heavy precautions. Are the authorities looking for this information?"

"They may have suspicions. This will be a major scandal. I can't say more. Will you do it?"

Max hesitated. "How can I be sure this isn't a trap, a test, or even a joke?"

"You have only my word and my thanks. I'm taking a big chance just coming here. But your ignorance should keep you safe. Will you do it?"

Max hesitated. Then, "Okay. I survived the Taliban twice. Maybe I've been kept alive for some greater purpose. I..." The envelope slid onto Max's lap and the stranger was gone. Max placed the envelope in the volume of Don Quixote he had found in the hospital exchange library. It took a long while for him to find sleep again. Then he dreamed of seeking Kitty among windmills with large black birds perched on their blades.

The next morning, one of his doctors met Max as he ate breakfast. During his initial examination of Max two days before, Doctor Bill Gillespie, a red-haired Irishman, discovered Max was a jazz musician. Max had asked him in jest if he was related to Dizzy Gillespie, the great black jazz trumpet player. Dr. Gillespie chuckled at the joke but admitted he was a jazz aficionado. He and Max had several conversations about jazz during the next couple of days between Dr. Gillespie's appointments. Gillespie had collected records by both Larry Delgado and Tiger Blakely. He was intrigued that Max knew them both well. Gillespie hadn't realized Max was the pianist on one of the records until Max mentioned it.

As Max ate his breakfast, Dr. Gillespie joined him with a cup of coffee.

"Max, I know you want to get back home in time for Christmas. You're scheduled to leave on a civilian flight the day after tomorrow. But it looks like we may be in for some heavy weather by then. Your flight could be delayed. So, if you're interested, I can get you on a military cargo rotator this afternoon. It won't be as comfortable, but it should get you to the U.S. a few days before Christmas. The passenger plane is bound for New York. The rotator will take you to Baltimore instead. Would that be a problem?"

"Heck, no. Baltimore will be fine. That would be wonderful, Bill."

"Okay. I'll arrange it. Your tests are all negative, so I don't see any need to keep you here any longer. Although I would love to continue our conversations about music. Maybe I should make you wait the full time."

"I tell you what, Bill. You get me on that cargo plane today and, when I get back home, I'll send you the latest recordings by both Larry and Tiger."

"Well, I guess it's a deal then," said Gillespie with a grin.

Max was on the cargo flight to Baltimore that afternoon. However, Dr. Gillespie forgot to cancel Max's reservation for the New York passenger flight, which left on time just before the storms would have delayed it.

***

The weather in Baltimore was cold and dreary. Dirty snow and slush quilted the streets. Max hopped a taxi from Andrews AFB to a hotel downtown. After checking-in and taking a long, hot, delicious shower, Max decided to walk around town. He needed to shop for clothes and other necessities he had lost in Afghanistan. He had been wearing the same clothes since leaving Kandahar.

However, his most pressing need was to get rid of the envelope. He walked a mile from the hotel and found a public mailbox. He tore open the outer envelope and slid the inner envelope untouched into the slot. Then he tore the outer envelope into pieces and put them in a trashcan.

Next, he went to a branch of the bank that held his account. He withdrew some cash and replaced his credit card. He bought a new cellphone and called Odetta at his law office. She squealed with surprise and joy when she heard his voice.

"Praise Jesus, Max, we thought you were dead! When we didn't hear from you for a month, we contacted the Associated Press. They said they hadn't received word from you in weeks. The military knew nothing about you either. You just disappeared."

"Yeah, I'm sorry about that, but it couldn't be helped. I got blown up in a Marine convoy. The authorities didn't know I was with the convoy. A friendly Afghan rescued me, and I lived in his village for the last six months. I'm fine now, just a little worse for wear. I'll tell you all about it when I get home."

"Max, Kitty has been worried sick about you too. She's been calling me every week since you left. When you disappeared, she was frantic and depressed. But she hasn't called me in over a week. Should I call her, or do you want to?"

"I'll call her. If I can't reach her, I'll call you back. I should be in Fort Worth in a few days. See you then."

Max was nervous about calling Kitty, afraid that Larry might grab her cell phone and become hostile. But Kitty answered, her voice quizzical, not recognizing his new number.

"Hi, Kitty, it's Max. I'm so sorry I haven't been in touch these last six months. I just arrived in Baltimore."

"Max! Oh, Max. Thank God! I've been so worried. Are you all right?" He could hear the relief in her voice. Then she was crying.

"I'm okay, darling, just a little banged up from a brawl with the Taliban. How are you?"

"Oh, Max, it's not me, it's Larry. He's been in the hospital for the last two days. He had a heart attack. They have him stabilized finally. And they say they now have a way to fix his heart defect. The surgeon plans to operate tomorrow. Larry's been asking about you, wishing he could talk to you. I think he wants to make up with you."

"In that case, I'd better hop a plane as soon as possible. Text-message me with the details. I love you, Kitty. I can't wait to see you."

He immediately called the airport and booked an early-morning flight.

***

Max arrived at DFW early the next morning and grabbed a taxi to St. Joseph Hospital. Kitty had given him the room number. He found her seated in the hallway outside the room, reading. She jumped up when she saw him, leapt into his arms, and kissed him.

"Oh, Max, you're so gaunt! But it's you, my darling, it's you!" Her eyes devoured him, and her arms locked around him. Max held her off the floor and whirled her around as if he were a dervish. He winced a little as she squeezed his cracked ribs, but he hugged her to him and did some serious devouring with his own eyes. He could hardly believe he was holding her after all those months of desiring her and dreaming of her.

"You should have seen me before I shaved my six-month beard and lost my burnoose. I had to look like an Afghan over there. Only the thought of you kept me alive."

"Oh, Max, I've missed you the whole time. But I've been worried sick since you disappeared. I was so afraid you had died, like my father. But I somehow sensed you were alive."

"It was my love for you that kept me sane and enabled me to return. Do you still have what I gave you when I left?"

"The torn two-dollar bill? Yes, it's right here in my purse. But you'll have to put me down so I can get it."

"No way, I'm holding on to you the rest of my life, one way or another."

But he reluctantly released her. She slipped her half-bill from its hiding place, then asked, "Do you still have your half?"

Max stooped down to remove the bill from his boot lining and handed it to her. "It's the only thing I didn't lose. I promised I'd come back to you, darling. I don't want to ever leave you again." They each held up their half of the bill and saw how they fit together.

"We can have an official joining of the bill ceremony tonight over wine, darling," said Kitty. "And I want you to tell me all about your adventures, but first you should say hello to Larry. I think he's still awake. They may come for him any time now."

"I'd much rather stay out here and catch up on kissing you."

"We will definitely do that a little later," she giggled. "But Larry is anxious to speak with you. I told him you were on your way. You'll want to hear what he has to say. I'm going to get us some coffee. I'll be back soon, and maybe the three of us can talk."

Max slipped his half of the two-dollar bill back inside his boot. He entered Larry's room. His friend was connected to several tubes and monitors with numbers jumping and squiggles flowing across their screens. Larry's eyes were closed, but he must have sensed Max's presence.

"Max, glad you showed up in time for my last solo, pard." Larry's voice was hoarse but clear.

"Why do you say that? I thought this new operation has a good chance of success."

"The doc says so, but he's prob'ly just trying to keep my spirits up. It's still 'sperimental. Anyway, I figure I might make a bigger splash dead than alive. The headline in *Down Beat* will read: 'Alto Sax Jazz Giant, Larry Delgado, Dies Too Soon, But His Music Lives On.' Did Kitty tell you I won the Grammy this year?"

Max sat on the bed to hear Larry better. "No, we haven't really had a chance to talk yet. Congratulations. I knew you would win it. But seriously, you've got to hang in there and be positive about this operation. You have a lot more choruses before the head."

Larry pointed at his head in the gesture of a jazz leader indicating the last chorus of a tune to his sidemen. "Maybe so. I've mellowed a lot since the pressure's off about the Grammy. Kitty's been depressed ever since you left. I realize now she loves you more than me; prob'ly always did. I tried to give her stability and security, but I reckon she needs more than that. 'specially since she can't have children. So, I decided if I pull through this heart thing, I'll give her a divorce. 'Course, if I die on the table, she won't need one."

"That's wonderful news, Larry. Uh, not the thought that you might die, I mean, but that we can be friends again. Thank you from both Kitty and me. I want us to jam a lot more tunes together."

"Yeah, I hope so too. I'm sorry I cut you off like I did. I was just awful angry about everything back then. I was working too hard, but nothing good was happening. I had trouble thinking straight. I guess you were just the most convenient target."

Max had been unconsciously fingering the scarab beneath his green plush pullover jersey. Larry said, "What's that you're worrying with under your shirt?"

Max pulled the scarab out and showed it to Larry. "It's an ancient Egyptian scarab amulet that an Afghan friend gave me just before a grenade killed him. It contains pills that are supposed to bring you back from death or assure you the afterlife."

"Evidently didn't help him."

"I didn't have time to give him one of the pills. But he gave me one for a severe leg wound that probably would have killed me. Also, his son recovered from a fatal stab wound within minutes after receiving a scarab pill. It was miraculous."

"So, you've got some miracle lifesaver pills in there? Well, you'd better give me one."

"It's not that simple, Larry. We put one in the boy's wound, and it healed. But you're not wounded. And it might actually be poison if you don't really need it. The pills are very powerful."

Larry's voice went sharp. "Give me one if you want that divorce. I mean it. I need every chance I can get. This is a new operation. The doctor told me the odds were only pretty good. I want better than that. I can be up there with Bird and Train if I live to keep playing. Give me the pill if you want Kitty."

"Damn it, Larry, are you determined to be an asshole your whole life? Okay, here." Max opened the scarab, removed one of the golden pills, and put it in Larry's hand.

Larry rolled the tiny pill between two fingers, examining it. "Looks like one of those Red Rider BBs I shot you with when we were kids. Yeah, I can feel its power in my fingers."

Kitty entered the room with two cups of coffee as Larry was eyeing the pill. He popped it in his mouth when he saw her.

"What the heck are you doing, Larry? What was that? The doctor said you should have nothing on your stomach before the operation. They are taking you in for surgery any time now."

"Max gave it to me. He says it's a miracle lifesaver pill. Or it might be poison. But I'm gonna take that chance. It's just a tiny thing, couldn't matter to the doctor."

"You're both idiots! I'm calling the nurse."

Larry said, "Now, don't go ballistic, baby, it's only—." He suddenly gasped and made choking noises. He fell back against the pillow, his eyes bulging, his face crimson. The heart monitor lines became erratic, and the machine beeped in a steady 2/4 alarm, like a metronome. Kitty screamed and slammed the coffees down on a table. Max ran to the door to call a nurse, but they were already on their way.

Several nurses and doctors rushed in and surrounded the bed. They shooed Max and Kitty out. Moments later, they wheeled the bed out and pushed it down the hall in a hurry.

Kitty glared at Max, her eyes blazing. "Why did you give him that pill? Do you really hate him that much?"

"Honey, no, I don't hate Larry at all. We made up. We're friends again. He apologized for shunning me and said he would give you a divorce. But then he threatened not to unless I gave him a pill. I didn't think he would actually take it. I warned him it could be dangerous." He tried to embrace her, but she pushed him away.

"I think you had better leave. I'll wait here and call to let you know how it goes."

"Kitty, please let me stay with you. Don't be angry with me, darling. There's so much I need to tell you."

"I'm just too upset right now, Max. I probably wouldn't hear half of what you said. Go on home. I'll be okay. It's all just too much right now."

She gnawed her lip and was on the verge of tears. Her eyes had a glazed stare.

"All right, I'll go, but let me give you this scarab pendant. It's important that you wear it. It can protect you."

"Protect me! Like it did Larry? I saw you take the pill out of that thing through the window. I don't want your magic pendant. Did Afghanistan make you crazy?"

"Okay, I'm going. Please call me as soon as you know anything. I love you, Kitty. More than life itself. Please don't make any hasty decisions when you're under all this stress and anxiety."

Max tried to catch her eye, but she refused to look at him. She sat trembling in her chair. He turned and paced in slumped dejection to the elevators. Instead of leaving immediately, however, he went to the hospital restaurant and had some coffee and a sandwich. He racked his brain for something further to say to Kitty to convince her he hadn't meant to harm Larry. He walked outside in the hospital's meditation garden, his mind in a whirl. *If Larry dies, will she ever forgive me? If Larry recovers, will he renege on his promise to give her the divorce?* Two hours later, Max remained totally dazed, confused, and agonized.

He called the nurse's desk and asked about Larry. There was still no news. He sighed and called a taxi. As he opened the taxi door, he felt something soft under his foot. He looked beneath his shoe and saw a dead toad that must have been run over by a car. It was squished flat as a steamrollered cartoon character. He gave a shudder of revulsion and entered the cab.

Chapter Thirty

"Body and Soul"

Fort Worth, Texas, December 2002

As Max rode the taxi home from the hospital that afternoon, his mind churned with anxiety, anguish, and desire. He would talk with Odetta about it. She always gave good advice. Then he remembered this was Sunday, only two days before Christmas Day. The office was closed. She would be home with her family. Well, tomorrow would be soon enough. He needed sleep anyway if he could manage it.

At the locked front door, he remembered he had left all his keys with Odetta. He went around to the back garden and retrieved the back door key from its hiding place under the stone toad next to the doorstep. The stone toad reminded him of the squished toad he had stepped on at the hospital. Again, he experienced a shiver of disgust. He had loved unlovely toads since childhood and enjoyed watching them patrol his garden with their beautiful golden eyes. He hoped the squished toad didn't portend Larry's death on the operating table. *How can I hope to get back in Kitty's good graces then?*

As Max put the key to the backdoor lock, he found it was not only unlocked, but slightly ajar. Odetta must have left it open for him. He stepped into the music room study, dropped his backpack, and started for the kitchen to get a beer.

Someone stepped out of the shadows and jabbed him in the chest with a finger. "We've been waiting for you, pal. Took you long enough to get here."

Max gave a startled yelp and turned to run for the back door, but another man had moved in behind him holding a gun. "Yeah, we don't like to be kept waiting. But as long as you're alone, that's the main thing."

They motioned for Max to sit in his leather Eames reading chair. He sat. Max was shaking, breathing hard, and struggling to believe this was really happening.

"Gentlemen, I don't know what this is all about. I think you must be here by mistake. I'm just back from overseas. I haven't been involved in my legal practice for over a year. So, if it's legal advice you need, I'll be in my office tomorrow. But if you're here to rob me, please, just take whatever you want and go. I won't remember what you look like. I have facial amnesia."

"Hey, now that's a really good speech. You know how to think on your feet even sitting down, Mr. Max Ballard. Yeah, we know your name. We know all about you. We know you were foolish enough to receive something at Ramstein Air Base. Something naughty. We're here to relieve you of it before it causes any more trouble."

Both men were large but not pudgy. They had short haircuts and dressed in similar dark business suits. One wore a red tie, the other a blue tie. Red Tie, with the gun in Max's face, stared unblinking into Max's eyes as if probing his mind. Blue Tie said, "Please don't make me hit you. I've been having a little arthritis in my hands."

Max licked his lips. "Listen, guys, yes, I was given an envelope at Ramstein. They didn't say it was anything dangerous or important. They just asked me to mail it when I got to the States, which I did in Baltimore. I was only doing a small favor for a stranger. Wouldn't you do the same? Look, I'm sorry if it was something illegal or inappropriate, but I was just the messenger. I really know nothing else about it. I don't know what was in it or who gave it to me. I'd give it to you if I still had it. Please don't punish me for doing an innocent favor."

Max realized he was blathering, but he couldn't seem to stop himself. His voice quavered.

"Okay, okay, take it easy, pal. I believe you," said Red Tie. "But you see our problem. Even if you did it in total innocence, which I'm not entirely convinced of, you now know the situation, and you've seen our faces." Red Tie turned to Blue Tie with a smirk. "Why didn't you remember to bring masks? That was an egregious oversight."

Blue Tie snapped his fingers, which was difficult with surgical gloves on. "Oops! My bad."

"Have a look through his bag just to make sure he's not fibbing."

Blue Tie rummaged through Max's bag. "Let's take it with us just in case."

"Yeah, and check his clothes, especially those boots."

Blue Tie patted Max down, checked all his pockets, then made him take off his boots. The two-dollar bill fell out when the thug shook the boots upside down. He held up the bill and inspected it. Then he flicked it away.

"Half a two-dollar bill! That can't be what was in the envelope. He must have mailed it like he said. Makes sense. Too bad they didn't find out he went to Baltimore instead of New York. Someone got sloppy."

"You seem to have all kinds of secrets, Ballard. You a secret agent of some kind? What's with the secret two-dollar bill?"

"You know I'm not a spy. As I said, I was just doing a favor for a stranger. I told you I mailed the envelope in Baltimore. I wasn't being evasive. The two-dollar bill was a personal thing, a lucky charm to keep me safe in Afghanistan."

"Okay. Okay. The problem is now you know there's a problem. We can't afford to have you blabbing about it. The two-dollar bill may have brought you back safe from Afghanistan, but you're in a bit of worse trouble now."

Max was sweating and trembling. "Look, if you kill me, there will be an investigation and the possibility that you'll be found out. Maybe someone saw you enter or leave my house. Maybe you've left DNA or other evidence. If you just leave, I promise I won't mention it to anyone. If I do, you can always come back and kill me later. I have no reason to tell anyone, since it would implicate me as well."

"Is this guy some heck-of-a lawyer, or what?"

"Desperation can do that. But Mr. Ballard makes a good point. Why don't we just clear off and let him live? You know, I think we can trust this dude to keep his mouth shut. No point in making a mess." He gave Max a slow wink like a guillotine, and regarded Max with the thin, remorseless smile of a snake.

Just then, the phone rang. All three of them looked at it. Red Tie shook his head. After five rings, the answering machine took it.

Kitty's voice said, "Max, great news! The operation was successful. Larry is going to be okay. I talked with him for a few minutes. He said he forced you to give him the pill. He's going to give me a divorce, as he promised. I'm so anxious to see you. I'm sorry for being angry with you. It was just the stress about the operation. I'll see you soon, and we can tape together that two-dollar bill. We'll frame it and hang it in our bedroom when we're married. I'm coming right over so we can talk about everything. I love you, Max!"

Max gasped and started up from the chair, hyperventilating. "Jesus, please just go. I won't say anything to anyone, ever."

Red Tie pushed him back down. “Looks like you have a lot to live for, chum. Unfortunately, we can’t take the chance of letting you live for it.”

Blue Tie said, “Hey, maybe this will make for a better scenario. When she gets here, we shoot her, then him. Lovers’ quarrel, murder and suicide. Happens all the time. Cops won’t even look twice at it.”

Max pleaded. “No! Please, just kill me now and leave before she gets here. I’ll even write a suicide note for you.”

“Well, I guess that could work, too,” said Red Tie. “Simpler. No sense offing a woman unless we have to. Could lead to complications.”

“Give me some paper and I’ll write the note. In fact, I have some poison pills in this amulet I can take. You won’t even have to shoot me.” He opened the scarab and showed them the pills.

Blue Tie looked at the scarab. “Poison pills! You gotta be kidding me. And you said you weren’t a spy. Why else have poison pills? But, hey, you can take ’em. If they do the trick, great.”

Red Tie said, “Here’s paper, write the note, take the pills, we’re out of here, and Bob’s your uncle.”

As Max scribbled the note, Blue Tie said, “Maybe I'll just confiscate this little bobble as a souvenir; it's kinda classy.”

“Nah, it might be missed and lead to suspicion. Better leave it.”

Red Tie grabbed the note from Max's shaking hand. “Okay, this looks good. Take the pills.”

Max swallowed all the pills that remained in the amulet. The men watched him closely. Max’s eyes suddenly blazed as he felt the pills’ energy bloom within him like a nuclear explosion. His body convulsed. His mind raced. Memories in excruciating visual and auditory detail flooded through him, consuming years in mere seconds, then returned him to the present moment.

Surely the pills will save me as they did Salim. I can feel them working. But they seem to be ripping me apart. I took so many. Too many! But surely God will save me to be with Kitty. I've waited seventeen years for her. Surely God intends for us to be together now to help heal the world. Surely my life means something more than the pathetic farce it's been so far. Surely.... Suddenly Max groaned and lost consciousness. He slumped in the chair, drool foaming from his mouth.

"Wow! Looks like he's gone all right. Maybe the pills really were poison."

"Wait, I still feel a faint pulse. It may be a slow poison, or they might just be sleeping pills."

"We gotta get outta here before she shows up."

"You got your throw-down?"

"Yeah. I guess we gotta make a mess after all."

Blue Tie took a cloth-wrapped parcel from his coat pocket. He unwrapped a snub-nosed .38 revolver. He put the barrel against Max's right temple and fired. Max's blood and brains sprayed across the room. Blue Tie wiped the gun with the cloth and pressed Max's dead fingers around the handle and trigger. He dropped the gun onto the chair and arranged Max's hand near it.

"Should we erase the answer tape?"

"Nah. They'll think he offed himself just before she called. Nice bit of irony, eh?"

The two glanced around to make sure they had missed nothing, then eased out the back door, leaving it unlocked.

***

When Kitty arrived fifteen minutes later, she tried the locked front door, rang the doorbell, then walked around back and found the unlocked door. Entering, she saw Max's left arm hanging lax from the side of the chair, the scarab pendant dangling from his fingers.

She whispered, "Max, darling, are you asleep?" as she walked closer.

Then, she saw his bloody head and screamed—and screamed—and screamed. Kitty knelt beside Max, wide-eyed, unbelieving, keening, and shuddering in anguish. She clutched his arm, then fell to the floor, gushing tears. Finally, she called 911 and waited for the police and medics to arrive.

While she waited in shocked disbelief, she found the note in his lap. It was spattered with blood and tear stains, barely legible. It read, "Kitty darling, forgive me. This was all I could do. Please take the scarab and wear it to remember me. My love for you is beyond words and time. Max."

In an anguished daze, Kitty took the scarab from his hand and placed it around her neck. She stared in agony at his ruined face and prayed beyond all hope, "Max, Max, come back to me!"

CHAPTER THIRTY-ONE

"SOME OTHER TIME"

FORT WORTH, TEXAS, APRIL 1985

Max awoke with a jerk, his heart pounding, frightened but not knowing why, utterly disoriented, unsure where or even who he was. He sat there for a minute, dizzy with general amnesia, his mind a floundering chaos, flapping about like a fish suddenly yanked from water. Images of people and places he knew he knew but couldn't put names to flashed about randomly in his consciousness. Finally, his mind cleared, stabilized, and captured and unified his careening selves. Abruptly, memory crashed within him like a tremendous ocean wave. He realized who he was, that he was sitting in his reading chair in his music room.

He remembered the two thugs who had forced him to swallow all the pills from the scarab amulet. He looked around in fear, breathing in ragged gasps. But they were gone. *My God! The pills must have worked. They've brought me back to life. Maybe they only caused the simulation of death. Either way, it must have fooled the killers. I'm alive! Kitty should be here soon, and then we can begin our life together at last.*

His heart was pounding like Gene Krupa's drumming on "Sing, Sing, Sing." He put his hand to his chest. The scarab wasn't there. Had the thugs taken it? He looked around the room for it, for them, to make sure they were gone. Yes, he was alone. He stood up, still disoriented, unsteady on his feet, his body trembling in reaction to the horrific memory of his forced suicide.

He glanced out the picture window to the back garden. Something was different about it. The big Shumard oak was there at the back. But the tornado of 2000 had uprooted it. Yet there it was. He turned and saw his beloved Baldwin baby grand piano. The tornado had destroyed it as well. And his reading chair. It was the comfy blue wing chair, from before the Eames chair, in which he—had died.

Something's wrong! What happened to me? He walked to the front office. It too was as it had been before the tornado. Likewise, his upstairs office and bedroom. There was his old oak bedstead rather than the new brass bed he had bought in late 2000 for his new house.

He looked in the bedroom mirror and gasped. He was different, younger somehow. There was no wrap around his injured ribs. He took a deep breath without pain. His clothes were different. He wasn't wearing his boots from Afghanistan. He went back downstairs. The calendar on his office desk showed April 1985.

Now, his whole body was trembling violently. He sat in his office and tried to think what could have happened. He explored his memory, recalling everything he could from when he met Kitty in 1985; her marrying Larry despite acknowledging her love for Max; their love affair; Larry's total renunciation of their friendship. Max recalled his ten months in Afghanistan; being blown up; living with Dawud and Salim; the dervishes' monastery; the battle with the Taliban; returning home; and then committing suicide to keep the two thugs from murdering Kitty.

The pills! I took all of them. They must have not only killed me, but sent me back in time somehow, as well as brought me back to life. I must be dead in 2002. Oh, God! I've lost Kitty forever!

Max staggered out the back door into the soft mid-morning sunshine of April 1985. He walked around the neighborhood for an hour, trying to think, but his mind was spinning like a Tilt-A-Whirl. His thoughts cycled between anguish, anger, and bewilderment. But walking finally calmed his agitation. He quit thinking, quit obsessing, and just observed.

It now struck him that this scenery looked the way he remembered but seemed also somehow fresh, extraordinary, and, yes, wonderful. The breeze through his hair, the dappling of sunlight and shadow on the lawns, the insouciance of birds and squirrels. He passed a playground where children were climbing on monkey bars and chasing about. *Why can't we adults feel that imaginative concentration of being like children? It's just a matter of remembering, of letting go the fetters of habit. Our* entire purpose *in life is simply to love and to live—joyously. Did I have to die and go back in time to understand that?*

He suddenly realized his life wasn't ruined. He couldn't do anything about what had happened to his future self, which was now somehow also his past self. Yet, maybe fate had given him a chance to start over. Perhaps the future, from this alternate past, wasn't determined to have the same outcome. *Maybe I can change the course of my life for the better in this new now. I can be the man in the Frost poem, but now able to return and take that other path to a truly better life.*

If this really is 1985 again for me, there must be a reason I came back to this exact moment in time. Surely it means I can find Kitty before she meets Larry and convince her to choose me this time.

Max returned home and went around to the backyard. It was so beautiful with the majestic oak. He remembered the little garden pond he had put in after the tornado uprooted the tree. Well, that would have to wait. But that wire sculpture. He could get rid of it before the squirrel caught its tail in the wire. That in and of itself would change history slightly.

As he opened the back door, he heard a high-pitched mewing. He looked in the shrubbery beside the doorstep. A tiny brindled kitten gazed up at him with needy green eyes and mewed again. "Well, look at you, Rilke, you little fur ball. You showed up just as I remember. You'd better come in and have some milk."

The kitten drank a tummy-full of milk, then went to sleep in the cardboard box Max made cozy with an old towel. Next, he checked the calendar in his office. It showed he had an interview with Odetta Randle the next morning for the position of Legal Assistant. He had a feeling he would definitely hire her.

The calendar also showed that he was scheduled to play piano with Larry and Joe at the Catfish Club a week from next Saturday. That was the concert at which he and Larry had met—would meet—Kitty. There must be some way to revise his fate from its previous future outcome. Max spent the rest of the day considering possibilities. That night his mind resisted sleep. It was a torrent of memories of those other times, then fitful dreams of other wheres and whens, of ecstasies and horrors.

***

The next morning, Odetta Randle appeared in the office promptly at nine. Max was exhausted from reliving much of his previous future while asleep. He felt like a junkie who had just survived a cold-turkey comedown. But he was ready. He had shaved and put on a suit.

Odetta was modestly but immaculately dressed. She looked great. He wanted to give her a hug, but he knew that would certainly be inappropriate and would cause her to bolt. He could see that she was nervous. Max was amused but tried not to show it. This was the woman who had been one of his best friends and confidantes for over fifteen years. Yet he was meeting her again for the first time. Max invited her into his office and fixed them both a cup of coffee. He knew just how she liked hers.

"So, Ms. Randle, I see you're in your last semester at SMU Law School, and near the top of your class."

"Yes, sir. I'm highly motivated to practice law even though I'm getting a late start. Becoming a lawyer has been my goal since high school, where I was valedictorian. That was in Chicago. And, as you can see from my CV, I graduated cum laude from the University of Illinois. Thurgood Marshall inspired me to become a lawyer. I wanted to be the first black woman Supreme Court justice."

"Wow, that's quite an ambition, and a worthy one. I hope you can make it happen. I could certainly use a friend on the Supreme Court. Uh, sorry, didn't mean to be flippant. Why are you looking for a position here rather than in Dallas?"

"My husband, Clarence, was in the Air Force when we married. He was stationed here at Carswell. Now he's out and works at the local post office. So, we've lived in Fort Worth for several years. I would have done law school here if TCU or TWC had one. But SMU is the closest, and they gave me a partial scholarship. I prefer the culture here in Fort Worth to the glitz of Dallas, anyway."

"Well, this position is for a legal aide, not a lawyer. And of course, you haven't yet graduated or passed the bar. Are you willing to consider it?"

Odetta gave a rueful smile. "Well, I suppose I've lowered my expectations a little since high school. I've become more realistic. Let me be candid with you, Mr. Ballard. I've interviewed at several high-profile law offices here and in Dallas. Despite my qualifications and expectations, they rejected me. None of them will hire a newly minted, mid-thirties black woman as an attorney to be. I should be able to do better than your legal aide, but I'm hoping if I do an excellent job—and I will—that you will promote me to attorney eventually." She looked at him with those probing eyes that had always seemed to know his heart.

"Ms. Randle, I've got a good feeling about you. Let's start you out in this legal aide position, and if you graduate in the top five in your class, I'll make you a lawyer here as soon as you pass the bar. We handle mostly low-profile civil rights cases for the ACLU and some public defender cases. You're probably not going to get to the Supreme Court from here, but maybe together we can do some good in this damaged world."

Odetta blinked at Max in surprise. "That, uh, sounds wonderful. I know I'm in the top ten of my class. I could be in the top five if I ace my finals."

"Well, go home and study for those finals. You've got a job here." Max smiled and shook her hand. He already knew she would graduate fourth in her class and would become his partner in two years.

***

Max spent the rest of Monday thinking, planning, and preparing his strategy. His first move was to stop by his bank and get some cash, including a crisp new two-dollar bill. *I wonder if Kitty found my half and the scarab. She must have; she wore it in my vision of her. Somehow the vision must have been about being thrown back into my past.* Then he got a haircut and bought some new, more fashionable clothes, including a new suit. JJ had always criticized his too-casual appearance. *JJ! That's who I need to consult.*

She's not dead now! She should be part of my plan to win Kitty. I'll call her when school is out this afternoon.

Max vaguely remembered that Kitty had mentioned playing in some recitals at TCU before she attended that fateful concert at the Catfish Club. He headed over to TCU to find out more. Max bought a TCU T-shirt to blend in with the student crowd. He wandered into the music school building and checked the bulletin boards. Yes, there would be a music students' showcase tomorrow night. Kitty was listed as "Katherine Kazinsky, tenor saxophone." She would play a classical sonata movement for tenor sax and piano titled "*Incandescence*" by Ida Gotkovsky.

Max worked up his courage and telephoned JJ. This could be awkward. How long had it been in this lifetime since they had talked? He hoped she wasn't miffed at him about something, as was often the case.

"JJ, it's so great to hear your voice."

"What do you mean, Max? We talked just night before last about the Catfish Club concert this month."

"Uh, sure, but it's always great to hear those golden vocal cords of yours. Uh, listen, I was wondering if you would care to have dinner with me tomorrow about six and then attend some student music recitals at TCU."

"Well, uh, sure, Max, dinner tomorrow sounds good. But student music recitals? Why do you want to go hear those?"

"I'll tell you tomorrow. It's a surprise. It will be fun. Maybe we'll discover the next great jazz musician."

"I thought those recitals were usually classical music. Oh, well, I see you're being cryptic as usual. That's just part of your crazy charm when it isn't utterly annoying. See you then." He could almost hear her eyes rolling through the phone.

***

The next evening, he picked up JJ at her house in Meadowbrook. She looked gorgeous, healthy, and vibrant with that huge sassy smile he loved. He wanted to hug and kiss her but feared that might freak her out. They drove straight to *Szechuan* Chinese Restaurant with little of their accustomed chit-chat. He was nervous about seeing her so young and vital when he so agonizingly remembered her in her coffin in 1996. After they sat down, he ordered the spicy *Szechuan* shrimp. She had *moo goo gai pan*.

Max could tell JJ could tell he was nervous. She had eyed him suspiciously during the drive. He wasn't sure what to say or not say without making a fool of himself. He mentally kicked himself that he wasn't better prepared. Max picked up a shrimp awkwardly with his shaky chopsticks. It went squiggling into the air as if still alive, landing on her plate.

JJ deftly retrieved it with her chopsticks and popped it in her mouth. She gave him the squint eye. "Max, what's wrong? You're twitchy as a pair of porcupines. Are you in some kind of trouble?"

"No... No, I'm doing fine. I just wanted to, uh, catch up with you and see how you're doing."

She pointed her chopsticks at him as if she were a judge in court. "We saw each other just last week. You're jumpy about something. I can read you like a children's fairy tale. Spit it out."

He finally got a shrimp into his mouth and washed it down with green tea. "Okay, it's just that I hired a woman as my legal assistant yesterday. She mentioned having had a scare about breast cancer recently. I just wanted to remind you to get yourself checked soon." He went for a bamboo shoot, which shot onto the table. Max switched to a fork.

JJ smirked. "Well, thanks for being so concerned about my breasts, even though you haven't tried to fondle them since college." She pinched a snow pea and chicken chunk skillfully with her chopsticks and conveyed them to her mouth. "Still, you've got a point. It's been a couple of years since I had a mammogram. I'll make a point to do it soon. But somehow, I doubt that's what this is really all about. What's your actual ulterior motive for inviting me to these recitals tonight?"

Max slurped his green tea and took a last bite of egg roll. "Well, uh, there's a student playing in them I want to ask you about. I think you may have seen her before. I'll point her out to you when we hear her play."

"Okay, Mr. Mysterious, I hope the music is worth it." She took a final slurp of her egg-drop soup. "Those student recitals can be brutal. You may have to try to fondle my breasts just to keep me awake. What does your cookie fortune say? Mine says, 'You will achieve your desire the second time around.' That's rather strange."

"Oh, I think you may have gotten my fortune by mistake. Let me see what this one says. 'Love will bloom in time.' Oh, maybe we each got the right one after all."

JJ gave an extravagant sigh. "Well, let's go hear those recitals."

***

They arrived at TCU a little late. The recitals were already under way, but Kitty hadn't played yet. Max and JJ found a couple of good seats. Attendance was sparse. When Kitty and the pianist took the stage, JJ heard Max gasp and felt his arm stiffen against her.

Max said in a hoarse whisper, "This is the girl I wanted to ask you about. I believe she used to be one of Larry's students when she was in high school."

"I can't say I remember her. She's probably matured quite a bit since then. She's stunningly beautiful. I can see why you're taken with her. But how do you know her?"

"Her name is Kitty. I'm in love with her. I want to marry her."

"You what! How long have you known her? Why haven't I heard anything about her before now?"

"I'm hoping to meet her tonight for the second first time."

"What is that supposed to mean? Oh, shush, they're about to play."

Kitty gave a terse smile and nodded to the audience. She took a breath, then began an energetic tenor solo while the piano remained mute. She exploited the entire dynamic range of the instrument and featured several unusual tonal effects. Her tone and technique were gorgeous. Then she went silent. The piano began quietly and simply. The tenor soon joined it in a romantic melodic sequence that expressed for Max the intense desire he had for this exquisite, young-again Kitty. *My God, she's beautiful!* The piece ended as both instruments descended into an extended minor chord of tender yearning.

"Wow! That was wonderful," said JJ. "She's terrific. Let's go introduce ourselves before she gets away."

Kitty was putting away her tenor at the side of the stage during the interval between performances. Max and JJ waited while a couple of other students congratulated her. Then JJ said, "Ms. Kazinsky, your performance was fabulous. The piece is well-named."

"Yes," said Max, his voice a little husky. "You were—incandescent."

Kitty looked at them as if trying to remember who they were. "Oh, thanks. It's a great piece that sounds good no matter who plays it. I'm sorry, have we met before? You look a little familiar."

JJ smiled. "We may have met several years ago. I'm Larry Delgado's ex-wife. We were still married when he taught you saxophone technique. This is Max Ballard, Larry's friend, and mine. He's a pianist."

Kitty shook hands with them, squinting deep questions into Max's eyes as they shook hands and Max's legs went wobbly. Then she turned back to JJ. "Yes, I remember now. I glimpsed you a few times at his house, Mrs. Delgado. Larry was a fine teacher. He inspired me to continue with the sax, and I got here on a music scholarship. I'm planning to attend his concert later this month at the Catfish Jazz Club. I want to thank him for giving me a good start in music. Will you be there?"

"Yes, both of us will be there. Max is Larry's pianist. I may sing."

"Ki—uh, Ms. Kazinsky, are you free this Thursday evening? I'm playing a solo set at the Rondeau Club. JJ will be there too. I'd love it if you could come and have dinner with us. We'll be glad to pick you up."

JJ raised an eyebrow at Max and then turned to Kitty. "Yes, please join us. It will be fun. I'd like to get to know you better."

Kitty hesitated. "Well, okay. That sounds nice. But I can't stay too late. I need to study."

"The gig is only from six to eight. We'll pick you up at five thirty. Write your address for me." He handed her a well-worn pocket notebook in which he jotted ideas and poems.

"Oh, looks like you're a writer, too."

"Max is a fine poet. He teaches creative writing at the community college."

"We'll see you at five thirty Thursday, Ms. Kazinsky," said Max.

"Please, I'm Kitty to my friends."

"I hope we'll become great friends, Kitty," said JJ.

Max smiled like a Christmas puppy and gobbled up Kitty with his eyes as she left.

As Max and JJ walked to his car through the gathering dark, JJ grasped his arm and said, "Okay, Romeo, you've got a whole lot of 'splaining to do."

Chapter Thirty-Two

"It Ain't Necessarily So"

Fort Worth, Texas, April 1985

Max and JJ sat in his car in the TCU parking lot after Kitty's recital. Max was nervous; JJ was exasperated.

"Let's talk right here while all this is fresh in our minds," said JJ. "You've been acting strangely all evening. You look like you're about to hyperventilate. You said you were going to meet Kitty for the second first time and you're in love with her. But it was pretty obvious that she's never clapped eyes on you before. So, what's going on?"

Max was glad she couldn't see his face in the darkness. "It's a little difficult to explain. And you may not believe me when I do. But I guess there's no way to avoid it. I need your help, and you need to know why."

"Jesus, Max, just tell me. I'll help you any way I can, but don't be so mysterious. It can't be that hard to explain."

"It's not hard, just unbelievable." Max gave a sigh of resignation. "And it will take a while. Why don't we drive to your house? We can have some coffee, and I'll tell you everything. I'll try to get my thoughts organized on the drive over."

He started the car and switched on the radio to the local classical station. JJ struggled to maintain silence during their drive, although her mind was rife with curiosity. Max could certainly be obscure or mentally byzantine, but she had seldom seen him at such a loss for words.

JJ fixed them coffee at her house, and they settled in the living room. Her Pekinese, Barkley, laid his head on her lap. Max was grim-lipped. "Do you believe in the possibility of life after death?"

"Sure, I'm a believing Christian. I trust there will be an afterlife."

"Yes, well, this is my afterlife. I died in the year 2002, and I woke up here in 1985, two days ago."

"You're right. I don't believe you, but let's hear the whole story. Jeeze, Max, this better not be another of your crazy-ass episodes. Have you been dropping acid or reading the adventures of Baron Von Munchausen?"

"I swear I'm telling you the absolute truth, although it may be hard to prove."

For the next two hours, Max patiently described his other life starting with the concert at the Catfish Club where they originally met Kitty; then Max's rivalry with Larry for her; Kitty marrying Larry; the tornado of 2000; Max's love affair with Kitty; the 911 attack; Larry's repudiation of their friendship; Max's sojourn in Afghanistan; his being blown up and seeing a vision of Kitty; Max's friendship with Dawud and Salim; taking refuge with the Sufi dervishes; the Taliban attack, with Dawud dying and Salim saved by the scarab pill; Max's agreement to mail the dangerous letter; and Max's return to Fort Worth in late December, 2002, only to be spurned by Kitty at the hospital, and forced by the thugs to commit suicide by taking the remaining scarab pills.

Max only omitted the fact that JJ died in 1996.

"My God, Max, I don't know what to say. Either that's the most elaborate confabulation I've ever heard or some sort of miracle happened.

It's hard to wrap my head around the idea that the future has already happened. If you're lying or joking, you'd better tell me now, or I swear I'll rip you a new one. I may anyway. This is just too insane even for you." She looked lasers at him for several seconds.

"It's absolutely true unless I've gone completely mad, and I don't think that's the case. My memory of all that happened is still vivid and specific."

"Can you think of any way you can prove that it's true?" asked JJ. "Like knowing the score of the next Super Bowl or some major historical event that will happen soon?"

"You know I don't care anything about sports, besides the Super Bowl is nearly a year away. I can't remember anything significant that will happen in the next few days. We can't wait for the tornado of 2000 to prove it happened. I'm concerned about the Catfish Club concert next week. That's when Larry made his initial impression on Kitty and eventually married her. I can't take a chance of it happening that way again. You've got to help me."

"Okay, Max, my instinct is to trust you even though this is the most improbable story I've ever heard. But look, you've already changed history by taking us to meet Kitty this evening. So, you've proved your future history ain't necessarily so. Maybe...."

Max interrupted her with, "I've got it! I think I know how to prove it to you." He took a deep, ragged breath. "I sort of lied to you about my new legal aide mentioning breast cancer."

He hesitated, then plunged on. "In my other life, you die of breast cancer in 1996 because you didn't get a mammogram in time. That's why I warned you today."

JJ stared at him with open-mouthed horror. "I'm going to die in 1996?"

"Not if you get tested now. They will catch it in time, and you won't get sick."

"Okay, I'll make an appointment tomorrow. We'll see what the doctor says. It's good Kitty agreed to go with us to your gig at Club Rondeau on Thursday. I'll be able to get better acquainted with her and maybe put a bug in her ear for you."

"Oh, God, thank you, JJ. I haven't told you everything about my love for Kitty, but the Sufi dervish said it's of great importance that she and I are married as soon as possible."

"Well, let's take it one step at a time. Go home and get some sleep. I'll see you Thursday evening. Pick me up first so we can talk before getting Kitty. Be sure to wear a coat and tie Thursday."

***

Max spent the next day tending to a couple of clients at the office and calling others to postpone all his appointments for the next two weeks. He doted on Rilke, giving him milk and lots of affection as he obsessed about Kitty. How could he gain her love before she could meet Larry again at the concert? A plan formed in his mind.

***

He arrived at JJ's house at five on Thursday. She breezed out the door before he could exit the car. She wore a cherry-red cocktail dress that matched her newly styled, chemically induced scarlet coiffure. Max held the car door for her.

"Hey, you look fab, girlfriend. You trying to compete with my love interest?"

"I couldn't even if I tried. No, I'm celebrating your not lying and my beating breast cancer. I managed to get a quick appointment yesterday. The mammo showed a tiny growth that the doctor biopsied immediately. I have to go back in a couple of weeks for a minor operation, but he said I was very lucky to catch it this early. Max, you literally saved my life!" She hugged him hard.

"Oh, JJ, I'm so happy for you. Attending your funeral was the saddest day of my life. And now I hope you can believe me."

"Not only do I believe you because of the cancer thing, but it occurred to me that you wouldn't have known who or where Kitty was if you hadn't already known her somehow. So that too verifies your story."

"Well, thank God I confided in you. Sometimes even a blind hog finds a rainbow."

JJ kissed him with a smack. "Max, you are the most lovably brilliant idiot I've ever known. If Kitty marries you, she will definitely have her work cut out for her."

"Well, slap me if I get too sappy. By the way, you smell great. What's that perfume you're wearing?"

"Poison."

"'Poison!' Why would anyone name a perfume Poison?"

"They're just being provocative, I guess. You should buy some perfume for Kitty."

Max grinned and drove them to pick up Kitty, who emerged wearing a filmy, cornflower blue dress that made Max sweat despite the air conditioning. She also emanated a fragrance that seemed to invade his deepest instincts of desire. JJ must have noticed. "Is that Opium you're wearing, Kitty? Love it." She arched her eyebrow at Max. "I think between my Poison and your Opium, Max is getting a little woozy. Maybe I'd better drive." Kitty giggled. She obviously loved JJ's sassy humor already.

"I'll be fine;" said Max, "though it is getting rather heady in here. You know, Afghan women wear really heavy, intense perfume because of the heat and heavy clothing they must wear."

"How would you know anything about Afghan women and their perfume?" asked JJ.

"Oh, uh, just something I read somewhere, I guess."

JJ gave him a squint-eyed, baleful look that reminded him of the nanny goat in Afghanistan.

At Club Rondeau, Max garnered a table near the piano where he could watch the girls as he played. They ordered food and wine. After his quick dinner, Max moved to the piano and improvised some innocuous jazz for two hours while the girls giggled, gossiped, and consumed another bottle of *Pouilly-Fuissé*. By the end of his session, JJ and Kitty were almost sisters. Kitty now had an elevated opinion of Max and knew he was "ga-ga" for her, but she didn't know why.

When Max took Kitty back to her apartment, he walked her to the door and asked if she would be interested in getting coffee on Saturday. "I would like to go out with you, just the two of us," said Kitty, "but I'd prefer to do some walking. I need more exercise. I'll bet the Botanic Gardens are nice this month."

Max could hardly believe his luck. His last date with Kitty at the Botanic Gardens had been wonderful, as he recalled, and it fit right in with his plans.

***

That Saturday, Max picked up Kitty and drove to the gardens in mid-morning. The sun was glorious among piled-high whipped-cream clouds. A light breeze carried the scent of roses, lilacs, and honeysuckle. Kitty was alluring in shorts, halter-top, and sunbonnet. Max brought a basket containing a quilt, a thermos of tamarind juice, some peanut butter and honey sandwiches (which he already knew Kitty liked), and a secret weapon.

They walked among the flowers for a while, smelling the blossoms, pointing out flamboyant blooms that caught their attention. He eventually guided them to the same secluded grove they had visited the last time he had taken her here in that other 1985, seventeen years previously for him. They spread the quilt and reclined on it, talking lightly of music, literature, movies, family, various likes, and dislikes. Max reached into the basket, removed the thermos and glasses, and poured them some cold fruit juice.

Kitty was about to take a sip but put down her glass with a frown. She cocked her head and motioned for him to be quiet. "What is that noise? It sounds like a kitten. And I think it's coming from your basket."

"Oh, yes, I almost forgot. JJ told me I should have a chaperone when I go out with you in case you try to make a move on me. So, I brought my new friend Rilke to keep an eye on you." Max reached into the basket and lifted out the now annoyed fur-ball who had been ignored too long.

"Oh, he's precious!" Kitty eagerly accepted Rilke from Max's hands and nuzzled the kitten. Rilke mewed piteously and licked her cheek. She cuddled him to her breast and stroked his fur.

"He showed up on my back porch a few days ago. I plan to hire him to guard my office when he gets some size on him."

"Oh, I wish I could have a cat, but I'll be moving from my apartment after this semester, unless I decide to stay and do grad school at TCU."

"Oh, you should definitely continue with your master's at TCU, especially if you want to do environmental work."

"What!? How did you know I'm thinking of doing environmental work? I don't remember mentioning it to anyone."

"Oh, uh, just a lucky guess, I guess."

"I don't think so. There's something really peculiar going on here. I've wondered how you happened to attend my recital. Even my mom didn't know about it. JJ said you invited her to it. How did you come to know anything about me? Have you been stalking me or something?"

Max reached into the basket and handed Kitty a small, doll-sized baby bottle of milk for Rilke. She took it and snuggled Rilke as he nursed from it greedily.

"Don't try to divert me with the kitten. You need to tell me why you seem to know so much about me."

"Please don't get upset, Kitty. I can explain. There's nothing nefarious going on. I swear I haven't been stalking you. In fact, in a manner of speaking, I wasn't even here until a few days ago."

"You've been out of town?"

"I've been out of this world. It will take me a while to tell you the entire story, but let me just say that I've been in love with you for the last seventeen years, since I first met you in—another 1985. I lost you in 2002, and now I've found you again."

"I'm sorry, Max, maybe you had better take me home. You're talking kind of crazy. JJ said you sometimes act a little weird even though you're basically a good person. Don't make me change my mind about that."

"Kitty, please give me a chance to explain. Here, maybe this will convince you that I've known you in another life." Max got out his billfold and removed the two-dollar bill, which he had already cut in half. He handed half of it to her.

Kitty looked at the severed bill. Her eyes became enormous, and her mouth gaped.

"Does that look familiar?" asked Max.

"It looks like the half of a two-dollar bill my father gave my mother when he went to fight in Vietnam. But it's not the same one. That one is old and wrinkled."

"Right, it's not that one. It's not even the same one I gave you in 2002 as a pledge I would come back to you from the war in Afghanistan. I, uh, lost that one. But this one proves I knew the story of the bill because, in my other life, you told me all about it. How else could I possibly have known that about you?"

Kitty now appeared totally confused but was no longer angry. "You're saying you went to Afghanistan to fight the Russians?" She hugged Rilke to her breast, absently caressing him.

"No, darling, uh, Kitty. The Russians will leave Afghanistan in 1989. But in 2001, America will declare war on Afghanistan because, well, never mind why. In my other life, I went to Afghanistan as a war correspondent in early 2002. You and I were in love. I gave you half of a two-dollar bill and kept the other half as a pledge to return to you. And I did come back. But I was killed soon after returning home. Never mind why."

Kitty looked horrified, her mouth agape. "You were killed?"

"Yes, that was in December 2002, two days before Christmas. Then, last Sunday, I woke up at my house in 1985 again. That's how I knew about your recital. You told me about it in my other life." He paused and then plunged on, "Kitty, you and I were lovers in my other life. We were going to be married. I lost you then, and now I've found you again. I couldn't bear to lose you a second time. Please don't be angry. Please believe me. God destined you and me to be together, to be married. I'll tell you why when we have more time and when you can believe what I've told you so far. I told JJ all this too. She will tell you why she believes me."

Kitty was trembling and biting her lower lip. The vertical crease Max wanted to kiss away was prominent between her brows. She closed her eyes and shook her head as if dazed. “This is just too much for me to process. It still seems crazy. How could it have happened? If I find out you’re lying, I’ll never want to see you again. You had better take me home.” She continued to cuddle Rilke as they walked silently back to the car.

Max was anxious but exultant with love as he drove her home. She said little but continued to hug and stroke the kitten.

“Rilke, is he telling me the truth? He had better not be lying or I’ll never want to see him again. And I’m already in love with you, little guy.” Rilke mewed piteously.

When they arrived, she kissed Rilke and put him in the basket. Max walked her to her door. “Kitty, call JJ and talk with her about what I told you. I’ll be happy to meet with you any time and go into more detail. I admit it seems unbelievable. I wouldn’t have believed it myself if I hadn’t lived through it. But I swear to you, it’s totally true. You and I belong together.”

“This is just so overwhelming I don’t know what to think. I’ve only known you for two days, and I like you, Max, but I don’t really know anything about you. You could be an axe murderer.”

Max walked her to her door. “I realize this seems awfully sudden and crazy and unreal. All I can say is I love you, have loved you for seventeen years, I love you more than life itself, and I’ll devote my life to your happiness if you’ll let me.”

Kitty stared at him glassy-eyed, then gasped and said, “Oh! How am I going to study for my tests now!” She shut the door before Max could say anything more.

***

Max drove home and reported to JJ what he had told Kitty and what her reaction had been. "She will probably call you for corroboration. JJ, you've got to make her believe me. I can't live with losing her again."

"Don't get melodramatic, Max. I'll vouch for you. Just don't do anything stupid in the meantime."

Max waited on tenterhooks for three days without hearing from anyone except Larry, who checked in with him by phone to make sure Max was still coming to the Catfish Club gig.

"Yes, of course, I'm planning to be there. It may be the most important event of my life." He hoped his now bitten-bloody fingers would be able to play by that night.

*Why do I feel I've never had any control over my life? Larry always seems so self-*confident, *even when he isn't in control. The only time I feel confident is when I'm playing music. But I may be so nervous next Saturday I'll embarrass myself in front of Kitty. That damn catfish may laugh himself loose from the wall.*

Larry said, "I don't know why this gig would be so important to you, Max. It's not that special of an occasion. Hey, you haven't maybe heard that a record producer will be there, have you?"

"No, sorry, nothing like that. I'm just hopeful about a personal situation."

"Okay, but you sound sorta glum, chum. You sure you're okay? I want to run the tunes by you before the jam."

"Yes, Larry, I'm fine. Just email me the list of tunes and I'll look them over."

"Email? What the heck is email? You on some strange weed, bro?"

"Sorry, I meant fax it to me. I'll see you there. I'm busy with clients right now."

Another day went by without word from JJ or Kitty. Max's anxiety was escalating. He called JJ.

"Oh, Max, I'm sorry. I thought Kitty was going to call you. I talked with her in person the day after your picnic. I think I convinced her that at least you believe you're telling the truth. But she's still somewhat shaken up by your story. And she's got tests this week. That's probably why she hasn't called. She said she plans to attend the Catfish concert, but, uh, she wants to come by herself."

"Crap, JJ, Larry's going to see her and turn on the charm. I'm going to be shut out again. I just know it. The details of history may be different, but the outcome is probably going to be exactly the same."

"Well, as a matter of fact, she did ask me why you and she were just engaged to be married in 2002 if you had been in love since 1985. I had to tell her that, in your other life, she married Larry even though she loved you."

Max gasped, "Oh, God, JJ, that will make her think she's meant to marry Larry. I'm doomed again!"

"Well, we'll just have to trust in the power of love. It brought you back. Maybe love's not quite finished with you yet, Max."

***

The Saturday of the Catfish Club performance arrived. Max got there early to check the piano and tried to calm his jitters. Larry was already there. Joe and Elaine soon showed up, and JJ shortly after. Max wanted to speak with her, but she and Elaine were gabbing like long-lost sisters. Larry ran the trio through a couple of tunes. Max could hardly contain his nerves. Larry kept glancing at him somewhat apprehensively.

The club soon filled up. JJ smiled and gave Max the 'okay' sign, but Max felt he might be sick. His stomach was trying to escape his body. He glanced at the catfish on the wall. It seemed to be leering and gloating. ***"Ready for a second round of ruined romance, sucker?"***

The trio settled into the first set, meshing nicely. Both Larry and Joe offered excellent solos. Max's solos were uninspired, and the catfish taunted his ineptitude. As they were about to finish the set, Kitty came through the door. She was wearing the same jeans and blouse she had worn that other first time, and she looked like a goddess with her hair flowing loose in the breeze of the overhead fans.

Max swallowed hard and played "The Girl With the Flaxen Hair." Larry leered and turned it into jazz, just as before. When the tune ended, they rushed to the band table as they had in that other 1985, and Larry again nudged Max out of the way.

"Who is our lovely guest, ladies?" Larry queried JJ while eyeing Kitty. "And to what do we owe the honor of her presence?"

Kitty fixed her sparklers demurely on Larry, her face flushing slightly, and said, "I hoped you might recognize me, Mr. Delgado, but it has been several years since you taught me to play tenor sax. I was only fifteen then. I guess I've changed some."

Larry gawked at her. "I remember now. I tutored several kids from Pascal High five years ago, and you were one of them. Yes, darlin', you have changed—a lot. And I apologize abjectly, but I can't remember your name."

Kitty opened her mouth to reply, but JJ touched her shoulder and said, "Let me relieve your abjectness, Larry. This is Kitty Kazinsky. She's a musician too, and a student at TCU. She's going to join us for the rest of the evening."

"Hey, fantastic! Let's get y'all some drinks. It looks like the waitress is ignoring us. Max, how about you and Joe go get the ladies some refreshment while I get reacquainted with Miss Kazinsky?"

Kitty hadn't yet looked at Max. He turned in dejection toward the bar, but Kitty abruptly stood and caught Max's arm. She glanced at him shyly (or was it slyly) then turned to Larry. "I certainly wanted to say thank you and hear your group, Mr. Delgado, but I'm mainly here to support Max. He's my fiancé!"

Max did a double take, assuming he had heard wrong. Kitty gave him a dazzling smile, put her arms around Max, and kissed him passionately. He went dizzy and collapsed onto a chair with Kitty on his lap. Kitty giggled and JJ guffawed like the co-conspirators they were.

Larry said, "Well, I guess I'll get the drinks. You musta been a busy boy of late, Max. Now I understand why you were so evasive on the phone. I'll want to hear all about this."

The trio played another set. Max was ecstatic. His fingers danced like magic (or at least like Bill Evans) along the keys. As they ended "Since Love Had Its Way," JJ came up and whispered to Larry. He announced, "Ladies and gentlemen, a rare treat. JJ Turner will honor us with the song: 'It Ain't Necessarily So.' Although apparently it is."

As Max played in an enchanted delirium, he glanced up at his fishy *bête noir*. It did a slow wink at him and said, ***"Well, it took you long enough, but you finally won her, chump, I mean champ. I guess she was literally to die for."*** Max looked at Kitty. She was smiling at him with the light of love in her magnificent eyes.

JJ sang with a slinky, noir intensity that combined Lena Horne with Billie Holiday. At the end of the song, while the audience applauded extravagantly, JJ whispered in Larry's ear, "Marry me again and I'll help you win a Grammy."

Larry looked at her as if gob-smacked both by her singing and her proposal. He nodded his head eagerly.

Then JJ rejoined Kitty and Elaine at the band table. "Kitty, I'm going to be Larry's manager now. You should come and make some records with us."

When the next break came, Max sat with Kitty; they hugged and kissed blatantly.

"Darling, I was so afraid you had rejected me. How did JJ convince you I was telling the truth?"

"Well, JJ was very persuasive," said Kitty with an impish grin. "But what actually happened was, I fell in love with Rilke, and I decided I would just have to take you along into the bargain. Is that going to be okay with you?"

"Kitty, I'm yours, body and soul, and for as many lives as we're allowed."

Chapter Thirty-Three

"What A Wonderful World"

America, 1985-2001

Max and Kitty were married in late 1985. Kitty finished her master's degree in math and became a statistical consultant for several environmental organizations. Max partnered with her to do environmental legal work as well as continuing to work for the ACLU and private clients. Max made Odetta his law partner in 1987. They hired Nancy Nguyen as their third lawyer in 2000, soon after the expected tornado destroyed Max's office/residence. He and Kitty had the house rebuilt, bigger and better. Rilke was the pampered potentate of the law office and never had to put a claw to any irate miscreants.

Instead of dying in 1996, JJ lived to help Larry earn his Grammy that year. Larry became highly successful as a jazz artist and record producer under JJ's management. Max and Kitty continued to perform with Larry, Joe, and JJ at the Catfish Club (the catfish finally ceased to taunt Max). They also performed at the Caravan of Dreams and other Texas and national venues. Max and Kitty traveled extensively to promote environmental protection and awareness. But they preferred to maintain a low profile.

Max and Kitty created the Blue Scarab Society in 1986 to recruit other loving couples who would knowingly generate love energy for what Max called the God Cosmos. Each couple was to seek other especially happy couples and indoctrinate them. Each member couple received a blue scarab amulet with the words "Only Love" on the reverse side.

Max wrote a treatise explaining how acting with love generates love energy to help nourish the God Cosmos, of which Earth and humanity are a part. Thus, love energy helps create a better, kinder, more spiritual world. Each couple who joined the Society also pledged to act with love and compassion toward all beings in their everyday lives.

Max met Dylan Moonbear and Tiger Blakely for the second first time in 1999, after Moonbear became engaged to violin virtuoso, Missy McKean, and Tiger married Missy's violin mentor, Lili Rendon.

JJ and Larry, who were married soon after Max and Kitty, became the first Blue Scarab recruits, followed closely by Joe and Elaine, then Odetta and Clarence. Missy and Moonbear became Blue Scarab members when they married, as did Tiger and Lili. Sally Landers became a professor of philosophy. Since she couldn't marry Max or Moonbear, she married Brant Lasker as she had announced when 14 (how that came to be is another story). They, of course, also joined the Blue Scarab Society. Soon there were hundreds of members, and the movement grew exponentially. However, Max wanted to make sure the Blue Scarab Society didn't become a cult or religion. There are no prescribed rules or rituals, no officers or titles, no publicity. The members are free to practice any religion or none. Their prime directive is: "Only Love." Within a few years, they could see beneficial results from their informed, dedicated, loving actions.

America, China, and the Soviet Union agreed to major nuclear disarmament. The Berlin Wall was dismantled early, as was the Soviet Union. Pan Am Flight 103 didn't explode. The wars in Kuwait and the Balkans failed to materialize (thus, Moonbear and Lasker met under other circumstances). Russia abandoned its incursion into Afghanistan two years early. The violence of the Irish Troubles ended five years sooner. The Rwandan genocide failed to occur. The world in general became more peaceful and cooperative.

The Clinton administration was hugely successful economically. Clinton put three justices on the Supreme Court, which prohibited gerrymandering of legislative districts, required only public funding of federal elections, and negated the idea that the Second Amendment gave unlimited gun rights to individuals, so guns were tightly regulated and gun violence decreased dramatically.

Congress passed a universal basic income and single-payer universal health care. NASA, during the Clinton administration, revived programs to explore the Moon and Mars. Clinton's vice president, Al Gore, was easily elected president in 2000 with no need of Supreme Court intervention in the election.

President Gore's security services detected and prevented Osama Bin Laden's plan to use commercial airplanes as weapons. Therefore, the American incursion into Afghanistan didn't occur. The Taliban made peace with other factions in Afghanistan, and a democratic government emerged. There was no American war with Iraq, but Saddam Hussein was overthrown by his own people.

The federal government heavily taxed the American coal industry, so it became uneconomical. Jobless coal miners were well-compensated and retrained for safer, better-paying green energy jobs such as solar panel and wind turbine work. The petroleum industry was tightly regulated and was required to finance massive carbon dioxide sequestration projects to minimize global warming. Higher taxes on the income of the ultra-wealthy were put into effect. Moderate tariffs stimulated business to keep strategic industries in America.

The national economy bloomed. President Gore promoted several major federal programs to protect and enhance the natural environment. Max and Kitty were heavily involved in that effort. Larry and Joe urged Max to take advantage of his knowledge of the future, but as he had told JJ, he didn't remember sports scores. Moreover, the economy changed so radically because of love energy influence, Max couldn't predict anything about the stock market. He and Kitty were quite content with their accomplishments in quietly improving society.

***

On the afternoon of September 11, 2001, Max, Kitty, and their twelve-year-old daughter, Gaia, were on the twentieth floor of the New York World Trade Center for a party during an International Peace Conference.

They saw a small crowd of people gathered around a young boy playing a strange multi-stringed instrument. Gaia, hearing the music, ran to the group, listened a minute in fascination, then took out her Chromonica and joined the boy. He smiled with delight at her, and they merged seamlessly into a dazzling duet of Afghan music.

Max and Kitty joined the crowd. Max told her the boy was Salim playing the *rubab*. Standing near the boy, Max recognized Dawud and assumed the beautiful dark-haired woman with him must be his wife, Suraya.

"Kitty, let me introduce you to a new old friend of mine." Max led her over to Salim's smiling parents.

"Good afternoon. I believe I have the honor of addressing Dawud al-Balhki, do I not? I'm Max Ballard, and this is my wife, Kitty."

Dawud stared at them for a moment in obvious surprise. "Yes, I'm Dawud al-Balhki and this is my wife Suraya."

"And I'll wager that is your son, Salim, playing music with our daughter, Gaia. It sounds very much like music for the dervishes."

"Yes, indeed, it does." Dawud knitted his eyebrows, trying to place Max. "What a beautiful and talented child, your daughter. But I'm afraid you have the advantage of us. Have we met before? I think I would have remembered."

"We have, but you wouldn't. I'll be glad to tell you about it if you would be our guests for dinner tonight."

"How kind, but I believe we are already committed for dinner. What do you think, Suraya?"

"Did not Rumi say, 'Be grateful for whoever comes, because each has been sent as a guide from beyond?'"

"Ah yes, my dear, you are right as always. We would be delighted to join you for dinner, Mr. Ballard."

"Wonderful," said Kitty. "I have been eager to meet you both."

"I'm sure it is mutual," said Suraya. "And, Kitty, I see you are wearing a blue scarab amulet almost identical to mine. You must certainly tell us about that. I sense that you have a fascinating story to relate."

Kitty produced her megawatt smile and said, "Oh, yes, I've been waiting fifteen years to meet you and thank you for the blue scarab. Max and I and you wouldn't be here without its miraculous powers."

Just then someone in the crowd said, "Hey, look, something is flying straight at the building."

Max panicked. "No! This can't be happening. Get everyone out." He pushed Kitty toward the exit and rushed to get Gaia.

He was about to grab her up when Gaia pointed outside and said, "Dad, look. It's an American eagle. I didn't know they had them here in New York."

The eagle flew straight to the window of their gathering and somehow lit on the shallow outer sill. It pressed itself against the glass and peered in with a fierce gaze. A crowd quickly gathered around the bird. It scanned the interior for a few moments, taped its beak against the glass three times, then lofted away and was gone. Max took a few deep breaths in amazed relief. *Was that an eagle or an angel? And why? Maybe Dawud will have a Rumi quote that explains it.*

Before the crowd could disperse, Gaia said to Salim, "Do you know this song?" She then led him into the jazz tune "What a Wonderful World."

END

Author's Note

Roll Back the Sun is perhaps the first novel to use knowledge of neuroscience in the development of its characters. Although it is a work of fiction, the ideas it contains express truths I want to make widely known. The idea of producing love energy to help heal society's evils is very real. It is the fruit of personal experience, spiritual knowledge from several sources, and scientific verification from anthropology, neurobiology, and quantum physics. To learn more about love energy, please read my essay, 'Humanity's Cosmic Purpose,' which is contained in my book of poetry, *The Only Important Thing*. I invite all true lovers to join the Blue Scarab Society (sorry but you will have to provide your own blue scarab) and to join in the effort of generating love energy to the sacred Cosmos, of which Earth and all its creatures are a part. There is no cost to join the Blue Scarab Society. Its sole directive is "Only Love." Thanks so much for your time and interest.

If you would like to know more about Dylan Moonbear, Missy McKean, Tiger Blakley, Lili Rendon, and Brant Lasker, read my novels, *Murder Music* and *Neanderthal Gita.*

About the Author

Michael Baldwin is a self-professed descendant of the Lakota mystic warrior, Crazy Horse, and will be glad to elaborate over a couple of beers. Baldwin was born and raised in Fort Worth, Texas. He spent his youth exploring the fields, rills, and fossil-strewn hills of North Texas. Baldwin also developed a keen interest in music, playing clarinet in his high school band and orchestra and taking part in jazz combos through his college years. Roll Back the Sun is the fruit of his lifelong love of jazz, poetry, philosophy, and spirituality.

Much of Mr. Baldwin's writing stems from an early and enduring love of nature and his exploration of it through science, particularly astronomy. As a youth, he built a Newtonian telescope and followed the progress of the space program closely, hoping to become an astronaut. But the eyes weren't quite twenty twice, so he became a writer of poetry, literary fiction, science fiction, plays, mystery thrillers, and children's books, which is safer than space travel and often quite as exciting.

Baldwin has maintained a lifelong interest in science and has used scientific concepts and facts in many of his writings. His children's book, *Space Cat*, takes children on a scientifically accurate tour of the solar system. His science fiction, of course, contains many scientific references and ideas.

Mr. Baldwin holds a B.A. in Political Science, a master's degree in Public Administration, and a master's degree in Library & Information Science. His career was primarily that of a public library administrator, but he was also a field operations supervisor for the 2000 U.S. Census, and a professor of American Government. Baldwin is now retired from the directorship of libraries and devotes himself to writing, creativity consulting, and community volunteer work.

Baldwin has a long-time interest in neuroscience and has developed three seminars based on neuroscience: *Find Your Creative Mind*: Using Neuroscience To Enhance Your Creativity; *Your Poetic Brain:* What Neuroscience Says About Poetry; and *13 Ways of Looking At Poetry Thru Neuroscience*. He also presents seminars on Famous Women Poets and The Nature of Nature Poetry. He and his wife, Helen, live in Marble Falls, Texas. Visit Mr. Baldwin's website: www.jmbaldwin.com.

Other Books by Michael Baldwin

A Slam Poetry Manual (American Library Association, 2003). [How to produce a slam poetry event and succeed as a slam poet]

Scapes: Landscapes, Heartscapes, Mindscapes, Soulscapes, (Eakin Press, 2012). [winner of the Eakin Poetry Book Award, 2011]

Counting Backward From Infinity, (Dancing Rabbit Press, 2012). [winner of the Morris Memorial Chapbook Award, 2012]

Murder Music (Inner Eye Books, 2014; 2nd ed 2018). [winner of Readers' Favorite 5-Star award] A mystery thriller for music lovers.

Passing Strange (Inner Eye Books, 2015). Science Fiction short stories, Volume 1 of the Passing Strange series.

Surpassing Strange (Inner Eye Books, 2016). Volume 2 of the Passing Strange series.

Beyond Passing Strange (Inner Eye Books, 2018). Volume 3 of the Passing Strange series.

More Than Passing Strange (Inner Eye Books, 2019). Volume 4 of the Passing Strange series.

Again Passing Strange (Inner Eye Books, 2023). Volume 5 of the Passing Strange series.

Chronicles of Frank (Inner Eye Books, 2016). Humorous Texas ranch stories. Illustrated by Gary Miller.

Lone Star Heart (Lamar University Press, 2016). Poetry of a Life in Texas.

Nominated for the Texas Institute of Letters poetry book award.

Space Cat (Cozy Kitten Books, 2017). True science adventure stories for children.

A scientifically accurate tour of the solar system by two kids and a cat. Illustrated by J. Darrell Kirkley.

The Quantum Uncertainty of Love: Poems of the Entanglement of Science, Philosophy and Spirit (Shanti

Arts Press, 2019). [awarded the Readers' Choice medal and nominated for the National Book Award]

Words In Concert: Anthology of Poetry About Classical Music (Inner Eye Books, 2019).

[proceeds benefit the Fort Worth Symphony Orchestra] Edited by Mr. Baldwin

A Few Bricks Shy of a Chevrolet: 12 Short, Strange Plays. (Inner Eye Books, 2019).

The Sublime Landscape & Beyond: An Artist's Retrospective & A Poet's Vision.

(Shanti Arts Press, 2021). Poems by Michael Baldwin, Paintings by Johnny Bowen.

Birds, Beasts, & Blossoms: Poems Based On Asian Art Prints, (Inner Eye Books, 2021).

Includes 65 full-color, full-page, Asian art prints with a poem for each.

Neanderthal Gita (Atmosphere Press, 2022). A novel of exotic high adventure.

Nightmarica**:** Poetry of Political & Social Issues (Inner Eye Books, 2024).

The Only Important Thing: Poems on Aspects of Love

With an Essay on Humanity's Cosmic Purpose. (Inner Eye Books, 2025).

All of Mr. Baldwin's books are available at a discount from his website:
http://www.jmbaldwin.com

www.ingramcontent.com/pod-product-compliance
Lightning Source LLC
LaVergne TN
LVHW020654110826
845149LV00012B/2003

9798993055602